DESIGNS

Dell, yearned to trust the love of three dynamic—and very different—men who desired her . . .

Danny, the design genius who swept Dell off her feet and into his marriage bed, sparked her passion, promoted her career—but could not control his secret sexual hunger . . . **Theo,** the award-winning architect who seemed to have everything—including a wife . . . **Rip,** the handsome, unforgettable lawyer in cowboy boots who stood outside the world of glittering surfaces where *everything* was for sale and for show.

But after Dell gave each of them her love and her trust—and her heart was breaking—she was finally ready to face the hardest choice a woman could make . . . and the greatest gamble a woman could take. . . .

INTERIOR DESIGNS

® **SIGNET**   ®**ONYX**   (0451)

LOVE, ROMANCE, AND ADVENTURE

☐ **PASSIONS by Christiane Heggan.** As Paige Granger finds herself torn between the ex-husband she still loves and the husband-to-be she should love . . . she is forced to heed the timeless needs of the heart to decide which passions are worth what price. . . .   (403533—$4.99)

☐ **THE PALACE AFFAIR by Una-Mary Parker, best-selling author of** *Enticements*. Three women of Society in London are caught in a web of deceit, desire, blackmail, and betrayal in this novel of Life in Royal Circles and a world of pomp, power and privilege. Scandal and intrigue only royalty can create. . . . "Delicious!"—*Sunday Telegraph*
(173090—$5.50)

☐ **TEXAS BORN by Judith Gould.** Jenny and Elizabeth-Anne were opposites in every way—except in the fiery force of their business ambitions, and their overwhelming desire for the same man. Theirs was a struggle in which the winner would take all—and the loser would be stripped of everything. . . .   (174216—$5.50)

☐ **INTENSIVE CARE by Francis Roe.** A beautiful woman and her doctor—a novel of love and scandal. . . . "Fascinating!"—*Tony Hillerman*.
(172825—$5.99)

☐ **MARGARET IN HOLLYWOOD by Darcy O'Brien.** In this extraordinary novel, the irrepressible actress Margaret Spencer tells her millions of fans all about her outrageously intimate experiences—on camera and off.
(170776—$4.99)

Prices slightly higher in Canada

Buy them at your local bookstore or use this convenient coupon for ordering.

PENGUIN USA
P.O. Box 999 – Dept. #17109
Bergenfield, New Jersey 07621

Please send me the books I have checked above.
I am enclosing $_____ (please add $2.00 to cover postage and handling).
Send check or money order (no cash or C.O.D.'s) or charge by Mastercard or VISA (with a $15.00 minimum). Prices and numbers are subject to change without notice.

Card #_____ Exp. Date _____
Signature_____
Name_____
Address_____
City _____ State _____ Zip Code _____
For faster service when ordering by credit card call **1-800-253-6476**
Allow a minimum of 4-6 weeks for delivery. This offer is subject to change without notice.

INTERIOR DESIGNS

by

Margaret Burman

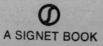

A SIGNET BOOK

SIGNET
Published by the Penguin Group
Penguin Books USA Inc., 375 Hudson Street,
New York, New York 10014, U.S.A.
Penguin Books Ltd, 27 Wrights Lane,
London W8 5TZ, England
Penguin Books Australia Ltd, Ringwood,
Victoria, Australia
Penguin Books Canada Ltd, 10 Alcorn Avenue,
Toronto, Ontario, Canada M4V 3B2
Penguin Books (N.Z.) Ltd, 182-190 Wairau Road,
Auckland 10, New Zealand

Penguin Books Ltd, Registered Offices:
Harmondsworth, Middlesex, England

First published by Signet, an imprint of Dutton Signet,
a division of Penguin Books USA Inc.

First Printing, November, 1993
10 9 8 7 6 5 4 3 2 1

Copyright © Margaret Rapp Burman, 1993
All rights reserved

REGISTERED TRADEMARK—MARCA REGISTRADA

Printed in the United States of America

Without limiting the rights under copyright reserved above, no part of this
publication may be reproduced, stored in or introduced into a retrieval system,
or transmitted, in any form, or by any means (electronic, mechanical, photo-
copying, recording, or otherwise), without the prior written permission of both
the copyright owner and the above publisher of this book.

PUBLISHER'S NOTE
This is a work of fiction. Names, characters, places, and incidents either are
the product of the author's imagination or are used fictitiously, and any resemblance to actual persons, living or dead, events, or locales is entirely coinci-
dental.

BOOKS ARE AVAILABLE AT QUANTITY DISCOUNTS WHEN USED TO PROMOTE PROD-
UCTS OR SERVICES. FOR INFORMATION PLEASE WRITE TO PREMIUM MARKETING
DIVISION, PENGUIN BOOKS USA INC., 375 HUDSON STREET, NEW YORK, NEW
YORK 10014.

If you purchased this book without a cover you should be aware that this book
is stolen property. It was reported as "unsold and destroyed" to the publisher
and neither the author nor the publisher has received any payment for this
"stripped book."

For Sheldon

ACKNOWLEDGMENTS

Three people top the list of those who have enhanced the writing and completion of this book:

Sheldon, above all, most of all.

Eileen Weinberg, sharp, literate, insightful . . . quite simply the best friend a writer could ever have. Reading and commenting her way through several revisions of the manuscript, she provided invaluable help, unwavering support, amusing lunches, tearful talks and, always, the enormous pleasure of her company.

Audrey LaFehr, this writer's dream editor. Meticulous, perspicacious, and inspiring, her impeccable judgment has won my complete trust.

In addition, I would like to thank:

Karen Abramovitz, dearest friend since childhood, who could rouse me from writer's depression and start me laughing again with a curt "Snap out of it!"

Irene and Jacob Rapp, my mother and father, whose pride in their daughter never ceases to delight her.

My brothers: Donald, who never let the three thousand miles between us ever separate us; Harold, for always being there; and Ralph, who has shared it all.

Dr. Paul Bradlow, whose wise counsel helped lighten the dark days.

Jeff Gerecke, my literary agent, who was there from the beginning.

1

THE WEDDING
Labor Day Weekend

The wedding. Pervious to the sky, the sun and the sea . . . and then, later that night, to the stars, it was the celestial climax of the heated, eight-month affair Dell Shay and Daniel Dannenberg had begun quite by accident.

The wedding, however, was no accident. Although it did have the look and feel of something impromptu, something slightly offbeat, avoiding, as it were, the conventional route to the altar and beyond, its singular splendor and dash were the result of meticulous planning. And, of course, money.

Those who were there called it a blessed blast.

And it was. A cheeky-chic marine dream, joyous and raucous, it was a ritual of sacred vows and profane revelry set on the eternal wash of the sea. Of course, looking back, it was neither the beginning nor the ending of anything, but at the time its significance seemed huge. And thereafter, it was assumed all of Dell's and Danny's days would peak on similar summits touching the heavens.

Three and a half years later, some still believed it, remembering the wedding . . .

They chose the last Saturday in August because that was the earliest that their matching white embroidered suits could be ready. Dell worried it might be too hot in a suit jacket, even if it was silk, and ordered a white satin strapless bustier, embroidered with the same passementerie of pearls, to wear underneath. Her copper-freckled arms were as thin and toned as taut rope; she could go strapless with confidence now. Today, even she had to admit that the results of eight months of rigorous weight training, begun almost the instant after she fell in love, were distinctly visible. And although Danny had begged her to wear her blazing red hair loose and flowing, she was right to sweep it up and allow romantic tendrils to escape. She knew Danny wouldn't really mind. He was always urging her to show off her "Modigliani neck." To show off, period.

"Be bold. Make them weep," he'd say. "You are *too* divine, but you have no ego. I must give you one, Dell, darling. Then you'll make them weep gladly. They'll look at you and sob!"

Oh, how he adored her. She was, to him, a prize. That's what he called her: "My prize." She had, he said, an uncommon talent, solidly grounded but fresh. He embraced it, he actually encouraged it. That he found her ravishingly beautiful and smart and witty was an endless surprise and pleasure. And sometimes she even believed it. But that he also found Dell talented fired in her a thrilling new energy and, at the same time, the most enduring and profound sense of pride she had ever known.

He was making her his partner.

So now she would be linked to him not only in marriage but in their own business as well. D & D, for Daniel and Dell Dannenberg, Design & Decor.

My husband. My partner.

At last, Dell thought, a life. A perfect life. And the look of it! Eclectic, elegant, like the rooms she liked to design. Status at last. And a prestigious future furnished with an odd but pleasing mix of eighteenth-century Venetian painted pieces, Etruscan artifacts, and one long, sleek leather Le Corbusier chaise. Eclectic but valuable. Unmatched but somehow unified. As were she and Danny.

She'd done it, the impossible. She'd made her past vanish. At last, she had it all. Was there ever a woman as happy, she wondered . . . or lucky?

They chartered an entire Fire Island ferry for the ceremony. *Summer Spray* was her name and she reclined at the pier like a wide-hipped lady on the deep green divan of the sea, lazy, jolly, and accepting.

"Flowers," Danny had said. "I want so many flowers that they fall off the boat and carpet the water, like one of those Indian funeral barges. Oh, I can see it, Dell. And it's going to be . . . to die!''

He *could* see it. He could see it all. The wedding came to Danny as a total vision. He always knew he could *use* the wedding, make it a precise, to-scale rendering of the boundless talents, the design daring-do of the new interior design duo, D & D. To promote business.

But when he actually *saw* the entire wedding scenario in his mind, he *knew* this would be his most spectacular creation. It came to him complete in every detail, from beginning to end, just as a vision could come to him while standing in a bare room and he would *see* it, finished, transformed, down to the final accent, the last gold-fringed overstuffed pouf, the pair of rare bronze sconces over the French burl commode.

It only remained for him to make Dell see it, to sweep her away. He could do it easily if he were careful about the business part. He was, after all, a kind of sorcerer, and Dell, forever eager for transport, said she loved him most for making his dreams realer than her own.

At any time he could sit her down and, like a storyteller, paint pictures in her mind, pictures of rooms, of grand houses, of spaces he would design for her out of his imagination or from actual commissions he was working on.

''And then what would you do?'' she'd ask, her blue-sage eyes wide as a little girl's. ''Where would you pick up the periwinkle blue chenille—in a side chair or an accent pillow?''

And he'd tell her, weaving her into his interiors, stroking her russet hair against a verdigris wall, biting into her freckled neck on a quilted paisley settee.

''Where do you want to ravage me today?'' she'd ask, waiting for him to escort her into his voyage.

And he'd think a moment, his eternally boyish face puffed in concentration. Then he'd tell her, ''Dijon, France, in a stone farmhouse, done in mustard tones and tiger skins and black patent leather benches.'' Or he'd take her south.

''In South Carolina, on our veranda, lacy white. You're lounging on a double chaise of Spanish moss chintz— Spanish moss is a good color for you. I climb in with you but it's too hot to move.''

"Too hot to move at all?" She delighted in every suggestive nuance the game offered.

"Mmmm, almost. Al . . . most. So I just make these lazy little pelvic circles . . . like this . . ."

"Oh. Such lovely little circles."

"Barely moving."

"Oh, God."

At that he'd have to smile and whisper to her that this could go on for some time. "We're waiting, you see, for the wind to start up and blow the delicate glass curtains I've gathered into the porch corners with white silk cord."

"Yes, I see. Oh, God, yes."

She would listen with her eyes opened wide, seeing with his eyes. She would go anywhere with him, lose herself in him to become the princess of his fairy tales. First he'd tell her how he'd do the room, then he'd tell her how he'd do her, making her see it, feel it, live it in her mind until she wriggled and squirmed with anticipation beside him. Only then would he do it, do *her,* taking his time, talking her through it, mesmerizing her with his words and his hands. He was, to her, a magician, an enchanter whose spells she craved like a drug. Before Danny, no man had ever absorbed her this completely. Before him, all she had ever felt was guilt. Thank God, she said, for Danny.

Knowing the extent of his powers and of Dell's receptivity, Danny couldn't wait to tell Dell about the wedding. He sprawled on the wicker sofa in Dell's mother's Fire Island house that first weekend in March and groaned with relief.

"I never cease to amaze myself."

Dell laughed. She had a high, open laugh, hilariously infectious to virtually everyone, even to Danny, who laughed with her now. "I should think you'd be used to your brilliance by this time," she teased.

"You can never take a *keppeleh* like this for granted."

Even though he'd pointed to his head, Dell looked unsure. "*Keppeleh* means head?"

Danny rolled his eyes but then he smiled at her. "Come here, you gorgeous *shiksa*. Sit down and listen. I know the look I want for the wedding. It's fabulous."

Over my dead body. Dell heard the house echoing and began to move, plumping pillows, sweeping up sand. More than anything, she wanted Danny to make her see the look of this wedding, the look of this whole new life. If she could see it, then perhaps she could truly believe it.

"Dell, did you hear me? I've got it. Stop that scurrying. Sit down and let me tell you."

But Dell was acutely aware of her mother brooding in the kitchen and the memories of her father echoing through the house.

"Over my dead body," Victor Shay would say when refusing Dell something, everything. "Why can't you try to please me? You used to be such a sweet girl. Now look at you. Not an ounce of meat on your bones! Razzle-dazzle, that's what you want now. Razzle-dazzle and—and—flash! A decorator? And work with all those fairies? Over my dead body." Well now he was dead, so why did it still bother her?

"And I want your mother to hear this, too," Danny was saying and called to the kitchen, "Gertrude? Oh, Gertrude!"

But just as Dell could have predicted, Gertrude Shay did not answer him. Her mother, Dell knew, was in one of her deep "broods." Unfazed, Danny turned back to Dell, his beloved, and studied her as she scurried around him.

Dell. She was the tallest woman he had ever known, and the most striking. His match, exactly. Once, she had told him, while walking trough Central Park, a *Vogue* editor had come up to her and told her that her cheekbones were "convex perfection."

"So are her breasts," he might have added if he'd been there. "And her outrageous ass. Like marshmallows upholstered in white velvet." They were the only two entirely unfreckled areas of her body, but of course, only he knew that.

"Do you think," he wondered aloud, grasping Dell's left hand, the one with the engagement ring flashing, "that your mother's still depressed over your father's death?"

He examined the diamond and midnight-blue sapphire ring that she wore on her middle finger, and felt a jolt of triumph once again, remembering the heady excitement when he heard, "Sold! To Number 149," and realized the ring was his. Of course, without his mentor, Christopher Beene, whispering bidding instructions into his ear, Danny might never have won this prize for her. But he didn't tell Dell that Christopher sat next to him at the Sotheby's spring estate jewelry auction. The less Dell heard about Christopher Beene, the better.

"Still?" she finally answered with uncharacteristic bitterness. "She's always been depressed."

And I'm the cause, she almost added.

"You're nothing at all like her," Danny said, thinking of Gertrude Shay sitting in the kitchen, large, mute, and unpardonably plain.

"You mean it? Nothing at all like her?" He had no idea of the effect those words had upon her.

"You don't even look like her—except for the hair. She did give you her one outstanding feature—her glorious red hair."

"Don't you often find me moody . . . like her?"

"You? My gem, my brilliante?" His dark, round eyes—indeed, his whole dark cherubic face—widened in bewilderment. "Never. Absolutely never."

Oh, he was so good for her! He was so certain of everything, so convincing. He said she was magnificent, perfect; he insisted she believe it. And she did, whenever his eyes were upon her. Just then, Danny's eyes were surveying the living room. When he grimaced, Dell grimaced, too. More clearly than he could see into people, Danny could see into a room—any room—and instantly respond to its scale and proportions, its period and detail, and see how it should be done. What came to him naturally, instinctively, Dell had had to learn—from him, but from others, too. Years of schools and irascible teachers, and then years of low-paying jobs assisting talented but starving designers until she came to Leonard, Melton, Inc., where she found her eye, and where she found the brilliant designer, Daniel Dannenberg. And where, at long last, she found love.

"*I'm* about to get depressed," Danny said, the grimace turning his boylike face not exactly old, but older, "unless we do something about this cheap maple wicker. How could she buy crap like this?"

Where earlier his praise had lifted her up to the height of her dreams, now his criticism let her drop with a dull thud.

"As you said," she told him, "it's cheap."

"But this house must be worth a fortune."

"Now, yes. Not when they bought it."

"When did they buy it?"

"*They* didn't. My father bought it. Two days after the hurricane of 1960, when I was an infant. Every other oceanfront house in this community was either flooded or washed out to sea. He called up the owners, who were in a panic. They practically begged him to take it off their hands."

"So he raced out here and took it off their hands?"

"Yes, but without telling my mother. When she found out he'd used up all their savings to buy a house behind her back, she got even with him by refusing to live in it."

"That's why you never summered here?"

"That's why." She didn't add the other reason, that it was to her and to her mother just one more dilapidated shack and she never saw its possibilities. "It was rented out, and only after Daddy died last year did we come here for the first time. Just before I met you."

"You knew me for four years."

"Yes." Dell smiled. "But you know what I mean. Just before we fell in love."

Danny sighed, remembering, and then shivered in the pale winter-sunlit room.

"It's freezing in here," he said, hugging his lean, six-foot, five-inch frame, and he warmed his hands at the old stucco fireplace.

Dell smiled at him from the sofa. Finally, she'd found someone tall enough for her. To gaze directly into his walnut eyes even she, at five feet, eleven inches, had to tip her head back slightly. "You're the beanpole," she'd told him more than once, "I've been searching for all my life." Not like her father—short in stature and short on love.

"What this place needs," Danny was saying, "is . . . everything. New insulation, new windows, and, definitely, new decor. Oh, let's redo it, Dell darling! In time for the wedding. Do you think your mother would like that? It might cheer her up.''

''My mother does not cheer up easily,'' Dell told him. Then, tremulously, she added, ''But when she does, everyone around her can feel it and it's like . . . sunrise.''

''Then it's settled,'' Danny said, envisioning settees, not sunrises. ''It's about time you took true possession of this house, anyway. Think of it—D & D's first job. We'll make it fabulous, too fabulous for words.''

He was transporting her again, transforming the ceiling above her into endless sky.

''And we won't even charge her.''

''That's nice of us.'' She hid her hurt behind her wit.

Despite himself, Danny laughed. For most of the four years they had worked side by side at Leonard, Melton, Inc., he saw Dell only as a wit, a fast-quipping designer who could make him chuckle. Profoundly lacking a comic sense of his own, he admired the insouciance of others. Always fretting, sweating, racing, late, he might never have laughed at all had it not been for Dell's irreverent humor. And if she hadn't come, flushed and sobbing, to his apartment for the first time that freezing night earlier that winter, he might never have discovered how else she could delight him, how else she could resurrect in him pleasures he thought impossible or dead. With Dell, he had become a man again. Oh, thank God, he thought, for Dell.

In the end there were enough flowers to satisfy even Danny. Reproducing his vision intact (''I want white. All white. Totally monochromatic. Even the guests will come in white. And you, Dell darling, will reign supreme, the pearl itself, white and luminous as the moon''), there were thirty bouquets of white orchids and white freesia, fifty tubs of gardenias, white jasmine, white dogwood, and, trained up the sides and poles of the decks, lattices of white roses that did much, with their fragrance, to soften the smell of boat oil and gasoline.

''Baby, let the good times roll!'' boomed from the loudspeakers, while the chamber quartet set up their instruments on the lower deck, near the white cement birdbath packed with iced magnums of vintage champagne.

Danny had wanted white food only, and perhaps because his demands for perfection were beginning to surpass her own, Dell was able to say, "That's going too far." Danny argued, "Real food will spoil the *look*!" but Dell was adamant, so finally he relented, grumbling, "I'm warning you, it's going to look tacky-tacky." Instead, he stood before a black mountain of caviar rising from a sculpted chunk of ice, blinis warming beside it, and had to admit, not for the first time, that Dell was right. The caviar worked. The baby ebony eggs provided an elegant contrast to the all-white boat.

As did the diminutive duck legs that were studded with grass-green scallions and shellacked with a honey and orange liqueur glaze.

And the mammoth fish platters just that moment being set down on white-draped tables before him: platters of bold orange lobsters climbing a fantasy seaweed tree; battalions of giant pink and white prawns marching toward a blue-black hill of chilled and herbed mussels; platters of crabcakes and whitefish rectangles and swordfish squares and trout triangles, all bezel-cut sea gems beached beside pools of blazing dipping sauces.

Behind him, early arrivals applauded as two waiters carried out an antique hand-painted porcelain of a mermaid and a merman swimming into each other's arms, the table's centerpiece.

Oohing and ahing, the guests hugged him for the vegetables. Never, they said, had they seen such red radishes and tomatoes, such purple eggplants, such green zucchini and avocadoes.

"It's the Garden of Eden!" his Aunt Molly cried, and kissed him.

"And get a load of this!" said his Uncle Sid Dannenberg, elbowing the others. Off in a corner of its own sat the "Dannenberg Banquet," as Dell coined it—squares of onion kugel; little rounds of potato pancakes with chived sour cream and maple-colored applesauce; and walnut-sized knishes stuffed with mashed potatoes and exotic mushrooms, broccoli and rice, kasha and onions.

Out on the water the sun's dazzling reflections made of the bay a sparkling sheet of aluminum foil. A sympathetic breeze blew across the dock, fanning the guests as they emerged from black, hearselike limousines, vintage Cadillac convertibles, snappy red or blue two-seaters, and rented Japanese compacts, and jeeps and motorcycles, and an occasional yellow taxi.

As the guests waited to board the boat they formed ragged, rowdy lines, breaking ranks to kiss and hug a new arrival, to capture a glass of champagne from the roving waiters, to display their all-white getups. Then down the rickety gangplank they descended, some inching along fearfully, others skipping and cavorting above the narrow ribbon of water. Most whooped with glee when they set foot on the boat.

"Hurry up!" they called to those on the dock, and the line quickened nervously. "We're casting off any minute."

Dell and Danny stood on the top deck beside Danny's cousin, Judge Morton Dannenberg, of the Suffolk County Municipal Court, his black robe flapping over his white suit. Later he would marry them, shouting hoarsely into a megaphone over the roar of the engines, but now he shook his head in wonder.

"This is some party," he said to the couple. "Strictly Hollywood. And we haven't even gotten to the Island yet. No cars allowed, I understand. Well, I brought my bathing suit and my dancing shoes. I'm ready for anything."

In the sunlight, in their matching, embroidered white silk suits, waving down to family and friends, the statuesque couple seemed almost unreal, like prisms of light, bright and ethereal. Everyone felt it; the assembled group looked up at Danny and Dell with expressions of devotion and reverence, which the bride and groom accepted with nods and smiles, for they knew. They knew they were priest and priestess of a new religion; they stood at the altar of the Temple of Style. Below them their flock waited, wallets opened wide. Here, everyone knew heaven was a home done in fawn suede sofas and fourteen-carat gold faucets.

"Take me to heaven!" their eyes begged.

They had seen, from the very first moments, that magic had been created here, and it had turned them worshipful. Now they knew who could save them from the most humiliating hell of all—a house without taste and without status.

"What do they charge?" they asked each other.

"Who cares?" they agreed. "Just get their card."

And Dell nodded and smiled because she, most of all, understood. On the upper deck, her long, slender legs, raised high in heels of raw silk, tapped and zigzagged to the music, to the excitement, the splendor of it all. Her hair, afire in the sunlight, blazed blue-red, gold, ginger, burnt-sienna. In the breeze, flaming wisps blew wildly, forcing her to ask Danny to help her don the pert little hat she was saving for the ceremony—a virginal crown of lilies of the valley and antique lace and pearls. The crowd, as if witnessing a royal coronation, roared its approval, and Dell took a deep bow.

Danny, a tower of white beside her, couldn't stop touching her, fingering her, turning her as he would a rare vase he was considering purchasing for a client's dining room table. Pointing at her with both hands, he turned to the crowd and asked, "What do you think? Isn't she exquisite, my prize?"

"Bravo!" they roared.

"Brava!" Carl Leonard and Philip Melton shot back in tandem. "Brava!" they corrected with disgusted emphasis. But it was a lesson lost on the Dannenberg clan and the Shays. Feminine suffix notwithstanding, they all continued to call out to her, "Bravo! Bravo!" with glee.

Dell took Danny's arm and squeezed it. "It can't get any better than this," she told him, and meant it. Today, she was truly happy. And beautiful. The fear had vanished. Oh, she was absolutely euphoric. She was loved. Loved! She had escaped at last. And today she had arrived. Now, all she wanted was this shimmering, melting loveliness. This perfection. Forever.

The crowd thickened on the boat. Dancing had begun on the top deck and the steady pounding reverberated everywhere, luring a steady stream of guests in whites gauzy as the sea's foam up the staircase. Even with all the seats removed, the open-air deck was packed tight with pulsing, perspiring revelers while the sun, a flaming pink ball, sank swiftly behind them.

"We should get started," said the captain.

Danny stopped dancing and peered over the railing. He watched as a Silver Cloud pulled onto the dock.

"Five more minutes, Captain," Danny called over his shoulders. "Guests are still arriving."

"Who?" Dell asked, joining Danny at the rail.

Down on the dock Dell saw Christopher Beene, Danny's oldest friend and mentor, climbing stiffly out of his Rolls, and her heart sank. He was not supposed to be here; he was supposed to be in Washington, redoing the president and first lady's private quarters at the White House. He'd sent a generous gift. All right, Dell reluctantly admitted, a fabulous gift. A complete set of antique, hand-forged silver flatware with an ornate *D* engraved on the handle of every piece, along with his regrets:

> *My Dear Danny and Dell,*
>   *I regret I have but one life to give to my country, and unfortunately our President needs it the weekend you will be married. Please do let me make it up to you later.*
>   *The silver, by the way, is early 19th century French, originally crafted for a landowner and his family by the name of Duchamps.*
>
>   *Congratulations,*
>   *Christopher*
> *P.S. Daniel, this changes nothing.*

But now, here was Christopher Beene, gate crashing at her wedding. His eyes, when he looked up at her, were coldly taunting, as if he were daring her to make a scene. Just as the postscript to his note aimed a defiant arrow, she was sure, directly at her. But as to the meaning of it all, she could not say, particularly since Danny kept insisting, "You two are going to be crazy about each other. Just trust me and give it some time."

"I don't believe this. You made it after all!" she heard Danny call to him. "The first lady didn't fire you, did she?" He was so lighthearted, he actually attempted a joke.

As Christopher laughed, a group of Dell's relatives piled out of a taxi that screeched to a halt directly behind him.

"Halloo! Halloo!" they called and swept Christopher Beene into their nervous storm.

"We're late! But you know us, Dell, always late."

They pushed Christopher in front of them as the captain blew the first horn.

"Quickly, quickly! Yoo-hoo, Captain, hold your horses. Here we come!"

In less than sixty seconds they were all aboard and *Summer Spray* headed out to sea.

When the sun melted into a shimmering sash of shocking orange belting the horizon, they all gathered on the top deck for the ceremony.

Down below, Gertrude Shay stood beside her daughter and held a mirror steady while Dell primped. Then she removed her jacket and her mother gasped. It was not the pearl-embroidered white satin strapless bustier that stopped her breath; it was Dell's arms.

"Look at them," her mother said. "Skinny as sticks."

"Do you really think so?" Dell asked, pleased.

With her free hand, Mrs. Shay grasped Dell's armpit and squeezed. "Not even half an inch," she said of the flesh between her thumb and index finger.

"I know," Dell agreed and, performing for her mother's eyes alone, pulled on matching long lace gloves that went over her elbows and had a removable ring finger. She let her mother fasten the twenty-five pearl buttons.

Her mother's hands slid to Dell's waist. "When did you get this figure? Just look at you! Have I been asleep, or what?"

"Sort of, Ma. Remember when I was seventeen and I lost all that weight? Well, I'm seven pounds less than that now and—"

"Seven pounds!" Gertrude Shay repeated, shaking her head as Dell reached into a large white box.

"And now," said Dell, "for the veil." As soon as she attached it to her hat, a fountain of embroidered tulle cascaded down over her bare shoulders.

Gertrude Shay stepped back to get the full effect and her enormous chest heaved heavily with emotion.

"Where did you get such style, Dell? Surely not from me." She looked down at her own plain, off-white dress for confirmation. "All I could tell you, all I could show you was what *not* to do." When she looked up, she saw tears in her daughter's eyes.

"Ma, you've come awake, like the sunrise."

"Oh, Dell. Where have I been? I think I'm seeing you for the first time. I never understood before who you really were. I was too worried and miserable with your father to really look.''

"Ma, promise me you won't sink back.''

Gertrude Shay shook her head, but Dell wasn't sure whether that constituted a promise . . . or a refusal.

"All this time,'' her mother continued in a broken, startled voice, "I thought I had to keep at you, warning you, pushing you, and I never stopped to notice what a beautiful, glamorous creature—''

"Dell! If you don't get your freckled buns up on deck right now you're going to be married in the dark,'' Jackie Knight, Dell's best (and only) friend was shouting as she clanked down the metal stairs in her white satin-bowed stiletto heels. "The sun is settin', girl,'' she said in her made-up drawl for, like Dell, she was born in Brooklyn— though she did move to southern New Jersey in her adolescence. "What y'all waitin' for?''

They watched Jackie rustle over to them in her white silk taffeta dress with the enormous bow in the back, finger-fluffing her blonde curls until she noticed Gertrude Shay and stopped short.

"Oh, you must be Dell's mother. We've never met.'' She introduced herself.

"Jackie Knight,'' Mrs. Shay repeated in bewilderment. "You're the first friend of Dell's I've met since she was in high school. I've never even heard Dell mention your name. Her private life is very private.''

"You're telling me!'' Jackie agreed. Dell tensed, but Jackie, who was scrutinizing Dell's mother, told her, "Y'all have real good skin, by the way,'' and Dell laughed with relief.

"Jackie writes beauty columns,'' Dell explained. Then she whispered to Jackie, but in a voice loud enough to include her mother, "In case you haven't noticed—though goodness knows, you've seen me naked often enough— my buns are not—I repeat—*not* freckled.''

"Oh.''

"My breasts aren't either.''

Jackie shrugged. "And I suppose you're going to tell me your suit's not freckled either? It came out gorgeous, by the way. You look so beautiful, you're beyond hating. You make me want to just . . . sigh.''

Jackie sighed. Then Gertrude and Jackie sighed together, making Dell believe, for one moment at least, that she was the glorious red-haired goddess reflected in their eyes.

They all wanted her to hurry now. They called to her from the top deck and the quartet played lively scherzos, but Dell hesitated. She watched her mother slowly climb the stairs and for the first time the lumpy back and girdle-flattened, panshaped buttocks did not repel her; Dell's gaze was uncritical and unswerving.

"Ma—" she called, and Gertrude turned. But there was nothing left of before in Gertrude's eyes. She had sunk back and the golden link between them had broken off before Dell could remember what she had wanted to say.

Danny was waiting for her on the top deck. He had insisted he should escort her down the aisle. "I give you away, and then, through our vows, I reclaim you. I'm mad for the symbolism in that."

Without her father's arm to hold on to, Dell was glad to break with protocol and, once again, to please Danny. She took his arm.

"Oh, Mary, mother of God," she heard her Aunt Betty sigh. "The angel, look at her."

"Magnificent, magnificent," someone repeated.

Then she saw her Uncle Al for the first time since the funeral, and heard him whispering to her mother, ". . . that he couldn't be here . . . his only daughter . . . is the tragedy."

Daddy, forgive me, but I'm glad you're not here, spoiling my day with your disapproval, Dell thought, then was instantly guilty.

The procession began, photographers and video cam leading the way. Out of the corner of her eye Dell spied Christopher Beene, his gaze fixed on Danny. *What did he mean?* she wanted to ask Danny for the hundredth time, but the music was luring them forward to the white-tented altar crowned with an Italian gilt baldachin, where her mother and Danny's mother waited, sobbing, and the waiters were scooping out handfuls of rose petals that the wind blew into perfumed swirls.

"See the way they float on the air?" Danny said, his mouth close to her ear. "That's the way our life is always going to be. Like roses on the wind. Magic."

"I love you, Danny. I love you so much."

It was true; she felt airborne already. She had fallen in love with Danny overnight, after years of knowing him. But when it happened, it was so zoomingly fast and weightless, it felt like a plane taking off. And suddenly her life had the promise of excitement, of glamour, of what her father used to call "razzle-dazzle." From now on, Danny had said, it would always be like this. She was so happy, she could hardly remember how it had been before.

Suddenly, she was impatient for the wedding to end and the marriage to begin. But there were hours yet of celebration. First, a sunset swim. Then more eating and dancing. And through it all, work. After the grilled steak dinner, but before the four-tier wedding cake was sliced, Danny would give a slide presentation and she'd work the room, unveiling D & D's portfolio to their friends and relatives. For the ferry ride home she'd offer each guest a white gift basket packed with white chocolate truffles and one white D & D business card.

"Don't forget Carl and Phillip. Make sure they each get a card," Danny reminded her. "You'll see. In time, they'll call and say they forgive us and wish us well."

If for now her two elegant ex-bosses seemed cooler and more aloof than usual, Dell couldn't blame them for being miffed, although Carl Leonard and Phillip Melton always knew they'd never be able to hold Danny. In the past year alone, Danny had drawn in almost as many big-budget clients to the firm as Leonard and Melton themselves had. No one quite knew how Danny, such a poor boy without any visible important connections, had achieved this. Christopher Beene, invisible until the actual wedding day, was immediately recognized but his presence there was not understood.

So it must have been Danny's brash confidence, everyone agreed, and the dazzling talent to back it up. And indeed, by now Danny did have his own following—returnees whose studio apartments he'd done ten years ago and who now needed him for the grand estate in Greenwich or the two filmmakers who'd formed a company in a downtown warehouse, and now, after their third blockbuster, were flying him out to Los Angeles to do their beach homes . . . and perhaps the sets for their next film. Oh, yes, he had a following.

Sometimes, it was Phillip Melton's very own clients. They'd call him and say, "Listen Phillip, I just saw the work of that young boy of yours, Dannenberg, in *Architectural Digest*. Met him in Washington a month ago. Quite a charmer. Anyway, my daughter just married Senator Cary Tieg, as you know, and they need their place in Georgetown done. Why don't you let Dannenberg design it? I'd be much obliged."

Or, "I've been hearing about a designer of yours, Danielberg, Danielstein, something like that. Anyway, I met him at the black-tie at the museum the other night. He's got something. We talked about my triplex. Let's face it, I haven't been too happy with the scheme you presented to me. But I really think this seven-footer with the baby face really understands what I want . . ."

Dell wasn't doing badly, either. Considered a workhorse, a meticulous planner at the firm, she was respected and noticed, and six months ago had been rewarded with an annual raise of almost six thousand dollars—a massive pay hike for a staff designer, even if it was deserved. But it was Danny who was the star. They gave him a secretary, and then an assistant, and then another. Still he was late with almost every project. But oh, his visions! Clients forgot the infuriating, interminable wait when they entered their own doors of paradise.

"It's heaven!" they cried.

"I never though an all-black kitchen would work, but you were right—the secret's proper lighting. It's sophisticated and sexy . . . just like you!"

"When my friends see my Turkish bedroom and the mosaic floors, they're going to hate me so much they'll beg for your name."

They hugged him, they gave him presents, and they never forgot him.

Nor did the interior and decorating magazines, which regularly featured his work. Their photographers competed to be invited to his installations, not only because pictures of a Dannenberg house virtually guaranteed publication, but because of the glittering parties given by grateful clients that would soon follow. Happily, they gave Leonard, Melton, Inc., a fortune in targeted free publicity, which did not exactly ill dispose the two partners toward Daniel Dannenberg. In fact, they gave him the largest Christmas bonus ever received at that firm. And they were thinking of giving him a sports car, something so fast and expensive that even their arrogant *wunderkind* might feel a sense of indebtedness.

It wasn't, however, enough.

On the first of July, Dell and Danny marched into Carl Leonard's office and resigned, announcing in hand-holding unity their plans to marry and form their own firm, D & D, Design and Decor. This was less than a year—just six months—after Dell had gone to Danny's place for the first time, the night he awakened her with a kiss and her life began.

Now, as she recited her vows, darkness closed in, and the heavens became a bejeweled ceiling, almost within reach.

2

Labor Day Weekend

Theodor Glass bent over the canopied Victorian cradle and marveled at his baby daughter's pink ears. Translucent as a china teacup and far more delicate, Cara's incarnadine ears made her father smile.

"They're bubble-gum pink," the great architect whispered to his wife. "Look at them. Did you ever see anything so fine?"

Erica Glass pulled her straight blond, precision-cut hair away from her face and showed her husband her own ears. "They're like mine, I think," she whispered. Then she laughed. "Theo, why are we whispering? Cara sleeps through anything."

Nevertheless, though Theo laughed with her, they both continued whispering, even as they carried the cradle with their soundly sleeping baby into the nursery next door. Now that Cara was two months old and sleeping through the night, she was moved from the side of her parents' bed to her own grand room, a cause for celebration of sorts.

"She's growing up," Theo said. "Soon she'll be leaving us for good."

"Twenty years is not exactly soon, so stop that and come downstairs. Let's have a cognac and toast her first night of independence." She took his arm and coaxed him out of the lacey pavilion. But at the door, Theo Glass looked back at his daughter once more and stroked his wheat-blond moustache.

"Let's not have any more. We could never make another one as perfect as Cara. Let's just concentrate on her, and savor it all while we can."

"I thought you wanted six. Didn't you make me promise to give you five while I was still on the delivery table with Cara?'' Erica teased, with little conviction and great relief.

They spoke in normal tones as they descended the great floating staircase. They were still so smitten with their new baby and their role as her parents, they were barely conscious of the splendors inside and outside the house Theo had created for them on a cliff overlooking the Hudson River.

Passing through the domed great hall with walls of Bohemian glass tile, they worried they might not hear Cara if she awakened, even though an elaborate and extremely sensitive intercom system was in place throughout the house. They hurried to the built-in sofas that ringed the circular living room (virtually every corner, every right angle and sharp edge in the house had been rounded and softened), where they could sit beside the speaker and listen for Cara's cries.

''Let's not have cognac. It's too hot. How about rum and lime on the rocks?'' Theo had noticed the fat, emerald-green limes Erica must have piled into his favorite bowl, an authentic Picasso footed ceramic. Like him, Erica had grown up with fine art and good design and, unintimidated, found domestic use for even their most priceless objects. A collection of second-century Roman marble busts had become, this summer, repositories for his baseball caps and her wide-brimmed straws. She used their Georgian silver platters as breakfast trays and their small Etruscan vases to hold her makeup brushes and pencils. However, she'd forgotten to fill the ice bucket.

''I'd rather have the rum neat than go all the way to the kitchen to get the ice,'' she said, tucking her bare legs under her. ''Unless, of course, you'd be willing?''

Theo Glass looked across the huge first-floor expanse, all the way to the swinging kitchen doors, and sighed. It was times like this when, tired and drained not only after a week of too much work but a whole summer of sleepless nights with a fretful baby, that this sprawling mansion seemed a monumental mistake. A one-room river cabin was all he really needed.

''Why did I do it?'' he asked aloud.

''Do what?''

"It's inhuman."

"What's inhuman? What're you talking about?"

"The scale, the scale!"

Erica saw him pound his stomach with his fists, and thought he regretted eating two portions of her mascarpone pudding for dessert. For Cara they'd both stopped smoking, but the five-pound paunch he'd developed drove him to fits of exasperation. Then Theo stood up and Erica could tell, from his flushed face and clenched fists, that he was about to deliver a speech. Theo made speeches about only one subject: work. His work, the work of other architects, or the state of architecture in general. Therefore, the "scale," she now realized, referred not to the weighing machine in their bathroom but to the grand proportions of this house. Theo was feeling guilty about his grandiosity again, not his girth.

"Do you realize," he began as if she were hearing this for the first time, "that in order to retrieve six little ice cubes from our five-thousand-dollar subzero refrigerator, I must walk, let's see, the diameter of this massive circle of a living room, which is forty feet. Then I've got to cross the width of the hall, which, for some reason, I designed as an entryway for guests arriving in groups of five hundred at a time. Five hundred extremely fat and tall guests. The hall is thirty feet wide. Then there's the dining room—another thirty linear feet. And because that stainless-steel monster is on the far wall, I've got to walk across the entire kitchen—another thirty-five feet—for a grand total of one hundred and thirty-five feet. Think of it, exactly forty-five yards for a measly six ice cubes! It's wrong to live this way. It's debilitating, it's dehumanizing, and it's indecent. What have I done? Oh, what a stupid folly!"

Erica stood up and gripped his solid but hunched shoulders. She peered into his blue eyes until he looked back at her. He did not think he could bear to hear a pep talk right now, but he knew that if he stopped his wife from delivering her sermon, her hurt feelings would be even harder for him to endure, so he let her speak. And to his surprise, he was somewhat cheered.

"Theo, I'll tell you what you did. Quite simply, you made a very big house that turned out to be a masterpiece. Yes, yes, it's big—but big in importance, not just in scale. Almost every critic said the same thing: 'A major event in residential design. Finally, we have in one structure, the sum of all that is best in American architecture.' And don't forget that *Architectural Trends* called you the Frank Lloyd Wright of the second half of the twentieth century.''

''I'm sure Frank Wright could get a cold drink on a hot night without trekking a mile.''

''*I'll* get the ice.''

Theo sank back down into the deep brown leather sofa under the carved wall of windows and gave his wife a grateful smile. He watched her race-walk from the room. Erica race-walked everywhere, and Theo had grown accustomed to the taste of salt on her skin and to the constant trickle of perpiration down her hairline. Unlike him, she never hunched her shoulders, yawned, stared into space, or gained a pound. So slim hipped she bought her jeans in the boys' department, she was, like so many small-boned women, endowed with an unlimited store of energy. That she was essential to Theo he would never deny. She navigated the course of his busy life with such efficiency and in such detail that he was sure he'd drown without her. And yet whenever she was near, her selfless devotion turned him churlish. Or sulky, like now, and he couldn't help calling out to her, ''Of course, it'll all be slush by the time you get back!''

Erica heard him and laughed to herself, but she did not turn back. Ordinarily, she would've race-walked right back to him because she liked to nip his moods in the bud. Perhaps she would've teased him or shook him, but certainly she would've argued his case again with more meticulously memorized quotes of praise from the articles she'd been clipping and pasting in an album begun on the day he graduated from Yale, over thirteen years ago. And if the critical praise didn't work, she could often brighten his disposition with her own biased but entirely plausible projections for his future. And if all else failed, she could always break down and tearfully plead with him to remember his mission, and fulfill his destiny, because the whole world needed him, and so did she.

She was, as she saw it, mistress to genius. And with a genius as towering as Theo's, care had to be taken that the structure didn't crumble. She knew the fragility of his ego, the danger of his crippling self-doubts and despair. It was up to her to keep him cheerful, to keep him going. She brought him his breakfast in the morning, spoke to him not less than five times a day, expertly critiqued his every project, all the while secretly monitoring and evaluating his moods. Several evenings a week she accompanied him to the balls and benefits hosted by his clients, or entertained them at her own lavish dinner parties. And each night before bed, she put him to sleep with a glass of hot cinnamon milk. Until now.

Until now, she did everything for him, forgetting nothing. With her husband's emotional well-being entirely in her hands, she could not afford to make mistakes. But that was before Cara. Now, after thirteen years, she finally had a real baby to protect and nurture, and . . .

Cara!

It could have been only the hiccups, but it also could have been a short coughing fit, or actual choking. Erica put her ear to the speaker to listen for the sound again, but she heard nothing more. And Theo was waiting for his ice.

"Did you hear?" she asked him, returning to the living room. "I think she coughed."

"Yes. I was about to run up and have a look at her but she settled down. She's quiet now."

"Too quiet," Erica said uneasily. Often she could hear the sound of Cara's breathing and her little grunts and sighs magnified throughout the house. Now there was a silence so empty, it was alarming.

"I'm going up."

"Erica, don't be silly. She's sleeping soundly. Have your drink and then I'll go up with you."

"You're right," Erica conceded, and forced herself to sit down beside her husband. But her uneasiness remained, souring everything, even her drink. It needed something sweet, she decided—fruit juice or cola. She set the glass down for the maid to clear in the morning. Lucille! she suddenly remembered with mounting agitation. Lucille, nonstop talker and endless vacuumer. The thought of a long, hot Labor Day weekend with Lucille chattering and clattering through the house filled Erica with unfamiliar dread, for she usually looked forward to

Lucille's company. And this damned house annoyed her, too. Perhaps Theo was right, after all, though she could never tell him. The scale of this house *was* inhuman. To be so far away from her baby that she had to depend on electronic transmissions of Cara's cries suddenly seemed monstrous. She yearned to press her nose into the sweet, powdery smell of Cara's skin, and listen, one last time this night, to the actual sound of Cara's sleepy sighs.

She stood up.

"All right, let's go," Theo agreed, for he understood his wife almost as well as she understood him. He could tell by her determined stance and the way her eyes were searching the ceiling that to prolong their "adult time" down here was pointless; Erica was all mother now. Once, he had occupied the entire field of his wife's vision. Now Cara did. He wasn't resentful, just rueful. He missed the attention.

Mechanically, he pressed the buttons on the central remote panel that turned down the air conditioning and turned up the hall lights. Another button turned off the exterior floods, and a switch even locked the doors. When all the buttons and switches had been pressed, he put his arm around his wife's doll-sized waist and together they went up to Cara.

"See? What did I tell you?" Theo said at the doorway. "Sleeping like a lamb."

They approached the silent cradle, a master carpenter's cocoon of spindled walnut, canopied and skirted in French lace and pink ribbon, for one last proud peek inside. Though there had been blazing sunshine all day, then a brilliant sunset, the night was dark and moonless. But a small porcelain lamp gave off a pale pink light, shadowy but sufficient. And it would always be those next few minutes—surely no more than three—that Erica, in the days and the weeks and the years to come, would relive over and over again. Much of what happened after that went by in a blur of incessant pain, but those three minutes she recalled in exact detail, even though—or perhaps, just exactly because—they filled her with a sense of unpardonable shame and unspeakable horror.

"You're right, she does have your ears," Theo whispered. "But she's got my brain, my sense of humor, and my teeth."

"How can you say she's got your teeth?"

"I can tell by her gums. She's got my gums."

"All right, she's got your gums," Erica conceded with suppressed laughter. "But she's got my body."

"As long as she's got my brain."

"What brain? You're the one who forgot to give us a master bedroom until I took a look at your plan and reminded you."

"Not that we've made much use of it this summer," Theo murmured in her ear.

She would always remember the exact weight of Theo's hand on her shoulder, kneading her flesh, and his question, curled in his smile, "Shall we tonight?"

And how she took his hand and placed it on her belly, still stretched but entirely healed, and how eagerly she smiled up at him in answer.

And then, how, arm in arm, they stood together above the silent cradle, their flesh alive with anticipation. And how his hands reached around her and caught her tiny breasts as she bent over the cradle, making her laugh out loud above Cara's still and silent form.

She would always remember the exact sound of her laughter that night. She might have been a young soprano trilling in song, skipping lightly up the scale to C. She never laughed like that again.

It was on the last note of her laugh that she heard it, and became convinced. What was so odd was that there was no other sign. If she could ever forgive herself for those three grisly minutes of gratuitous gloating and doting, it would be because, in all fairness, everything else was so normal. For instance, everything *smelled* normal. The faint scents of powder and baby lotion, urine and fresh laundry, the slightly humid air, and even Theo's after-shave, all mixed together into one utterly familiar, normal atmosphere. Only the silence was unusual.

"C'mon, let's go to bed. We were supposed to do this after your six-week check-up. My patience, I believe, is finally about to be rewarded," Theo may have said, but Erica was no longer listening to him. All she could hear was the silence, slicing through her like a baby's scream.

She pulled the blanket back.

* * *

Where Erica's memory left off, Theo's began.

All that long, sun-drenched weekend when everyone else was at the beach Theo watched and listened, absorbing every detail but reacting to none of it. It all seemed to be happening like a disaster movie on a large screen right in front of him. He saw the earth rupture and then slide away, like mud and rocks down a mountain. He heard the enormous roar but he did not feel the vibration. The doctors said he was affectless due to shock and grief, but they didn't know the depth of Theo's guilt. Guilt had not anesthetized his pain; quite the opposite, in fact. But now he no longer felt entitled to any other feelings. He had no right to them. What he wished was to transform himself into a zombie, a living, working, aching zombie.

During those first few hours, when Erica could only sob, his guilt seemed almost useful. It kept him steady.

He saw the way Cara's head flopped back limply when Erica lifted her out of the cradle, and he knew, but he did not perceive.

"Please, no," Erica was whimpering. "Please, oh, please, no."

And already, a part of him knew it was his fault. Still he resisted, not quite believing what he was seeing. In fact, at first he took a step back, into the shadows, almost afraid to look. His wife was behaving like a lunatic, waking their baby, taking her to the dressing table, shining the light in her little face. He told himself that in one more second Erica was going to be extremely sorry because Cara was going to start screaming her head off. Why was she doing this? Waking Cara up, turning her upside down. He was furious. She had to be stopped. Except that Cara wasn't crying. Cara wasn't making a sound.

He took over then, pushing Erica out of the way, but as soon as he grasped Cara's tiny wrists, he knew with certainty, and his heart turned to stone. Still, he persevered, gently tipping Cara's head back to open an airwave. He'd practiced infant CPR one night in their group childbirth class, and although it all came back to him, he couldn't help remembering, too, that then he'd worked on a plastic doll and that he'd laughed and joked and his hands were deft, not shaking.

"She's not . . . she 's not . . ." Erica was weeping.

He covered Cara with his mouth and gave her four of his gentlest breaths. Then he checked her carotid and the brachial pulse on the inside of her arm.

"She will," he said. "She's just . . ."

"I know. She's just . . ." Erica eagerly agreed, nodding and crying.

He only did one more cycle of rescue breathing, then he switched to chest compressions, giving her one gentle breath after every five compressions.

"She's still not . . ."

"She will, but Erica, call Emergency."

"Oh, my God!" Erica cried.

"Call 911. Do it now!"

"Wait. Let *me* have her," Erica suddenly insisted and tried to push Theo away. "She'll breathe for Mommy. She just needs to burp. You'll see. Let me—"

"Shut up. You're throwing my counting off."

"Oh, God, she's still not . . . and I just stood over her . . . and laughed. Even then, she must have been . . . but I thought she was—"

"Listen to me, Erica. Dial 911. Get an ambulance. Get the police. She'll . . . be all right," he heard himself say. "But call *now*!"

As he labored over his infant daughter and listened to his wife crying into the phone, he felt remarkably calm. His hands, though shaking, performed automatically, as if they'd practiced these procedures hundreds of times. It left his mind free to think, so long as he avoided thinking of her pulse. When he checked for Cara's pulse and couldn't find it, panic pounded at the door of his heart, threatening to break through. So he locked the door and threw away the key. He was sure he'd never need it again.

One hundred thousand minutes, he calculated as he straddled Cara along his forearm, face down. A father for 1,700 hours. With the heel of his other hand, he gave Cara four short, careful back blows, expecting nothing and receiving nothing. But he didn't think about that.

Supporting the baby's head with one arm, just as he'd been taught, he turned her over again and resumed the chest compressions and rescue breathing.

How odd, he thought. Not once in all those one hundred thousand minutes did he ever wish for his daughter's tears . . . until now. Her squalls had always filled him with instant sorrow. Erica was even worse. Sometimes her own eyes would fill with tears at just the sound of Cara's cry. Always, their impulse was to quiet her. Hush, hush little baby. And yet, what wouldn't they give this minute just to hear Cara scream again at the top of her tiny lungs? To turn red, even purple. Shuddering screams with her little fists slashing the air. Gasping for breath, but breathing. Breathing out loud.

Erica had returned. He felt her behind him. He tried to make his mind calculate how long it had taken her to make the call. How long since he'd last checked Cara's pulse. Then Erica's face was in front of him, and her voice had a new insistence.

"They said to check her pulse. You found one, didn't you? I didn't, but you did, right? Theo, tell me she has a pulse!"

Theo touched the carotid, then the brachial. Then he looked up at his wife.

"Yes," he said, but his cheeks were strangely wet, and it was not Cara's sobs he heard, but his own.

Theo sat with the metal tin, the size and shape of a coffee can, on his lap. There hadn't been time to purchase an urn. Perhaps, Erica had suggested, he'd design one. He glared at her. Perhaps, she said, they'd look for one together, but the image of a shopping expedition such as that made him hate her for framing it in his mind. No, he preferred this simple cannister. Inside, nickel-size white chunks, weighing, he calculated, one-half pound. Cremains. All that was left of Cara.

"Don't," Erica implored him. "Please don't."

They were sitting beside each other on the brown leather sofa, in the same places they'd occupied on Friday night. It almost could have been Friday night. The limes still sat in the footed bowl. There'd been another spectacular sunset, but now the light show was over. If only it were Friday again, and not Sunday, a million years later.

But it wasn't Friday. It would never be Friday again. Now, family and friends wandered through the house in hushed groups, lingering at the entry way to the living room rotunda, but avoiding the sofa, as if they were stopped by an invisible fence of grief.

And because it was Sunday, on Theo's lap sat the half-pound can. And his wife was saying something to him, interrupting his one-car train of thought. He'd been thinking, *Her life, like her death, was over this fast.* And then he'd snap his fingers. And kept on snapping them, because more accurately than words, the sound of that quick, dull, thwicking snap gave expression to death's incomprehensible swiftness. Crib death, the doctors had said. *Snap.*

"Oh, please, Theo. Don't," Erica said again.

Her eyes were the color of blood. Tears had bled from her swollen eyes almost continuously for forty-eight hours and still they trickled down her cheeks, her neck, and into the cup of her collar. Her words were soaked in tears.

Thinking she meant the snapping, Theo folded his hands over the cannister on his lap. But she continued to plead with him.

"You've turned away from me. Don't, Theo. Please."

Now he understood what she meant, but he was aware that, even as she begged him not to turn away, he was staring out the window at the darkening panoramic outline of the Palisades cliffs and that his hands were still folded in his lap, not reaching out for her, not even touching her. He would not, he could not comfort her. He wouldn't even look at her, for he knew that if he did, she might try to hold onto him, and he to her, like two drowning swimmers in a sea of sorrow . . . and be saved. But Theo didn't want to be saved. What right had he to be spared? To keep the memory of Cara alive, he must keep the pain alive. He had no right to seek relief. For the father who caused the death of his child, no less punishment would fit the crime.

"I'm just . . . thinking," he told her in a monotone.

"What are you thinking? Let me in."

"I can't. The door's locked."

He heard her begin to weep again but he wouldn't allow himself to touch her.

"I knew it, I knew it," she cried. "I knew this would happen."

Theo said nothing.

"First, you'd turn away. Stop talking. Go into your

own world. Before, I could always guard against it. But now . . .''

He heard her blow her nose. He felt her touch his shoulder. He pulled away.

"See? And soon, you'll leave me altogether. Oh, Theo, don't! Please don't leave me.''

Now, Theo told himself. *Take her in your arms.*

He stopped himself with a will of iron, but he did turn to face her.

"Leave you? You mean pack my bags, go out the door and check into a hotel? That kind of leaving you?''

Erica nodded, sobbing.

"I don't understand where you got that idea,'' he told her without masking his irritation. This was not a conversation he wished to have now. It was repugnant to be discussing marital relations at a time like this. And on Friday night, it had been an obscenity. If it hadn't been for marital relations, Cara might be alive. He cursed his cock and his balls and everything that lived below his waist.

"I'm not leaving you,'' he said, hoping that would be the end of it.

"Not now,'' she agreed, despondent. "But you might next week, next month. And I don't think that then I could go on. To lose you, too . . . oh, Theo, I don't know if I can go on anyway. It doesn't feel like only forty-eight hours; it feels like I lost her a year ago. Like I've been missing her every day for a year. And the weight of it—the weight of missing her—just keeps building, getting heavier, getting worse every minute. I keep hearing the sound of my own laughter.'' She covered her ears with her hands. "Help me, Theo.''

"How?'' he asked.

"Just stay here with me. No! Don't turn away! I feel so alone. So empty.'' She clutched her belly. "Promise me.''

"Promise what?''

"That you'll stay. I have to know I won't lose you, too. Ever. I need you to promise me . . . and mean it.''

When the metal can arrived from the crematory and the mortician placed it in Theo's hands, Theo carried it to a corner table and carefully lifted the lid. What he saw inside made him gasp. He didn't find the gray ashes he'd expected; instead, he saw the remains of his soul. He too was mixed in there with Cara. He too had been reduced to dry, white bone. He doubted if he could ever bleed again. Yet Erica still wanted him. Of course, he had no intention of leaving her—he had no intentions, period. But if she needed his promise, then that much he would give to her. He'd make the promise, and mean it. And then she'd know she'd always have him—whatever was left of him.

"I'll never leave you," he vowed. "You have my promise. No matter what, you won't lose me, too."

3

Dell liked to say that her life began on Christmas Eve 1987, the night she fell in love with Danny, the night his first kiss awakened her from the thirty-year sleep that was her life. Just like Sleeping Beauty.

"That was some kiss," she liked to tell him. "A Sony alarm clock with lips."

Except, of course, that she wasn't sleeping when Danny kissed her. She was crying.

All day she'd sat at her slanted drawing board with a room plan on the quarter-inch graph paper tacked to it. Dispiritedly, she pushed plastic-coated furniture templates around on the Burnett apartment plan, trying to find the impossible: a balanced, graceful arrangement for too many oversized pieces in a room whose dimensions were no more than adequate.

"We must have a king-size bed," Molly and Charlton Burnett, the clients, had insisted with an embarrassed laugh. "We do everything in bed. Everything!"

Then why, Dell had wondered, did they insist upon a six-foot desk, an upholstered chaise longue, a wall of electronic video and music equipment, a skirted break-fast table with two pull-up chairs, and various bureaus and cabinets? Of course, she'd attempted to explain to her clients that their apartment's meager master bedroom of only three hundred square feet could not accommodate all the pieces on their wish list, but her clients kept calling and pleading with her to squeeze in just one more must-have item, as if Dell were withholding from them their desk, their breakfast table out of some inexplicable selfishness. As if, by pressure and importunings, she could be talked into being more generous.

"Look here, Dell," Mr. Burnett had said on the phone only that morning, "my wife is an impossible person to live with when she sets her heart on something. She simply won't stop until she gets it.''

''What has she set her heart on, Charlton?''

''A frilly dressing table.''

Dell blew up. ''A frilly dressing table?'' she repeated. ''But she never even put it on the list!''

Charlton Burnett coughed conspicuously for several seconds. Then he admitted, ''I know that, and she does, too. That's why I'm calling for her. Dell, last night my wife cried in my arms, her longing was so great for one of those Hollywood-style dressing tables with the ruffled skirts. She's wanted one ever since she was a little girl— but because she didn't put it on the list, she was afraid to tell you. So I told her she could have one. Now she's got her heart set on it.''

No other designer at the firm would permit this, certainly not the autocratic Danny Dannenberg, who worked down the hall. They all had the same credo: ''I know exactly what you need. Trust me; I'm the expert here.'' She'd overheard Danny boast, ''*I* tell my clients what they need, not the other way around.'' But not Dell.

''Oh, dear, I see,'' she said with more understanding than her client realized. The yearning. Was there anyone who'd endured more of that deep, gnawing need than Dell? Oh, she knew all about being a little girl who grows up living every day with that excruciating longing inside of her. But because she was feeling slightly sorry for herself, she said, with less sympathy that she felt, ''Nevertheless, I've already done over the bedroom scheme three times and there's no more floor space.''

''As a special favor to me, Dell. Please try.''

And she would, of course. She'd go right on trying until she got it right. Until it was perfect. The least she could do was make their dreams some true. Her own were quite another story.

The wish list was entirely Dell's idea. She always asked her clients to make up a fantasy list of favorite periods, pieces, looks.

''Are there any special pieces of furniture you always dreamed of owning, any special look you secretly want?''

''Are you sure?'' she'd urge if her clients drew a blank. ''Because I can't promise I'll find it, or be able to fit it in, but I know I can make at least some of your dreams come true.''

Usually, that's when they told her of their secret yearnings. A Scottish real estate tycoon yearned for an all-plaid study to remind him of the kilts of his native home. Haltingly, a fashion designer admitted that although he didn't know how to cook—"I am terrified of the stove. Terrified! I make only cold things, tuna sandwiches, sliced cheese, fruit"—he wished for a large country French kitchen loaded with old wood, quarry tile, marble, and brass.

"The kitchen is the soul of a house," he said. "I want my house to have a big, generous soul. I want it to *look* like I cook and eat and live in my kitchen. Big, hearty French peasant meals bubbling on a six-burner stove in shiny copper pots. Of course, if I ever ate like that, I'd gain fifty pounds in a week. I exist on lettuce—Romaine, arugula, chicory, Bibb. That's it. But I love to be near food, to be near other people who are eating. I love kitchens because, to me, they're more illicit than bedrooms!''

They confessed to her their idiosyncrasies, their fears and desires. Like a psychotherapist, she encourage them to dig deeply, remember, dredge.

"Did you like your bedroom wallpaper when you were a child?''

"Did you ever walk into a room and say, *Wow!* Yes? Okay, close your eyes and tell me what it looked like. What about it made you love it?''

She asked all of them to make a wish list, but only some of them did. Several actually wrote pages to her, even affixing pictures they'd clipped and collected. These were the ideal clients; from them Dell received a specific direction toward which to head. With them she need not wander aimlessly. They knew what they wanted and she was experienced enough to know how to fill a space with their dreams. They told her where they wanted to go and, like a travel agent, she planned their trip. But for more than just professional reasons, Dell loved these clients. With them, she felt less alone, for they allowed her, even for a moment, to peer into their familiar souls.

Then there were some who wrote one-word descriptions of their desires. Dell understood them, too.

''Kitchen—efficient.''

''Bedroom—restful.''

''Living room—traditional.''

She knew how to bring them out. By interviewing them in their old surroundings, often she learned what she needed to know.

''Are you sick of this place or do you still like the look?''

She'd wander through the old rooms with them and ask them to suppose they could take only three things with them.

''What three things would you choose?''

When the clients had already moved to a new, bare space, she'd lug over her photo portfolio and a couple of glossy picture books of interiors, and sit with them on the floor, flicking the pages while encouraging them to tell her which ones they liked and which ones they hated. She never tired of hearing their secrets and their dreams, of learning their preferences in decor and style. In this way, she learned that a ''traditional'' living room meant a profusion of English chintz and portraits of dogs on the walls to one client, and to another it meant graceful nineteenth century French chairs facing a multicushioned sofa upholstered in pale cream silk.

Even more, she learned how to structure an environment that answered their particular dreams—an ideal environment that gave them status, comfort, happiness. It was no more than what she wanted for herself. Perfection. But giving it to them was easy and fun. Finding it for herself had been a lifelong search.

So she grew to love her clients, love making them happy. Even the ones like Molly and Charlton Burnett, who began by admitting they hadn't a clue about decor and wanted Dell to make all the decisions, but ended up having an opinion about everything—particularly those technical areas, like whether the ceramic tiles should be eight or twelve inches square, and whether the table height should be twenty nine inches or thirty inches.

Nevertheless, even Dell would admit that it wasn't Charlton Burnett's fault that her mood had sunk so low. Certainly it was frustrating to rework the plans for the fourth time and to conclude that her scheme was still not perfect.

But it wasn't Charlton's fault that at four-thirty on the Friday before the Christmas holiday weekend she sat all alone at her drawing board with no plans, no love, no life to look forward to.

All afternoon she'd watched the other designers and staff at Leonard, Melton, Inc., where she'd worked for over three years right down the corridor from Danny Dannenberg, pass the open door to her office bundled in overcoats and scarves, and wave good-bye. When even Leonard and Melton themselves had left, calling "Joyeux Noël, Dell! Don't work too late. Even your nasty old bosses don't expect you to work late tonight," she was sure she was entirely alone.

How was she to know Danny was still working too, buried in the swatches room, searching for a certain puce pinwhale corduroy, when everyone else had left hours ago? She assumed he had, too, and that she was finally entirely alone. Otherwise, she never would have burst into tears with her door open, much less lamented out loud. Usually, she cried quietly, but today she was so sure everyone was gone that she let herself go and her sobs turned into screams. That's when Danny came running.

He grasped her doorway, white with alarm, and peered in. Dell could see, through her tears, that he had expected nothing less than disaster, that the way he was bracing himself with his arms meant he was sure he'd find her ripped or roped or raped. His eyes searched wildly for an assailant, for the blood. Under the circumstances, to be merely miserable, hysterical but intact, was utterly humiliating. She hid her face in his chest.

"What happened?" he asked above her bent head.

"Just hold me," she pleaded, and he did, but not without a certain self-consciousness. This was the first time he'd ever held her inside the circle of his arms, and he touched her gingerly, his fingertips jumping with surprise at the unfamiliar softness.

Dell, too, felt awkward, stiff, and touched him carefully even as she sobbed. Her hands traced a hesitant path down the bony spinal center of his back, grasped his slender torso, and then quickly let go. Inwardly she groaned, *He's skinnier than I am*! and for several seconds hated him irrationally. Maybe ten pounds, she calculated. No wonder she couldn't stop crying.

"What is it? What happened?" Danny still wanted to know, his spidery arms still entwining the sobbing Dell, his nose inhaling the shampoo scent of her flaming red hair. Coconut. He inhaled deeply. Now that it was obvious Dell wasn't physically hurt, her tears somehow made it safe for him to stroke her, sniff her. He felt almost parental, protective. Usually, it was he who wished to be taken care of, but today with Dell he felt something completely new. Her tears had touched an unused part of him and now, though he wished her no pain, he also hoped her tears would never end.

"Danny, I'm so embarrassed," Dell muttered into the polka-dot satin of his tie. "I didn't know anyone was here, and now I'm completely hysterical and I don't think I can stop crying."

Danny patted her back and held her tighter. "It's all right," he crooned, as if to a colicky daughter. "I know how it is. You feel as if you'll never stop crying, but you will. I promise, you will." He kissed her forehead.

The kiss on her forehead unnerved Dell. It was as if he'd licked her ear. It made her shiver. But at the moment, she disliked herself too much to enjoy feeling shivery. And, in any case, there was no point feeling shivery about a man like Danny Dannenberg. She preferred to hate him.

"Stop being so nice," she said, and pulled away with irritation. "I can't stand it. You're making me cry harder."

"Someone's nice and it makes you cry?"

"When *you're* nice. It makes me realize, among all my other millions of mistakes, that I also have misjudged you terribly."

"No! I don't believe it." He stepped back in mock shock. "The snooty Irish redhead is finally wrong about something." He was angrier than he realized.

"I'm not Irish."

"And I'm not the nasty, rotten rat you seemed to think I was."

"Not nasty, just cold. I thought you were cold. You *have* managed to ignore me for over three years," Dell said, and realized she was no longer crying. The depression that had enveloped her like a black, airless cloud had lifted slightly.

"Well, you haven't exactly knocked down my door to speak to me," Danny shot back, feeling a strange desire to laugh. This was so weird—having an argument with a woman.

"You set the tone right from the beginning." She could remember her first day as if it were last week, and the way he didn't even bother to look up when she said hi to him. "You'd been here for almost a year before me. You could've extended a hand. This is a very large, competitive place. I was so . . . scared."

"How was I to know? You didn't seem scared. And anyway, they keep me so busy here, I don't have time to play Mr. Nice Neighbor."

Suddenly, they both were silent. Danny stared at her with dark, heartbreaker eyes and Dell stared back at him with her mutable blue and sage eyes, each of them aware that this was the first intimate conversation they'd ever had together.

"So," Danny said slowly, "why were you crying?"

Dell's stomach tightened as her mind searched for a way to explain her fit of hysterics to him. Or rather, to find a way to hide it. For surely she couldn't say, "You would cry, too, if your life hung suspended morning to night between unrelenting loneliness and an overwhelming need to succeed." She liked that he'd thought her snooty. It was so much better than terrified, or obsessed, even if they were more accurate. She meant to maintain that particular illusion about herself. Snooty. Yes. Another useful illusion to add to the collection.

"Oh," Dell sighed, "I guess everything just got to me all of a sudden."

"Why isn't a gorgeous *shiksa* like you home eating ham and singing carols for Christmas?"

Somehow, the question stabbed her and her eyes filled with tears again.

"What'd I say?" Danny asked helplessly, pulling out a linen handkerchief. He rose from his chair and handed it to her.

That he, of all people, would be the one to use a linen handkerchief seemed to her a propitious omen, though she was not usually superstitious.

She dabbed at her eyes, streaking the cloth with her mascara, and told him in a shaky voice, ''My father used real handkerchiefs.'' She even managed a smile. ''I never thought, after he died this September, that I'd ever meet another man who did. I thought the age of handkerchiefs died with my father.''

Though Danny had never met Victor Shay, he nevertheless felt strangely complimented to be linked with him. Danny's handkerchiefs, which Christopher Beene had bought for him already embroidered with his initials, were suddenly some sort of badge of honor. He could see that Dell saw it this way and her admiration made him feel proud of himself for keeping up an antiquated but refined custom that added ten dollars onto his weekly—and already excessive—laundry bill.

Dell, he mused, was having an unusual effect on him. He seemed to be enlarging right before her extraordinary blue-green eyes. He seemed to be bursting out of his shirt. And he couldn't stop smiling.

''I am the keeper of a number of outmoded customs,'' he told her as he glanced at his antique watch.

That does it, Dell thought. *It's over*. She knew he always did that when he wished to break away and run off someplace else. She'd seen him glance at his watch, frown, and then disappear from staff meetings, from clients. And now he was about to disappear from her. She forced herself to shrug indifferently. She prayed for the protection of apathy. Apathy dulled the sharp edge of rejection so that she could endure it. All she had to do was not care.

She looked at her own watch and pretended surprise.

''Oh my! It's so late.''

She became a whirlwind, powdering her face with a huge sable brush, reclipping her earrings to her ears, straightening her desk, gathering her things. Only after she'd wrapped a camel cashmere scarf around her neck, thrown her alpaca coat over her shoulders, and slung a bronze leather bag over one arm did she look at him.

''I suppose you have plans?'' he asked, slumped in his chair, staring up at her with those heavy-lidded, soulful eyes. ''Ham and carols?''

''I don't celebrate Christmas. I'm not religious.''

''Fabulous! Neither am I.''

"You mean *you're* not busy?" The possibility that she might not have to spend this evening alone stretched out before her like a lighted airport runway. She circled overhead, not quite ready to land. "I don't think I've ever seen you when you weren't running off somewhere. I thought—"

"And I thought, the way you were hurrying, that you had an appointment." He was grinning ecstatically. She was a study in ecru, camel, bronze, and rust. He adored the way she'd wrapped her scarf round and round her neck. If he brought her home he could unwind the scarf and kiss her warm neck. But would her soft breasts delight him? He felt ready to find out. Now.

"I did," she lied, "but I just canceled it."

He roared with laughter and rose to help her on with her coat, shaking a finger at her.

"You're really terribly sharp and naughty. I can't believe I never noticed that before."

Dell had to bite her lip in order not to say, "Maybe because I'm a woman." The only people the men in this office ever looked at with any real interest were each other.

He brought her back to his place, walking the seven blocks briskly with her arm curled around his, talking into her frosty ear of all her remarkable traits that, for some reason, he'd just become aware of.

"Look at you! You must be—what?—almost six feet, yes?"

"Five eleven."

"My match! Fantastic."

"Well, not exactly. You still tower over me," she said, looking up into his big, dark eyes.

He stopped in the middle of the cold, damp street and looked back at her. "Still, you feel like you're my match." She was the tallest woman he'd ever known and her shoulders seemed to come up to his shoulders. He looked at her padded shoulders in the alpaca coat, at her smooth jawline above the cashmere scarf. Her flesh looked juicy, succulent; her posture was impeccable. He loved the way she held herself, erect yet loose. He held her shoulders and ran his lips along her jawline.

"Mmm," he murmured. "Your skin is as smooth and cold as ice cream."

"A premium brand of ice cream, I hope."

He laughed again and hurried her along the frigid streets until, too chilled to remove his hands from his pockets, he pointed with his chin to the building on the corner.

She nodded that she understood and allowed him to rush her into the lobby, her mind in complete turmoil. On one hand, she could hardly wait to see the great Danny Dannenberg's personal interiors. She had thought she would wander the rooms, accept one glass of wine, and when her curiosity was satisfied, leave. But that was before he began doing whatever it was he was doing to her shoulders and her face on the street. Suddenly, it was a whole new ballgame and now the question had to be asked again, "Is he or isn't he?" Could it be she'd made an entirely incorrect assumption about him years ago—several incorrect assumptions, actually—and that she'd been as blind to the real Daniel Dannenberg as he'd been to her? To learn the answer, however, meant once again facing the danger of rejection . . . or its opposite. Involvement. Both terrified her. But it was too late to flee; Danny had unlocked his door and pushed it open for her. She had no choice but to enter.

"Oh, my!" she gasped, eyes fixed upward, as she shuffled down the long foyer, gazing at the barrel-vaulted ceiling painted the exact blue of midnight and scattered with stars of gold. The stars shot forward and receded on the inky ceiling, and, Dell discovered when she looked down, on the floor, too. Gold stars were woven into the indigo carpet runner, which gave her the dizzying sensation that she was walking on the sky. Ahead of her, on the far wall, an opalescent moon beckoned.

Then, suddenly, she *was* dizzy—dizzy enough to faint. She fell against Danny, who steadied her by grasping her shoulders again.

She could feel her head flopping back and her eyes closing and his hands sliding under her to support her arched back, but she was alert. She just didn't have the energy to tell him.

"My God, Dell! Are you really going to faint? I didn't know women did that anymore." His warm breath blew on her chin, making the rest of her face feel cold and unprotected.

She opened her eyes. ''Between your handkerchiefs and my faints, we're really two very old-fashioned people.''

He laughed, but instead of pulling her upright, he pulled her tighter into him, squeezing her waist, grinding his hips into hers.

''Don't wake up. Faint. I like saving you.''

She smiled and closed her eyes again. Her arms hung straight down and her fingers grazed the indigo carpet while her breasts pointed straight up at his eyes. She tried to make herself faint. She was willing to do anything he asked, so long as he held her like this, gazed at her like this, covered her with his warm breath.

When he lifted her up, grunting with the effort, she kept her eyes closed although she was completely awake. It was just that she'd never been carried anywhere by anyone since she was an infant, and she was afraid to let Danny see how much she was enjoying it. Even more, she was afraid to see whether he was enjoying it or not. Every second she kept expecting him to turn from her, revolted.

He dropped her on a quilted peach bed and immediately pulled an afghan over her. As he tucked the blanket around her, she felt tears suddenly splash out of her eyes and down her cheeks again.

Before he could say a word, she sobbed, ''I'm sorry. It's just that you've been so incredibly sweet.''

He sat down on the edge of the bed beside her and blotted her tears with a tissue. When new tears fell, he leaned over and kissed them. When she curled an arm around his neck, he climbed onto the bed with her.

''You really have to start getting used to people treating you well without bursting into tears,'' he said, smiling. ''Although I do adore the taste of your tears. Clam broth, exactly.'' Which reminded him he was hungry. He pointed a warning finger at her. ''Don't move. I'll take care of everything. Sleep a little. Go ahead. I'll wake you when dinner's here.'' He stood up without touching her, flicked out the light, and left her alone on his bed.

What am I doing here? she asked herself. Headed for more heartbreak, she answered without pause.

The next thing she knew, he was kissing her awake. Little-boy kisses. On her cheeks. Heartbreak kisses.

"Feeling better?"

She nodded, almost ready to cry again. The loneliness was infinite, the aloneness even more intense because he was standing right there but she couldn't have him. For years she admired him, hated him, ignored him, spied on him. Tonight she allowed herself to want him. But now she knew for sure, as he bent over to wake her with his prissy little kisses, that she could never have him because he kissed her like an older brother. Without desire.

And that's when his mouth slid across her cheek to her mouth, circled her lips, circled back, and enveloped her.

Much, much later, when the bowl of soup he'd brought her sat on the end table thoroughly cold, she wanted to remove her bronze sweater, but he stopped her. They had not yet spoken, only kissed. And kissed.

But now he said, "Let me. Let me do everything to you. For you." He touched her breasts through her sweater. "Let's pet, make out like we did when we were in high school, with our clothes half on. Remember how hot that was?"

His hands, his words, made her remember. Through her clothes she felt his hands on her more acutely than if she'd been naked. At first, his touch was tentative, exploratory, and overwhelmingly arousing. The nervousness of his fingers brought her back, back to the same hurricane of sensations she'd experienced when she was young. Then, when a boy kissed her, touched her, made her wild with excitement beneath her panties and her half-buttoned blouse, the force of her sexual hunger frightened and shamed her. She was afraid she'd be accused of liking "it" too much. Now, with Danny, she somehow knew she could never like it too much. She gave in to the storm inside her.

"We are in a Caddie convertible," Danny whispered. "The seats are tomato-red leather. This is the first time for both of us."

"Yes," she eagerly agreed, and he smiled.

"You're paralyzed with fear. You need me to take charge. You need me to touch you . . . like this."

"Yes. Oh, yes," she groaned. With her eyes closed she could almost smell the red leather car upholstery, although she'd never been in a Caddie convertible. But tonight she was there.

"And to feel you through your sweater."

"Yes."

"And through your pants." His hands went between her legs and were busy for some time.

"Yes," she heard herself moan.

"And to help you off with your sweater," he said at last, his fingers moving deftly, expertly now.

She ached as he slid the sweater up her midriff, devouring her bare skin as it was exposed. She wished he'd rip the sweater off in one swoop, and she also prayed for ten more arms, so that he might never stop inching the sleeves up, up as he found new flesh to squeeze in his teeth.

"You need me to undress you."

"Yes," she ardently agreed.

"But I'm not going to remove your bra yet."

She arched her back in the bed beneath him, oblivious of the peach-quilted walls, the wonderful old wrought-iron garden bench with cushions of cotton piqué, and thrust her breasts up at him, as if they were begging to be bared, as if they were saying, "Please. Oh, please!"

"I'm making you wait because I want to touch you for a while in your little lace bra."

"Oh."

"And to look at you. I love how you're almost bursting out of those little cups. Do you like when I squeeze them like this?"

"Oh, so much, so much."

A paradise of months seemed to go by before he said, "I'm going to unhook you now."

She wanted to lift up, help him, but he told her not to move and she liked that, too.

"Oh! I could cry!" he exclaimed, kneeling above her. "I never thought they'd be this white and this round. Oh! And with darling, hidden nipples. I must coax them out."

And he did. He'd discovered her flaw—breasts without any nipples at all—and he set out to correct it. For more than an hour all she could see of his was him dark, silky head, clamped to her chest, but she could feel what he was doing to her down to her toes. He was producing sensations in her that traveled down to the bottoms of her feet, congesting her toes until they sat up stiffly.

She felt him as she'd felt no one before, partly because no one had ever paid her this much attention, or set such a languorous pace to lovemaking. Danny seemed willing to devote the entire night to pleasure. Absent was a sense of urgency to finish, to end; only the present existed, continuing on and on in exquisite tension.

Down in her stiff toes she felt his teeth and his tongue on her breasts, then his wide open mouth covering them, devouring them. He was turning her breasts into instruments of pleasure so sensitive, he had only to blow on them to make her whole body convulse. He'd blow hot little gusts, then long, whispery breezes, and smile as he watched the effect.

"Look," he said, amazed. "They've popped out."

And there, at the bumpy centers of her aureolas, were her inverted nipples, nubby, raw, and dark pink, seen by her for the first time.

"Daniel, Daniel, you don't know what you've done. Look at them. They're like pink erasers on a pencil." Her fingers closed around them. "I've got little rubber erasers on my breasts and I never knew it. Daniel, I never saw them before."

They stared solemnly at her nipples as she stroked his head and told him how she'd pinched herself black and blue, slapped ice cubes to her chest, and once, even stuck herself with a safety pin.

"To force the little buggers out," she said with a laugh.

"And other men?" he asked, suddenly feeling such a powerful mastery of this unfamiliar terrain that he risked hearing the answer. "No one ever could?"

"No one," she said, shaking her head emphatically. "No one, ever."

At that he cried, grinning through his tears. It was the first time she'd seen a man cry. At her father's funeral some months before, she'd looked down into his face in the open casket and thought he looked like he was crying.

Tears of regret, perhaps? Or an apology? She'd wondered. Finally she concluded they were tears of disappointment, a frown of disapproval, for why should he be any different in death than he was in life?

But Danny's tears were joyous.

"Oh, Dell," he said. "Dell, darling."

Darling. He called her darling. She looked around the bedroom for the first time. She hadn't wanted to peek until now. She took it all in—the peach-quilted walls, the garden bench, the cushions and the table skirt in those refreshing fabrics—piqué and plissé—the walls of mirrors and closets, the thick apricot carpet, and the framed photographs. Of his father? Mother? Brother?

I would change nothing, she thought. This is it. It was the heaven she'd been journeying toward in her dreams. Perfection. If she lived here, with him, she'd fall asleep smiling with him beside her and awaken in his arms, and everything would be tinged a pale, pale pumpkin.

She thought of the peeling walls of her room when she was a child, and the walls, picture-laden, in the tiny apartment where she lived now. One week she brought home three new pictures, the next week five. The walls were covered with art—watercolors, pastels, pen-and-ink drawings, ancient Oriental masks, and architectural ornaments—but still she shopped for more. She shopped for anything and everything. But if she lived with walls like these, of quilted pale peach polished linen, she'd never hang a thing to cover them. Nothing.

What, she wondered, would her mother think of these walls? She wasn't sure. And of this lanky, adorable, excessive, arrogant, tender, passionate, naked—

"Oh, my!" she said, turning back to Danny. "I see you have a Christmas present for me after all."

4

In the beginning, they discovered they loved to shop. Together.

Of course, what they meant by "shopping" wasn't the ordinary, mundane march to the market to buy a carton of milk, or even the purchase of a sleek new designer suit at an exclusive boutique. And it certainly wasn't the kind of driven, numbing shopping that could overtake Dell when she was feeling most alone and vulnerable.

No, this was the specialized, professional shopping permitted only to designers, architects, and decorators at to-the-trade-only showrooms. Work. But all that first winter and spring, Danny and Dell elevated their work onto a pedestal of delight because they were falling in love, and to young lovers, anything is delightful if it's done together. Especially shopping.

So together they hunted in the jungle of design buildings centered on the city's East Side, stalking the exclusive showrooms for bleached python-skin desks and carved horn chairs, for imported brocades in bird-of-paradise prints, and for unusual tassels to finish custom chenille sofas and damask drapery swags.

"What do you think of this? Of these?" they asked each other without identifying which client, which room they had in mind. They didn't have to. They knew.

After that first rapturous Christmas weekend, they were never apart again, even at work. They talked over all their design projects, improved on each other's solutions, learned everything about each other's clients. So they knew.

Everyone at Leonard, Melton noticed. Daniel Danenberg and Dell Shay were the talk of the design field. And although the happy couple weren't particularly discreet, no one could quite believe what they were seeing. Into the austere, professional, and unteamlike viciousness of the Leonard, Melton workplace, Danny and Dell had brought harmonious cooperation, creative generosity . . . and heterosexual love.

Eroticism dripped and rubbed on everything they did, everything they said. With them, sex and work were so intermingled, it was difficult to tell where one left off and the other began.

"Those two," a fellow designer observed, "have redefined the word inseparable."

After a couple of months of the new affair, everyone expected things to die down. They certainly never expected it to last. To their surprise, the intensity only mounted, and some said Danny flaunted it in public like a proud peacock. It was never more obvious than when they shopped together. Wading through the metalassés and pongees, some part of Danny's anatomy always seemed to be touching some part of Dell's.

But no one would deny that, despite all the touching and grabbing that went on, they were always working. They worked incredibly long hours, partly because working together was such fun. And the best part, the most fun, was when they went shopping.

Consulting her list, Dell would say, "I need vinyl kitchen flooring for the Delmans—you know, the shoe designers with the huge family."

And Danny would whisper in her ear as they flicked through vinyl samples, "Mmm, this one feels particularly resilient. We could get down on the floor and test it."

And Dell would have to insist, "Danny, stop it! Someone might see. Get up!"

"Come with me to find an embossed velvet for the Roths' Victorian sofa." If Dell were at her drawing board, Danny would come up behind her, take her breasts in his hands, and suggest they go shopping.

"And what do *you* need?" he'd ask, pressing into her back. "Don't you need lighting for your corporate dining room?"

"Yes, and an enormous oriental rug."

"Ah, Dell, darling, I'm thinking of a hundred and one things I'd love you to do to me on an enormous oriental rug. Let me tell you ten of them."

"No!"

"Five?"

"Let's go shopping." Sometimes shopping saved them. She was sure of it. And sometimes, shopping only increased the heat between them, setting them on fire while they flicked through panels of hand-painted wallpapers and scrolled borders. Often, they served as scouts, leaving a scorched trail behind them as they picked out two or three reproduction Chippendale dining chairs or two Directoire-inspired chandeliers for their clients' final approval. Then, retracing their steps a few days later, only this time with a client in tow, the trail seemed not scorched by passion but juiceless and desiccated. In the presence of their clients they had to stifle all foreplay, and only remember how much fun it had been to test the French beds upholstered in toile de Jouy.

That winter and spring they kissed and flirted their way through hundreds of showrooms, and made purchases totaling hundreds of thousands of dollars. Yet few showroom managers or receptionists would waive the registration process and simply usher them through, even though they greeted Danny by name.

"Good," Danny told them, nodding approval. "Never let me buy you or charm my way in here. Keep your standards high."

Happily, he signed his name and resale number at the front desks, pleased to see that the manufacturers and wholesalers were protecting him and professionals like him by keeping the general public out. Whenever he saw the familiar sign on a showroom door, "All Clients Must Be Accompanied By Their Decorator," he'd smile at Dell or nudge her approvingly.

"Aren't you carrying this love of exclusivity a little too far?" Dell finally confronted him.

"Absolutely not."

"But you have to admit the system smacks of a certain snobbishness." For the first time, a note of irritation crept into her voice. "It's like an exclusive club, closed to the 'wrong sort' of people. Doesn't this remind you of the way we used to practice anti-Semitism in this country—*we* would keep *you* out of our clubs."

"It's still done," Danny sighed with exaggerated patience, "but this is different. This is a system based on economics. It's business."

"Snooty business."

"Look, why do you think we have to register our company's name before we can even look through the samples? And why are all the fabric and furniture prices in code?"

"Oh, come on, Danny. I've been in the business almost eight years. I know how it operates."

"You know *how* it operates," Danny agreed, "but not *why*."

"Okay, I give up," Dell said, folding her arms tensely across her chest. "Tell me, professor, why does the business operate this way?" She was fuming but she didn't know why. Something about the way Danny so cheerfully accepted being scrutinized by the front-desk staff, the way he excused their haughty attitude and toadied up to them, actually giving them compliments, irritated her immensely.

"The system," Danny said, oblivious to Dell's irritation, "is based on the fundamentals of economics— supply and demand. We take Mr. and Mrs. Client to see the gorgeous chintzes at Mr. X's showroom. Mrs. Client is crazy about the chintzes. Mr. Client takes out his checkbook. 'I'd like to order five yards,' he says. But Mr. X says he only takes orders from designers, so Mr. and Mrs. Client are forced to come to us and pay our fees and our markups if they insist on having Mr. X's gorgeous chintzes. And Mr. X can count on large orders from us—not five yards at a time, but more like fifty or a hundred yards."

"Yes, yes," Dell said shortly. "Of course I understand that Mr. X creates a demand for his supply by being so exclusive. Do you think I'm an imbecile? Of course I understand that he protects our business, precisely because it brings him more business. We, who represent dozens of clients, will make larger and more frequent purchases than a single customer."

"Then what, Dell, darling, is troubling you?"

"I don't know!" Dell cried, covering her reddening face with her hands. "It's me. No, it's you!"

"Moi?"

He swung an arm over her shoulder and glanced around

him. Fighting bored him, but *that*—in a windowed show-room display sat a chair covered in calf stenciled in a leopard pattern—simply thrilled him.

"Oh, look at that hide. Isn't it to die!"

Dell just shook her head. All her life she'd avoided fights because they always turned into tense, mean-spirited affairs that went on too long and solved nothing. As a teenager she was always fighting with her mother, but even when she won, she really lost. Afterward, her mother would sulk silently, making Dell feel guilty for speaking out. Even if she sobbed an apology, her mother would take days to come out of it.

Then there were the arguments with her one-and-only high school best friend, Tamara, in which Tamara's superior debating skills left Dell defenseless. On the few occasions when she'd fought back, she was more miserable than if she'd never lost her temper—fearing she'd lost not only her temper, but her best friend too. So she resolved to avoid all fights for the rest of her life—a resolution she was able, for the most part, to adhere to by remaining aloof. The less she interacted with people, the less chance there was for friction. But with Danny, all that changed. He'd forced her back out into the world. And now, he had forced her to break her resolution. But just as she was roused to the point of inflammation, he simply walked away from it. And she was inexplicably disappointed.

"Aren't we going to finish our fight?"

There, in the busiest corridor of their favorite design building, Danny burst out into roaring laughter. His shouts bounced off the slick polished-stone walls and floors, the sound magnifying in the narrow corridor. People turned and stared, which only made Danny hold Dell tighter.

"You're completely *mashuginah*," he laughed, "begging to keep a fight going that already ended."

Unable to break free without making more of a scene, she said to his face, "I hate you. And I hate when you lecture to me, and when you're critical of me, especially when you find it funny."

"But how can you be sorry our fight's over?"

"I don't like leaving things in the middle," she offered lamely.

"Good," Danny said and swatted her rump. "Remember that when we become partners, and make sure to finish every project you start."

Dell stood completely still. Only her eyes moved, rolling and blinking and flashing electrically.

"When we become . . . what?"

"Partners."

"That's what I thought you said." She was so stunned, she didn't think to stop his hand from rubbing her rump. She threw her arms around his neck and for once was completely unconscious of the spectacle they were making of themselves. "But what," she whispered tearily in his ear, "do you need me for? If you stayed, I'm sure Carl Leonard would make you a partner. You could have your pick of anyone. So why me?"

"Oh, Dell, darling, how many times do I have to tell you you're the first and only woman I've ever loved?"

Though she never tired of hearing it, she never really believed it, either. "How about your mother? Didn't you love her? Doesn't she count as the first?"

"My mother was wonderful company for me in my loneliest young years. Wonderful. But I could never really love my mother because I absolutely despised her taste."

"Oh, Danny, be serious. We've known each other less than three months. Do you really think we could—and should—become partners?"

"Why not? We work fabulously well together. Fabulously," he said again and gave her rump another rub, as a fellow designer from Leonard, Melton couldn't avoid noticing as he walked past them.

"Well, it is true you know absolutely nothing about upholstery and finishing techniques," she teased, "as we discovered when you ordered Turkish corners for all the Ketchums' knife-edged sofa pillows. Without me, you might make even worse blunders."

Avoiding the packed elevators, they made their way down the stairs to the lobby. Then Danny moved her into a phone booth with him, but couldn't get the door to close around them.

He kissed her mouth until his own lips were red with her lipstick. Behind him an annoyed but curious line formed to use the telephone.

"Think of the sensation we'd make. Look around you. Already we create a sensation wherever we go."

"That's because you refuse to keep your hands away from me," she laughed, trying to block her breasts with her own hands, "even in public, even when a crowd of people who want to use this phone are staring right at us."

"Don't look at them. Look at me. Better yet, close your eyes," Danny commanded. "Then picture this: We're partners in our own company and every day, a new and fabulous client hires us. And every night, we go home and make fabulous love."

If Dell was embarrassed to express affection in public, Danny was her exact opposite. He seemed to want every passerby to know that not only was he kissing Dell's lipstick off, but that he really wanted to rip her clothes right off. Sometimes, it even seemed to Dell that he touched her more in public than he did in private, but she refused to find fault with him, perhaps hoping that then he couldn't possibly find fault with her. Theirs was a miraculous union, she told herself, of opposites—a perpetually shy and embarrassed redhead who hates calling attention to herself and a flamboyant exhibitionist who adores the spotlight.

"Public mortification," she told him, "really isn't as awful as I expected. In fact, I'm getting used to it. Oh, I still blush when you try to feel me up in public, but I don't die on my feet anymore. I just get a little queasy now."

She loved to make Danny laugh. And now, if they became partners, she could keep him laughing forever.

"Partners," she sighed. She could hardly believe it. But she had to get him out of that telephone booth, so she asked him, "What are you doing for lunch?" knowing the answer in advance, knowing Danny, once revved up, rarely stopped midday to eat lunch. Though he enjoyed elegant dinners, lunch was the time for junk food, fast food, food-on-the-run food.

"Lunch?" he asked, incredulous. "You know I don't—"

"I know, I know. Just give you a frank with mustard and sauerkraut and you're happy. But I thought, partner, that today you just might have second thoughts."

"Hmm, on second thought," he said, catching her meaning immediately, and leading her out of the building, "a leisurely lunch is just what I had in mind." He took her to his apartment, undressing himself in the elevator until he was barechested and shoeless. But once they were alone, he would not be rushed, even if they were on their lunch hour.

"I detest quickies," he stated after an hour, and called the office to say they wouldn't be back that afternoon.

"We're shopping. And we have to go all the way up to the Bronx to the furniture framer. So if anyone asks," he told the receptionist without a trace of dishonesty in his voice, "we're seeing sources in the hinterlands and we'll be in tomorrow."

"But once we're partners, once we have our own company," he warned Dell, returning to bed, "we can't do this anymore. No sneaking off work for the afternoon. Promise?"

"Of course. We'd only be screwing ourselves—literally and figuratively," she laughed, delirious at his vision of their future together.

And to Dell's surprise, Danny agreed, despite a sexual appetite that was almost insatiable.

"D & D comes first," he announced.

"D & D?" Dell shouted. "D & D? Oh, God, I can't believe it. You've even thought of our firm's name. And it's . . . it's pure poetry!"

Two months before their wedding and month-long honeymoon through northern Italy, they took offices in an old industrial building downtown. Its unlikely location was so far downtown that when Christopher Beene got the announcement, he told Danny, "I get nosebleeds below sea level." Most of their colleagues told them they were crazy.

But Dell and Danny knew they were destined to be ground-breakers. Liberators. Messiahs. Eventually, others would follow them. And meanwhile, the rent was ridiculously cheap.

They began with a budget of a hundred thousand dollars—a collection of bank loans, family loans, personal savings, and an outright gift from Dell's mother. Almost all of it went toward redecorating their offices, but even then, Danny fretted it wasn't nearly enough.

"D & D needs a million-dollar face and all we can afford is cheap cosmetics."

"But Danny, that's just what we want to display—our own bag of decorating tricks. We don't want our clients to say of us, 'Oh, my, they're richer than we are.' We want them to say, 'Oh, my, they certainly are cleverer than we are.' "

"Maybe so," Danny conceded, "but I don't feel very clever."

For once, a design scheme did not come to him. He stood in the center of the huge loft and squeezed his eyes shut but he couldn't see a thing. Just blank white walls. In just three months—on October first—the office was scheduled to open officially and all decoration would have to be completed by then. Danny hadn't felt this kind of dread since he was a boy, before he discovered his special talent.

Now they shopped together in a frenzy, looking not to buy, but for ideas. There was sadness, too, in their search, for they knew that once they were married and D & D was open for business, they'd rarely be able to shop together again.

"One of us has to cover the office—to be there for the phones, for walk-ins, to do the furniture layouts and the color schemes. We can't both take off to the showrooms. We've got to divide up the work."

"I know," Dell agreed, but she was disconsolate.

"But we'll always be together when we meet with new clients," he offered as a compromise. "We'll make it a rule to do the first consultations together. Not that I'll be needed. When new clients see you for the first time, Dell, darling, they'll agree to double their original budget, just to see you smile."

Dell smiled, but she knew it was Danny who got clients to double their budgets, and got them to agree to it willingly, even gratefully. She'd seen him do it.

"Only one and a quarter?" he'd said to Dell's Aunt Annette and her new husband Ralph only last week. Hearing that Dell and Danny were opening shop after their wedding, Annette and Ralph invited them for dinner and then a short tour of the new suburban house they were in the process of purchasing. They said Dell was the only decorator they knew.

"And I said to Ralph," Annette told them proudly, "that yes, one hundred and twenty five thousand is a lot of money, but I think we should keep it in the family and give you kids our vote of confidence."

And Ralph said, elbowing Danny and winking broadly, "Think that chunk of change is big enough for you to create a little paradise for us?"

"Frankly, no," Danny had told them. "I know it sounds like a lot of money, but D & D will stand for quality. And there's no way we can do the interiors of an entire house—even a not overly large house like yours—for less than two hundred and fifty thousand dollars. You've seen our work in magazines over the years and you've seen the newspaper publicity D & D is getting in advance of its opening. Already, we're one of the front runners in the field, but we're big budget."

"What do you mean by a not overly large house?"

"Look," Danny said, holding up his hands, "I'll be happy to recommend a small-budget designer who—"

"No, no!" Annette cried, grasping Ralph's arm. "We want you!"

"But we can't do the job you want—we can't give you New Orleans decadence with just the right touch of peeling paint and new, made-to-look-faded upholstery and lace drapery—for less than *three* times your budget. It's a fabulous look but it has to be done just right. The colors must be faded and dusty but never muddy. And we'd have to take down that tacky railing immediately and put up a filigreed balustrade. I have an iron forger who will—"

"*Three* times our budget?" By now Ralph was swallowing rapidly. He seemed to have something caught in his throat. "Didn't you just mention a figure of two hundred and fifty thousand?"

"Well, that would be cutting it extremely close, but since you are family, I suppose we could try—"

"Yes? You're sure? Oh, thank you, Danny. We really appreciate it. Bless you both."

Dell had seen him do it a number of times, first at Leonard, Melton, but now that he was starting the practice at the unborn D & D, she felt as protective as a mother-to-be.

"D & D must establish an impeccable reputation immediately," she said, half in love with Danny's silky manipulativeness and half remorseful.

"My poor aunt and uncle are spending much, much more money than they ever intended. It's not right. Danny, aren't you at all guilty?"

"Of course not. Dell, darling, we are not monsters who trick innocent clients. And if there is one thing your aunt and uncle are not, it is poor! They're responsible adults with oodles of money. Oh, God, Dell, oodles! And they *want* to spend it. They want to spend a *fortune,* don't you see, so they can complain loudly to all their friends about just how much it cost them. Don't worry, they can afford it—they just need to be coaxed a little."

Coaxing was his specialty. He could coax her into anything, convince her of absolutely everything. He was always so sure of himself that she was embarrassed to tell him her fears. Now, suddenly, he was the one who was afraid. He stood in the middle of the empty D & D loft and moaned, "I'm lost. I'm completely blocked. I can't think of a thing to do to this place. I hate everything."

She knew better than to try to suggest some design motifs to him. On their most recent shopping jaunts, he'd expressed distaste for every display she'd admired. It was true; he hated everything.

"I hate Bauhaus, I hate post-modern, I hate English country. I mean, I hate it for us, for D & D. We shouldn't be identified with any one look," Danny said, pacing and perspiring. "And yet we want it known that we can do an interior in any period, give it any look the client wants and that's appropriate. So what do we do here?"

Dell stood beside Danny and stared at the white walls, the high white ceilings, and suddenly, it came to her.

"Well, I love your idea for our wedding," she said slowly. "For doing it entirely monochromatic. We could do that here. Just paint everything out. It's a cheap and unifying solution."

"Gray," Danny said, coming alive.

Dell just smiled and let him think out loud.

"We could do the walls in in a low-luster gray patent leather. It'll give almost the exact effect of lacquering and cost half as much. And we could do the floors in a gray pinstripe industrial carpet that wears and wears."

"Gray. Yes," she said, nodding. "Tailored. Professional. Yet the patent leather will give it just the right touch of dazzle. I like it."

"Yes, I do, too. I think I've finally found the winning solution."

She wanted to remind him that she'd come up with the monochromatic idea and that *they* had worked out a solution together, but he was still creating aloud, and she didn't want to stop the flow.

"We could do fabulous charcoal-dipped nailheads around the perimeters of the walls. And gray frosted glass doors."

"Oh, Danny, I see it, I see it!"

"And it won't be entirely monochromatic. We'll do an accent in rose," he said.

"Rose. Yes," she agreed.

He was cooking now, bubbling over but even he recognized he could thank Dell for most of it. She was the source of some of his best inspirations. With her, he could do no wrong. She freed him. With her, he soared. Only one other person adored him this much. *Oh, God,* Danny thought, *how I love to be loved!*

"Ah, Dell, darling, it's going to be fabulous!" he rejoiced, swooping her up in his arms.

He stood there and let Dell cover his face with kisses. Staring out past her red hair to the blank walls, he thought of Christopher Beene. Only Christopher would know where to find the perfect gray low-luster patent leather for the walls.

Poor Christopher, Danny thought, sighing inwardly. Would he ever get over Dell? Or, as Christopher would say it, "that overly tall redhead."

Christopher had been ignoring him, sulking, ever since Danny told him about Dell. But this had been going on long enough. Today, Danny would call him. Tomorrow, perhaps, he would see him. Even with Dell right there in his arms, he missed Christopher. Until this moment, Danny hadn't realized how much.

5

"Don't let him cow you, my darling. He's a bit of a snoot. So if he tries to pull his Great Architect routine—like he did with me—just remember, he can advise but he can't dictate. The house is to die, but now that his fun is almost over, ours is just beginning. D & D has a legitimate say about all interior space. All. And it's right there in the contract."

"Yes, but you know how he works," Dell said, her upper lip a moustache of milky foam from the cappuccinno she'd gulped hurriedly. "He even designs the coffee mugs and sheets for the beds. A Theodor Glass house is always just that—his—from top to bottom, exterior *and* interior. Every square foot bears his imprint."

"Well, not this time," Danny said gleefully, still in his robe. He took a napkin and reached over to dab at her lip, but to his surprise, she pulled away. Her gesture was noted and then disregarded, for Daniel Dannenberg was as certain of Dell's innocence as he was of her love.

And for his love of her, hadn't he dragged himself out of bed at seven after only two hours sleep? True, he had an important installation today, but that wasn't until ten. No, he adored their morning cappuccino ritual; he wouldn't have missed it for the world. What went on last night had nothing to do with this, with the two of them. For love of her he was here now, alert and eager to chat, to advise and support her before her big day. And if she was less appreciative than he'd expected, well, he reasoned, she was probably nervous. Poor Dell was still ruled by fear and even his great love for her had not yet cured her.

"The world-famous Theodor-I-work-alone-Glass signed his name to it," Danny continued. "Don't ask me why, because I never would've believed it, but in a way, I don't think he cared. There's something dead about him. And yet haughty, too. As we shook hands, he actually said, 'I look forward to our collaboration.' The putz.''

Dell listened as she searched in her bag for the keys to the car she'd rented last night, stifling a yawn, stifling the whole dreadful night of anxious waiting that was now over but not nearly forgotten. She'd awakened when Danny finally got home, and after an hour of tossing, finally got up. When she was dressed, she packed a large leather shopping bag with rolled-up plans, a tape measure, fabric swatches, paint chips, her work notebook, a nightgown, and a map of Long Island with the route to the Southampton house outlined in red. Then she headed for the stainless-steel kitchen to prepare cappuccino, which always relaxed her, subduing the morning storms of unhappiness and doubt that she increasingly awakened to, with the comfort of a well-practiced routine.

But even more pleasurable than the seven simple steps that produced the black, aromatic coffee and the steaming milk was the machine itself. It was enormous, of gleaming copper and brass, and performed with such gusto that she formed a kind of emotional attachment to it, cooing and patting it each morning, just as she might a household pet. A house-warming gift from their secretary, Angie Romano—shipped by her prosperous family in Rome whose factory manufactured the machines—it sat, fat and imperial, just waiting for a bellyful of cold water, a cup of milk, and a few scoops of espresso to begin its dyspeptic belching and spewing that never failed to make her smile. Except for today.

Danny was still talking as he helped her on with her shearling coat.

''Ah, Dell, I could just scream that I can't go out to the house with you today because it's going to be such a giggle.''

''It won't be a giggle,'' Dell disagreed, ''but it just might be awesome because he's awesome. I love Theodor Glass.''

''You never even met him.''

''No, but I've loved every building he's ever done. And don't call him a putz for being a little stiff and shy when he met you.'' By now, she knew that putz meant stupid little prick, a word that usually made Dell groan and then laugh in spite of herself whenever Danny used it. But not today. "I like shy people," she added.

"Dell, darling, what in the world is wrong with you this morning?" He held her by her collar, forcing her to see his genuine bewilderment. "Aren't you going to tell me?"

Actually, she hadn't planned to tell him. If she had any plan at all, it was to close her eyes and hold on. To squeeze her eyes shut and hope that when she opened them, she'd see how wrong she'd been. Being wrong was infinitely preferable, she'd learned early on, to being right but loveless.

But Danny kept insisting, "Tell me." His eyes were bruised innocence, his demeanor entirely free of guilt. Of course, Dell almost laughed, that was because Danny never suffered guilt about anything. All during their first year together, she joked that somehow she'd inherited Danny's Jewish guilt while Danny had the genes of an authentic I-don't-give-a-shit WASP. "Talk about mixed marriages," she'd say, and laugh. But even now, a year later, a part of her still believed him, believed that if he felt no guilt, he must be innocent. Therefore, she could risk asking him. She still loved him that much.

"Where were you last night?"

Danny let go of her collar but his eyes were steady.

"I woke up and you weren't there. It was almost five. Then I heard you come in. It happened last week and the week before. All those nights." Her eyes filled with tears. "Where do you go? I want to know. Tell me. There's another woman, right?"

Danny sighed with an amused kind of relief and took her into his arms.

"Oh, my pet, my one and only love, is that what you thought? Another woman?"

She sobbed yes into his shoulder.

"Don't you know you're the only woman I've ever loved?" He was careful not to rub his unshaven face against her flushed cheeks, but he held her tightly. "Aren't you my prize, my partner in everything?"

"Yes, but where were you?"

He let go of her and ran his hands through his thick brown hair. "You know that when I'm tense I can't sleep.

And you know that when that happens, I've got to be alone to walk and work it out.''

"I know," Dell said, and searched for signs of anxiety on his smooth baby face. "But what are you so tense about? Tell me."

"Are you joking?" He grabbed a clump of his hair and pulled. "In two and a half years, D & D has grown faster than even I predicted. We're both swamped with work. We've outgrown our office. This apartment is a dump. I can't hire junior designers fast enough. I've got the Kriter installation today and the Jackson party tonight, and I don't have time to get a haircut. And then, I'm sorry to say, you make it all worse. You accuse me of having another woman and you tell me how much you've always loved Theo Glass, no doubt because he's an architect and I'm only a lowly interior designer."

"Oh, Danny, that's not true!" Dell cried and awkwardly threw her bulky arms around his neck. "You know I think you're a giant. I worship you." Overheated, she brushed back her damp hair but would not let go. "Please don't be angry. I was wrong, and I'm sorry. But I love you so much that sometimes I imagine I'm losing you to something dark and secret and scary. That's why you must never keep any secrets from me. Okay?"

"Who has time for secrets?" Danny said, hiding his face in her radiant hair.

"Me, too," Dell agreed with about as much conviction.

"Fabulous," Danny said and took her arm. "Now you better get going." He walked her down the long foyer with walls the blue of midnight and held the door open.

"Drive safely."

"I'll drive straight to the office tomorrow morning and see you there."

Displaying nothing, Danny asked, "So you're definitely staying over?"

"Yes. It's supposed to snow tonight and the Elkins said there's an inn in town open all year round. And hell, they're paying."

"Our first night apart." Danny looked utterly disconsolate.

"Oh, Danny," Dell said, smiling at last, "I love you so much."

* * *

At first she thought they were piles of old clothes, but as she got nearer to her car, she saw they were people—living people—sleeping in the corners of the parking garage. One man was awake and came toward her as she stuck her key in the car door. She looked around wildly for the guard.

"Don't, Miss. Please don't give us away." His hand had grasped her arm as she was about to pull open the car door.

"I won't, but you must let go of me."

Immediately, he raised both arms over his head, as if he were under arrest.

"We ain't gonna hurt you. We just need a warm place to sleep, is all." He was wrapped in rags.

Dell looked over at the sleeping mounds. Two were children.

"My family," he explained. "We're waiting to be placed. It shouldn't be much longer. It be nine months." He opened his mouth to laugh. "And no baby yet!" His purple gums were swollen. He had no teeth.

Dell pulled twenty dollars from her wallet. She might have given him all the cash she had if she didn't need it for her trip. Nine months, and still cracking jokes.

"Bless your heart, beautiful lady."

"And bless your heart, too, sir," she said, and shook his gloved hand.

Out on the highway past Queens and the airport exits, eastbound traffic lightened and Dell, cruising at sixty with the heater on and the radio off, relaxed her tight grip on the steering wheel, expecting to begin enjoying the two-hour drive any moment now. Certainly, nothing in the bare and flat February landscape commanded her attention, but her mind skipped wildly over a vast terrain of subjects, unable to concentrate on anything. Every thought touched on a different aspect of her life, but they all produced the same sensation in her chest and throat: strangulation.

First, she thought about the incident in the parking garage, and for a moment, actually felt elated. Why not, she wondered, start a project to design and build low-cost housing for the homeless? Not dreary, faceless dormitories, but gorgeous, award-winning dwellings conceived and executed by the greatest architects and designers of our time. Each artist's model setting new standards in stylistic yet practical housing, and each built upon the rubble of urban decay. So advanced, so well-publicized, and so beautiful that the rich would actually welcome the poor into their neighborhoods and want to live beside them.

If ever she could get a man like Theo Glass to sign on, others would follow. But then that reminded her that she was about to meet him for the first time and panic seized her, tightening around her like a turtleneck ten sizes too small. Choking off the idea of a project that excited her because it could put her design work in balance, in harmony. On one hand, she could continue to enhance the lives of her wealthy clients by providing spectacular interiors, and on the other hand, try to ease and grace the lives of the poor. But would Theo Glass share such an idea? She already knew the answer; she didn't have to ask.

Not that he'd give her the opportunity to ask. *He'll keep me at a distance,* she decided. Oh, he'd be polite, but formal and superior, just like he was when Danny met him. He'd tell her to measure the window returns, and she would, and he'd loathe the seafoam green Berber wool carpeting she chose, and he'd go away never even knowing her first name. To him she would always be inconsequential, while to her he had already become unforgettable.

"Unforgettable?" Danny might well ask. "What about me?"

Indeed, what about Danny? How could she betray him with thoughts about a man she'd never even met? She drove on, faster, tenser, berating herself in precisely the same scolding tone of voice she'd hated as a child.

"How could you . . . ?"

"Be careful, Dell, or . . ."

"Don't you see what you're doing . . . ?"

It wasn't that Danny had ceased to be the center of her universe; his behavior was so unstable and erratic, there was hardly a moment when she didn't think of him. One minute—or rather, one night—he was the master of delight, weaving his sexual spell on her, over her, in her.

The next night he was simply absent. At work, though they divided the projects that came into the office equally, she wound up behind the drawing board while he went shopping with clients. He was out of the office so much that she'd stopped asking, "Where are you going?" because he always said the same thing: "To get more business for *us*."

Where, she wondered, had he been last night? Did she forget to ask or did he forget to tell her?

It doesn't matter, she decided, and eased her speed back down to sixty again. *I'm loved. Danny loves me, loves me mightily, and I was a fool to doubt him. No man has ever looked at me the way he does. He's proud of me. Proud. I am, to him, perfection, a prize. And an asset as his partner.*

It was true. D & D was their baby, but two one and a half years she ran the company day to day, assigning work to the junior designers; opening accounts at every major fabrics, carpeting, furniture, lighting, window, appliance, and floorings house in the city; signing thousands of purchase orders and invoices and bills to clients. Money was flowing in so fast that she had to hire a full-time bookkeeper, then an assistant, and even a purchase order expediter. She only had time to do what she loved most—create perfect interior environments—an hour or so each day. Financial planners urged them to buy real estate, buy a building to house their offices. "Fabulous," said Danny, "but who has time to shop for buildings?" Nevertheless, she heard him on the phone with real-estate agents while she made scale drawings on graph paper, trying to find a niche in her clients' newly designed kitchen for their heirloom Belgian armoire so that they could display their collection of antique linens.

"What would I do without you, my prize?" Danny would say. But what would she do without him? It was he who could look at a floor plan while sipping champagne with a client and devise an entire scheme in his head, describing it to her later as she took rushed notes. It was he who guided her days, filling the long hours with excitement and magic.

And her nights.

What he did to her nights was too much yet never enough, so that she was always waiting for more. Before him, no one had ever made sex an epic, an all-night event, an almost endless journey to deeper and deeper sensations. He spent hours teasing her, beguiling her, kissing the padded knobs of her knees and the soft flesh where her thighs began, refusing to let her undress, just tracing the outlines of her underwear until she could feel his touch more acutely than if she'd been naked. Before him, she'd never whimpered, begged for it, died for it. Now she often lived on three hours of sleep.

And yet there were nights when he'd warn her he'd be home "very late," or he'd awaken and prowl the dark city while he thought she slept, and she'd wander the apartment that she'd once thought was heaven and now imprisoned her in a lonely hell. Those were the nights when pain returned, like a former chum, to keep her company and occupy her mind. For two and a half years she'd been telling herself she'd arrived not where her mother feared she might end up, but at the other side of the rainbow. The place of dreams. But now there were nights when it was her father's voice she heard, irritated, disapproving, making her stomach churn with confusion. Somehow, she had lost his love, and blamed herself. On nights like this, she still did.

Dell checked her directions on the seat beside her and turned right onto the dirt road that went south, right down to the Atlantic Ocean and the white, deserted beach. Even from the start of the road, the house was clearly visible, rising and undulating with Theo's signature curves of cedar and rose stucco on a high dune. Graded but unlandscaped, the sloping gravel approach led up to the porticoed entrance, an airy colonnade of trellises that circled the house. Bare now, in time she knew they would support an array of exotic vines. She knew this from Theo's printed notes in the margins of his plan, and later, from his elaborate model, displayed on a coffee table at the clients' apartment.

Technically, this northern facade with its main entrance was called the front, but Dell knew most people considered the true front of a beach house to be the side that faced the sea. Nevertheless, rear or front, here was nothing less than a miracle, and of this Dell was absolutely certain from her first breathless glimpse. The house was a miracle because it spoke—no, *sang*—not so much of volume and mass and space and light, but of joy. Joy! You could feel that joy even half a mile away.

Danny had said there was something dead about Theo Glass, but how, she wondered, could a dead man make a house that so definitively celebrated the joy of living? There was exuberance in the palette of pastel colors, there was ease in the public spaces sympathetically shaded by arches and trellises and deep overhangs, and there was fun and surprise in the curves of the walls and the wavy ribbons of window. The house itself was like a spirited family of architectural elements, all living cheerfully under a rosy clay tile roof. It made you yearn to be invited in.

Theo was there, waiting for her, on the other side of the house. Glowering.

She saw him, unfriendly eyes, lapis blue, haunted, blond hair and moustache, handsome, about her height, gloved hands balled into fists, wearing a shearling jacket identical to her own and the same tan lace-up work boots. And jeans, of course. They were dressed like twins. She smiled and waved. He didn't wave back.

She pushed through the soft sand and the oceanic wind, and climbed the planks to the unfinished deck, uncharacteristically confident. She felt she knew this man. She felt it whenever she saw pictures of his work, and she felt it now, seeing him and remembering one other time when she felt it.

The eyes made her remember.

Beneath his blue stare dark circles sagged like sacs of pain, reminding her of what she'd heard about him. Everyone in the field knew about his tragedy almost immediately, but because it occurred on the same weekend as her wedding, she first heard of it long after she and Danny had returned from their honeymoon, from their luscious, indecent time eating and shopping and loving their way through Italy, where, for a time, sorrow didn't exist. It was an expert Norwegian carpenter who'd done some work for Theo Glass who told her.

"Poor Theo," she'd cried. "Poor, poor Theo!" As if she knew him and could feel his pain. She felt the same way now.

Theo watched her from the far side of the deck as she

strode, lean, long-legged, and shining, toward him. The day was gray and threatening, but she seemed lit by the sun. Her hair blazed, her skin shone. Even her wide-mouthed smile was sunny, jaunty. He could not take his eyes from her, and he hated himself for wanting to stare at her. When she was before him, he turned his hate on her.

"You're late," he said. "Not that I'm surprised."

Dell had checked her watch a hundred times on the trip out. She knew she was a half hour early. She also thought she understood why he was doing this. But when he spoke again, it was as if he were trying to punch her face in with his words, and she forgot all about feeling sorry for him. She hit back.

"I've worked with you Leonard, Melton decorators before. You're always late and you're always—"

"Designers, Mr. Glass," Dell interrupted. "As you well know, we're trained to do a lot more than simply choose the draperies and upholstery. Of course, unlike you, we can't move mountains, but we can move walls, reroute wiring and—"

"All right. You made your point. I apologize. *In*terior designers."

"Thank you. Also, I haven't been a 'Leonard, Melton decorator' for almost two years. I have my own firm now, D & D. But of course, you knew that."

Then she smiled. She'd just told the Great One off. She couldn't remember the last time she'd done such a thing, but she was enjoying the triumph immensely. It lasted only three seconds. What she hadn't realized was that this was only round one. He wasn't done with her yet.

He folded his arms across his chest and looked her up and down. Slowly.

"You're not so beautiful," he finally said.

"Wh-what?" she asked with an unsure laugh.

"I heard you were a knockout. You're not."

"Then I guess they lied to you," she shrugged, and patted her flaming hair, unaware of what her gesture was doing to him. She only knew that her own hands were trembling, and she hid them behind her back.

"You're surrounded by a bunch of liars, Mr. Glass," she said, thinking, *Oh Danny, you'd be so proud of me!*

"They told you I was a—how did you put it?—a knock-out. Disappointed, are you?"

"No, I—"

"No? Well, then, if you're not disappointed, you must be pleased. Which is it?"

"I'm neither pleased nor displeased."

"Okay, but clearly you're in agreement with what you heard about me. That I *am* a knockout. Not that any of this matters, of course, unless you were thinking of making me up into a two-armed chandelier over the dining room table."

Great, he thought. *Now she detests you.* An ideal working relationship. But at least she wasn't sorry for him anymore. He sure dried up all the pity swimming around in those funny eyes of hers. One minute they were blue, the next, they were green.

"Time out," he called, making a T with his hands. "Look, maybe I was a little out of line, but I'm under a lot of pressure and I just assumed—wrongly, I admit— that you were going to waste my time with a lot of ideas—"

"You were right."

He looked at her, but then he had to look away because the gold and red and cinnamon in her hair flashed like fire, and it was burning into him.

"I do have a lot of ideas, but first, I want to hear yours. Would you take me through the house now? It's getting cold out here." She shivered slightly. "Aren't you cold? You realize, don't you, that our clothes are identical?"

He bent down and pulled one leg of his jeans up past his knee, revealing gray long underwear beneath. Then he looked up at her, smiling for the first time.

"Not entirely identical, I bet."

So she rolled up her pants and showed him her pink tights, posing cutely.

She has the legs of an Arabian pony, he thought. Big smile, big teeth. Everything about her was big, but as sleek as a russet colt. *Oh, God, Cara, forgive me!*

"Just as I said, not entirely identical." He led her into the house.

"I still don't concede. For all I know, you're wearing pink jockey shorts." Then she laughed and held up her hands. "That wasn't meant as a dare."

Nevertheless, he began unzipping his pants.

"Wait!" she cried, laughing. "What are you doing?"

"You're not going to believe it."

He pulled one side of the waistband down low enough to show her his shorts. They had wide stripes of pink—dark pink, light pink, fuschia. And after that, Theo would recall almost every morning of his life, *We met in laughter.*

They laughed, at first, in embarrassment and relief. The wry grin Theo wore as he buckled his pants and the surprised gasps Dell muffled behind her hands erupted simultaneously the moment they looked at each other. Like a rusty fountain, their laughter spurted and sputtered at first, then picked up momentum, becoming a rising and falling roar of hilarity. They had only to look at each other to break out in a new jet of foot-stamping guffaws that doubled them over and sent tears from their eyes.

"Oh, I don't believe this!" Dell cried and tried to get control, but as soon as her eyes met Theo's, she was off again, clutching her sides as she shrieked with laughter.

They turned their backs on each other and the fountain slowed to a dribble. Dell dabbed her eyes; Theo took a few deep breaths.

"Ready?" he asked with his back to her.

Then they both about-faced and immediately bent in half, almost sobbing with hysterics, although they never could have explained what it was they found so funny.

He took her on a tour of the house, and although she often cried when stirred by great beauty, this time she laughed. And he laughed with her.

"All the windows open and close electronically," he told her.

"Yes," she nodded, and pulled samples of pale linen micro-slatted blinds from her bag. "Which is why I thought these would work so well. They can be controlled on the same system."

Without a word, Theo led her to the master bedroom on the second floor. A cut-off section of a pale green linen micro-blind lay on the floor. He held it up to the window.

"Just what I was thinking," he said, and looked at her.

They had a big laugh over that, but when she showed him her seafoam green carpeting sample, he roared.

"Don't tell me—?"

He fell against a wall and shook his head yes, yes, yes, too hysterical to speak.

She laughed at all the bedrooms on the second floor, at their ribbons of windows and interconnecting decks and bathroom silos. She laughed at the grace of the central staircase, crafted of a wood she'd never seen before. And even at the first level's grand expanse, made larger by the walls of glass and the soaring height of the unfinished ceiling, though by then, she also felt close to tears.

He laughed at all her ideas, even the ones he himself had never thought of.

"It's as if you knew me, knew exactly what I was thinking. It's uncanny."

"I know," she agreed.

They walked down to the water's edge and looked back at the house.

"Of all the pastels—I used nine, by the way—how did you know it was the sea green I wanted to employ as the primary background?" He watched her hair blow across her face, hating himself no less now, but not hating her at all.

"Theo—may I call you Theo?"

"Dell, don't be so formal." He laughed heartily at himself as soon as he realized what he'd said. "All right, I admit I behaved like a pompous idiot. I meant to give you a hard time . . . and I did. I didn't want to think much of you professionally, and I didn't want to like you personally. I can't explain it, but I'm sincerely sorry."

Dell looked up at the sky. "It's begun to snow."

They returned to the house just as the carpenter arrived, and they assembled in the kitchen so Dell could show them how she wanted the cabinets done. Theo said nothing.

"And here," she said, pointing to the plan and then to the actual spot on the unfinished floor, "I thought we could put a nine-foot-round central island. If we bunch the appliances and cabinets like this, it would give a two-foot overhanging lip for quick countertop dining. A round island is less practical than a rectangle or oval, of course, but it does echo all the round forms of the house rather nicely, I think.''

"I do, too,'' Paulie Mixon agreed, fingering one of several hammers hanging from his carpenter's belt. Then he patted his ample belly and announced, "Lunchtime. I'll bring back sandwiches.''

When he was gone, Dell waited expectantly for some comment from Theo, but he had withdrawn into himself and stared silently out at the falling snow. As soon as Paulie returned, Theo carried his sandwich and coffee out to the car, where he could make business calls on his cellular phone. Then, all at once, the glazier, the tile layer, the landscape designer, the painter, and the stone cutter arrived. Serving as general cocontractors, Theo and Dell spent the remainder of the afternoon organizing, guiding, and scheduling the work of the local tradesmen and their crews. It was dark when the last pickup truck pulled out of the driveway.

"Shall we have a drink in town before we head back?'' he asked as they locked up the cold, dark house. She couldn't make out the expression on his face, but she could hear him yawning.

"Fine,'' she agreed, "but I'm staying over.''

His face came close to hers and she could see the smile on his lips. "Are you?''

"Mm-hmm,'' she mumbled, her cheeks flaming. She dove into her bag for her car keys, trembling from the cold, and from the nearness of him.

"Excellent idea, Freckles.''

"Freckles? I haven't been called that since I was a girl.''

"This afternoon I counted thirty-three freckles, from your chin to your forehead. You're asymmetrical, you know. And more beautiful than they said. I lied before.'' He took off his glove and touched her cheek. "More beautiful than I was prepared for. I think I went a little crazy the minute I saw you.''

She was shaking all over now, and so was he. Their teeth were chattering, but still, neither one moved. He was watching the little smile on her lips. Marveling at the way she could make her wide mouth into something so small. And pulpy, like the inside of a summer peach. He yearned to cover her mouth with his, to nibble her lips, to taste her saliva, to breathe in her warm air, but it seemed to take forever to reach her. So much stood in their way. Then he felt Dell's arms reaching up, pulling his head down, sliding her mouth into his, warming his nose, his cheeks, his neck, his belly, and even that part of him that had been lifeless for so long. It was a kiss that lasted seconds, then minutes, locking them in a hungry oblivion while the wind raged and almost blew them off the deck.

When they finally pulled apart they were both so surprised that they began to laugh. Laughing and shivering, they crunched through the snow and hardened sand to their cars.

"See you at the inn," he said, and slammed her door behind her, too cold now to kiss her again.

They were distant strangers when they met at the bar, five minutes later.

For Dell, it happened the instant she was alone. *I must have been mad,* she told herself, grateful for the snow and the wind and the empty, calming streets. By the time she parked in front of the old, white-columned inn, she felt sane again—or, at least, no longer mad. *I'll tell him I'm exhausted. I'll tell him I must have been mad. Then I'll tell him good night and go straight up to bed.* No apologies. No touching. Just a cool, professional good night. She must get this working relationship back on track. It was a nice kiss, a lovely kiss, a grand and unforgettable kiss. But why did she do it? Why was she so aggressive? The challenge? To triumph over the Great One? If that were so, she should be satisfied. She got what she wanted. And she didn't want him to kiss her again, did she?

But she needn't have worried. He didn't kiss her again. He didn't even remove his coat. He arrived a moment before her, and although he was waiting for her, he didn't look at her.

"On second thought, I think it's best if I get right home," he told her.

It was what she wanted, what she was sure she wanted, but hearing him say it almost crushed her under a weight of unexpected disappointment. The surprise of his words so jolted her, she could hardly mask her true feelings.

Unless she got control of herself, she might even burst into tears.

"Yes, I think that's best, too. Best all around," she said stiffly.

"Dell—"

"No, really. It's best. It's right." She put a finger to her lips. "Now, let's not say anything more about it. Good-bye . . . Mr. Glass. Drive safely."

He watched her lug her bag to the reservation desk. He waited, but she did not turn around. He stepped out onto the porch and closed the door behind him.

The night had no moon and no stars, but for a while, it had given him Dell, and he'd known pure laughter again, and shuddering delight. And that was impermissible. When Cara died, an essential part of him became cold and lifeless, too. He'd willed it so, but tonight, his cock had defied him. That was impermissible. For Cara's memory, for Erica's sake, he'd continue to atone. And perhaps in time he'd be able to erase the vivid memory of Dell from his mind and his heart.

He stepped down into the snow and walked rigidly to his car.

6

She didn't think she'd ever see him again—certainly not so soon, definitely not just one week later. She wasn't ready yet. Seeing him was like having a subway train rumble right through her, lurching first to one side and then to the other. The roar was deafening. She clearly saw yellow lights flashing, but she didn't know whether she wanted to slam on the brakes or hurtle right into him. She had seconds to decide.

"Hold this, please," she said to the hardware store clerk behind the counter.

Then she hooked her finger under the lip of the metal tape measure and pulled. Backing away from the counter where the tape holder sat with the clerk's hand on it, she let out a six-foot length of yellow measure tape.

"Good. It doesn't buckle. I'll take it," she said, not looking to her right, where she had last glimpsed him. But surely, she thought, he had to have heard her voice and recognized it. After only one week, he couldn't have forgotten.

"It's the two-inch width," said the store clerk. "They finally made one wide enough not to buckle."

"Yes," Dell agreed, "you're right. But it's also a thicker, heavier metal, and that helps to keep it stiff, too." She hoped she wasn't speaking louder than usual. There was such a racket going on inside her head that she couldn't tell.

The store clerk was staring at her. "You an architect?"

"No, an interior designer."

"Yes, well, I didn't think you were a carpenter or a tiler because your nail polish isn't chipped. So you had to be either an architect or a decorator."

"Why is that?"

"Because they're the only ones who buy up all my tape measures. The main tool of the trade, I guess."

Dell nodded and paid for her purchase. She wished the store sold quarter-inch-square graph paper and pads of tracing paper, the decorator's true tools of the trade. Then she remembered that she was uptown, far from the D & D loft, and that her three shopping bags were full of cuttings and samples, several glossy catalogues, and a set of Louis XV brass door levers and keyhole plates that she wanted to use on a client's scrolled doors that led into a magnificent salon lined in pecan *boiserie*. Her arms could support not one ounce more.

Carefully, she turned to the left and walked to the door, though she was fairly sure he must have noticed her and decided not to approach her. He may even have sneaked out, hoping not to be recognized, but if so, she hadn't heard the tinkle of the overhead doorbell. *What does it matter,* she asked herself, trying to adopt an indifference she didn't feel. *He doesn't care about me, and I don't care about—*

"Dell, wait. Here, let me help you with the door." Theodor Glass's hand reached out in front of her and pushed open the door.

"Theo! What a surprise!" she cried, turning back to face him with a look she hoped displayed startled authenticity. Then she changed her mind, and she could feel a rush of instant relief even before she said a word. It was as if she decided in only an instant that this time she would begin with a truly clean slate. No lies, no games.

"Actually, it's not a surprise. I saw you before, out of the corner of my eye," she said, standing in the open door.

"Why didn't you—"

"I was afraid you wouldn't really want—"

"Are you serious?" Theo said, transferring two of her shopping bags to his arm. There was no need to complete their sentences; they understood each other immediately.

"Would you please shut that door!" the clerk called to them from the back of the store. "You're letting in the cold air."

"Sorry!" they both called and, laughing, inched their way out into the bitter, sunless late afternoon. It was as cold as the last time they were together, but this time they didn't draw together and sink their mouths into an endless kiss. They stood shivering and stamping their feet in front of the hardware store, trying to have a conversation.

"So, what's been happening in the last seven days?" Theo asked, turning up her coat collar for her. He preferred being out here in the cold with her, out on a busy New York street, in public, and in daylight. It was safer. And although he knew that there was a comfortable cafe just down the street, he didn't suggest they go there.

Dell motioned with her chin to her shopping bags, the interior designer's identifying emblem. "Work and then more work," she said, aware that Theo was looking at her, touching her as he had on the deck one week ago, just before he'd kissed her. As if nothing had happened between them after that. But too much had happened . . . and yet not enough. She decided to break away.

"I'm afraid I still have to run back downtown to the office—"

"You've never seen *my* office, have you?" Theo interrupted her, unwilling to hear her say she was leaving. "It's only a block and a half away."

Dell hesitated.

Theo locked her arm in his. "Ten minutes?" he smiled, nudging her forward. "Just to warm up."

The opportunity to see the great Theodor Glass offices was almost irresistible, but Dell could hardly breathe, hardly talk, and a voice deep inside her kept asking, "Are you giving him the chance to reject you all over again, you fool?" She believed that voice and yet she couldn't say no. But she could protect herself. She could be cool and professional. And she could be the first one to leave this time.

"I really do have another appointment downtown," she said as he nudged her forward. "So I'm warning you—"

"I understand," he said, but his smile was ecstatic.

"Oh, Theo!" she gasped as soon as the elevator door slid open onto the thirty-fifth floor.

The gently curving pierced copper wall—a segment of the circle whose center served as the reception desk—struck her first. Light from the round south wall and north wall windows glinted, even on a gloomy day like this, off the gleaming copper. Other than one long black leather bench, there was no furniture. No art on the walls. No plants or vases of flowers. The eye was meant to focus on the copper wall and the copper drum of a desk without distraction. It was pure. Spare. But because of the warmth of the copper, the drama of its pierced pattern, the rounded and curving shapes, the space wasn't cold at all. It was stunning.

"Seven minutes of contemplation is more veneration than this reception area deserves. Seven seconds is more like it," he joked modestly, but clearly was pleased by the intensity of her interest. Nevertheless, he took her elbow and guided her into his office, where he wished she'd spend seven years in contemplation.

He showed her photo murals of houses he'd done and drawings of projects he only dreamed of doing. She was surprised to see that mostly his walls displayed these imagined projects.

"Fantasies," he scoffed, dismissing the framed sketches and elevations of a futuristic cluster of dwellings ringing a series of cookie-shaped parks and courtyards. "Low- and middle-income fantasies to salve my political conscience while I go on making houses for millionaires."

"You just dream these up?" she asked.

"Well, I pick a real New York City street in a depressed area and I make the client an imaginary tenant group in the community who got extensive city and bank funding. Then I just go ahead and try to dream up, as you put it, a workable scheme for them."

Dell was examining one of his "fantasies," in which the buildings looked like nothing presently on a New York street, yet somehow, the flat-roofed drums and cylinders looked like they *should* be. The shapes seemed to complement the New York skyline and, as was usual with a Theodor Glass design, there wasn't a sharp edge or square corner anywhere.

"Your work seems to embrace the rounded form more and more," Dell told him, not taking her eyes from the drawing hanging on the wall. She wasn't avoiding him; she was genuinely interested.

" 'Embrace' is a really apt word for it. The older I

get, and the more I see of human suffering, the more convinced I am that what we need is more compassion, even in architecture.'' He didn't look at her either as he spoke, but he felt her close beside him . . . extremely close.

''Compassion in architecture?'' Dell was intrigued. She forgot that it'd only been a week since she'd kissed him. She even forgot the kiss. Most of all, she forgot that, in the end, he'd turned away from her. She forgot how that had hurt.

And of course, she forgot nothing; she remembered it all. The kiss as well as the hurt. And the relief. But with him standing right beside her, so close she could hear a slight rasp in his breathing, she was able to put aside the hurt and the longing, and just, simply, be.

''On one level,'' he was explaining, ''I mean a compassionate architecture of softened edges, of, yes, embracing forms like the circle and the arc. And on another level, I mean a whole new architectural movement that would make kindness and compassion its first priority. Our buildings would make living a little easier for the ones who have it the toughest. A little easier, a little more attractive, and a lot cheaper. Sounds idealistic, huh?''

Dell sat down opposite Theo and looked directly into his deep blue eyes for the first time that day.

''Idealistic, yes, but what's wrong with that?''

Theo ran his stubby hands through the blond waves of his hair and sighed audibly.

''Some people—my wife, for instance—think these—'' he waved an arm at the drawings on the wall—''are unrealistic, maybe even downright silly.''

His smile was slightly embarrassed, his expression slightly vulnerable, Dell thought, but she stifled an impulse to lean forward and clasp his hands in hers and try to comfort him. *It's all over if you touch him,* she told herself. *This way, at least you can be friends.*

So she folded her hands in her lap and asked softly, ''Because low-cost housing can't afford good design like this?''

Theo nodded. ''Exactly.''

He too had an impulse to lean forward and touch some part of her. First, her hands, then maybe her forearms, then her shoulders. What he really wanted to do was yank her out of her seat and pull her to him, pull her right into his lap. And then he wanted to bend her over so her hair could fall in her face and leave the back of her neck clear. He didn't know why he wanted to kiss that part of her—the back of her long, regal neck—so much right now, but he recognized the impulse as madness, and stifled it.

"I want to tell you something," she said, smiling mischievously. Something, she realized, she could only tell him. For Danny would call it *mashuginah*. And he, it suddenly occurred to her, ruled their business. D & D was really *his*. Now if, however, she had a design firm of her own . . .

He watched her smile change from something mischievous to something dreamy. He loved all of her smiles because they made him smile, too. It was impossible not to join her. Yet he also felt some slight sense of dread. Not sure what she might be about to say, now that he'd regained his own professional composure, he hoped she wouldn't try to compromise it. He gestured for her to continue, but he couldn't look at her.

"Last week, driving out to the Elkins' house to meet you, I had a thought: What if designs for low-income housing were donated by some of the greatest artists of our time? What if the furnishings were donated? And many of the building materials?"

Theo couldn't help it; he turned and looked at her. But now it was not so much because he wanted to touch her, but because he wanted to hear what she was saying.

"What if these artists created an urban environment that was artistically pioneering and utterly brilliant? So beautiful that the wealthy would want to live beside it—even in it!"

"Okay," Theo agreed, playing devil's advocate. "What if?"

Dell stood up, and as she rose so did her color, until she was entirely flushed. Theo remained seated and watched her with the illicit thought that beneath her clothes—between her legs, above her breasts, on her belly—she was probably as pinkly blotched as were her cheeks. Towering above him, her eyes flashing excited sparks of electric green, her presence was simply too beguiling for him to pay attention to her words. So reluctantly he made himself look away again.

"What if?" she asked back at him. "What if? Why, then there wouldn't be any more ifs. We'd just do it."

Theo laughed, his eyes in his lap. "Just do it, eh?"

"Oh, I don't mean to sound simplistic. I know this is a big, complicated idea and I don't know how I could find the time to fit it into my schedule. And I don't even know if it's doable. But I do know this is how many big projects get started—with a great, big exciting idea. And I think it's exciting. Don't you?"

At the same moment that Theo allowed his eyes to travel up from her black woven leather heels, her sleek, racehorse legs, her black wool suit until they passed her white throat, her slightly pointy chin, her flushed and freckled cheeks, and finally rested upon her luminous eyes, a discreet knock on the door silenced the answer he was about to give her.

"Come in," he called instead, and instantly recognized a waft of his wife Erica's lemony fragrance that preceded her into the room.

Entering briskly, Erica headed straight for Theo, a manila envelope marked "photographs" tucked under her arm.

"I've got the—" she began, holding out the envelope to him. But when she saw Dell standing at the window, she stopped short while everything froze inside her.

"I'm sorry. Terry didn't tell me you had someone in here with you," she managed to say to Theo, but her eyes were on Dell and in that one sweeping glance, Erica Glass had taken all of her in. She absorbed Dell's tallness and the bigness of her bones, from the length of her fingers to the size of her feet. She absorbed Dell's coloring, even noting the shade of lipstick she wore and the matte jade shadow in the crease of her eyes. She was able, too, in that brief glance, to gauge exactly how many feet Dell stood from her husband's chair and how many minutes she had sat on the sofa where she or Theo had thrown her coat. She noticed the coat label: Georgio Armani. She noticed that the black wool suit was probably Armani too. The slit up the long black skirt emphasized Dell's slim, black-stockinged legs, forcing the eye to her graceful calf, her bony knee, and a suggestion of taut thigh. Finally, her eyes rested on the sapphire and diamond engagement ring and the gold wedding band on Dell's left hand. But still, she was afraid.

If she could have put her fear into words, Erica probably would have said, "This woman's my exact physical opposite."

Where Erica was small and pale and blonde, she was big boned and colorful. And where Erica was tense, efficient, and mostly unsmiling, she suspected her rival was witty and expansive.

She's what he'll want if he continues to tire of me, she told herself.

Theo rose and introduced them and Erica watched the way Theo presented her, the way he spoke her name. Dell.

He wants her now, she realized. *It's worse than I thought*.

"Dell is doing the interiors in the Elkins house out in Southampton," he said. "She and her husband, Daniel Dannenberg, own the design firm D & D."

"Ah, yes, D & D. You're becoming superstars. I see your name every time I open a magazine," Erica said with a tight smile. She noticed that Theo avoided looking at Dell and that Dell avoided looking at him.

Guilty thoughts, she decided. *That's why. Oh God, that's exactly why.*

"D & D has been very lucky," Dell conceded softly. "I myself was surprised at all the publicity we got. It just seemed to snowball. But you must know what that's like since you live with a real superstar!"

Dell couldn't help sneaking a quick glance at Theo. He was laughing at her superstar remark but he stopped abruptly when their eyes met. Suddenly, there was silence.

Oh, God, help me! Erica silently prayed, watching the two of them trying not to look at each other—and failing. She took hold of her husband's arm.

"I don't think it's the same thing."

"No, of course it's not," Dell said quickly, feeling entirely deserving of Erica's antipathy. At the same time she also felt an immediate kinship with Erica that made it impossible to be angry or hurt. She knew that this woman had endured the death of her baby; she didn't want to be the one to make Erica suffer any more. She would not fight with her.

"But now I've got to dash." Dell looked at her watch and groaned. "I warned your husband that I was only staying for a minute. I've got a client arriving at the office in five minutes, and in this rush hour it'll take me a half hour to get downtown." She pulled on her coat as she talked, backing away before Theo could help her on with it.

Erica held onto Theo's arm. "How unfortunate we didn't have more time to chat."

Theo was about to suggest that the four of them have dinner together one night, but Erica squeezed his arm and Theo knew, after over fourteen years of marriage, that his wife was sending him a message to keep silent. With uncanny prescience, she often anticipated exactly what he was about to say. And Theo had learned at those times when she intercepted his thoughts and commanded, with a pinch, that he remain silent, his wisest course of action was to obey. Which is what he did now. Otherwise, he knew, Erica would torment him with accusations of insensitivity and endless demands that he explain himself. "Why did you invite them?" "Why didn't you heed my warning?" "Why didn't you care about my feelings and wait until we were alone so I could tell you why I didn't want you to invite them? Why?"

It was her fear, he knew, of losing him. Fear of another loss, of being left entirely alone, made her go rigid at times, and scratch and thrash about as if she were dreaming her worst nightmare.

"I *am* dreaming my worst nightmare," she once told him. "Just promise me you won't make it come true."

He promised and promised, but there weren't enough promises in the universe to convince her. She remained vigilant in her mistrust, her eyes keen to any signs of misbehavior. But until Dell, Erica had no cause to suspect him. Now, in the space of one week, everything had changed for him. He too had a recurrent dream, only his was of Dell, and it wasn't a nightmare.

Dell managed to back out of the office with a smile and a wave and an awkward "thank you," her coat buttoned up and her shopping bags hanging heavily from her arms.

Im-pos-si-ble, she said to herself, parsing the word into separate syllables of equal meaning. Impossible. Not able to happen. Impossible. Unacceptable behavior. Impossible. Unendurable. Impossible. Doomed.

The high-speed elevator dropped to the lobby in the space of one long, low mournful wail. But when the doors slid open, Dell emerged dry eyed.

She tried to tell herself that what most disappointed her was that now they couldn't even be friends. For a few moments back in his office, she thought she'd aroused his interest in her concept for funding low-cost "designer" housing. She even thought they might become cosponsors of the project. At the very least, they were professional colleagues, but now even a professional relationship seemed impossible. She would complete the interiors for the Elkins house, consulting the clients, but not him. As of here and now, she was cutting off all contact with him.

But how, she wondered as she stepped into the icy air, could she cut off the images of him, as sharp as photographs, that she kept seeing everywhere she went?

Time, she told herself. *Give yourself time.* Like photographs, in time her memories would yellow and fade. She could foresee a time when the mention of his name would no longer make her hands shake. When she'd no longer be able to recall the exact sound of his voice. And all she'd be left with would be this longing for him, which she knew might never fade at all.

7

Despite Dell's background—or perhaps precisely because of it—Dell had an aversion to clutter, to dust, and to old and musty accumulations. She had grown up amid acres of rubbish and scrap, where nothing was ever new or clean or whole. So it was Danny, not Dell, who could not pass a pile of junk on the streets of New York without sifting through the contents for "found" art or unrealized treasures heedlessly thrown away. It was he who compulsively collected old things, amassing baskets full of old eyeglasses, watches, pens. And it was Danny who couldn't bear to throw anything out.

Where Dell had spent her childhood, old things had none of the panache of Danny's found objects; old things were merely other people's discards, possibly reusable. Long before the notion of recycling, her father had found a meager profit by trading in the nearly obsolescent. Danny's profit, to be sure, was greater, and the quality of his merchandise grander, but she couldn't help feeling oppressed by certain similarities.

With one hand she wished she could sweep it all away—the dust, the memories, and most of all, the shame.

She lived inland, only a few tiny blocks from the water, from the picturesque promenade and the fishing boats and the gulls and the seafood restaurants of Sheepshead Bay. But it could have been miles. She rarely visited these attractions. Instead, as a child, her playground was the vast junkyard that spread out before her. There, cracked and rusted items lay heaped and strewn about as if an overloaded armoire had toppled, spilling domestic samples of a familiar yet obsolete culture over two and a half acres, all the way to Neptune Walk.

There were always piles of tires and hubcaps, bathroom vanities, carved wood moldings, doors and panels. Next to them on the sparse clumps of grass were the crates loaded with unmatched cutlery, lidless pots, crockery and glassware. Everywhere there were warped window frames and warped rowboats and warped chairs.

White porcelain sinks, commodes, and claw-footed tubs were grouped in the center of the lot and became strangely sculptural, like mysterious totemic artifacts, like a modern Stonehenge.

A ramshackle shed provided some protection for a collection of the rusted and corroded—typewriters, electric fans, toasters, radios, car mufflers, vacuum cleaners. The octopodan arms of brass chandeliers, now the color of green mud, ghoulishly beckoned as if from the deep.

Barbed wire topped the aluminum fencing, but a large sign cheerfully announced:

WORTH SAVING CORP.
Your Scrap, Junk, Household Items
Are Worth Saving!
SH-6-6666

Half hidden at the far end of the lot, on Neptune Walk, what looked like a long, once-white railroad car was really a house. The Shay house. And it was there that Dell lived from the day they brought her home from the hospital, seven days after she was born on May 7, 1957. Home.

From her window Dell could look out over the entire wasteyard, and on clear days she could see through the mesh of the fencing to the green trees that lined Shoreside Parkway. The trees themselves held no particular interest for Dell, yet she cherished the sight of them because they lined Shoreside Parkway, which was the most direct route to Manhattan, and that was where Dell yearned to be. Manhattan was her green landscape, her "nature," her rolling, verdant hills of freedom.

Manhattan. For years she neared it, even touched it without really feeling a full part of it. Commuting by subway to college in the city, she dreamed of penthouses and sparkling wines and men in tuxedos. By the time she entered interior design school, she was living almost entirely in the interiors she created in her mind.

But then, she'd been creating private worlds of her own since she was a small child, perhaps because there were no toys in the Shay house. According to her mother, Gertrude Shay, a toyless environment was beneficial for a child.

"Be creative," she told her daughter. "Create your own toys. If you're creative, you'll see toys to play with everywhere."

To her husband, Victor Shay, she said, "Don't you dare bring any toys into this house. I don't want that child depending on anything but her own God-given resources."

But the truth was that there was simply too much junk for Gertrude to keep track of already. Toys accumulated, broke, became so much more junk. And they were expensive; they were not essential.

But at the age of three Dell didn't understand her mother's admonishment. She thought *creative* was another word for good. It was as if her mother had said to her, "Be good and you'll find the toys. Just don't bother me now. Go play and be good."

Where were the toys? Dell wondered. She was always searching for the toys, wondering where they were hidden.

On Christmas morning there had been gaily wrapped presents pulled down from hiding places. No toys. A hat and scarf, a pink nylon nightie, new pink slippers. And nothing since.

"Where are you hiding?" she'd mutter to herself as she wandered. By then she'd learned that to bother Mommy was to bring upon herself the most dreadful of punishments—banishment. Mommy walked around with a clipboard and three freshly sharpened pencils, checking inventory, answering phone calls. She typed up bills and receipts and business letters on an old black Royal, curly red tendrils falling onto her wide, florid face. But mostly, she stared into space, completely distant and alone. If Dell pulled at her, she was dumped into the wooden playpen off in a corner of the lot. At first she would scream for hours.

"Crying won't help," her mother told her matter-offactly. Then she'd throw into the pen an old crate, a couple of spigots, a piece of round brass pipe.

Sometimes Victor would rush across the yard and implore Gertrude, "Can't you pick her up? The customers are beginning to wonder."

"She has to learn," Gertrude would tell him. "Life is no picnic and the sooner she learns, the better."

"How can you stand the crying? I can't take it, I tell you. Listen to her. She'll break a blood vessel. How can you stand it?"

"I can stand this just as I've stood everything else in this miserable life." Folding her arms across her enormous chest, she'd insist, "I can stand it because I'm strong as a rock. I've had to be. So does she."

"Pick her up, goddamn it to hell, you bitch, you! Pick her up!"

At those moments a sly but mirthless smile would bend the corners of Gertrude's tight mouth. "You've got your filthy junkyard to rule over, but don't try to rule me. I'll decide when to pick her up. And I'll teach her what she needs to know—self-control and determination—so she won't listen to a man's empty promises and end up in a pigsty the way I did. She's going to learn from my mistakes. She's not going to wind up with a man like you!"

She knew how to defeat him. There was nothing for him to do but to about-face and run back to his customers, to his world of business and sales where apartment-building landlords bought his porcelain commodes by the dozens. Here, he could wear his white shirts that his wife starched and ironed for him and his secondhand suits and look almost as prosperous as his customers. He had the gift of sales. He sold his garbage as if it were gold, as if the goddamn priests had anointed it. But not if he let her rattle him. She was a fork-tongued bitch, no question about it. She could sour his most promising sale.

"You snake," he snarled under his exhausted breath as he ran. "Poisonous snake. You poisoned my business and now you're going to poison my daughter. But you won't rattle me, you snake. Not me!"

In time, Dell did learn that crying was ineffective. She learned that if she wanted freedom from that remote, slatted prison, she'd have to be quiet and appear content with the junk toys. She'd have to develop skills of patience and determination and self-control, skills few if any three-year-olds possessed. But Dell was a most unusual child. Perfect behavior achieved her release from prison and a rare hug from her Mommy.

But her real reward, discovered after months of scrupulous searching, was Mimi. Spotted under a porcelain tub, the soiled and scuffed rag doll was Dell's first and only dollie. But as Dell tugged it free, it instantly became apparent that Mimi was an utterly impossible little girl and that Mimi was the ideal name for her. "Me! Me!" was her constant plaint. "Hold me! Mommy, play with me. Give me, tell me, take me. Me!"

Four-year-old Dell had her hands full with Mimi.

"Stop following Mommy. Mommy has work to do. Stop hanging on Mommy. Stop it!"

Bad as Mimi was, Dell was thrilled to have found her. It was because she'd been so good, so perfect, really, for so long, that she found Mimi at all. Other rewards lay hidden, she was sure. And she would find them. It was just a matter of being good and of making Mimi shut up and stop whining for her Mommy.

Once Dell was free to roam, and the hated wooden pen was dismantled for good, she made the entire scrapyard her playground. And within its walls of barbed wire and metal fencing, Dell did flower.

Her thick, deep red hair was left free, unbraided, abandoned by Gertrude, who could sustain neither the patience nor the gentleness required to comb through the nest of knots that amassed year after year under the top layer of the child's curls.

Eyes that switched color, alternating from blue to green a hundred times a day, stared out from lashes that curled up like the points on two tiny tiaras across her lids.

The extraordinary cheekbones, of course, weren't defined yet. Instead, baby fat puffed out her face and dimpled her arms and layered her belly. But the freckles were already in place, small and coppery, like pennies spattered over her white skin.

She was considered a marvel, an ideal, the best-behaved child that the small cluster of relatives (both Gertrude's and Victor's) had produced.

"Such self-reliance!" they cooed and clucked. "Such red hair! Doesn't she ever whine or have a temper tantrum?'' they asked, watching helplessly as their own children raced heedlessly around the yard.

"Don't give her ideas," said Gertrude. "I'm teaching her independence and self-control."

"But she's so young to learn so much."

"She's Daddy's good little girl. Want a cookie, Dell?" said Victor, ignoring Gertrude's glare.

The relatives, bewildered, kept silent, eager to make an early escape from the tension and grime that pervaded the Shay house. Their own houses were large, grand. Their children had clothes, toys. From each of her visits, Gertrude Shay brought home bags of hand-me-downs. Clothes; never any toys.

"My rich sisters married men who let them lead charmed lives," Gertrude told her round little daughter. "They look down their noses at me, but I don't care. They don't understand what it's like to be trapped and nearly penniless. They don't understand how I could let myself go, just give up. But you're not going to be like me. I'll make sure your life is different, that *you're* different. They don't understand that you're going to be nothing like me. Or like him, either. This is one fight your father's not going to win. He's not going to turn you into me. You're going to have it all."

But Gertrude did resent her sisters' superior attitude, and visited them less and less. Shame and bitterness consumed her. She refused to invite the neighborhood women and their children over at all. As the years of her marriage and her misery compounded, she grew increasingly mute and reclusive, not speaking for weeks at a time. She grew fat, slowly picking at packaged cakes while Dell played by herself in the junkyard.

"Bad girl. You bad, fat, ugly thing!"

Though Dell's doll was badly behaved, Dell built monuments for her, fantasy homes created out of the detritus of the real world. Inside plastic shower-curtain walls were rooms with ripped rush stools, teacups, chipped vases filled with dandelions. The floors were covered with muddy rugs and there was always make-believe music from dead radios.

And in the center of it all, Mimi was propped upon a white plaster pedestal, her tiny panties bulging like a badly soiled diaper. Loaded inside were the crumbs of the chocolate cookies Dell inserted and then pulverized with repeated spankings.

"That's it. Play nicely," Gertrude told her daughter.

"Come see Mimi's house, Mommy. Come inside."

To enter, it was necessary for an adult to get down on all fours and crawl through the opening.

"Not now," Gertrude told her, too large to bend all the way over.

"Please, Mommy. Please."

"Don't whine, Dell. I need peace and quiet."

Sometimes, desperate for someone to witness her doll's interiors, she turned to her father. Once, she dressed up before taking the big walk across the yard to him.

"Daddy! Daddy! Mimi's house is finished. Come see it," Dell called to him, hobbling along on her dress-up shoes. "Go home!" she told her father's customer. "Get away. Get away."

"Dell!" Victor Shay was aghast.

Dell took his hand and began pulling him. She was surprisingly strong and actually yanked him several feet, convincing his browsing customer that the child meant business. He raised his hand to his hat and said to Victor Shay as he left, "I was only looking, anyway."

It was true. Victor hadn't really expected a sale. Nevertheless he was annoyed, and although his customer had smiled at Dell, Victor found her behavior embarrassing. In a few minutes he was expecting a big customer, one of the landlords who regularly shopped his yard, the one he secretly called "Mr. Loaded," and he wanted to be rid of Dell by then.

"Daddy, come on. Don't look at your watch. Just come see Mimi's house," Dell kept urging him. "See, the man went home, just like I told him to."

This wasn't amusing. Even if he weren't expecting a customer, he wouldn't want to scramble onto his knees and crawl into a shower-curtain playhouse. He didn't like to play with his daughter unless there was some moral, some lesson that could be learned. Mothers played with children; fathers took care of business. He still believed this was really the only way, despite all the shouting. It was the way he was taught when he was young; he hadn't changed. So why wouldn't Gertrude play with her daughter? Victor was not a man to crawl around in the dirt.

Dell's sandaled feet were stuffed inside gold high heels with broken straps. Tripping on the loose straps, she fell against her father. As he lifted her upright, he seemed to take notice of her for the first time.

"Wait a minute. What's this?"

Holding her chin, he pushed her head back so he could examine her face. He searched for her cherubic little lips, but they had disappeared under a thick, bold slash of magenta. The same magenta colored her cheeks in two hand-drawn discs that had been partially hidden by the scarf tied under her chin and pulled forward, old-woman style. But it was the violation to her lovely blue-sage eyes, circled in charcoal until they were no longer her eyes but the eyes of a raccoon, that froze him.

"What's this getup?"

"I'm a grownup lady, Daddy," Dell announced proudly.

"I see."

"Do you like it?"

"I like certain kinds of grownup ladies."

"Me? Do you like me?"

"I like plain ladies, like your mother, who have some meat on their bones and who don't paint their faces."

"But Mommy wears lipstick sometimes. And she said I could."

The protest, accompanied by hot tears, tore out of Dell despite herself. Her mother, she remembered, had told her it wasn't too early to experiment with makeup, that it took years to learn how to apply it expertly. And something about ingraining in her the habit of "keeping up." Whatever that meant, Dell knew enough not to tell her father. Gertrude Shay had said, "There's no point keeping up for a suspicious man like your father. If I buy a new dress, he thinks I've got a secret lover. So why bother?"

Victor Shay bent down and rubbed Dell's cheeks with his white handkerchief that he moistened with his tongue.

"Don't cry, Dell. I just want to clean you up."

Ever since Dell spoke her first words at seventeen months, Victor Shay had been teaching her how to be a good girl. He spoke to her as he would to an adult. He taught her as he would teach any mature student, with advice gleaned from his own bitter experience. Except, of course, that Dell was just a child. And all these stern warnings from her father only made Dell see the world—and him—through frightened, overly cautious eyes.

"There are really only two types of women. There are nice women, good women like your mother," Victor Shay pronounced.

"What's the other kind, Daddy?"

"Tarts."

The only tarts Dell knew were the ones in the nursery rhyme. She knew the rhyme by heart and whenever she recited it, she grew hungry. She'd always wanted to taste a tart. It was something sweet, she knew, pielike, but also something bad now as well. She'd have to be careful; perhaps macaroni, her favorite supper, meant something bad, too. Bad elbows.

"A tart lady is a bad lady?"

Victor Shay nodded.

"Why, Daddy?"

Victor Shay took a deep breath. He was uncomfortable with this subject but, as always, took Dell's instruction seriously.

"Because she's artificial."

"What's arti-fishy?"

"Arti-fishy?" Victor Shay began to laugh. "Oh, that's a good one! Arti-fishy!" He picked Dell up in his arms and hugged her.

"Do you love me, Daddy?"

"I love you when you're not arti-fishy."

"I promise I'll never, ever be arti-fishy."

"And you'll never like all that razzle-dazzle?"

"Never!" Dell vowed.

"Or think you're too good for us and go sailing off?"

"Uh-uh."

"Promise?"

Dell hugged him tighter, tighter.

"In that case, Dell, I love you."

Dell got down on her knees and crawled through the narrow foyer of shower-curtain walls to Mimi's house. Mimi was whining, as usual. Dell put the doll on her knees and shook her.

Mimi closed her glass eyes and sniffled that she wanted her own dollie to play with, and her own bed with ruffles, a whole new prettier house to live in.

"Okay," said Dell. "I can do that for you."

It was easy. Dell simply closed her eyes and imagined pictures hanging from the shower-curtain walls and white shelves lined with dolls and toys. She could see every doll, every colorful toy in its place. She'd redo Mimi's house as a toy store, or as a palace. Yes, definitely a palace!

"Here," she said, and gave Mimi a filigreed white iron bed with millions of lace and ruffled pillows. And a pink, cushy chair with a skirt of ruffles. She gave Mimi an extra room—a ballroom with marble floors and little gold tables. On the tables were pink and gold bowls filled with chocolates.

"Do you like your palace? Isn't it better than Cinderella's?"

Mimi said it was the prettiest palace she'd ever seen. "Perfect."

"And do you like me now?" Dell asked her.

Mimi said she was the best mother in the whole world. "Perfect."

And so, for a short while, Mimi didn't whine, she didn't buck. For a very short while, home was heaven.

8

Dell was awake, but she lay abed with her eyes squeezed shut, feigning sleep, forestalling disaster. Lately, disaster hid close by, coiled, ready to spring, ready to swallow her whole.

Listening to the sounds of Danny shaving and showering in the bathroom, she was reminded of other mornings, not so very long ago, when the two of them still could not bear to be parted, and even bathroom rituals were performed while clinging to each other, talking, kissing. Those were the mornings when they brushed their teeth shoulder to shoulder and actually saw something sacred, something symbolic in the way their saliva intermixed in the porcelain sink. That was when showering together was just an excuse to slide soapy fingers over wet skin, caress contours, enter slippery crevices. Such sensual mornings! She still missed them, but now it was Theo's face she saw when she opened her eyes.

Theo. It had taken her almost a year since that day when she ran out of his office to find an excuse believable enough to justify her calling him, and by then she was afraid he'd forgotten her. Or had entirely lost interest. So she spoke to him only of the Embassy she and Danny had purchased and of the work that had to be done, and when he expressed a willingness to get involved in the renovation, she said to herself, *Thank God for the Embassy*.

Thank God for the Park Avenue mansion-in-shambles because now she saw Theo regularly. She'd be seeing him today. But that only increased her sense of longing. Because of Theo her mornings had become heavy with new desire and old misery. She'd come to hate her mornings, to dread the start of each new day, and lay abed later and later in a turmoil of yearning and apprehension.

* * *

Danny stood before the mirrored doors of the thirty-foot-long bedroom closet, naked. By shifting to the right or the left, he could see his genitals reflected in all ten floor-to-ceiling mirrors, a sight that made him smile wearily. Such excess, such vanity! Guilty of both, but not yet finished with either, he stepped into tapered black silk boxer shorts and assessed with more confidence than anxiety his body's major assets.

He began with his broad shoulders and could find no fault there. And although even he would admit that his arms were too slender, he was quick to notice that they were, nevertheless, nicely toned, even fairly muscular.

"Not," Danny liked to say, "because of any efforts on my part. Nothing jock whatsoever." He claimed his biceps and triceps were a complete mystery to him. Loathing almost all sports since childhood, he'd been continually surprised that his body, nonetheless, grew on, becoming the ideal prototype for a basketball player: very tall, very lean, very strong.

Standing in profile, he congratulated himself on his midriff. At thirty-six, his belly still was not merely flat, it actually sucked inward under the cliff of his ribcage.

Only his butt was a bedevilment. When had his buttocks begun to pucker? It reminded him of the crinkles and puckers of the cotton plissés and piqués, attractive but rarely used fabrics he'd resurrected and often featured in his interiors. He'd even used them here, in this apartment, on the bench cushions and the skirted table in the bedroom. When Dell saw the place for the first time that Christmas weekend over four years before, she fell in love with it, convinced the brilliance of the decor reflected the depth of Danny's soul. Surely he must be an outstanding person, she had reasoned, to be gifted with such an outstanding sense of style. She loved the walls in the foyer that were the exact color of midnight, and the gold intaglio stars and the hand-painted clouds on the ceiling, but what made her clap her hands to her mouth in complete awe of him when she awoke on Christmas Day in the quilted peach bedroom was the sentimental rediscovery of cotton plissé.

"After all these years! My favorite dress, when I was a girl, was made of this fabric," she told him, fingering the striped table skirt, unaware that the orange and apricot stripes exactly matched the highlights in her hair. "What's it called?"

She goes with everything, Danny remembered thinking. *She belongs here.*

"Plissé," he told her.

"Plissé," she repeated, sighing with nostalgic pleasure. "I think you're the only designer in New York who knows this fabric exists. You should win the plissé award."

That was almost four and a half years ago. The plissé award became a private joke between them. In the beginning, whenever he did something that pleased her, she'd give him the plissé award. Now, after three and a half years of marriage, the "award," like so many other golden qualities between them, had tarnished with disuse. In fact, all that had endured intact were their secrets, so meticulously hidden from each other that perhaps they each deserved an award for deception.

Danny returned to the mirrors and to his self-appraisal. In the beginning, he hadn't wanted Dell to know how preoccupied he was with his appearance, and approached the mirrors with circumspection. Then he began catching Dell, stomach sucked in, staring at herself more and more often in front of these same mirrors, with mounting agitation. Danny found this perplexing since Dell had never looked better.

Once, when he came upon her, she looked up guiltily, and cried, "There are too many damned mirrors in this apartment. It becomes an addiction."

He recited his credo for her, "An apartment can never have too many mirrors."

"No!" she insisted with surprising vehemence. "Being addicted to your own image is wrong. It's harmful."

To Danny, wanting and endeavoring to look good could never be harmful, though he recognized that others could think him vain, or worse. But these days Dell slept late and he had the mornings and the mirrors all to himself. He took his time, pausing after each step in his dressing routine to appraise the effect. So far, except for the tie, everything met with his satisfaction.

* * *

Behind him, Dell was buried under the covers, unseen, unseeing, listening to the metallic click of his belt buckle, the swish of his silk tie. She wondered if he was wearing the blackberry tie.

"I take it you're not coming into the office this morning?" Danny talked to her slim mound under the peach comforter while studying his pocket appointment book.

He waited, but there was no response. Not that he honestly expected one; they had argued the night before and gone to bed in sulky silence. She was angry because he hadn't bothered to tell her that he'd be home late, but if she knew he was with Christopher, she'd have been even angrier. Still, she was right, he wrong, yet he withheld an apology. He never called to warn her he wouldn't be home, and he never apologized, though he knew she resented his behavior. But apologizing would have far-reaching implications, entrance to a door of discussion he kept firmly locked. So he ignored the tension between them and contained it by avoiding it. But the pressure was building and one day, he knew, the door would blow open. On that day his world would shatter like a smashed mirror. He was a man with much to lose, but most of all, he did not want to lose Dell. And he didn't want her hurt. That was why the door was locked. For her protection, he told himself. For Dell.

"One o'clock, then, Dell. Sharp. At the Embassy."

The Embassy. He loved calling it the Embassy even though he knew that, technically, it should really be called a consulate. "I can't say 'our New York Consulate,' can I? What else can I call it?" he'd argued. "Our shed? Our little Park Avenue lean-to?"

Under the covers Dell sighed but said nothing. Danny slipped his appointment book into his pocket and spoke to her supine form without actually looking at her.

"Did I tell you Theo wants an hourly consulting fee during construction? A hundred and sixty an hour. So don't be late, Dell—not even five minutes." He didn't bother to look at her. "I'll meet you at one."

He was dressed in a British hacking jacket with a mauve tint in the tweed, mauve-gray slacks, and a gray silk shirt. The blackberry tie had been considered—it lay snaked on the window seat—and rejected. He was waiting for Dell to lift her head from under the peach pillows and notice his outfit. To give him her whistle of approval that she needed two fingers to execute. She knew he was making a design presentation for the Garsons' nineteen-room penthouse at a breakfast meeting this morning, but only her right pinky emerged. It bent and twitched slightly, a good-bye gesture.

Sighing, Danny turned and caught himself again in the mirrored doors of the wardrobe. By the time he was seventeen he'd grown to his full height of six feet, five inches, but he hadn't known his almost endless legs were really an asset until he began draping them in custom-made slacks, more than fifteen years later.

"Custom work makes all the difference," he used to tell his clients.

The clients he had now didn't have to be told. They insisted on the best. As did he. There wasn't a project in his office for less than a quarter of a million dollars. Several were budgeted at well over a million. Two restaurants would top the five-million mark and one hotel conversion might go as high as ten or twelve. And most likely a palace. Some Arabs wanted to talk to him about the futuristic Islamic residence they were building.

"Modern, modern, modern," the three brothers had chanted in unison. He could hear them giggling into the three-way phone across ocean, desert, time. He imagined them nibbling dates and thought he heard one spitting out the pit.

"Wait," one brother cautioned the others. "We must not tell him modern. Tell him progressive. The architect calls our palace progressive. There is a difference."

"Modern? Progressive? Nonsense! Royal. We have a royal compound, now we need royal furnishings. Mr. Dannenberg, you understand royal, yes?"

"Of course," Danny nodded into the phone. "Royal. Colorful mosaics, rich tapestries, and perhaps a progressive hint of western classicism?"

"Ah, we love Doric columns."

"You want the future but you want the past, too, yes?" Danny said.

"Exactly," they agreed with relief. "All of time in a single space."

"All of time. I can't wait to see it. And to meet your architect," Danny said dryly.

''Then you'll come?''

''Send me a plane ticket. On second thought, send me at least five tickets.''

''Ah, he travels with entourage.''

''Then he is beloved.''

He understood them, all of them. Most aroused in him a rather sneaky curiosity at first as he poked through their homes, measuring their bedrooms, peering into their closets. But too often the curiosity turned to disappointment and vexation. People were so maddeningly tasteless. Even the rich. Especially the rich, who should, he insisted, know better. That was why he warned them he only worked with clients he liked.

Only last week, speaking across the slab of granite that was his desk, he told his newest clients, a couple who wished to redecorate their entire seven-bedroom Westchester home, ''You and I will be working intimately for perhaps the next year. Intimately.''

At that they had nodded, pleased he'd emphasized intimately.

''That's why I insist I must like a client before I take him on. All my clients ultimately become my friends.''

This was what they'd hoped, and the Westchester couple couldn't help grinning luckily.

''If I don't like you,'' Danny warned, ''I can't work with you.''

The couple frowned as if they'd just heard horrible news.

''Because if a job isn't fun, I can't create. I can't think fabulous. I can't think drop-dead draperies and unboring color schemes. I just can't. So I'm warning you. But if I do take you on, if we do go to contract, I'll give you a look that'll make your neighbors weep with envy. You will die and be reborn in beauty. Really. This is not conceit; it is just that my best is *the* best. And I can only do my best when I love my clients.''

That he happened to love all those clients, and only those clients, with budgets of over a quarter of a million dollars did not seem to matter. He convinced them it was an honor to have been chosen by him. He was that good. He was a master.

As Danny tied the laces of his gray wingtips from Milan, he thought of the Garsons. Edgar Garson would appreciate his outfit. He had dressed for Edgar Garson, and now, Dell forgotten, Danny was eager to get to the office and wait for Edgar Garson, for that moment when his client would meet Danny's dark eyes, hold them for a pulse too long, and then turn guiltily away to his wife.

Danny nodded into the ten mirrors as if he were being introduced to his reflection. A dark, unsmiling visage stared back at him. A handsome, boyish face, but the eyes were unforgiving.

You'll be sorry, they warned.

He whirled around and looked to the bed, to Dell to stop him, but she was still hidden under the covers. He thought of crawling under there with her, burying his face in the white dessert of her breasts where he used to feast deliriously, where he used to find shelter. But first he'd have to face her wide, accusing eyes, and he could not even face his own.

So he turned back to the mirrors and thought of Edgar Garson, surely at this moment dressing with unsuppressed eagerness for the morning's meeting. That silver-white pompadour would be teased to new heights and that beef-red neck would be drenched with Italian cologne, of that Danny was certain. In just one previous meeting Danny, with a combination of professional bravado and titillating innuendo, managed to nudge the haughty old man close to hiring him for a three-project deal; today he would sign. And what's more, feel lucky to sign. Lucky to be in the clever hands of Danny Dannenberg, of D & D, designer of dreams.

Danny let himself quietly out of the apartment and prayed that Angie, Danny and Dell's secretary, had remembered the raspberry preserves, and to pack the French crocks with butter. He himself would pick up hot croissants and scones on the way. He was hungry for something frothy and sweet, cappuccino the way Dell made it. Dell again. The thought of her stabbed him with a sharp and twisting point. He should let her go, he knew, but he couldn't. Or change his ways, then, but he couldn't. *You'll be sorry,* he warned himself, *very, very sorry.*

Dell's eyes snapped open as soon as she heard Danny close the front door. For two stiff hours she had been faking sleep, lying still while her heart pounded with foreboding and her mind sped through all the things she wanted to say to him. Perhaps if he'd touched her, held her, she wouldn't be feeling this ravenous yearning now, this voracious need. Perhaps if she hadn't pretended . . . but no, it was better this way. Better to let him think she was angry. Because she was angry.

Suddenly, she threw back the covers, and stood, naked under her untied white velvet robe, before the wall of mirrors, just as Danny had done earlier. In a kind of daze, she moved slowly but fixedly to the bathroom, her breasts with pink pindot nipples and her taut, exercised belly and her penny-spattered thighs were alternately exposed and draped by the folds of her white velvet gown.

There, Danny's damp peach towels and robe lay in a pile on the Italian hand-painted tile floor. Usually meticulous, he'd left them in his hurry to get to the office for his breakfast meeting with the Garsons.

I should really be there, too, she told herself, and the emptiness inside her widened. *I came up with the pagoda concept and the entire nineteen-room color scheme.* A *Chinoise* motif throughout. Inspired. Palest jade greens for the master bedroom suite. Window shutters carved from purest jade—and a jewel cutter lined up who would do it.

Jade deepening to juniper, then bluing and yellowing to turquoise in the long foyer. And a red lacquered entry and dining room with a Chinese pagoda enclosing a semicircular lacquered table looking out over the view. *My* inspiration.

But Danny was annoyed with her. She could tell from the sound of his voice when he said, "I take it you're not coming into the . . ." Actually, he was relieved. That's what he really was. Glad she wouldn't be there. So he could have his bitchy little clients all to himself, take all the applause. Clear the stage! Give Mr. Dannenberg room, lots of room.

God knew she didn't crowd him. *Where does he go when he flies out of here? Is he really gone? I want him back. No, I don't. I have pride.* She didn't want him. She wanted a new suit. That black velvet fitted evening suit she'd seen on Madison Avenue. If the size six fit, she'd buy it. Black velvet heels, too, if she could find them.

And new bedsheets and shams. She was tired of all peach. She'd shop for a new floral fabric and have their upholsterer make up a new quilted spread. The bedroom was looking a bit worn. With a little effort, she could make it perfect. And Danny would love the black suit. He adored it when she looked glamorous.

"That's what I'll do," she told herself as she turned on the shower. "I'll go shopping."

Now that she had a mission of urgency, Dell dressed quickly. Flinging open the mirrored doors of the thirty-foot-long closet, she flicked through the sleek suits with short skirts hanging beside silk shirts and satin blouses, beaded jackets and dresses, clingy, billowy, long, slit, all meant for late evenings. She chose a belted, knitted dress of creamy cashmere.

At the mirrored vanity displaying a collection of antique crystal perfume bottles topped with tall and fragile stoppers, she sat on a peach linen tufted bench and applied only one layer of mascara to her lashes and one tint of cocoa gloss to her lips because she was in a hurry. Across the room a photograph behind glass sat on Danny's nighttable. It was a picture of Dell, a first-anniversary gift to him. Her hair was longer then, but no less radiant. And her magnificent face, the face of a freckled Garbo, was dazzling, sunlit, and laughing.

Where did that laughter go? she wondered.

"I'm going shopping now and this time I'm going to get it right," she said firmly, out loud. She'd do herself over, do the apartment over, and this time everything was going to be perfect. He'd see. He would love it. He'd never want to leave.

The black velvet evening suit was gone! In its place in the window a headless mannequin was wearing a brown tweed dress. Danny hated brown. He insisted that she hate it, too, but there were certain times when she secretly liked the color, especially the way it was used here in the tweed dress.

It was too early! The shop wasn't even open yet. She jiggled the doorknob but it was locked tight. She checked her watch. Nine-thirty. A half hour until it'd open. And she had to be at Willa's Way Studio by 10:50 for her advanced double class. There was so little time to get so much right!

Hurrying down Madison Avenue, she was dismayed to find virtually every boutique not yet open for business.

"A bunch of lazybones!" she said under her breath, remembering all her years of rising at dawn to complete drawings or plans or meet with busy clients. On the other hand, Dell reasoned, a shop that opens later in the morning can stay open later in the evening. "And who, Dell, darling," she could almost hear Danny ask, "feels like shopping for evening clothes at nine in the morning?"

"Who indeed," Dell muttered to herself and ducked into a coffee shop to use up some waiting time. Facing her at the long formica counter were trays of buns and muffins, sweet rolls, hard rolls, scones, and Danish pastries.

"Just coffee," she told the waitress, but to herself she said, *Eat one of those and you'll be out of control. Then you'll have another and another and you'll wind up looking like you-know-who.*

Not since she was seventeen, when she lost twenty-seven pounds and thought she'd changed her life, had she ever loosened her grip on herself again. Sometimes she longed to let go, to give in and not care anymore. Lately, perfection had become exhausting. It didn't make her happy, and it obviously couldn't hold Danny. She had a sudden desire to apologize to her mother for somehow letting her down. It was a scary feeling, and it drove her out of the coffee shop and back up Madison Avenue, to the boutique with the brown tweed dress in the window.

The door was open but the saleswoman still had her coat on.

"Please come in. I didn't have a chance to take my coat off because the phone was ringing as soon as I unlocked the door." She held out a container of coffee to Dell. "I brought this for my assistant, but that was her, calling in sick. Would you like some coffee? I'm afraid it's black—"

"I take it black, thank you," Dell said and accepted the container, knowing this would make her third cup this morning. Three cups, but zero calories, she reminded herself.

"I drink my coffee almost white. It's the only chance I get to include some milk in my diet."

"Calcium," Dell said as the saleswoman hung up her coat. She whirled around to appraise Dell through sixties cat's-eyeglasses.

Dell smiled at the dark, slightly chubby woman and turned to flick through the racks.

Clucking her tongue, the dark woman said to Dell's back, "You young women. You don't know how to relax."

Dell found the brown tweed dress, the one featured in the window. Ideal for the office, she thought, holding it up.

"You all keep buying clothes for the office," the dark woman continued, "but what you need to do is get all dressed up and go out and have a good time. And do I have the outfit for you!"

There, behind the paneled closet door that the saleswoman pulled open with a flourish, was the black velvet evening suit, as stunning as she'd remembered it.

"Let's see," the saleswoman said, assessing Dell's figure. "I'd say a size six."

Dell held up her beautifully manicured hands with nails flashing lobster red and protested, "Only sometimes. One big dinner and the next morning I go up to a size eight."

"Well, this is a six. It's the only one we have. Would you like to try it?"

She was out of her clothes and into the black suit in just over a minute, but she didn't recognize the statuesque beauty with the silky red hair staring back at her in the mirror.

"What do you think?" the saleswoman finally asked.

"I don't know. What do *you* think?"

Sighing deeply, the saleswoman said, "It's a shame you don't know how beautiful you are. You look just like that French actress, Catherine Deneuve, except with red hair, of course."

"Is the cleavage a little too risqué?"

"Madam, I am inspecting you all over and there's nothing for the tailor to take in or let out. It fits you like a custom order. It's perfect."

"Do you really think so?" Dell stared at herself, and back. "It's rather . . . sexy."

"Oh, yes," the saleswoman agreed. "But extremely elegant."

"And extremely expensive," Dell added, looking at the price tag. But the sight of herself in that suit was making her feel slightly lightheaded, as if she'd just had a glass of champagne. "I'll take it," she said at last. "And now I think I'll try on the brown tweed." She took that, too, and kissed the short, dark saleswoman on both cheeks as she left the store, two slick, slim boxes tucked into a handsome shopping bag.

"Come again, Mrs. Dannenberg. Just for coffee and to talk. I'll remember—black, for you!"

Oh, it was thrilling to buy beautiful things. Shopping erased all the fear and gave her hope again.

She turned left and headed east to the cluster of design showroom buildings on Third Avenue. Making her way to her favorite fabrics house, she checked her watch and began flicking frantically through the hinged wings of color-coordinated fabric panels. She knew what she was looking for—a silk pongee in palest apricot or cognac, and a cotton eyelet or lace for her dressing table. Then she wanted a butter-soft leather in cognac again, to re-cover the garden bench. It was time to replace the piqués and plissés, despite her fondness for them.

Of course, she should be discussing all these changes with Danny, she scolded herself. He'd be furious.

Right, she answered herself bitterly. If he even noticed.

Then she had to laugh to herself. Thinking of all the millions of women in troubled marriages down through the ages, she knew she stood out as unique. Who else would rush to bedroom reupholstery as a solution?

She had bought some exquisite new lingerie a few weeks before but it still remained folded and unworn in her drawer. She wasn't sure why she hadn't worn it yet, but somehow it'd seemed a waste to crease and wilt the precious silk satin and delicate handmade lace. If Danny wouldn't appreciate it, then why bother?

She collected the pinking-edged little swatches and the larger memo samples, and hurried home to drop off her packages. Then it was on to the exercise studio. Her day was planned: She was going to work out her body, rush to the Embassy, and then redo her bedroom. Tonight she'd ask Danny to take her out to dinner and perhaps wear her new velvet, beaded suit. But she still needed suede heels and new linens for the bed.

Oh, there was still so much to do to get her life just right! And a part of her was tired, so very, very weary from the endless striving. She longed to let up, to just stop, but she couldn't. Not now. Not when she might lose Danny, her husband, her magician, who was supposed to turn everything abracadabra, into a dream of joy . . . and love.

9

Dell flung her leg warmers, green with stripes of metallic gold thread, onto the dressing-room floor. It had been a frantic morning, but punctuated with small triumphs. First, she'd awakened to that familiar feeling of emptiness again and despair over her marriage that made her want to stay in bed and hide all day. But she overcame that temptation. There was triumph, too, when the size-six black velvet suit fit and when the chubby little saleswoman told her she was beautiful. She'd even managed to collect some fabric samples for the bedroom makeover before taking two advanced exercise classes. As a result, she actually felt quite pleased with herself, a sensation so rare that it made her want to sing.

It had been a thrilling morning, because everything she wanted, she got. And everything fit! Usually, her height of almost six feet made alterations mandatory. But not today. And the fabric swatches she'd collected were just the fresh, elegant touch her bedroom needed. It was almost unbearable to wait to see everything recovered and redone. Tomorrow she'd have to do the measurements, order the reupholstery, and shop for black shoes. There was a small shop on Madison Avenue—hardly larger than a shoebox itself—where she knew she'd find heels to match the suit. Oh, she could hardly wait!

Leg muscles trembling, Dell shimmied out of her shiny green unitard, humming Butterfly's hopeful ''Un Bel Di.'' She gathered up all her damp exercise wear and stuffed it into an enormous black leather pouch that she'd brought back from Italy when she was there on her honeymoon, three and a half years earlier. Soon, she and Danny would be returning to Milan where once, for three days and nights, they were so happy that they claimed they never slept at all.

"We lost the need for sleep. Honestly. It was completely amazing."

When they returned home, no one was surprised. Everyone said, "Those two are running on love."

Now she and Danny were scheduled to return to Milan for a whole week. Milan! Home of the great International Furniture and Design Biennale, where D & D was to receive the Innovative Small Design Firm Award at a gala dinner. The award was one of the most prestigious in the field of design. Milano!

But suddenly, Dell's elation evaporated as she thought bitterly, *If only this were a year ago. No, two years ago. Then I still would've been ecstatic.* But not now.

Once, a nostalgic return to the land where she'd found such happiness, highlighted by a gala where Danny's and her hard work would be rewarded, might have filled her with intense anticipation . . . when she was still sure of Danny's love, and of her own. But now, she thought, one week without seeing Theo . . . she didn't think she could stand it.

"Shower time, thank God!" Jackie Knight announced and Dell, naked and damp with sweat, followed her friend's dimpled buttocks into the shower room.

Three times a week, Jackie took the twelve o'clock advanced class with Dell. Afterward, they sometimes shared an all-vegetable salad lunch at the vegetarian cafe nearby, but not today. Today Dell had whispered that she wasn't available, which was just as well with Jackie. She was sick of the salads Dell always insisted they eat, and looked forward to a nondiet hamburger-and-French-fries lunch for a change. After a workout, she craved indulgence, not abstinence. She refused to be rushed. She refused even to be dressed. Eschewing a robe or even a towel, she preferred to lounge and chat and apply her makeup entirely in the nude.

"We're all 'jes l'il women," she said in her sweet but fake drawl. "We all got the same things," she'd say, giving her buttocks a little slap, "some a mite smaller, some a mite bigger. That's all—so why we hidin' what we got?"

She set the tone for the Willa's Way Exercise Studio. Eventually, most of the other women shed their pink towels and walked around naked, too, albeit not entirely freely. A certain self-conscious stiffness remained, clinging to them like sweat.

"I'm drained," Jackie groaned with exhaustion, and piled three pink bath towels on the shelf beside the shower—one to dry her hair, one to dry above the waist, one to dry below.

"I really belong in the beginner's class. Why do I torture myself?"

Dell rolled her eyes. Jackie whined before and after almost every class. They'd been through this before. But today Jackie was particularly sulky. She glared at Dell's trim body with envious resentment, even though her own pert and compact form was usually a source of intense personal pride. Today, however, Jackie stared only at Dell.

"I do. I torture myself. But you, Dell, are totally beyond belief. Why do you do it to yourself?"

"Me?" Dell asked reluctantly.

"You."

Jackie's blonde curls were plastered to her cheeks. She brushed at her wet face impatiently. Then, with a recently tanned arm she tested the water temperature at the one pink shower in full operation—the Willa's Way Exercise Studio's pink renovation was not quite completed and the inconvenience, at these prices, was galling.

"Yes, you. Of course, you. Why do *you,* Dell, do it, day after day?"

"Do what? Oh, what did I do now?"

Annoyance suddenly replaced the disappointment she'd been feeling. She did not want to be the focus of Jackie's theatrical jealousy in front of all these strangers.

"Two one-hour advanced classes, back to back," Jackie continued, tipping her head back so she could look Dell in the eyes. At five feet, eleven inches, Dell towered over Jackie's petite frame. "I could almost hate you. You're like some kind of fierce, magnificent giantess in class. An Amazon. Yes, an Amazon! While we're huffing and puffing, you're humming and hopping. I *do* hate you."

"Jackie, it's Wednesday. You're always tired and cranky on Wednesday. You don't hate me. You hate Wednesdays," Dell told her.

It was so easy to subdue Jackie's storms and coax a

smile out of her. Ever since their first days at the American School of Design and Decoration, where Dell was a full-time student and Jackie had enrolled for one course, "Color-Coordinating Interiors," Dell had been just the stabilizing foil Jackie unconsciously craved. Cool and reassuring, Dell surprised even herself that Jackie's chaotic moods and frenzied tirades didn't shake her. In fact, Dell found something to admire in Jackie's wild, emotional swings. Jackie would say, "I don't know why I took this class. I still don't know what color to paint my apartment. I hate green. I hate blue. I hate beige. I hate colors! What am I doing here? I'm a writer, not a colorist."

And Dell would tell her, "You don't hate colors, you just hate choices."

Amazed, Jackie would agree. "How did you know? That's it! I do! I hate choices. So you choose for me. What color should I paint my walls? I'm hopeless."

And Dell would tell her with a kind of admiration, "You're not hopeless. You're emotional. But at least you don't hold your craziness inside you. You get it out before it poisons you."

That always stopped Jackie. She'd look up at Dell and wonder, Is she talking about herself?

But it was just this alert scrutiny that Dell was always trying to shun. Friendship demands revelation, but Dell had managed in her one grownup and close friendship to avoid intimacy by skirting around the edges of her life, and concentrating on the center of Jackie's. Still, Jackie could be insistent.

"Just tell me. Why do you push so hard?" she said now, folding her golden arms across her bare chest.

"Nervous energy, I suppose," Dell conceded.

"What have you got to be nervous about?"

"Oh, Danny and I had another silly fight last night and—"

"Another?"

"Jackie, stop probing, will you? We're fine."

"That's the trouble. Now I'm really jealous. How can two people look so perfect together, be so perfect together, and only have silly, perfect little fights? When Dominick and I fight, we don't speak for weeks."

"Did you have a fight this weekend?" Dell had noticed dark circles under Jackie's eyes, an imperfection Jackie rarely left uncovered.

"No, we made up." Jackie's smile was a wet-lipped leer. "I got a total of twenty minutes of sleep, and it hurts to sit."

Dell smiled a half-smile of ambivalence. How she envied Jackie her passions. While Jackie spent the weekend with Eros, Dell had teetered dangerously, like Humpty Dumpty, on the edge of a high wall. If she weren't careful, the elaborately embellished eggshell enclosing her marriage would crack. She had become exceptionally fragile. Jackie was lucky. Jackie could tell the whole world everything and fear nothing. But Dell, who feared imperfection more than anything, could not tell anyone when things were going wrong. Instead, she had to strive harder to make herself and her world impervious, perfect. Until then, she must never let up. Never.

Dell caught Jackie just as she was about to climb under the foaming shower. Pressing Jackie's clammy shoulder, she pushed ahead of her.

"Listen, do me a favor and let me get into the shower first. Your interview isn't until—when? Two? And I'm supposed to be at the Embassy five minutes ago. Danny's going to be furious. We're meeting Theo Glass there."

"Who's Theo Glass?" Jackie asked and let Dell pass, stealing a glance at Dell's white breasts that always seemed so tightly massed, so full, that they hardly jiggled when she moved. Then, unobserved, she enviously examined Dell's buttocks until they disappeared behind the shower door.

A spray of irritation washed over Dell. How could Jackie live in this world and not know Theodor Glass? And how dare she!

"Jackie, everyone has heard of Theodor Glass—even you!" Dell shouted more loudly than she meant to through the shower door.

Jackie shrugged impassively. There were few leading actresses or top New York models whom Jacqueline Knight had not heard of. Many she'd met and interviewed, and several were among her closest friends. These were the only people worth knowing anyway. The beauties. Dell, too, was a beauty, but she could be so damned aloof and secretive. It brought out Jackie's wickedness. With a spiteful but hidden smile, Jackie contented herself with the thought that, though Dell's body was perhaps the most perfect she'd ever seen, it did indeed have one flaw: no nipples. No nipples at all!

"Didn't Glass do the new Rockefeller Museum?" asked Cathleen, the advanced aerobics instructor, as she entered the shower room. She leaned her bony but startlingly powerful body against an unfinished shower stall. When completed, the Willa's Way Studio would have six pink showers, but for now Willa herself warned everyone not to complain.

"Not a word. I don't want to hear one complaint. I'm paying the workmen double to come in late at night, just so I won't have to close and you won't miss your classes. I do this all for you, so no whining, ladies, please."

"I remember reading an article about it," Cathleen continued. "It opened a few months ago, didn't it?"

Behind Cathleen two more naked women entered and they formed a lush line that was echoed in the wall of mirrors opposite the showers.

"The Rockefeller Museum and the Seventh Avenue Synagogue and the American missions in Kyoto and New Delhi. As well as half the waterfront in New York, and that hot new rock group's glass house—I believe it's called the Cracked Globe House," Dell enumerated from under a lather of bubbling anger.

"Oh, an architect."

"Not just another architect, Jackie. Theo's been called the Frank Lloyd Wright of the late twentieth century."

"Who's Frank Lloyd Wright?" Jackie teased, and everyone but Dell laughed.

"He's hot, red hot." Some part of Dell knew she was protesting too much, but she couldn't resist poking her head out of the shower and adding, "And he's a hunk, too. An unbelievable hunk." Which only made her infuriated with herself. And made Jackie curious.

"He must really be something," Jackie said, winking at the other women, "because I've never heard you rave about another man before. Except for Danny, of course." To the women on the shower line she explained, "They've been married more than three years, and they're still on their honeymoon. A three-and-a-half-year honeymoon, can you believe it?"

Dell scrubbed her head and wondered how she could have demeaned herself, and especially Theo, by calling him a hunk. She'd never used the term before about any man. She didn't think that way about men. She didn't.

Jackie waited, but the pink shadow behind the frosted-glass door scrubbed furiously and said nothing more. Clearly, Jackie saw she had struck a nerve with Dell, but its exact meaning eluded her. If Dell had been a different kind of friend, Jackie might have suggested, "Let's do dinner. This is too big for a lunch. I want all the time in the world to discuss this most interesting new interest of yours." But she knew that Dell would deny everything while accusing Jackie of nosiness, perhaps even insanity, and Jackie would end up doing all the talking. Not that Jackie entirely minded; Jacqueline Knight happened to be her all-time favorite subject of conversation. But even Jackie yearned, at times, for more balance in the relationship.

"It's not that Dell isn't an intent listener and a wise adviser; she is. It's just that her own psyche remains a complete mystery to me and I've known that girl for ten years," Jackie was always explaining to Dom after their lunch dates.

Rarely did Dell ever reach out, needy and confused. And even more rarely did Dell ever seek Jackie's advice. How could Dell ask for help when she refused to admit to even having any problems?

Nevertheless, over the years Dell had left a trail of teasing clues that Jackie did not fail to notice. Most surprising of all was this newest clue: the architect Theodor Glass. It suggested something might have soured in the dazzling Dannenberg union after all, but Jackie knew she mustn't push. More than once Dell had warned her, "Back off, Jackie," maintaining a remote distance for weeks afterward.

So Jackie turned to the assortment of reflected breasts and pubes in the mirror. All her life she had been curious, even obsessed by women's bodies—their tits, their buns, their bellies, their collarbones, their inner thighs, their underarms. She wished she could examine them all and compare them with her own—every silvery stretch mark, every rosy, bumpy aureola, every inverted navel, every cinched waistline. Sex was emphatically to be enjoyed with men, but it was the female form that held for Jackie a competitive and therefore compelling fascination.

"Three years," Cathleen, the instructor, sighed. "I can't imagine being married for three years." Her rack of ribs rose and sank as she sighed again. "Three years must be like an eternity."

Jackie guffawed. "Oh, right, a millennium."

"No, really. I had my first affair three *months* after I was married."

There was a collective intake of breath.

"I didn't say that to boast," Cathleen said quickly. "I didn't mean it that way, really. And of course we're divorced now. But what I am saying is that it's still so difficult. So impossible."

"What's so impossible? I don't understand," the last woman on line asked, barely masking her impatience. She was about fifty-four, her hair was almost entirely gray, and her abdomen, soft and spongy, draped like a weary web from her waist, an emblem of the four children she had borne.

Jackie, childless, glanced down at her own midsection and sucked it in. Even Dell, who emerged from the shower swathed in pink terry, tightened her belly. The sight of that weak and sagging abdomen served as a warning that everyone seemed to hear; all the women pulled in and up in unison and stood straighter and taller by several inches. The vacant shower dripped, but no one made a move for it. No one wanted to miss a word of this conversation.

"I mean, it's so impossible to remain faithful to anyone—or anything, for that matter."

"For more than three months," the older woman said dryly.

"I know what I must sound like to you, but doesn't anyone here know what I'm talking about? The temptations. How can you resist them when they're everywhere?"

"Everywhere," Dell agreed in a small voice.

"Exactly. Everywhere," Cathleen said to her, nodding. "Men, sex, drugs, clothes, furs, jewelry, cars . . . *things*. All those things are out there, flashing neon lights at you, calling to you like the sirens. You have to strap yourself to the mast to hold back. Or be turned off entirely, in your own world. At least, that's the way I see it."

"It's one big supermarket. Everything's tempting. Everything. And it's all available. But you want to choose the right thing, the perfect thing. You don't want to make a mistake, but you do," Dell said, her voice stronger now. The discussion was drawing her in, embracing her. There in that tight and steamy tiled room she suddenly felt safe. She wasn't alone. And the possibility existed that she might even be understood. She let her towel fall.

"It's true," the woman standing behind Jackie said, nodding to Dell. "Life is a goddamned glitzy supermarket. The *things* out there. Oh, God," she rolled her large, brown eyes, "I go crazy with the yearning. Things I don't need, never needed. Things that could *hurt* me! Things I don't even know what to do with, or have room for. Things, especially, I can't afford. I want them. I want them all."

She was thirty-three, Jackie's age, but Jackie couldn't take her eyes from the woman's huge breasts. She nodded to the breasts in the mirror, and they swayed slightly as if in answer.

"Pretty things, beautiful things," Cathleen said, adding to the litany. "They stick them in front of your face and what are you supposed to do?"

"You do exactly what we all do in the end—you give in," Jackie said without bitterness. To Jackie, the temptations of big-city life made for a delicious struggle, the delights outweighing the frustrations. She was like a restaurant diner who wanted everything on the menu. Which exact item to choose was always the problem. She didn't resent excess, only the fact that she couldn't have it all right now, right here.

"But if you give in, you pay. You always pay, one way or another," Dell said darkly, thinking of her father. He'd never forgiven her for breaking away, for daring to dream of more than the meager lifestyle he'd provided, for growing up. And to this day, for that great crime, she was still paying.

When Dell heard several murmurs of agreement, she looked up, surprised, too, at herself, at her own participation in this confidential exchange.

Exposure! She'd actually risked exposure. It was for just that reason that she usually avoided such encounters, particularly with women.

Women. She longed to talk to them, cry with them, make friends with them, but they were dangerous. Too dangerous. Unlike men, women were so eager, so ready for exposure that even in the unlikeliest settings—cramped and steamy bathrooms like this one, for instance—one spark of intimacy was all they needed to unite them, and then they were off, revealing and sharing the details of their most personal selves. They hid nothing, and they expected you to do the same. Oh, it was terrifying!

"It's the 'why not?' age. Forget about payment," the woman with big breasts was saying. "If it feels good, why not?"

"On the other hand," said the older, gray woman, "I've spent my whole life obeying one strict set of values, refusing to succumb to empty temptations. I've never owned a pair of high heels, for instance. Or slept in a hotel with a man other than my husband. And yet . . ." she hesitated, her eyes on Jackie.

Oblivious, Jackie stared only at herself. *Five pounds.* If she was going to buy that red catsuit, she'd have to lose at least five pounds.

"And yet what?" asked the woman with big breasts.

"And yet I can't help feeling I've missed out on something. As if that part of life—the superficial, seductive, consumer-manipulated part that you're all talking about and which I always condemned—was the best part, after all. I don't know . . . it just seems like more fun. And you all certainly look great, whereas I . . . Which reminds me, may I ask you a personal question?" she said directly to Jackie.

Jackie shrugged, but her body tensed. She felt nothing but scorn for ugly people, and went out of her way to avoid them. Ugliness, up close, made her physically ill, headachy, nauseous. Ugly people made her angry. What she couldn't understand was how they themselves could tolerate their ugliness. Why they didn't do something to fix themselves up. Women, especially.

"We're always in the limelight, so we've got no choice.

We've got to keep up,'' was the way her mother put it,
and Jackie entirely concurred.

Mrs. Knight taught her that everyone looked at women
more, even other women. ''Women look at us more than
men do, and when they look they *see* more, if you know
what I mean.''

Jackie knew what she meant. Movie stars understood
this, too, and it was what made Jackie's work so appealing. Interviewing beautiful women who understood the
necessity and the techniques to cultivate their beauty.
Showing Jackie how they applied their egg masques and
their chilled-cucumber eye soothers, their cinnamon
cheek contour and the six shades of beige eye shadow on
their lids. Demonstrating how they did their abdominal
exercises and how they concocted their high-energy
breakfast drinks so Jackie could show her readers. Edu-
cate them, really. And inculcate her own personal doc-
trine (which also happened to agree with her magazine's
unspoken but basic precepts). Jackie, like the beauty
magazine she worked for, subscribed to the gospel that
beauty, not religion, could save a woman's soul. With
missionary zeal she spread the ''word,'' and every time
she saw a plain woman wearing expertly applied eyeliner
and cheek blush, she was sure she had gotten through.

''Uh, where do you get your legs waxed?''

Jackie scrutinized the gray woman quickly, and then
averted her face as if fending off a bad odor. Then she
glared back at her again. The woman's hands flew to her
abdomen. She spread out her fingers to create more cover,
but she couldn't hide from Jackie's sour stare.

''If I were you,'' Jackie said, ''I'd treat myself to a
whole day at Elizabeth Arden. They call it a day of
beauty, but there've been times when I could've used a
month.''

There were laughs of agreement, but when Jackie continued, everyone listened in uneasy silence, appalled and
yet amused at the same time.

''I'd get my old, gray hair colored. My God, you look
about seventy! I'd get a facial, get my eyebrows tweezed,
get my legs waxed, yes. And,'' she added no less tact-
lessly, ''I'd clean up that bikini line. Prune your pubis,
honey, and you won't recognize yourself in a bathing

suit. And if you get yourself on a diet, your husband might even sit up and notice you again.''

"Now wait a minute. I don't have to listen to—''

"Oh, yes, you do!'' Jackie retorted, finger pointing straight at the gray woman. "I'm the only one who'll tell you this. It's what I do. They'll only think it—'' with her chin she indicated the other women—"but I'm the only one who'll say it. It's more than my job. I've devoted my life to edifying women like you—smart women who don't know a thing, not a thing worth a real damn.'' She paused, breathing fire again. "And I'll tell you something else—''

"Jackie, don't,'' Dell interrupted, her hand on Jackie's shoulder, trying to quiet her, stop her. But Jackie wouldn't be stopped.

"No, let me tell her what a fool she is.'' Jackie turned to the gray woman and scowled.

"You say you wonder if you've missed out on something and all I have to do is look at you to know you have.''

Everyone groaned at her words but the gray woman folded her arms in front of her chest, stuck out her chin and said, "All right. What do you see when you look at me?''

"I see a woman who's been completely co-opted. A dope. What idiot convinced you that if you have a brain you have to look like you just got out of Intensive Care?'' There were a couple of awkward snorts of laughter, then silence. "Get yourself to Elizabeth Arden's. It's the best university in the world.''

The gray woman tried to smile but her face went rigid with humiliation. Dell grabbed a towel and offered it to the stricken woman. Then Dell and the woman with the big breasts wrapped their own nakedness in large terry towels, and Cathleen folded her arms across her narrow chest. Everyone had a new and uncomfortable sense of modesty.

It's gone, Dell thought miserably. The intimacy. The trust. Shattered. And we're all forced back, all we modern women, to an era when female rivalry made us all enemies.

It was Jackie who had done it, but they'd all had a part.

They'd listened and laughed maliciously, and now they could hardly look at each other.

Jackie escaped into the shower, leaving an uneasy silence behind her. Dell wandered back into the dressing room, her private thoughts encased in lead again, as carefully guarded as an explosive. It would be a long time before she'd wish to share her thoughts with a woman friend again, but she couldn't imagine ever wanting to tell anyone what she was thinking now.

Sex. She was thinking of sex. As she dressed, she stole glances at herself in the mirror and tried to picture Danny's hands on her bra, pulling it off, his bare thigh rubbing against hers. But she couldn't picture Danny's hands on her bare skin. She couldn't remember when he'd last touched her with desire. The truth was that he hardly looked at her body at all.

"Nice," he'd say, admiring a pair of her earrings, dangling them in his hands as once he'd played with her breasts.

Oh, how he used to love fondling her breasts! But no more. So what was she trying to prove? That she could win back her husband by working out like an Amazon? Isn't that what Jackie called her—an Amazon?

Suddenly, she stopped. *If I'm trying to win Danny back*, she realized for the first time, *then I've already lost him.* A wave of sorrow washed over her.

And that was when Jackie entered, talking. "Did I ever tell you about my junior high school report on Amazon women?"

She waited for Dell to finish pulling on her red leather boots, but Dell merely grunted. Jackie continued anyway, seating herself on a pink terry chaise.

"The Amazons, according to my report, had this initiation rite that was totally embarrassing to read out loud to a class of twelve-year-olds. So, naturally, I wanted to."

Despite herself, Dell smiled. Back there a few minutes before, she'd discovered a new and virulent cruelty in Jackie, and she'd wanted nothing more to do with her. But even Dell recognized she couldn't afford to lose her one real female friend. Then her loss and her isolation would be complete. Perhaps, if she had a child, Dell mused to herself, she wouldn't be so afraid of being alone. But Danny said he wasn't ready for "diapers and doo-doo," and, Dell supposed, neither was she. It was difficult enough dealing with her life as it was. The added burden of a helpless baby seemed to her an overwhelming responsibility; she doubted that she could handle it.

So without a child of her own or a full-time husband, Dell turned to Jackie and forced herself to listen attentively as she prattled on. But when Jackie began talking about her mother, Dell didn't have to force herself to listen. The sense of familiarity was so intense that already Dell was nodding her head in unconscious agreement.

"I asked my mother whether or not I should read my report out loud. I told her about their initiation rite, but she didn't seem revolted, or even interested, for that matter. She said, 'Wear the white, open-necked blouse.' It didn't matter to her what I said so long as I looked good when I said it."

Applying several more coats of mascara to her already stiff and blackened lashes, Dell made no comments but listened to every word as Jackie leisurely continued.

"You see, my mother was shaped by one solitary event in her life—the morning her husband, Thomas Knight, took off and never came back. She was left with their five-year-old daughter—me. My mother went around the house blaming herself. 'I let myself go,' she told me over and over. 'And a woman should never do that. She's got to keep up, or you see what happens.' "

That's it! That's what unites Jackie and me—our mothers! Dell suddenly realized. For although no two mothers could ever have been more different on the surface, their message was the same. Gertrude Shay, too, had let herself go, and blamed herself for giving up. But she hadn't given up on Dell. "Don't end up like me," she warned Dell over and over. "You can be different, happy. Make me proud of you, Dell."

She *had* become different. She'd become a kind of Amazon. And still, she kept trying.

"What was this brutal initiation rite?" she asked Jackie, half-listening.

Jackie shuddered. "To prove their strength, they would cut off—or burn off—the right breast. It seems it got in the way of the bow and the javelin. But can you imagine?

They literally gave themselves voluntary radical mastectomies!''

Dell nodded; she *could* imagine those ancient warrior women searing off a breast for the appearance of strength. Hadn't she been willing to do as much, in her way, for appearance? But when she looked up at the clock on the pink wall, the thought sliced through her that in less than a half hour she'd see Theo again, and she grew frantic to leave.

''So, did you look good?'' Dell asked with a smile as she began gathering her makeup from the counter.

Jackie smiled back. ''Yeah. The white blouse was a hit. My mother, as usual, was right.''

Dell whisked on her black leather cape, blotted her lips one last time, and sprayed the air around her with her own personal scent, a concoction of perfumes that she combined with the exactitude of a chemist. It made her smell, Danny had once told her, ''as irresistible as freshly baked cake.''

Danny! Fearful of Danny's wrath, she checked the time once more. Eager to see Theo, she headed for the door. At the doorway, she waved to Jackie.

''Bye. I've got to run.''

Suddenly, Jackie was on her feet and at Dell's side. She held onto Dell's sleeve with one hand and her wraparound pink towel with the other, blocking Dell's way.

''I've got a big, beautiful secret, Dell, and I'm just burstin' to tell you.''

Intrigued, Dell waited. Secrets. Jackie had a million secrets; Dell tried to imagine this one. She tried to imagine thinking of a secret as ''beautiful'' and of wanting to reveal it to a friend.

''I'm moving in with Dominick.''

Dell's heart sank and she couldn't help exclaiming, ''Oh, no, Jackie. Not again!''

Remembering the last time, how she'd lugged Jackie's cartons and car packs through a snowstorm to Dominick's apartment, how excited Jackie had been, and then how stricken, she shuddered inwardly. It was the first night in February the year before and all the New York City taxi drivers had gone out on strike that afternoon, as the snow began to fall. Jackie sailed past the doorman, two paintings under her arm, and chattered excitedly as they rode the elevator to Dom's penthouse. But a note taped to the door told her why her brand-new key would not work:

> *Call me a rat, call me chicken, but I just can't go through with this . . . yet. I thought I was ready, but I need more time. I've gone to the Coast for the week-end. I changed the locks—what else could I do? Don't hate me. I still love you and I will make it up to you, I promise. Dom.*

"He means it this time," Jackie insisted. "For a whole year he's been making it up to me."

"Until he has to make a commitment," Dell argued.

Jackie wanted to shoot back, "And what about your perfect husband—the raving fag?" But she didn't. She wasn't sure what Danny Dannenberg was. There were times when he seemed to her entirely swish, and she wondered what Dell was doing, married to a man who was so obviously gay. At other times, Jackie found Danny one of the more sensitive and affable men she'd ever known. Even rather attractive.

Not that she had anything against gay men. She'd be the first to say that some of her favorite conversationalists were gay men. They shared her spectrum of interests and were willing to discuss subjects straight men disdained as strictly feminine, like cosmetics or body fat. It was only when she pictured them in bed together that she felt less tolerant. What irritated her was the waste. As a rule, gay men were much more concerned about their appearance and infinitely prettier than straight men, and she couldn't stand having to relinquish such a good-looking group of men. Why couldn't only the ugly, pimply, fat men be gay?

One thing remained clear, however: To attack Dell's husband was to risk unleashing a protective, and possibly lethal, loyalty in Dell. Jackie could never be sure of Dell; she remained a mystery. While most women cursed their husbands now and then, they never wanted to hear *you* curse their husbands. Dell, on the other hand, never cursed anyone. How close, and how loyal, she remained to Danny was unclear, but Jackie knew better than to test it.

"No, he's genuinely sorry about last time," Jackie said

with controlled patience. Her fake Georgia accent was
thick. "Why, he was so sorry, he broke right down and
cried in my arms. Now, there are only two things a man
can't fake, and one of them is tears." Though she giggled suggestively, Dell remained impassive. "I mean it,
Dell, this time he's ready."

"I hope so," Dell conceded and glanced at the clock
again. She had wanted to get to the Embassy early. She
always wanted to get everywhere early, do what was expected of her, be the good little girl. But what did they
want of her? Oh, she'd do anything to avoid their anger
and their disappointment, but the harder she tried, the
emptier she felt. Fancy chocolates and shopping and exercise used to be the antidote, but not anymore. Not since
Theo. To sate this grinding emptiness inside her, she
needed Theo, she needed love.

Feed me love. Theo, feed me love!

What was she saying, thinking? She and Danny were
the anointed ones, the glitter couple. The entire international world of design was opening up to them. In just
three and a half years D & D had become the hot firm,
the in team. Danny and Dell. They had purchased a fairy-
tale mansion, their very own embassy, and they had the
singular Theodor Glass to help them restore it. Theo, the
brightest star in the universe.

No, no. Think of Danny, she told herself. *Think of our
future. Of D & D. Think!*

Soon they'd be flying back to Milan and to the parts of
Italy where they'd honeymooned for one delirious month.
It wasn't too late to recapture all they had lost in the three
and a half years since then, to find their way back to
bliss. Why, they were, after all, not much more than
newlyweds. So how could she be thinking what she was
thinking, feeling what she was feeling? How could Theo
be doing this to her?

Stop it! But how? she wondered.

Just the thought of Theo made her feel instantly restored and whole, as if he somehow completed what was
missing in her. To think of him was like being on vacation in the Caribbean. He was its sunlight, its juicy tropical plants and fruits, its vibrant fish and bird life.
Perhaps it was his coloring—his peach cheeks, his lemony hair—that reminded her of island breakfasts of pa-

payas, plump melons, pineapples, bananas. He was perpetually tan. At seventeen, she'd gone to Jamaica with the hope that it would change her life. Now Theo was truly changing her life. His dazzling eyes, bluer, deeper than the Caribbean Sea, were changing her life. His walk, slow and deliberate, the very opposite of Danny's, was changing . . .

No, no, this must stop, she told herself harshly. *Can't you do anything right? What kind of wife are you anyway? No wonder Danny's disinterested in you. He's disappointed. They all are.*

She'd married Danny because, unlike her father, he always said she was divine, his partner, his feminine ideal. And for a time she believed it. Just as she'd once believed her father. When she was a girl, he too told her she was his favorite. But then he changed and she never knew exactly why, only that it was her fault, all her fault that he never loved her again.

As a child, he took her to watch the fishing boats in Sheepshead Bay. She loved to go at four o'clock, when the fishermen sold their day's catch from their boats at the piers. Bravely, she watched the men gut the fish, their knives wet with blood, and fillet the flesh for the waiting customers.

"When I grow up, I'm going to be a fisherman and catch a great big fish like that one," she told her father, Victor Shay. "I'll sail away on a big ship and—"

"You'd sail away and never see your Daddy again?" Victor Shay probed, only half-joking.

"No, Daddy. Never!" She grabbed his hand and held it tightly. "You'll go *with* me. Won't you, Daddy?"

Victor Shay shook his head. "No, sweetheart. I want to stay right here in Brooklyn, in my little house with my little family and never, ever sail away."

"Me, too. I want to stay right here with you and never, ever sail away."

"That's my good girl, my best girl."

When Dell was older she begged her father to allow her to take dance lessons and reluctantly he finally agreed.

After several months of lessons Dell told him exuberantly, "I've decided. I'm going to become a ballerina!"

"Ever see a chubby ballerina?"

She grudgingly shook her head no.

"Know why?" Because ballerinas never have any fun. They can't eat Oreos or candy. They can't have cookies and milk at bedtime with their father the way we do. They have to practice, practice all the time and if they gain an ounce—that's it, they're out!"

"But my teacher says I'm talented."

"And I'm sure you are. You can do lots of things. You draw pretty pictures, too. But a big, tall girl like you isn't built to be a ballerina. I'm surprised you're so gullible."

"Even Mommy says I could lose weight."

"And become a skinny belink? I like you just the way you are. Don't we have a good time? Isn't it cozy right here, safe and cozy? Okay, then, forget that razzle-dazzle. That's not for you."

"Well, what *is* for me?"

"I'm surprised at you, Dell. You're nine years old. Don't you know by now? Don't you want to make your father happy? Don't you like it here?"

"Yes, but—"

"No ifs, ands or buts. Just be a good girl and settle down now, Dell. Make me proud."

But in the end, he died angry. She never could do what would have pleased him, though she never stopped trying.

Today, soon, she'd be seeing Theo again. But each time she saw him—she often saw him now, during this frantic period of renovations—she fretted, What does he expect of me?

Oh, Theo!

She couldn't take the chance. She could never have him. It had nothing to do with Erica, for even if there were no wife, she still could never have him. Because he must never know her, never know how thinly the razzle-dazzle veiled this scared, unhappy little girl. If she ever gave in, let go just once, she'd lose control and end up obese and depressed like her mother. And a failure like her father. Theo mustn't see her like that.

With Danny, it was different. He never wanted to look at the insecure little girl hiding behind the glamorous veil. Always darting off somewhere, gone from her so many nights, distracted when he was home, Danny expected her to be his beautiful gem, always shining brightly, and nothing more.

But she wanted it to be different with Theo. She wanted to begin anew, fresh and clean. It was unimaginable that she would keep secrets from Theo. And just as unimaginable that she could tell him that inside her lived a fat, lazy, miserable girl just longing to give up and end all this striving. She felt split in two: She couldn't tell him the truth, yet she yearned desperately for him to know her. The first time they all met at his office to discuss the embassy renovation, she found herself drifting into the personal, telling him details of her childhood, bringing them one step closer.

Closer to what, she didn't know.

She looked at Jackie, who had returned to the pink terry chaise where she was slathering pink lotion over her smooth and shapely legs. Jackie, she knew, would tell her to go for it.

Abruptly, she was jolted back into the present. She heard Jackie saying, "This time he's not going to bolt, believe me," and Dell realized they were still talking about Dom.

"Dell, you ought to see him. He's something else. He's determined to do it right this time. He's going all out, moving me himself, in style. By limo. Three limos, actually. Or, as Dom says, 'Hey, if we need ten, we'll get ten.' "

Dell couldn't help herself. She whistled.

"This man does have a certain kind of style," she had to admit.

She thought of Theo. Of Dom. Of Danny. Of men with a certain kind of style. Men who could take your breath away. Once, for a time, Danny had left her breathless. Now, when she thought of Theo, she was sure she'd never felt *this* breathless, *this* exhilarated. As if she'd just climbed five hundred steps. Never. And this quivering lightness in her chest and her knees that made her grab hold of doorframes, ledges, anything—surely she'd never felt this before. Perhaps no one in all of time ever had. It was singular, entirely unique, yet she had no difficulty in identifying it. It was really quite simple.

Dell was in love.

10

"A red pagoda. Hmmm."

"A *lacquered* red pagoda. And cushioned in your red silk velvets."

"A red pagoda," Edgar Garson repeated, frowning at the watercolor rendering of the dining room that Danny held up for him. "Interesting."

"Interesting?" Danny exploded. "Come on, Edgar, it's to die and you know it."

Garson smiled. "Perhaps."

"Perhaps," Danny mimicked with sulky derision, yet his client continued to smile at him. Even Danny was appalled at himself for his blatant lack of professionalism, but there was something about this haughty old queen that made Danny want to scream. Garson was leering at him boldly, accelerating everything, toppling Danny's expectations. Then Danny remembered the contract. That came before anything. He pulled himself into control.

"Perhaps we need some coffee."

Garson nodded and Danny came around in front of the huge polished pink slab of granite desk and stretched his long body across it, somewhat like a chanteuse might do with a grand piano, and buzzed Angie to bring the coffee. The effect was not lost on Garson, but his appreciation was quieter and more disinterested than Danny had expected.

"Lovely, Daniel. Now that, without question, is lovely," Garson said, and then examined his nails with great care.

It was maddening. Garson was supposed to gasp at the pagoda, blow kisses to the boy genius, and be oh so grateful when this *wunderkind* deigned to descend from his perch in order to pose and be petted. Instead, it was

Garson who smiled with condescension while Danny fretted with uncharacteristic self-doubt.

But though Garson had succeeded in unnerving him, Danny wasn't unhinged. Like the rare actor he might have become, he held onto a fierce determination not to blow this audition, and continued to pose for Garson with his dark, half-closed eyes and his long, lean body lounging suggestively. Some undoubting part of him remained convinced that if he just kept at it, did what he usually did so well, he'd eventually arouse the old man's delectation to the point of hunger, need, weakness. That was where he wanted Garson—on his knees.

So he continued to stretch and loll lazily, letting the old man drink him in. The smile never left Garson's face, yet slowly, imperceptibly, it changed and, just as Danny had predicted, softened and rounded with undeniable desire.

The tip of Garson's alligator shoe, resting over his right knee, found Danny's leg and brushed up and down against it. There was an ever-expanding silence in the room, broken only by the rustle of Garson's foot sliding on Danny's shin, and the scraping sound of Garson's raspy breathing.

Garson was flushed a brilliant rose and his head felt as if it would burst. But he felt young again and he couldn't stop smiling.

Oh, this boy was insolent, though, Edgar Garson told himself. He wasn't used to such insolence, to being treated without a certain fawning deference. Well, it was all right, Garson allowed. It was even refreshing. Endearing, actually. *My insolent equal.*

He wished he could take the boy in his arms right now. It would be delicious to hold him, pet him. Or, if he persisted in being disrespectful, Garson could teach him the pleasures of submission. On the other hand, perhaps it would be Danny who'd force Garson to his knees, compelling him to clutch the cool, naked thighs of this gangling giant and beg, tearfully, for more, more. *Either way,* Garson sighed, *so long as I have him.*

Angie entered and, guiltily, he twisted around to see if she'd noticed anything, but her deep-set black eyes were lowered as she bent over the découpage tray that she'd placed on the turquoise tinted glass coffee table.

"I'll be back with your breakfast in a few minutes. The scones are heating in the microwave," she said, and when no one responded, she let herself quietly out of the room.

But the mood was broken and Danny was selling again, setting up the black steel desk easel that he'd designed for just these presentations and displaying the large blueprint of the apartment floor plan, while passing to Garson chips of marble, mirror, carved jade, Italian ceramic tiles, airbrushed designs for a mural, fabric swatches. The color scheme, room by room, was illustrated in watercolor renderings with small swatches attached to the borders. The renderings were packed in an antique paisley portfolio tied with a red silk cord. Nineteen renderings of nineteen rooms of gradated color, from the brilliant vermillion of the entry hall and the dining room to the palest jade of the master bedroom suite. Yet Garson perused the paintings listlessly.

Once again unnerved, Danny wondered if he should end this decorative tour of the apartment's color scheme if it was generating no excitement. Certainly Garson, more than anyone else in the field today, understood fabric, color, texture, design. His eye was unerring, cultivated, and it was said of his sense of touch that his fingertips were actually antennae. His business was textiles and he'd built it into an empire with his extraordinary acumen, yet he barely looked at the portfolio Dell had so carefully constructed. He barely touched the samples Danny offered him with unsuppressed eagerness.

He sighed. Then, still smiling, Garson settled back in his chair to enjoy this charming, although unnecessary, performance; Daniel Dannenberg would be hired, no matter what he said or did. No matter what, Edgar Garson was going to have Danny all to himself, and soon. Danny just didn't know it yet.

That damnable smile! What did it mean? Danny could not tolerate the man's brazen confidence. Sweat drenched the armpits of his gray silk shirt, and his upper lip began to bubble. Danny's body found almost any excuse to perspire, but now, with Garson's lewd and liquid eyes licking up and down the length of his body, he felt as flushed and moist as if he'd been tongued.

"I don't know whether you're smiling because you

know I'm right," Danny said, looking into Garson's pale eyes, "or because—"

"I'm still resisting?" Garson teased.

"No one is less resistant to exceptional design than you, Edgar," Danny said truthfully. Then he mopped his brow and drove his point home. "And you know that this lacquered red dining room with its own dining pagoda is exceptional design. Furthermore, *I* know that you know it."

"Oh, ho!" Garson chortled.

Danny gripped the rendering of the red dining room. "We've just given you a taste, so to speak. Just the color scheme. We'll work up detailed drawings for every room, of course."

"I would hope so, Daniel," Garson agreed, patting his white hair. "I would certainly hope so."

Forcing a smile, Danny took a sip of his coffee. The cup rattled when he replaced it on the saucer. He could not lift his eyes to meet Garson's again. Not until he'd gotten himself back into control.

Who's seducing whom here? he asked himself. *What does he want? Does he like the pagoda? If he thinks he can demand major changes so early in the project, then it means he really hates my work, but I'd rather quit first than let him ruin the red pagoda.*

Oh, if only people would stop intruding upon his elaborate constructions! Fuming inwardly, Danny remembered that once he had thought that he might become a set designer because a set, at least, remained intact once it had been designed and constructed. But when he realized that actors would have to sit in his chairs, even if they were precisely placed, and deflate his plumped cushions, that they would knock over his vases and slam his doors and perspire on his brocades, he saw it would be no different. People would inhabit his spaces and there was just no way around that. His perfect constructs would forever be tarted up, pared down, altered—and therefore ruined—by the mere existence of his clients in the rooms he had designed. Designed, for the most part, without them in mind. Real cat hair on the faux leopard bergère, fingerprints all over the mirrored bathroom doors, ghastly paintings on his pastel walls—there was just no way around that. And yet they begged him to take them on, they hailed him a genius.

All except Garson. With him it was quid pro quo; something for *something*. Gross. He was no prostitute, goddamnit! He was an artist. Here was a design scheme Garson should have been drooling over. Reverence was customary these days and Danny, like Garson, had come to expect it. Something even more than reverence. Danny had hoped to receive something from Garson that he could not even name, but he knew how it would make him feel—loved, embraced. If the old man had looked upon Danny with eyes of fatherly love, Danny might have done the entire nineteen-room apartment for nothing, for "family feeling." But as it was, Garson wouldn't let Danny forget that this was a battle for control. Not that Danny was particularly worried. In the end, he realized, he'd get the job, one way or the other.

"All in good time, Edgar," Danny countered with newfound control. "But we must reach an agreement before we can proceed. So I want you to visualize this."

Garson sighed again but this time Danny ignored it.

"You'll dine in the pagoda, surrounded by mirrors and giant red gloxinias. The pagoda, as you can see, is raised on a two-foot platform to take advantage of your spectacular city views. The trelliswork, lacquered red, of course—very Chinoiserie—will cost a fortune to do right, but just think how your red silk velvets will look done up as seat cushions."

On their first, very brief meeting at the bare, unfurnished penthouse site, Garson had said, "All of our residences must be showplaces for our fabrics, without being commercial showrooms."

"And we trust you understand the difference," Tina Garson had added.

Oh, the bitch! Danny had thought, perspiring heavily. But his tone was level, his manner cool when he answered, "You know my work. And you've already checked me out or I wouldn't be here, not even for this preliminary meeting."

We. He should have said we. *Our* work. He'd caught himself too late and Dell, standing next to Tina, had glared at him. But he couldn't help it, no matter how insulted Dell felt. She insisted they were a team, equal partners; he knew better. *He* was the firm. It was *his* vision they all wanted. He, Daniel Dannenberg, *was* D & D.

"On the other hand, I think your concern is entirely understandable," Dell added impulsively, touching Tina's sleeve. "You haven't worked with us before and you're concerned about whether we understand what you want."

Later, Dell would defend what she said to Tina, when she and Danny argued about it in their peach bedroom. She would insist she had to do *something* to soften Danny's cold arrogance. They were, after all, Mr. and Mrs. Taste, as *Architectural Trends* had labeled the Garsons in its last issue. A husband-and-wife tour de force.

"And when *Architectural Trends* says Garson Textiles, Ltd. is owned by two of the most knowing and listened-to arbiters in the field of design today, and you're trying to win them as clients, you don't sneer at them."

"I don't need a lecture from you on how to win clients," Danny had shouted.

"Yes, you do!" Dell had shouted back. "Garson Textiles is only the largest and most renowned fabrics house in the country—in the world, probably. Kings, presidents, movie stars—even Nobel Laureates—everybody!—does their homes in Garson fabrics. They've got showrooms and mills all over the world. And an art collection worth over fifteen million."

"And they chose us. Why? Because they know D & D is the best. Remember, Dell, we don't have to kiss their feet in gratitude. If anything, they should kiss ours. They wanted the hottest design team in town, and they got it."

"Not yet, Danny. They're only considering us. They haven't signed any contract."

"They will, Dell, darling. They will."

But Danny was tiring of Dell's toadying ways with clients. Though well-meaning, she actually exacerbated certain tensions between him and their clients, and this incident proved it.

Encouraged by Dell's words, Tina Garson couldn't have agreed more.

"We're *very* concerned," she said coldly, emphasizing her displeasure.

"Of course. It's understandable," Dell nodded eagerly.

But Tina Garson was no longer addressing Dell; she was looking straight at Danny, and only at him.

"You're small, extremely small, compared to the firms we would ordinarily deal with."

Danny wanted to pull all the red hair out of Dell's head. With just one mewling comment to Tina, Dell had undercut the confident, not particularly eager posture he'd been trying to establish. Suddenly, instead of a team, he and Dell had begun working at crossed purposes. He missed the days when their eyes would meet and they would share a knowing smile in the midst of a meeting much like this one. Now the only looks they exchanged were flashes of irritation. What in Dell was now most exasperating to him had once evoked keen sympathy. In the beginning he had labored to improve her self-esteem by drenching her in a shower of adoring words. But when it became clear his therapy wasn't working, he took it rather personally, convinced Dell was withholding success from him by clinging to a diffident, self-deprecating persona she'd long since outgrown. Meekness was no longer appealing in marriage, but it was downright repugnant in business.

However, Garson rescued the moment—at least, for Danny.

"Size isn't the issue," he said to his wife with iced exasperation. "It is *not* the issue," he repeated. "Vision is." Then Garson turned to Danny.

"There must be a compatibility of vision."

Tina appeared to be ticking ominously. Even her dainty high-heeled shoe tapped to a beat of syncopated fury. But what to do with her displeasure? Usually, Danny won the women first. Wives especially adored him. They all spoke the same language—hyperbole.

"Now, this, *this* is utterly magnificent!"

"Oh, I can't stand it. It's too, too gorgeous!"

"Ooh, I must, must have this. I must!"

But this most important wife, Tina Garson, spoke with a rancor that shocked and perplexed Danny. What could she possibly have against him? The question was unanswerable, baffling, so he turned his complete attention to her husband who, he suspected, made all the important decisions anyway.

"Now, there I agree with you completely, Edgar. A

compatibility of vision is absolutely essential. Uh, may I call you Edgar?''

Garson assented by flicking his brown-spotted hand and then replacing it on the sink. Danny walked across the enormous, bare white kitchen that first day, and stood next to Garson, his hip slightly grazing Garson's spotted hand. He kept his hip there and Garson didn't pull his hand away. The only movement Garson made was to shift his weight to his right foot, hoping to block the angle of his wife's view, but Tina saw—she always saw—and she fumed not entirely inwardly.

From Dell's position—her back leaning against the niche where the glass-doored professional refrigerator and sub-zero freezer would eventually be placed—she too could see a hand, a hip, a certain pressure. And then she didn't see it anymore. Her eyes darted away as if they had spied something forbidden, and her mind followed her eyes into a blank wall.

Staring blankly, she didn't ask herself why she was feeling this combination of uneasiness and depression. The answer, she knew, would make her feel even worse.

Meanwhile, Tina continued tapping and Danny fixed his eyes on Garson's.

''You want a design firm that can translate your vision into your interiors,'' he told the white-haired master unctuously. ''You're saying that there must be a complete harmony of understanding between you and your designer so that it is *your* aesthetic, ultimately, that is expressed.''

Garson nodded agreeably, blinking his watery eyes. He let his trapped hand remain right where it was.

Confidence restored, Danny shrugged nonchalantly. ''And I'm saying that's the only way I work, anyway.''

Danny didn't dare look at Dell; she knew how he really worked, the bursting ego and personal statement he invested into each job. Once, she might have suppressed a hoot of amusement at his nonchalant subterfuge. Or teased him later, sarcastically laughing, ''Yeah, right, that's just the way you work—whatever the client wants. Ha ha! I can't believe you told him it will be his aesthetic, *ultimately,* that's expressed. Just wait till he discovers you've hung an oil painting over the bathtub and he'll ruin the painting and the look if he ever gets that wall wet. Just wait till you tell him you hate his antiques and family heirlooms and that he should start with a clean slate. Just wait!''

Once, she might even have prodded a wicked laugh out of Danny. Or embraced him, feeling a mixture of amusement, awe, and repugnance to hear him say, ''Fuck him. Fuck them all!'' Not realizing *he* meant it, really meant it.

But now he couldn't be sure of Dell. He couldn't take the chance of meeting her eyes—he might find almost anything there. And he certainly didn't dare look at Tina. Of course, it was her husband who Tina really resented, but Danny was in her line of fire and, as he saw it, was bound to take some flack.

''My husband and I have very strong tastes and opinions. Are you quite sure you're willing to subordinate your own will to ours?''

''Tina!'' Garson exploded. ''How can the man possibly answer a question like that? It has nothing to do with subordination. As I said, it's a matter of compatibility. Will you stop making this so unpleasant?''

''Compatibility. That's a laugh.''

''Tina—''

''You of all people, championing the cause of compatibility.''

Tina's open hostility coaxed Dell out of her hiding spot to observe it. The spectacle of another woman publicly venting her rage was both revolting and thrilling at the same time. With one hand Dell wanted to clamp Tina's mouth shut, and with the other hand cheer her on.

Rage. Something so seemingly simple for Tina to expose, and yet so impossible for Dell.

''Tina—''

Garson had moved away from Danny and his fingers were curling around Tina's upper arm, which was narrower than a man's wrist. Tina violently shook him off. She was unstoppable now, as if that ticking, that tapping was building to just this, this detonation. She wriggled, she pushed, she pummeled, but she couldn't break entirely free of Garson's grasp, so she bent her head as if she were going to kiss his hand . . . and then she bit it. Hard. In an instant she was free.

''Animal!''

"He's calling *me* an animal!" Tina cried. Looking wildly around her, from the plaster ceiling medallion to Garson, then down to the poured concrete floor shot with reflective bits of mica, her focus finally settled on Dell, backing into the niche with her.

"Mr. Compatible over there! Mr. Compatible hasn't been compatible with me since—forever. I live with a man who won't even say good morning to me, much less—much, much less—good night. But, oh, he knows all about compatible when he meets a tall, tanned, young, handsome—"

"Tina! That's enough! I've warned you I won't allow our domestic squabbles to be put out on the table like so much rotten fruit in a bowl."

"Rotten fruit?" Tina asked with a derisive laugh. "Exactly. Well, have it your own way. I, like a fool, always let you, in the end. But just remember, as long as we share the same nest—and we always will, Edgar—I get the right of first cut. Isn't that how they say it in Hollywood? I get the right of last refusal." She scowled at Danny and continued. "Every last ashtray. Every slab of marble, every desk, every sofa this—this *kid*—puts in here. Or else I don't move in at all. And if I don't move in, Edgar, that will cost you more than just money."

"Are you threatening—"

"Moi?" Tina asked with wide, innocent eyes. Then she about-faced, flung her chestnut sable coat over her shoulders, nodded quickly at Dell, and hurried, high heels clacking on the teak parquet of the foyer, to the front door.

"Where are you going?"

"To Paris," she shouted. "And to hell with you!"

Nevertheless, Danny had expected to see Tina Garson today. But Angie whispered when Danny arrived, "Garson's in your office. Alone. But you can smell him from here." She held her nose with her two red-lacquered fingers and said, childlike, "Pee-yew."

Danny was surrounded by women who hated homosexuals. With Angie, it was intense but selective. She rather liked young, good-looking, articulate gays, even if they were swish; it was the old ones she hated. Dell was offended by all of them, though her political position was in complete support of gay rights. It was just that the very word homosexual evoked in Dell the most graphic pictures of naked men having painful anal sex. To avoid the pictures, she avoided thinking of gays at all. For the most part, they didn't exist as long as she kept her eyes averted. And Danny's mother, who even hated heterosexuals, detested gays as well.

Knowing that these most important women in his life were, to one degree or another, homophobic, yet did not regard him as a hateful candidate, was both comforting and unsettling to Danny. At any moment, any one of them could turn on him. No wonder he was always sweating. He took a tissue from the box on Angie's desk and blotted his brow.

So Garson had come alone, Danny gloated. Without even the pretense of a wife this time. For surely Tina Garson had returned from Paris by now, or wherever it was that she'd run off to in a huff.

It proved the job was in the bag. Jobs, really, for the Garsons had three other residences that Danny knew of besides the nineteen-room penthouse on Fifth. There was a villa near Rome, a grand estate in Greenwich, and a newly purchased, multitiered cliff house in Puerto Vallarta stripped bare and absolutely begging to be done over—according to none other than Christopher Beene who ("simply exhausted!"), probably was the only designer in the world who could *afford* to turn down the Garsons. That Christopher would recommend D & D in his place was not, however, entirely altruistic.

And there was also the new textiles showroom in London. Endless jobs, if he could just sign the old queen up. But first, of course, there was the presentation to get through. Selling. His family forte. An entire family of Jewish salesmen. But he was a seller of dreams. He traded in passports to heaven, or the closest stop to it—a sky-blue ceiling with creamy clouds and perhaps a light coat of gilt on the moldings.

Heaven. Heaven was where you combined *your* taste, *your* creativity, *your* technical proficiency, cultivation and high sense of style with *their* bank accounts. Heaven was where you gave them an environment that screamed *Status*! Heaven was your client's exalted position in society taken form, indoors.

"Take me to heaven!" their eyes begged. "Where a castle is a home done right."

It was like a new religion. The religion of the "How About?" and the "Why Not?" How about a heaven with an Aubusson rug so rare the housekeeper must whisk it by hand with an extra-soft toothbrush each morning? Why not a sofa of imported French calfskin, as soft as the finest gloves—and as expensive as a luxury car? Why not? And how about a waterfall, twenty feet high, that tumbles into the grottoed bath? Why not an English Gothic library with a hidden door in the fireplace and the original bookshelves from Blenheim Palace? And the Czar of Russia's marquetry table in the dining room? Or Marie Antoinette's paneling in the bedroom? Why not an electronically controlled household, everything push-button from the phone-message system to the revolving pantry shelves in the quarter-of-a-million-dollar kitchen? Why not?

And he was their messiah, the anointed modern captain who could fly them to heaven on a George II rare silver platter. Even Edgar Garson had come to worship at Danny's altar. All he had to do was buy a ticket at the door.

Of course, Danny mused, *tickets are pricey, but that's because I've bought a giggle of a place, Edgar. Actually an embassy. A very large embassy that I've got to pay for, so be generous, Edgar.*

All right, here I come.

He swished through the doorway to his private office, tall and sleek as a giraffe. *Watch me*, he commanded mutely. *I know that's why you're here—to feast your eyes on me once more. I'll do my dance for you, I'll take you all the way to heaven—but you better come through, Edgar. I don't dance for free anymore. Not for years. Not since I was twenty-three.*

"I'm curious," Garson said playfully, a smile still at the corners of his thin lips. "How did you come up with the idea of a pagoda?"

"I read an article about you in *Newsweek*—"

"*Newsweek*? My Lord, that must have been 1985. I remember because that's when Tina and I bought our chalet in Manchester and the magazine photographed us in our striéd velvet ski suits sitting in the chair we did in the same fabric. It was, you know, one of those small, newsy pictures, but they happened to catch us in a most favorable light, so we got hold of the transparency and had it blown up. I was particularly fond of the line of striéd velvets we did that year. I was mad for the house, too—Chinese Deco in Vermont, of all things.''

Just then Angie entered with a basket of croissants and scones and another pot of steaming coffee. She had long, shapely legs and shiny, dark hair that she wore in a boy's cut, which showed off her good facial bones and deep-set mocha eyes. Her clothes were expensive, but Danny had heard she could well afford them, having been awarded a huge divorce settlement the year before.

Dell and Danny had met Angie while honeymooning in Italy. At that time, Angie was still married to Fabrizio, and living in Rome. When she moved back to New York, she asked Dell for a job and Dell hired her. But Angie remained an enigma to Danny.

Why would a young, beautiful, rich American who not only spoke fluent Italian but several other languages as well, be satisfied being underpaid and overstressed as a secretary here at D & D? Dell said Angie needed to restore her belief in herself, that after the divorce, Angie felt like a helpless failure.

''I can help her,'' Dell said. ''I understand her.''

But so far, Danny could see no signs of improvement. Angie remained fiercely loyal and grateful to Dell, but otherwise shy and unambitious. She had an even weaker ego than Dell's, but no one (like Danny) to save her. Poor Angie, Danny sighed. What a waste!

Poor Angie, he thought again as he sat down beside Garson on the rose and gray jacquard sofa and watched in silence while Angie set out the gray striped plates and the clever gray checked napkins that were really French scarves. The two men stared off into space, into the corner of the room where a huge rose-colored urn sat. The urn looked and felt exactly like incised terra cotta, but it was made of some lightweight plastic. It was the only ''fake'' in the office, and it fooled Edgar.

''Nice,'' he said. ''Mexican?''

Danny just grunted while Angie inefficiently shuffled back and forth from the office kitchen, carrying one or

two breakfast items at a time until there was no avoiding
it; Angie would have to hear Danny taking the credit for
Dell's ingenuity and resourcefulness.

"Yes, I remember now. It *was* a 1985 *Newsweek*,"
Danny said, avoiding Angie altogether. "When our first
on-site meeting was, uh, cut short, I tried to supplement
what I needed to learn about you at the library. I took a
gamble that you and Tina never did get that pagoda you
both wanted."

Unable to stop himself, Danny glanced over at Angie
after all. She was, of course, glowering at him.

Angie Romano had been standing right there when
Dell, barely containing her proud excitement, wordlessly
placed the sketch of the pagoda on Danny's desk. Dell
was the one who'd researched the Garsons at the library.
In an old *Newsweek* article, she read a caption under a
picture of the famous Garsons at their unusual Chinese
Deco mansion in Vermont: "Now, all we need is a pagoda, an intimate little Chinese-style gazebo on the lawn
for al fresco dining, and this place will be pure paradise."

Immediately, Dell called the Manchester Registry of
Real Estate Records and learned the Garsons had sold
the house three months later, right after Tina suffered a
severe skiing accident.

"Chances are they never skied again—and never got
her pagoda," Dell said, standing behind Danny while he
studied the drawing.

Angie had waited in the open doorway, grinning at
Dell like a nervous coach on the sidelines.

How these women looked to him, awaiting his judg-
ments with the tittering intensity of schoolgirls! Of
course, he enjoyed it, and would probably be willing to
admit he even encouraged it. They made him feel infinitely wise and important and capable, yet he couldn't
help wondering why these women didn't feel that way
about themselves.

"It's the Chinese gazebo they both wanted and never
got. A vermilion pagoda," Dell repeated as Danny
frowned at the flaming house-within-a-house. "It's our
ticket—if they go for the pagoda, they'll go for us all the
way. The whole China motif—the red and jade color
scheme, the brass-lined niches, the penthouse-as-temple

theme. It's risky, but the pagoda's the only smashing idea we've got ready to show the Garsons so far. At least,'' she hesitated, ''*I* think it's smashing.''

Still, Danny said nothing.

''So, what do *you* think?''

He could feel his wife's eyes, round and uncertain, beseeching him, awaiting his word. Why didn't she know? Why did she need him to tell her? And tell her over and over? For a moment the burden was unbearable. Yet, at the very same time, he loved being the one to tell her, being the only one who could tell her.

''Isn't it wonderful?'' Angie Romano couldn't help asking him.

''Yes,'' he agreed, meeting her loyal dark eyes. ''It's wonderful. Smashing.''

There was simply no denying it, yet he was disappointed. Not in the drawing, but in her. He had thought, because Dell was so tall, so mysterious and closed off, yet with such aggressively red hair, that she was strong, like his father had been. Strong and distant. But he had married a woman like his mother, he realized, bereft of the qualities he most esteemed.

''Beautiful work.'' Indeed. He had to admit the pagoda and the Chinese motif were an audacious design solution. He never said Dell wasn't talented.

When he looked up at her, she covered his face with grateful kisses.

''Thank God!'' Angie gasped and crossed herself. ''Or should I say 'Mazel tov'? With you two I never know.''

''Well, here's how to tell,'' Dell giggled. She was flushed, positively florid, as Angie had seen her only once before—the night she'd first met Dell, the third night of Dell's honeymoon.

''You see, no matter what it says on my birth certificate, I'm the Jew because I'm the guilty one. Guilty, guilty, always guilty. While this one,'' she ruffled Danny's silky black hair, ''this one could be only one thing, despite his name, despite his nose, despite his knishes at our wedding. Protestant. WASP through and through. And do you know why?''

Angie shook her head, already laughing.

''Because, silly, he never feels guilty. He doesn't give, as he himself puts it, a flying shit!''

At that they all laughed, and hugged Dell, and toasted her with ironstone mugs of cold coffee. And for a moment it was the way it used to be at the beginning.

"To my partner," Danny said. "The first D in D & D."

He called her his partner, but he couldn't quite give up the notion that Dell was his assistant. Oh, she was marvelous, of course. A tireless worker, except for lately. How determined she'd been to make D & D a success. And occasionally she even came up with brilliant designs and solutions, like this pagoda. But this morning she was home in bed, and Danny was here with Garson, and if he made a business decision that required a little white lie in the interests of expediency, then no receptionist, no matter how overeducated and underpaid, no matter how darkly beautiful or loyal to his wife, was going to make him feel guilty.

He wasn't going to feel guilty about anything. Period. So when Angie left them, closing the door softly behind her, Danny moved closer to Edgar Garson on the sofa.

"Edgar, let's stop fencing. You know I'm going to transform the apartment into exactly, exactly, *exactly* what you want. You will have the most breathtaking showplace in the city. I told you—it's going to have the hushed feeling of a Far Eastern temple and it's going to be to die and you're going to want to get down on the floor and kiss my feet when you—"

"I want to kiss them now," Garson whispered. "Let me kiss them. Let me."

He laid his cheek on Danny's lap and caressed Danny's ankle.

"Edgar, please . . ."

"No, let me see you, touch you."

Danny lifted him off with both hands. "Not here."

"Where then?"

Quickly glancing around the room, at the high ceilings and the huge, factory-like windows, the long and roomy sofa and the sound-deadening, triple-layered industrial carpeting, Danny asked and then answered his own thought: *Why not?*

"Here," he said, "but later. Tonight."

Garson reached into his jacket pocket and pulled out a small lizard datebook. "I could be here at eight."

"I'll order up some sandwiches."

"My darling boy, all you seem to want to do in this office is feed me." Garson watched as Danny laughed. "You do understand I will not be coming here tonight for the, ah, cuisine?"

"I understand everything, Edgar. Everything," Danny whispered and pressed Garson's knee. Garson trembled and his smile was no longer haughty. He covered Danny's hand with his own, but Danny rose. As soon as Danny was standing, Garson lunged at him, imprisoning him in his arms.

"Intelligent. A very intelligent boy. Understands everything. I knew it from the first moment," Garson murmured, exploring Danny's back, lean and compressed, that bulged suddenly into two fleshy melon halves, surprisingly soft and ripe.

"Oh, yes," he sighed, "we are going to be extremely compatible."

"Don't be late," Danny said breathily and bit into the soft, puffy lobe of his client's ear.

"Better late than to come too early. Don't you agree?" Garson's hand shot to Danny's groin and Danny couldn't ignore the sensation that began to sizzle out from Garson's touch. The man knew just how to touch him—pressing his scrotum, avoiding grabbing firm hold of his hardening cock, teasing him maddeningly.

But a phone began ringing in an outer office and a typewriter began clacking away, reminding Danny of business—more specifically, of Garson's contract that had yet to be signed. He held off Garson with two hands.

"Don't forget to bring a good pen along tonight. It's a big contract and your signature is needed in a million places."

"Daniel, Daniel, have you only a head for business and no heart for romance?" Garson asked with true disappointment. But then he reached for Danny again, and Danny had to hold him off more forcefully this time.

"Please, Edgar, not now. I've got a staff of five out there. Anyone could walk in here, you understand. This is definitely not the time." He backed away until he was safely behind his desk, leaving Edgar Garson's romantic heart slightly broken. And though Garson struggled to regain control, at sixty-nine, these exertions exhausted him more than he was willing to admit. More, even, than he knew. Weak with love's last longings and the body's Herculean efforts to keep the engine going, he agreed, breathily, to Danny's demands. And by demanding that they end this meeting now in order to resume it later, Danny, though unknowingly, saved Edgar Garson's life . . . for a little while longer.

As soon as his client left, Danny buzzed for Angie.

"Angie, get Scott to clean up this breakfast mess. I need you to draw up a contract for the Garsons. I'll bring you the numbers and fees in a second, and you can fill them in on the forms as usual. Meanwhile, I'll be out of the office. I've got to pop over and see the new furniture line at Import International. Then at one, I've got to be at the Embassy." Angie nodded but refused to meet his eyes. He decided not to tell her where he'd be in the late afternoon.

"Angie, this is important," he called to her as she headed for the door. "I must have the contract, complete, before you leave tonight. By seven. Put in a voucher for the overtime."

Still, Angie refused to look at him. But so what? Danny thought. Yet in her silent and familiar rebuke, Angie was getting to him. For all his determination not to feel guilty, he was soaked with sweat and remorse, still the very bad little boy who dreaded his mother's punishments, her "silent treatments" that could last for weeks. He thought of Dell and groaned inwardly. She, too, would be filled with silent rebuke tomorrow, after another of his unexplained late nights tonight. And another contract success captured without her.

But he was a superior husband, superb, he insisted to himself. She knew nothing, absolutely nothing, of his other life. She knew he loved her. It's what she said she needed more than anything. She had what she needed. *I love you.* He gave her that, the words, over and over, in all their infinite variations. *I love you. You're my equal, my partner, my perfect one. You're beautiful, you're divine. You're my wife for life. My wife. Forever. I love you.*

So what did she want? What did they all want?

11

Like a stubborn but adored baby brother, the three-story former Cuban Embassy squatted beside its slim and towering siblings along Park Avenue, where it was tolerated, with affection, for more than a century. It sat well back at the corner of Seventieth Street, the shortest structure for seventeen blocks, yet somehow the loftiest, the most elegant, and the sun's favorite. No one could pass it without turning back for a second glance. Passersby stared despite its unkempt front lawn, its several broken windows, its apparent abandonment . . . or, perhaps, precisely because of all that. The neglect broke your heart.

Its style was a hazy loan from the Greeks that had been revived (several times) and revised, but still managed to retain a certain stately grandeur. The facade, in particular, was arresting.

Four colossal stone columns with Tuscan capitals supported a richly ornamented pedimented portico. The massive, expertly carved double doors were the original. Eight stone steps led up to the entrance, and though weeds grew in between the cracks, the wide, graceful steps made a dramatic approach to the house. Ribboning the entire structure were rows of limestone fretwork, and embellishing many of the windows and doors were rosette and leaf-carved moldings. A protection of black iron grillwork with a lavishly curlicued gate surrounded the building on three sides.

To Danny, it was a Park Avenue miniature of imperial Rome, and it thrilled him to stand on the top step under the portico and survey the urban vista that extended past the wrought iron gate, all the way across the avenue to the other side of the street.

"Isn't it a screech? Isn't it a giggle?" he'd ask Dell, nudging her with his elbow, each time they arrived together to have a look. "Our very own little Embassy. Isn't it an absolute screech?"

The first time he brought her to see it, she began pulling off her coat in the street even though the air temperature was twenty-one degrees.

"What are you doing? It's the middle of January," he said and tried to push the coat back on her. "At least wait until we get inside. But I'm warning you, there's no heat, of course."

"It's so warm. Aren't you warm?" Clearly flushed, she fanned her neck while staring up at what looked to her like a wing of the Metropolitan Museum of Art. "Suddenly I feel very woozy."

Danny was there behind her to catch her as she began sinking to her knees.

Later on, Dell adopted a droll attitude. She'd say, "I can't figure out what about this place makes me want to faint, but I always do. Maybe it's that I'm so completely baffled by its style. After all, this must be the only extant example of that forgotten period in late nineteenth-century architecture—you know, the Miami-Hollywood-Athens School."

"It's to die and you know it." Danny insisted, refuting her sarcasm. Usually they agreed on all matters of taste—tasteful decoration, that is. That she would deride their magnificently impressive Embassy was simply unacceptable. "Say it's to die."

"I know one thing. It makes me *feel* as if I'm dying . . ."

Misunderstanding her, Danny caressed her paternally. "Numbers always scare you. It's a big nut, but we can handle it. We've got the billings, and with an Embassy we'll have clients lining up at the door. It's an unbelievably posh piece of real estate. A Park Avenue Embassy. My God! And for a steal! No one would believe the price, not in a hundred years."

"Two million dollars is not exactly my idea of a steal."

Danny rolled his eyes, but he rather enjoyed the fact that big numbers scared her . . . and didn't scare him.

He was right, of course; big numbers did scare her. Or rather, shame her. She would think of her father, arguing with some plumber over a four-dollar piece of pipe, and feel stabbed with shame at so surpassing him. It was no good telling herself it was what her mother always wanted for her. Her father had been dead for almost five years, but it was his feelings she still felt she was hurting.

And was it really true that this was what her mother wanted for her? Now that she'd done it, done what her mother said she wanted—become her mother's opposite—she felt guilty. She'd gotten a grand house, a grand figure and wardrobe, a grand husband, a grand life, gotten it all. But it still wasn't enough. The more she escaped her mother's destiny, the more she transformed her own identity, the guiltier she felt. She was guilty for finding it thrilling, and just as guilty for leaving her mother behind.

And to make matters worse, now Danny was rolling his eyes at her, making her even guiltier.

"For such a smart aleck, you can be pretty naive sometimes. You still think a couple of million dollars is a lot of money?"

"It's not?"

Danny refused to laugh. "Stop talking stupid, Dell. I know what's scaring you. I saw your face when Mittendorf kept whining about real-estate taxes, calling this place his albatross. You're afraid we've bought his Embassy—and his burdens."

"It's been vacant almost thirty years."

Danny nodded. "Mittendorf's loss is our gain. Lucky for us he couldn't hold on to it any longer—just when the market's at its softest. We owe Christopher something fabulous for tipping us off."

Christopher Beene again. "Why did he?"

"I keep telling you, he's a darling friend."

"And I keep telling you there's something unhealthy in the way he lavishes gifts on you. It's . . . improper. You're . . . taken."

At that Danny guffawed. Then, sobering, he pressed his eyes with the palms of his hands and said, "Christopher's dying."

"Dying? Dying of what?"

"A very rare, very fatal blood disease."

"AIDS?"

"Maybe. He doesn't name it. He just says he doesn't have very much time left."

Dell couldn't help asking, "So, you've seen him recently?"

Danny looked away and told her what she wanted to hear. "I only spoke to him on the phone. I haven't seen him. But I do speak to him regularly. Dell, he has no family, no children. He doesn't even have a lover anymore. So that's why he gives to me. I'm all he has."

"He doesn't have you," Dell said tightly. "*I* have you, and you're all *I* have."

"No, I'm not. You've got an Embassy now, too," Danny reminded her, looking back at the house. "Two gems. You're rich."

Long after they purchased it, Dell still struggled to uncover what she really felt about their Embassy. The opportunity, in New York, to combine a vast living and working space in an elegant, private structure on perhaps the city's most luxurious avenue was thrilling. Dell could listen forever to Danny's daydreams of how gorgeous it would all look when it was done. But when Danny wasn't there to convince her, when she made secret visits to the building by herself, doubts would creep in. Sometimes she couldn't bring herself to go inside. She would climb and traverse the steps outside while asking herself, Is this really the one? Is it too old? Too expensive? Will it really be perfect? *Oh, do I love this Embassy or hate it?*

"It's not that I really hate it," she tried to explain to Danny, "but I just don't believe it's going to turn out fabulous."

"Because you're not visualizing. You always worry that every project won't be good enough, won't be perfect."

"I'm just not sure this Embassy is such a gem."

"Believe it, Dell, darling. Open your eyes. It's a ruby, a sapphire. And it's yours, Dell. Yours and mine. And it will . . . be . . . fabulous."

She agreed, nodding, but she couldn't wait to go shopping and fill the place with splendid examples . . . of what? French furniture? American? Spanish? If she could see it finished, complete, maybe then she'd feel sure that at last they had arrived at perfection. But what style to choose? Thank God for Theo. He'd help them, lead them. He'd give them a structure, a skeleton for their dream. Then, with each purchase, they'd flesh it out, fill it in. Make the dream real. Oh, she couldn't wait to shop for custom furniture frames and to order rich tapestry upholstery and silk tassels and braided trims and three-tiered window treatments and collections of antique perfume bottles and Chinese porcelains. To shop for a dining room table and gold faucets for the bathrooms. To fill every corner of every room of this massive dream, this . . . Embassy.

But first, Theo would have to do his magic because the interior was a complete nightmare, the opposite of a dream.

Walls once covered with rich fabrics and French paneling were now fire blackened and peeling. Cigarette butts carpeted all the marble floors. A forgotten photo-portrait of Fidel Castro teetered on the edge of a grimy Spanish walnut mantel. And every teardrop on the massive crystal chandelier had been smashed and crushed into the parquet floor of the main salon.

On the upper floors many of the doors had been fitted with plated locks and the rooms still seemed to hold secrets within them: shredded papers, iron-barred windows, a stained and befouled chair, an unlocatable smell of decay.

All the bathrooms were damp, rank, and henna colored with rust. The kitchen tiles were etched with angry gouges.

"It would seem," said Theo when they brought him here for the first time, "that the Cubans abandoned this place in a violent twit."

Yet it was a former Embassy, a building of high and historic credentials, and that alone was reason enough to purchase it. That fact alone was worth the final, brilliantly negotiated, drastically reduced selling price (fifty percent of which was paid in cash, the result of two massive fees delivered in Gucci suitcases by the Japanese owners of a new London hotel). An embassy. That fact alone would be the subject of numerous publicity releases received by every client and every guest long before entering the new design offices and residence of Dell and Danny Dannenberg. D & D in an Embassy. That alone was enough to keep them afloat. The Embassy would do it because . . . it had to. Because . . . they were sinking, they were drowning under the weight of their secrets. Because . . . they needed an answer, an anchor, a mooring on which to hold fast. They could not, anymore, hold onto each other.

Theo Glass stood at the windowed French doors of the Embassy's third-floor master suite, smiling. Dell always made him smile. He watched as she emerged, red boots first, from the taxi. This time it was the red boots that made his thin lips beneath the camel brush of moustache curl up in amusement.

"Big feets, big teats," she'd chanted to him. When? Was it only three months ago at their first big meeting? For over a year she'd disappeared from his life. Then, suddenly, her phone call, and that big, delicious meeting.

All three of them were sitting in his office when Dell suddenly looked down from the rolls of architectural blueprints to her feet. Theo, who had been watching her, followed Dell's eyes to her gray suede slingbacks.

He watched as she flexed and pointed, flexed and pointed. A nostalgic little smile played at the corners of her wide mouth when she turned to him. Somehow, with the superior peripheral vision that, in his experience, only women seemed to possess, she knew that his attention was upon her . . . and that Danny's was not.

"When I was sixteen or so, a black kid in my class used to sit behind me and whisper, 'Big feets, big teats.' You have no idea—I mean, having big teats was bad enough, but big feets was the final humiliation."

Theo watched her pink mouth curl to the words. It was amazing to watch such a wide mouth shorten and pucker until it was as cherubic as a Raphael *putto*, then lengthen and open like the basin of a Bernini fountain, then smile as faintly and mysteriously as the Mona Lisa herself. It was an elastic mouth, classic in its shape and fullness, but overlarge. Perhaps more than any other, it was the much-celebrated lips and mouth of the Statue of Liberty that Dell's most resembled. Lady Liberty. With big feet.

"I'd already grown to my full height—I was a five-foot, eleven-and-a-half-inch giant. I mean I could look down on the dandruff and the combed part on the top of every girl's head in the school."

Now her mouth was as thin and taut as a horizontal slash above her chin.

"And I was fat."

Yes, somehow it was all right to tell Theo this much of her ugly past. This much, but no more. Not yet. Nothing about the utter disappointment in her mother's eyes. Or the rest of it.

Danny, of course, knew that she'd been fat as a child. Telling Danny had been particularly easy since he was essentially uninterested in the details of her past. But telling Theo was different. And telling him here, in his very own office with Danny present, added to the strangeness. Yet it also freed her. They were here, she knew, to plan the interior renovation of the Embassy, yet she felt an uncommon urge to reminisce and talk openly about herself. Perhaps Danny's presence served to establish her position as a married woman, and therefore protected her from any accusation of impropriety. Or perhaps it was Theo's presence that somehow unleashed this flood of memories in her, and the desire to confide them to him. Perhaps both were true. In any case, she was so caught up in the memory of her years of fatness that she felt close to tears . . . so she laughed. And continued.

"Now, suddenly, I was afflicted with this grotesque combination—top heavy and big-footed. Do you have any idea how revolting I was?"

Theo shook his head of curry-colored curls.

"Dell, I'm sorry but I can't picture you as anything but . . . exquisite."

There was a sudden stillness in the room. Remorseful, Theo hoped Dell somehow had not heard what he'd just said, and concentrated his gaze down on Dell's gray shoes. Dell, pink-eared, prayed that Danny somehow had not heard what Theo had just said. In that, Dell had no cause for worry because Danny hadn't heard a word. Nevertheless, Dell sadly recognized that Danny's obliviousness to the two of them was yet another sign of how far apart they'd grown.

Danny sat at a long table spread with architectural drawings and floor plans. Without looking up, he groaned, "Oy, yuy yuy. Sixteen-foot ceilings. We'll need the furniture of a palace to fill this frigging space." Then, realizing that a palace was exactly what he had in mind, he laughed to himself.

Pink ears, Theo was thinking. When she blushes, her ears turn the pink of a newborn baby's toes. Cara! For an instant he squeezed his eyes shut. When he opened them, he could contemplate Dell's ears comfortably again, even longingly. Unconsciously, he ran his tongue over his lips and hungrily waited for her to lift her eyes from her lap.

"What size shoes *did* you wear?" he finally asked her.

He'd been searching for something to say to keep her talking, to erase the discomfort he'd just caused . . . and to make her show him those extraordinary eyes of hers again. When she called him after more than a year, that was the first thing he secretly thought of—her eyes. At last! he rejoiced. Ever since she'd sat here in his office that first time more than a year ago, he'd struggled to define in his mind the exact color of her eyes—not quite blue, not quite green, sometimes almost turquoise, yet at other times, a kind of heavy marine color, as deep and variable as the sea itself. Now, seeing her again, he knew the struggle was useless. The color of Dell's eyes was in constant flux, and while definition was impossible, admiration was not.

Not that he didn't want to know her shoe size. Irrelevant details, when they had to do with Dell, took on a significance that sometimes he was helpless to hide.

"At sixteen. I mean, did your feet grow bigger after that? And now? What size do you wear now?

That seemed to release her from her embarrassment. She laughed and her eyes skittered bouncily off the sleek surfaces and cabinetry of his office until they at last found his.

"That's the most intimate question anyone has ever asked me!" she gasped in mock horror.

Does she know she's flirting with me? Theo asked himself. *Flirting with me while her husband is sitting fifteen feet away? Flirting with me despite our history, our past failures and withdrawals? Despite our spouses? Flirting with me, yes, despite it all!*

It made Theo's heart hammer nervously, exuberantly. He saw Dell as someone daring, dashing. She took risks! *This* was a risk. A *big* risk, and it made him want to laugh until tears rolled down his cheeks, laugh and shout.

Always, when he was near Dell he felt a giddy sense of abandon, a passive recklessness. At any moment, he expected her to take his hand and tug him into a world of hilarious adventure. He realized—and not for the first time—that he hoped she would.

And what then? he asked himself.

If you take my hand and lead me, I will gladly follow. Anywhere. I'm sure I would. That is. . . I'm almost sure.

"Same size as I wear now. Ten and a half," Dell answered, inhaling a feigned breath of courage. "There. I admit it. Ten and a half. But at sixteen? Gro-tesque! Even my father didn't believe it. He'd tell the shoestore salesman, 'Give her a nine. Let her try on a nine.' He'd tell me, 'Dell, don't try on anything larger than a nine and a half.' "

"Why?" he asked, completely absorbed in her tale.

"My father was convinced the salesmen were just unloading their unsold sizes on me. He insisted on buying my shoes, even when I was more than old enough to shop by myself, because he claimed, 'I understand these villains better than anyone.' "

"Did he?"

"Of course not. They were villains merely because they were salesmen. 'They'll give you a ten and a half over my dead body.' Everyone was a villain to him, but especially salesmen because he was one, too, and he thought he knew them. But he didn't. He just had a persecution complex."

She was digressing, she knew, rambling. This was the first time she'd seen Theo in over a year and she felt as if she'd been storing up all this personal information, unconsciously awaiting just this outpouring. But with his lapis-blue eyes so intently upon her, encouraging her, it was impossible not to continue. She'd vowed to herself to keep this, and all future meetings they'd be having, entirely professional, but he seemed fascinated by her revelations. And in the face of Danny's continued indifference, Theo's fascination freed her to talk . . . and yes, to flirt.

"If only I lived in ancient China. I pined all through my adolescence that if I'd lived in China, my feet would've been bound, my chest would've been bound—everything—and I'd have remained petite forever."

Petite, he mused. She wanted to be like Erica. But then, she wouldn't be Dell at all.

''Petite,'' she repeated, her lips pursing playfully. ''Would you believe it's still my favorite word?''

Dell. Did she have any idea that Dell was his favorite word?

She decided not to go on, not to tell him how, at seventeen, she found the will to change her shape and found the rigid control to maintain it all these years. Because then she might tell him that she was always only one moment away from breaking out of her self-imposed prison, of letting herself go and becoming exactly like her mother. That what she really longed for more than world peace, more than universal prosperity, was not to be burdened by her own impossible expectations.

Because she was really a wild woman. One part of her loved all the razzle-dazzle, the glamour, the power and admiration. Loved it so much it made her sick with guilt. And the other part of her longed to quit, to just give up and return to the place where her mother had warned her she might end up. The place of shame. Home.

No, she could tell him none of this, for then he might be disappointed in her. So, instead, she turned facetious.

''Big,'' she said and rolled her eyes. ''And big is my least favorite word.''

Theo smiled at her but he could feel his mood changing, sinking. He'd been trying, for the last few minutes, to remember his own wife's shoe size, and had finally given up. Even though Erica usually preferred to shop alone, over the sixteen years of their marriage, he'd certainly accompanied her often enough to know her basic sizes. He could see Erica even now, one shoe off, one shoe on, asking the salesman for the size she wanted, but he could no longer remember what size that was. They had shopped together for her first mink, and her first ball gown, and he could remember she wore a size four dress, but he couldn't remember the size of her feet. *Sad, very sad.* He saw it as a symbol of just how far apart they'd grown. While secretly he was growing closer to Dell.

Dell. He could listen to her for hours. There was something quite profound in these little personal revelations of hers. Profound, and touchingly intimate. Suited entirely in gray, sitting on the edge of her chair, elbows on her knees, long neck lunging toward him, Dell pretended to be prattling aimlessly. But he knew she was giving him a part of her most private self. Right here! It was a small but alien kind of bravery and daring, the kind of risky openness he most esteemed but could never equal—except when he was near Dell. If he could be alone with her again, he was sure anything—everything— would be possible. Even his own freedom. Except, of course, that it was all impossible. For he would never again be alone with her. Never.

"Theo?" She caught him staring at her feet and wriggled them. "How do you like them twinkle toes, eh?"

Theo remembered how she'd lifted him up out of his sunken mood and made him laugh. He chuckled a little now, remembering it, remembering her.

He stood at the Embassy window now and watched Dell unlatch the wrought iron gate, wishing he'd video recorded this moment so that he could replay it again and again. From his safe perch on the third floor, this stolen glimpse of her in those audacious red boots (was she defiant now in adulthood, telling the world, "I may have big feets but I'll wear red boots, shiny red boots, if I want to"?) and the sleek, black leather cape that made her look like a Little Red Riding Hood in reverse, filled him with such competing measures of delight and despair that he groaned against the windowpane, "Dell. Oh, God! Dell!"

And immediately, she looked up. One moment, chin tucked into her neck, she was pushing against a wall of wind up the path to the Embassy steps. And the next moment, as if she heard him groaning at the closed window, as if she knew all along that he was watching her, suddenly, impulsively, she stopped and looked up at him.

Automatically, he pulled himself back from view. He knew she saw him but the impulse to hide was overwhelming. Shame made him hide. Such a deep, personal shame that it turned him rigid, stiffening even the camel hairs on his arms and locking his ocher-lashed lids against the vision of the woman he nevertheless carried inside him night and day.

It was the wanting her that shamed him. He had no right.

He was as good as diseased. Worse. At least there were cures for many diseases, or even the hope of a cure in the future. But for him, he knew, there was only continued torment. It was as if he were slowly dessicating like those herb branches Erica hung up in their kitchen to dry.

Erica. She too still mourned, but after almost four years hers had become a silent sorrow, internalized, showing itself most in little things: her slower gait, her vacant stares, her resumed smoking habit. She seemed, for the most part, intact. Besides, she still had him. And what did he have? Nothing. Not even himself. Inside, he was as white and dry as little Cara's bones and ashes in the half-pound metal can. On the day his baby was cremated, it was as if they also burned something out of him—his humanity, his vitality, his masculinity.

Dell. She was the only thing that reminded him he was alive, but just barely. No matter how much he thought of her, wanted her, his body remained dead. Yet even this doomed wanting of her enlivened him in a meager way. Deprived of her, he experienced a continuous, gnawing hunger, like that of a starving man. The continuous longing for Cara didn't compare because that was like mourning for an amputated limb. The limb was gone; Cara, his beloved little Cara, was gone. But Dell was here, and although he had no right, he did continue to want her.

He'd been able to control the wanting for almost a year after she went completely out of his life. Mornings, for some reason, were the worst. Waking from dreams of her, waking to daydreams of her, he began each day with a longing so sharp, it made him wince. But once he was up and dressed, work occupied his mind and his equilibrium returned.

Then she called. All he had to do was hear her low, slightly husky voice, and he would've agreed to anything. As it was, he agreed to this project because it meant he'd see her. And he had seen her. Twice. Once, at the meeting with Danny. And once, rather briefly, when she approved the preliminary plans. But seeing her had changed him. It changed his mornings. It even changed the nature of his longing. Despite himself, he was coming alive.

Now, here she was again, climbing the outer steps, red-cheeked and windswept in her fantastic red boots. He dared to look out again and caught a last glimpse of her.

Dell!

She was the reason he was here. *She* was the.Embassy. Dell!

"Enough!" he roared out loud.

He'd held himself in until he'd almost vanished. But no more. He'd had enough. He was ready to dare to live again. This time, he was ready.

He clattered down the formal circular staircase, unleashed.

Dell!

He slid like a boy on skates across the marble floor of the grand but littered entry hall of the Embassy.

Dell!

She was there before him as he pulled open the massive walnut doors, a frosty, faintly perfumed gust blowing in ahead of her. Then she blew in, and with her, all of Nature—crisps of brown leaves, wind, dirt, dust and sunlight.

Her black leather cape flapped like a black sail in front of her, propelling her forward, making her laugh. Or perhaps that wasn't what was making her laugh, making her eyes green as emeralds. He only knew he had his arms around her, pressing into her back, urging her in, into the room where he could tell her that he was ready at last.

"Dell!" This time he didn't just think her name, he said it. "Dell."

At last he was ready. At last he could tell her, and touch her and hold her and kiss her and have her. At last.

But first, they both had to heave on the door to close it against the wind. And that's when he saw it, the second yellow cab shuddering to a stop exactly where Dell's had a minute before. He even saw the gray Italian shoes and those long, long legs kick open the door wider, wider.

Then, without a word between them, with only a glance and a nod of resignation, Theo and Dell tightened their grip on the brass knobs and pulled the double doors all the way open again.

Dell called, "Hi, darling!"

Theo managed to wave.

And there they stood, avoiding each other's eyes once more, while they waited for Danny to come between them.

12

"You have to see it. Christopher, my Embassy is gorgeous."

"I will. I will."

"Of course, it's a mess now," Danny continued, holding a paper-thin goblet of wine.

Almost every Wednesday for at least eight years, Danny visited Christopher Beene here in his living room. There had been nights when Danny had stayed very late, but this would not be one of them. This evening was just a "stop-by," the kind of quick visit that, according to Christopher, allowed Danny to "take, take, take with no time to give anything in return." In the past, Christopher would've been very miffed. This evening, he hadn't even asked Danny how long he was staying. It seemed to be of no interest to him.

Danny pressed on. "I have to hand it to Theo Glass. He had his construction crew taking down walls as soon as the plans were approved. At the same time he's putting up a curved, pierced wall in what once was the dining room and study to enclose the offices. You know the marvelous work Glass does with curved forms—this wall will wiggle around work stations like a snake. The dust is, of course, horrible, but already it's really too beautiful and I can't believe you haven't seen it."

"I know. I know."

Christopher Beene reclined on a Napoleonic daybed in his living room which, this month, contained unusual early nineteenth-century French pieces, as opposed to last month, when it was arranged with rare Hepplewhites and Sheratons. Virtually all the furnishings in Christopher Beene's private rooms were transient, destined for his vast shop two floors below in the building he had owned for the last seventeen years. But however impermanent the fixtures, the rooms themselves remained a timeless, cream-colored backdrop, an elegant way station for his ever-changing shipments of cabinetry, carpets, mantels, and mirrors. "My orphans," he called them fondly and gladly took them in until a permanent home for them could be found.

Danny, who was determined to enliven his moribund old friend, sat on a chair already tagged and catalogued; tomorrow it would be gone, most likely. He estimated he'd sat on more than one hundred chairs in this very spot over the years, but this was the first Wednesday evening Christopher failed to point out the provenance of this latest orphan. Usually, there'd be a rhapsodic, well-informed lecture, but tonight the classroom was closed. During the four years when Danny had worked for Christopher, he took notes, learning the history of furniture design in a haphazard order as each new shipment arrived. But now his mentor was sunk in indifference and lassitude.

Danny was used to hearing Christopher say, 'I'm a healthy son of a bitch for a dying man." Christopher knew what he had, but the effects of his disease had eluded him for years . . . until these past few weeks. The sudden disintegration was unbearable for Danny to watch. Just to see Christopher's slim but imperial bearing now so weakened that he slumped was heartbreaking. But although Danny felt genuine pity, he also felt outraged. Christopher wouldn't dare leave him now. Not when Danny needed his guidance for a million things, and his encouragement. No. Danny wasn't going to let him.

"I thought you liked this white Burgundy."

Danny refilled his own glass and replaced the bottle in the silver cooler. Christopher's glass sat untouched beside his daybed.

"Say something," Danny insisted. "Do you or don't you?"

"I do. I do. But the medicine I'm taking—"

"Why are you saying everything in two's?"

"Am I?" Christopher asked wanly. He heard the irritation in Danny's voice and added, "Don't be cross."

Danny melted, mortified with himself. He ran his long fingers through his dark, silky hair.

"I'm not angry. I'm just . . . frustrated. I can't seem to spark your interest."

"I'm not much of a host this evening, am I?"

"You? Oh, right, you're a terrible host," Danny agreed with such a heavy coating of sarcasm that even Christopher had to smile. "Only a ghastly host would make lavish dinner parties every other Wednesday just so I could make important contacts."

Christopher's smile grew wider.

"What a bore! And don't forget all those working dinners when you had your chef prepare homemade corned beef so we could eat sandwiches while we analyzed the first schematic plans I did at Leonard, Melton. Oh, you were terrible, absolutely terrible. Remember that first Wednesday night when I called you in a panic, and you said, 'Come right over'?"

Christopher bowed his head but the smile stayed.

"And all the Wednesday nights since then—what is it now? Eight years? Eight years of expert meals and old cognac, and expert taste and expert advice and not a single boring conversation. And you know, you *know* how rare *that* is! Right. You're one horrid host."

Christopher leaned over and patted his hand. "Thank you. But the fact remains that's all history. I am no longer the man I was."

"No?" Danny smiled. "Don't you want to know how it went with the Garsons? Did you forget I had a meeting with them this morning?"

The mention of the Garsons worked first on Christopher's posture, prodding him into an upright position that was as erect and squared as it was formerly slouched. Then it registered in his eyes, which became alert and focused for the first time that evening.

Poor Christopher! Danny thought, picturing what a bore Christopher's days had become. There were no new shopping trips planned to Europe or the Far East, and Christopher sat in his shop, feverish and disinterested, turning away customers. He took on no new design projects and lately had begun referring his "A-list" clients to Danny. (He never spoke the name of the firm, D & D, because one of the D's was for Dell.) Like his shipments of orphans, his "A-List" clients were his darlings, his privileged subjects. But until Danny mentioned the Garsons, Christopher didn't realize how hungry he was for news of the kingdom he was forced to give away. He opened his mouth and his chin shot forward in the position of someone expecting to be fed by spoon.

"Tell me everything," he said.

"Well, as I told you, the penthouse is stunning . . ."

Christopher caught Danny's hesitation. "But?"

Oh, it was such a relief to see Christopher hanging on his every word, just like it used to be! He was not going to die and leave Danny all alone. He was here, adoring and protective as always.

"It's just that Edgar's wife is such a bitch. I told you about the scene she pulled at our first meeting. It was instant hate."

"I can't imagine why," Christopher told him dryly, meaning the exact opposite of what he said.

"Neither can I," Danny agreed, missing Christopher's sarcasm.

"Was the bitch as bitchy this morning?"

"She wasn't there."

Christopher's eyebrows raised quizzically. "Not there?"

"No. I suppose she just refused to come. Which is just as well because I have absolutely no rapport with angry wives."

"And Edgar?" Christopher asked carefully. "Did you find a . . . rapport with Edgar?"

"Edgar's in my . . . lap." Danny's confident grin was aimed directly at Chrisopher. "Of course, you probably wouldn't agree, much less approve, but some people find my lap irresistible."

Christopher's forehead creased in a deep frown, which only encouraged Danny to continue taunting him.

"In fact, I must run," Danny said, looking at his antique watch, "because he's meeting me back at the office to sign the contract. Don't worry about your precious old client. I'll see that Edgar's extremely . . . comfy."

"It's not Edgar I'm worried about," Christopher said, lacing his stiff fingers together. His kingdom was forgotten as he concentrated on his heir apparent, his wayward, worrisome, wonderful offspring.

"It's you who worries me, Danny. Be careful," he warned, not for the first time.

''Whyever why?''

''Because you've got a big problem, my friend.''

Oh, no, here we go again, Danny thought, rolling his eyes. *But you asked for it,* he told himself. *This time you really begged for it.*

Now that he'd provoked Christopher and a finger-wagging scolding was imminent, Danny hoped he hadn't gone too far. Christopher Beene was the most generous of guardians, but also the most possessive. To Danny this possessiveness was both insufferable and inexplicably re-assuring. He secretly adored having Christopher to worry about him, fuss over him, mold him, shape him, guide him . . . even scold him. At times it got to be too much and he'd begin to feel suffocated. But those weren't the times when he struck out and tried to hurt Christopher. Danny could never hurt Christopher for petting and ador-ing him. But when Christopher turned away, when he *stopped caring*—or when Danny became afraid that he would—Danny would try to regain his attention by tor-menting him. Then, realizing what he'd done, he'd fear that this time he'd gone too far, this time Christopher would never forgive him. Even if the fear lasted only a second, it left Danny momentarily shaken before he put it out of his mind. How could he get satisfaction from making Christopher jealous, he asked himself sharply. It was despicable behavior, but he knew he might very well do it again . . . perhaps even tonight.

He tried, instead, to think of all that Christopher had given him. Certainly, in the field of interior design, there wasn't anything, or anyone, that Christopher didn't know, and all of it he shared with Danny. From his private list of coveted craftsmen and remarkably secret sources, to the personal secrets and scandals of his most celebrated clients, Christopher filled Danny's ears as well as his heart. He guided Danny's career with seasoned shrewd-ness, calling in experts on finance and management to help build an investment portfolio as thick as Danny's burgeoning design portfolio. And everywhere he went, from Tokyo, Milan, London, or even from midtown Manhattan, he sent Danny colorful postcards with tips about new restaurants, art events, vacation spots, hab-erdashers, architectural wonders. Because of his vast and influential contacts, D & D received a barrage of public-

ity from the moment they rented an empty loft downtown.
(Or rather, from the moment Danny phoned Christopher
and said, "I know you're mad at me about Dell and D &
D, but I miss you so terribly that I'll absolutely die if we
don't make up.")

Danny would've been the first to agree that Christopher Beene was a munificent mentor. But though he gave
and gave, he held back, too. And what he held back,
though seemingly slight at first, grew more and more
important by its absence over time. Thus, however much
Christopher offered, and however grateful Danny was for
all his generosity, the gap between them widened. And
the hostility cut deeper.

"Yes," Christopher was saying, "you've got a very
big problem."

Again Danny rolled his eyes like an insolent child,
inviting Christopher's wrath.

"Don't roll your eyes at me! I'm telling you something
important, something for your own good."

"You're just jealous of Edgar. You hate that I have to
leave you to go see him."

Christopher's pale, sunken cheeks reddened slightly
with the fire of his anger but his eyes swam with sorrow.

"You're sick, Danny, a sexual sicko. You're a junkie
and sex is your drug. Why do you think I've never let
you near me?"

"Oh, no, Christopher, that's not it. You're the one
with the problem—and you know it."

"Really? And what's my problem, aside from having
devoted my life and everything I have to you?"

"Not everything. You hold back the one thing you
know I want more than anything."

"And what is that, may I ask?"

"Your blessing. You've never forgiven me for going
my own way, for leaving you to work for Leonard, Melton, and then for marrying Dell. So you withhold your
approval, your full acceptance. You're always more than
a little displeased with me. And we both know why."

"Why?"

"Don't make me say it. You're not well. We can stop
this now."

"No, go on, Danny. Say it, goddamn it!"

Danny sighed through narrowed lips. He wondered

how Christopher had the strength for this. He himself was tiring of the tension and bickering. Fighting essentially bored him. He longed to return to friendlier relations. But Christopher was waiting.

As gently as he could, he said, "Christopher, you want my total devotion. And I can't give that to you. You want to be everything to me, just as I am to you. But I've told you over and over, I can't and I won't. I must go my own way and you mustn't stop me. I can't let you be everything."

"Because you're spiteful, willful."

"No, no, no," Danny insisted with a rush of tenderness. "I don't want to hurt you. I never meant to hurt you."

"Is that why you went ahead and married the redhead even though I warned you and warned you against it?"

"Dell. Her name is Dell."

"And is that why you came over here and won't stay for dinner and tormented me about your flirtations with Edgar Garson?"

Chastened, Danny bent his head. "I don't know why I said those things. I'm sorry. Sometimes your possessiveness brings out the worst in me."

For a few minutes there was silence while Christopher dined on the sweetness of Danny's sentiments. Delicious, he thought. As delicious as Florida key lime pie, meringue-topped, tart and springy. Whenever Danny was at his best, he made Christopher think of the pie, a pleasure he had savored since his Florida childhood.

Danny, meanwhile, sipped his wine and stole peeks at Christopher, trying to assess the deterioration. There was, of course, his loss of weight but because Christopher had always been slender, with prominent cheekbones and a beak of a nose, it was difficult to say how many pounds he'd actually lost. All Danny knew was that now Christopher looked positively gaunt. At times, Christopher's breathing seemed labored and raspy, but at other times it seemed normal. There was, however, a nasty sore on his forehead just like the one on his neck. But to Danny's surprise, Christopher began to smile and rose and walked steadily across the room to the fireplace. He rested an elbow on the marble mantel, held his short, thin body stiffly, and for the first time appeared to Danny very much like the old Christopher Beene.

''I remember every detail of that day you told me you were leaving me to work for Leonard, Melton.''

Danny groaned, but Christopher motioned with his free hand that he wasn't trying to start another fight.

''I gave you a hard time. A very hard time.''

Danny could hardly believe his ears. Christopher was never one to admit his mistakes publicly, much less to apologize. This was beginning to sound like such an ominous departure that Danny wanted to hear no more of it, but Christopher wouldn't let him interrupt.

''I've come to realize you were right to strike out on your own. I don't resent it. I respect it.''

''You respect it?'' Danny was incredulous.

''I've been meaning to tell you for some time. I know that if you'd stayed with me here at the store, as I wanted you to, you never would've developed your name. You'd have inherited mine.'' He looked down at his bony hands and smiled. ''There would be no D & D. So it was the right move.''

''But even today you called me spiteful—''

''Oh, don't mind that,'' Christopher said with another wave of his hand. ''Lately, I've been feeling entirely too sorry for myself. The truth is that you walked into my shop, a tall, skinny, lost boy, just graduated but without direction—and within one week I could see that you had it. You were going to become one of the true great ones. And that's all I ever really wanted—that you fulfill the brilliant promise you showed right from the start. I'm not God, after all. I do make mistakes, but I think you'll agree I've always valued your future almost more than you do.''

It was an apology of sorts, and the closest he'd ever come to giving Danny his complete blessing. Not quite complete, not quite everything, but enough to partly fill the empty space inside him. He smiled at Christopher and closed his eyes for a moment, almost content. When had he last felt this satisfied? It was as if he'd just enjoyed a meal so completely filling that it promised to sate for all time the usual feeling of emptiness that gnawed away inside of him. He actually felt almost loved enough.

To be loved enough. Oh, how he longed for it. As a boy, how he'd yearned to know how it felt *not to* yearn for his father's love. To just have it. Anytime he wanted it. Because it was just sitting there, like air, always available. That's what he wanted. To receive the warmth from his father's golden smile merely by walking into the room and saying, "Hi, Dad." Like the way his brother Norman was loved.

"Hi, Dad," Norman would call out, his voice cracking slightly, and immediately, father and son would be on the floor, tumbling, tickling, wrestling, laughing. Sid Dannenberg rolled on the carpet, threw softballs, shadow-boxed with his oldest son while Danny clung to his mother, the only parent who would have him, and prayed that his father would turn to him, play with him, love him next. But he never did.

Danny knew that his father found him excessive, even eccentric. Once, when he was eleven, he heard his father say to his mother, "I can't talk to that boy. He's weird. Sitting there knitting with you all night long. How could you teach him all those pansy things? He knows more about number-eight knitting needles than he does about baseballs. Half the time I don't know what he's talking about, but if I tell him, he starts to cry. That kid cries more than any girl I ever saw. Muriel, you go knit with him, embroider with him, cry with him. Take him! I give up. Just leave Norman to me. You ruined Danny, but you're not going to ruin Norman. Norman's my son."

But after that, Sid Dannenberg was less available than usual. Even Norman never saw enough of his father. No one got enough of Sid Dannenberg because he lived two separate lives. Pastrami slicer, sandwich maker, counterman, and part owner with his brother Joe of a deli in Scarsdale, Sid kept a small room in Westchester (and a middle-aged mistress who was married to Lou, the deli's third partner).

Sid returned to the family apartment on Kings Highway in Brooklyn unpredictably, at an unfixed time after a variable absence of two days, nine days, for an equally transitory and uncertain stay.

But much as Danny missed him and suffered through his absences with an intolerable longing that his father's arrivals did nothing to relieve, Danny admired him. Distant and unknowable at home, his father was even a more mysterious figure when he was gone. Mysterious but fascinating. The object of Danny's dreams.

If, for only a moment, he could get close enough to his father, and could somehow be assured his father wouldn't sneer at him or roll his eyes impatiently, then Danny had a million questions to ask him. What did he do without Muriel to fix his coffee and his breakfast every morning? What did he do with his nights? At home, he often took Norman to a sports event on the weekend. What did he do in Westchester without Norman? And what did his room look like? Did he have only one room, or several? Did he have two of everything—two toothbrushes, two razors, two wives?

Most of all, Danny wondered, would his father one day take him into that other world, take him into that mysterious, magical place, take him into his father's other life? And leave his brother Norman, the big, blond jock, home.

For that, Danny waited his entire childhood. They all waited for Sid—even Norman, who popped in and out of the house with the same question, "Heard from Dad?" Between basketball practice, track, and later, dates with girlfriends, Norman, tall, big-boned and honey-blond like their mother Muriel, would run into the kitchen calling, "Heard from Dad?" But as soon as he saw his brother and his mother keeping vigil together at the formica table, knitting their scarves and sweaters, he'd turn on his heels and about-face.

"Sick," he'd say. "Really sick."

Endless nights of tea and the click, click, click of their knitting needles.

"You're pathetic," he'd tell Danny. "Completely perverted."

Still, Danny and his mother sat, stuck in their mutual waiting, stuck with each other, knowing that when Sid did come home, it would always be to Norman he returned.

Years later, here he was, still yearning for total love. Once, when he was twenty-three, he thought he'd found it. Now, he knew better. Now, he lived only for the search, and sometimes he even forgot what he'd wanted so much to find. Only the hurt endured. Its meaning, its purpose were almost entirely lost.

13

He was twenty-three and on his way. When he stepped off the plane, he was still wearing his plaid wool overcoat. The heat of Haiti was waiting for him. It greeted him like an invisible official, rising up to embrace him in a moist and heavy welcome. Entirely unexpected. Somehow, he'd imagined finding the same February chill here at the Port-au-Prince Airport that he'd left a few hours before in New York. He'd never been to the Caribbean. He'd never been anywhere. But now Danny was twenty-three and he was on his way.

"I didn't realize the heat would start the minute you get off the plane," Danny told Clive, shaking off his coat.

"Actually, it began before that," said Clive meaningfully. "It started *on* the plane."

Clive was right, of course. It had begun on the plane, the minute they boarded. Danny had just strapped himself into the window seat when Clive Sumners appeared, hovering above him on the aisle like some darkly beautiful bird of prey. He held onto the overhead rack with arms spread out like wings.

"I beg your pardon, but I'm afraid you're in my seat," he said in an accent that could have been British.

Danny looked at his boarding pass and reddened. "You're right," he admitted, unscrunching his long legs, banging his knees.

"Actually, it really doesn't matter to me," Clive said, touching Danny's arm to stop him. "Why don't you stay put?"

"All right, if you're sure—?"

"I'm sure." Again he touched Danny's arm. "Actually, I prefer the aisle seat here. A bit more freedom."

He pronounced the word actually as *ackshuwalley*. When he smiled, his caramel-tanned skin wrinkled at the corners of his penetrating eyes, softening them agreeably, and his white teeth gleamed. Though he was an inch taller than Danny, he slid into the aisle seat in one smooth, athletic movement, but Danny noticed that his knees, like Danny's, pressed up against the seat in front.

"We're really both too tall for these seats," Danny said.

"What is your name?"

"Daniel Dannenberg."

"Well, Daniel, haven't you learned yet that you can never be too tall?"

Danny shook his head, not sure what to say.

"The secret is to wear only custom-made trousers. I'm Clive Sumners. Where are you staying in Haiti?" He hold out a tanned, immaculate hand for Danny to shake.

"Hotel La Fantasia." Danny slipped his hand into Clive's and the electricity was immediate. He wasn't surprised. And when Clive didn't release his hand, he wasn't surprised, either. Somehow he knew, from the moment he looked up into Clive's dark, strong face hovering above him on the aisle, that they would . . . touch. There had been others—girls, at first, then several young men, then a female associate professor at college, and then her brother. Danny had had experience, but he'd never been in love. With Clive, it was immediate, violent, overwhelming.

"La Fantasia." Clive smiled again, still caressing Danny's hand. "It can only be fate." His nose was large, powerful, his lips wide, his cheeks prominent; in fact, he bore a strong resemblance to Hollywood's version of an American Indian chief. Only his feathered headdress was missing.

"We were destined, Daniel Dannenberg. I'm convinced of that now."

How Danny wanted to resist. And how Danny wanted to surrender! A certain worldliness, however meager, counseled Danny to be cautious. This tall chieftain was coming on very strong, and very fast. Too fast. How could Clive be so sure Danny would let him take his hand and hold it almost forgotten, like a set of keys, in his lap? How did he know Danny wouldn't punch him or at least shout an objection? Given that this Clive Sumners was exceedingly sure of himself, nevertheless he was taking an incredible risk.

On the other hand, it was the audacity of Clive Sumners's assumptions, the boldness of his approach that thrilled Danny. Nothing circumspect, halting, half-hearted here. Without testing the waters, Clive just bravely dove in. And Danny after him! For here was a dare worth taking. Clive's fearlessness was infectious. And the promise—the promises—were therefore infinite.

"You mean you're staying at the Fantasia, too?" Knowing the answer didn't prevent Danny from relishing hearing it confirmed.

Clive nodded significantly. "Fate," he said.

Danny gave a laugh of incredulity, wanting, expecting to be convinced, taken in.

"Don't you believe in fate?" Clive asked, not waiting for an answer. "Do you really think we happened by chance?"

Danny had been seduced before, but always on the most practical level—for sex. Never because of destiny. Never for love.

"I don't know," he answered honestly.

"Something like this doesn't just happen. We were hand picked by the gods, Daniel, and set down in these two seats next to each other to begin our journey together. There is no other explanation." Clive's manicured hands sliced the air with finality.

Staring into those eyes of impenetrable charcoal, Danny could think of no other explanation either. All thinking, in fact, had stopped. Like a man adrift on a leaky raft, Danny had only one thought from the moment he set eyes on Clive: I'm going to be saved. At last, I'm going to be loved!

Their first hour was a series of discoveries. They discovered they both despised the color brown and the word "pretty." Politics, they agreed, bored them.

"Especially American politics," said Clive. "At least in Europe, a sex scandal is rather chic. Here, it's just tawdry."

And reproduction furniture. Danny said, "I hate new trying to be old."

"I can spot the real thing in a whole sea of copies," Clive agreed.

Long was their list of pet peeves, medium irritations, and major hates. It positively cheered them to find they shared so many of the same exasperations. A negative universe united them.

"I can't believe I'm going to tell you this . . ."

"Tell me everything," Clive urged.

"I have this problem. I sweat. I sweat until I'm soaked and I hate it." Even as he spoke, sweat bubbled over Danny's lip. When he ran his hand through his hair he discovered his sideburns were wet. "See? I'm doing it now!"

"Listen to me," said Clive with all the authority of a specialist. "Mainly, perspiration is your body's way of cooling you off. It's your internal air-conditioning system, so to speak. If you sweat a lot, it must be because you're overheated, internally. Are you?"

Danny smiled. "I'm absolutely . . . torrid."

Clive smiled, too. "I thought so."

Words. How Danny loved the words, the dance, the flirting. Why had he had so little of it in his life? Even his own sexual fantasies were stripped bare, as if the sin was in making them playful, making them fun. So whenever he permitted himself to dream, it was of the act itself—"That's it. That's good. Blow me. Blow me!—" without any richness of detail. His fantasies were as blue and thin as skim milk.

But now for the first time he was traveling on his own, getting away, and he began to relax his own peculiar but strict self-control. He was having fun. He was twenty-three!

"You're very reassuring, do you know that?" With a dramatic flourish, he pulled the linen handkerchief Christopher Beene had given him from his pocket, and blotted his forehead. "Look at me. I'm cured. I sweat openly now, without shame. Thank you, doctor."

"You'd be amazed at the number of closets I've unlocked."

The line crept through customs in the sweltering terminal. Danny's coat, wrapped over his arm, felt like a heating pad. As Danny inched up in the line, right behind Clive, he noticed heavily armed guards in the corners of the terminal and guns and bullet clips prominent on the belts of the customs officers. Tension mixed with the heat on the line, and Danny's eyes finally rested on the one object of beauty in the fluorescent-lighted terminal—the back of Clive's immaculately barbered head.

As soon as they were outside, Clive gave his bags to Jacques, the Haitian driver he'd hired, and motioned for Danny to do the same. Holding open the door of the dusty Plymouth for them, Jacques said, "Don't forget, Monsieur Sumners, close your eyes and breathe through your mouth. There are many unpleasant sights on the road now, even more than last time. I will drive through Port-au-Prince *rapidement,* as always. Never fear, you will be in your paradise *tout de suite,* yes, yes.''

"He knows you!"

"Actually, he drives for me every time I'm in Haiti. I call him from New York, or wherever."

"Why did he tell you to close your eyes?"

Clive sighed deeply. "He knows I can't bear the city. The filth, the stench, the cripples simply break my heart." A shudder of revulsion shook his huge, powerful frame. Out of his pocket came a black eye mask that he placed on his lap.

"I doubt if you'll be able to stand it either," he added. "Nor should you. You deserve only the best."

Only the best. No one had ever said that to him before, yet it was what he'd always suspected. Instead of the best, he'd received the dregs. Only his boss, Christopher Beene, seemed to think he was special—or, at least, worthy of improvement. But not until today had anyone ever reached inside him and admired his core.

"I do hate suffering," he agreed. "Why can't everything just be beautiful?"

"You're exactly like me," Clive told him. "You demand very little—only that each little thing be magnificent. You want life to be a series of perfect jewels in one long, perfectly matched necklace. No inferior stones. No plastic, no horror. And why not? A life dedicated to beauty, to perfection—*that* is a life worth living."

"You're incredible." Danny shook his head. "Four hours, and you know me better than anyone in my whole life. You understand—but not only that, you *approve.* You're the first person I ever met who made me feel . . . legitimate."

Clive patted Danny's knee and said, "You've had a ghastly childhood. But we'll fix all that. Just put yourself in my hands." The hand remained on Danny's knee, massaging it.

The car took the main highway that led to Port-au-Prince and beyond, to where the green hills began. Along the way, Danny looked out at the sparse palm trees and the brown and green mountains in the far distance. Aside from several uncompleted and abandoned construction projects, Danny saw nothing seriously upsetting. What's all the fuss? he wondered. Isn't this what it's supposed to look like? True, there was no sea, no beach on this side, but the skies were blue and there were palm trees and the island heat was penetrating.

Just then a cloud of smoke blew toward the car, carrying with it a revolting smell of burning dung, grilled goat, rancid oil, human feces. Immediately Clive clamped his eye mask on and began open-mouth breathing, but Danny stared out the window, vaguely curious.

Picking up speed, Jacques raced the car past a group of Haitians sitting round a fire by the side of the road. They passed another group, then another. The stench and the smoke filled the car, making Clive cough despite his open mouth. When Danny began coughing too, Jacques seemed about to break down in tears.

"Unfortunately, we are traveling at the worst possible time of the day. They eat only this one meal. Firewood is expensive; they must use other fuels with the bad aromas."

A clothesline flapped, hung with the merest shreds of rags. Then they passed a group of shacks that seemed to be built of twigs and flattened-out metal cans. Then more fires and more settlements, one right after the other, crowded with people so small and skinny they looked like children.

"Squatters?" Danny asked Jacques.

"We are a very poor country. I am ashamed for you to see how we must live out in the open like animals. Our president says it upsets the foreign tourists to see this."

"Then why doesn't he—"

"Eliminate it from your mind," Clive said, lifting his eye mask momentarily. "It's not our business. All you'll do is upset yourself. Believe me, it's too hopeless. Don't look, Daniel. There aren't any jewels for your necklace here. None.''

Clive was right. From now on, Danny would pursue perfection, filling his life with beauty, and only with beauty. There was nothing for him to see out that window. Slowly, he closed his eyes, too.

''Hotel La Fantasia, Mr. Sumners. We are arrived.''

''Thank God,'' Clive muttered and pulled off his mask.

Danny opened his eyes and blinked out at Eden. He stepped from the car and immediately a fit of giddiness overtook him. Under a canopy of towering palms and massive ferns, exotic flowers were bursting from the earth in an explosion of color. Meanwhile, all manner of birds—screaming birds, singing birds, cooers, cacklers, cluckers and choppers—seemed to have awakened at the same riotous moment. Somewhere, an unseen waterfall clattered down, emptying into a gurgling rock pool at Danny's feet. He could see the brilliant goldfish darting through the clear water.

''Well, what do you think?'' Clive asked with a proprietary sweep of his arm. ''Will this do?''

Danny laughed in disbelief. ''This is beyond real, beyond even . . . heaven!'' He didn't know what he was doing. He threw his arms around Clive and hugged him. ''Thank you, thank you,'' he repeated over and over, as if Clive were somehow responsible for the hotel's beauty and for Danny's being here at all. Then, embarrassed, he pulled quickly away.

But when Clive counted out money for the driver and refused to let Danny pay a penny, Danny was once again overwhelmed. He wrapped an arm around Clive's neck and kissed his cheek.

''I thank you, and I'm sure even God Himself thanks you.''

They had entered the gates of paradise where excess made modesty seem absurd. Here, everything was permissible, everyone laughed merrily at his public expressions of affection. Yet except for his mother, Danny had touched no one, kissed no one in public view, ever. If it was done behind locked doors, unseen, then it hardly existed. Here, two men in high heels and capri pants wiggled by, demanding to be noticed, admired. Here, everything was possible. Danny felt free.

Clive canceled Danny's room and arranged for a suite with separate bedrooms, connected by a large sitting room of dark wood and cool breezes. Beyond the shutters a balcony with breakfast table and lounge chairs hung over their private turquoise pool.

"I think I'm delirious," Danny said from the balcony. "Feel my head."

"Quite, quite feverish," Clive agreed without touching him. "I believe the patient must be put to bed immediately."

"Whatever you think best," said Danny, holding out his arms to be led wherever Clive wanted him.

Clive led him into the first spacious bedroom, where Danny stood obediently while Clive unbuttoned his shirt.

"Are we playing 'passive petunia' today?"

"It's not a game," Danny said. "I think I'm out of my mind."

"Hmm, sounds serious." Clive unzipped Danny's pants and they fell to his ankles. With a kick he was free of them.

"It is serious," Danny agreed. "You're going to have to save me. Will you, Clive?"

"Actually," said Clive, undressing and folding his silk clothing with care, "I'd much rather ruin you."

All that afternoon, that evening, night and dawn they remained inside that shuttered room, unpacked, unshaved, unfed.

"We're disgusting," Clive said, sniffing his armpits as sunlight sliced through the shuttered slats.

Danny lay still, sated for the first time in his life. Upon waking, he had simply gazed at Clive's face, dark and dramatic even in sleep. Then his thoughts turned to Christopher Beene, his boss, perhaps because Christopher was the only person in the world who would understand what had just happened to Danny.

In some ways, Christopher Beene and Clive Sumners were startlingly alike. Certainly it wasn't a physical similarity, for no two people could look more different. While Clive's presence was enormous, Christopher was so pale and slight that his shoulders seemed no wider than a boy's. Yet they did have something in common—

their pursuit of perfect beauty. Without even realizing it, the pursuit had become Danny's as well.

Always afterward he would think of that sixth and final morning at the Fantasia as an initiation into a secret sect. It was then that he became a lifetime member, a blood brother. But at the time, of course, he thought it more an ending than a beginning.

The morning was like all the others—steamy, shuttered, and still. Reaching across the bed, he was surprised to find it empty because he could hear Clive, distinctly hear his familiar moans. But the sounds, he realized, came from the second bedroom, the one they'd never used.

He stood in the doorway for some time before they became aware of him. The boy, a local who worked at the hotel, hid under the covers, his white jacket and black pants a heap on the floor, but Clive stared straight at him from the bed.

Years before, his brother Norman would stare at him with the same steady, unrepentant gaze while Danny sobbed. They'd stand on the sidewalk where Norman had dragged Danny to force him to catch softballs.

"Catch, goddammit. Catch, you faggot."

But Danny would just stand there, his hands at his sides, and let the balls pound into his chest like punches. When the tears came, Norman gave up. But in his eyes there was no mercy, only exasperation.

Clive's expression held some of that same exasperation as Danny stood in the doorway and sobbed, "But why? Why?"

Clive shrugged. "Because he's absolutely adorable."

"But what about us? You said it was fate, remember?"

"It was."

"So why . . . this?"

"Why not this, too? I deserve it. I deserve every lovely jewel. So do you."

Danny sighed. "I thought I found my jewel. You."

"And here's another one. Don't be sad, Danny." He held open his arms. "Come let me show you this little pearl. Think of this as just one more ornament on your long, long necklace. Come, Danny, join us."

Just then there was movement under the bedcovers and

Clive's bed partner emerged, smiling shyly. He too held out his arms.

"He does have a lovely smile," Danny admitted.

Yes, Danny thought as he boarded his plane for home, *Clive was right. I appreciate it, therefore I deserve it.* Few people loved it the way they did. They were a rare breed, special. Clive was special. He didn't lose Clive. He *added* him to his collection of exquisite gems. *I'm rich!*

He was actually chuckling as his eyes scanned the plane, looking not for his seat, but for something else. Something arresting, exquisite. Something he couldn't live without—at least for now, for this moment. Then he saw it. The smile was knowing, unmistakable. The nose was perfect and the hair, though blond, reminded him of Clive's slick head.

He walked halfway down the aisle.

"I beg your pardon," he said in an accent that could have been British, "but actually, I believe you're in my seat."

14

At nine o'clock that night, Theo could wait no longer. He telephoned Dell at home. It was risky, he knew, but if Danny answered, he'd simply hang up. He let the phone ring ten times before Dell finally picked up. If she hadn't answered, he might have let it go on ringing all night.

There in her stainless-steel kitchen, Dell heard the ringing phone reaching down to her, rescuing her, just when she thought she was drowning. It was a slow swim up; she'd been quite far down—years, in fact.

She was sunk in memories, back in high school again. Not revisiting, which would connote a friendly stay. Rather, she was reliving. She was there. Reliving and crying and bingeing on chocolates, all at the same time. Her emotions, like her memories, were in anguished disorder. She had eaten a great many gold-foil-wrapped chocolates—an expensive gift from a grateful client—but still she ate more, unable to quiet the demanding emptiness inside her. And as she ate chocolates, she listened to the taunts of Russell Mullins.

"Big feets, big teats. Big teats, big feets. Oh, Momma, which are bigger—your feets or your teats?"

Russell Mullins sat behind her in history class her sophomore year of high school and he liked to lean forward and taunt her until the white skin under her foxy freckles turned the same color pink as his mother's Saturday-night dress.

"Hey, Red! What size shoe you wear? How come you gots such big feets? Big feets and big teats, they go together. Right, Big Titties?"

She had this crazy hair, the color of fire, and when he walked home from school, he often carried with him the image of that hair at exactly eleven o'clock in the morning, when the sun from the classroom windows set it ablaze.

She was too fat, too tall, too shy, and definitely too white, but there was something about her—her muteness, her softness, her vivid coloring—that both repelled and fascinated him. He wasn't the only boy who stared at Dell and secretly found her flesh appealing, but Russell Mullins was the only one who bothered to approach her and say something to her, even if his words cut and shamed her.

Perhaps that was why she never told on him. It was *something*. And not entirely untrue. *Something*. Negative, but nevertheless, attention. Therefore she allowed him to hiss his insults into the back of her neck while she stared straight ahead, hot-cheeked, pink-eared, until he became temporarily bored or distracted. Until even Russell Mullins lost interest in tormenting her, and everything returned to nothing again.

Publicly, she ignored him, but privately Russell lived inside her, goading her, taunting her awake each morning. She memorized Russell's chants and repeated them to herself as she dressed, practicing a kind of self-punishing litany. Unlike her mother's warnings and disapproval, Russell's taunts aroused her hopes and determination as much as they deepened her abasement.

Okay, fat titties, today is the day!

Nodding in agreement in the mirror, she was moved to try again.

Hey, big feets, get on that diet!

She was almost seventeen, almost thirty pounds overweight, almost in complete despair. If she could just escape this junkpile she lived on top of, she was sure she'd find bliss: a magnificent home with millions of rooms to redecorate; an adorable, adoring husband; a glamorous, gratifying career; and loads of money to buy all the clothes and all the furniture and all the things she'd been deprived of owning her whole life.

But she'd never get there looking like a huge cow. The first step was to get skinny, and to stay skinny. Oh, if only she could! Every morning she promised herself she would. Every morning she was determined anew to take that first step. But by about four each afternoon, the step grew higher, impossibly higher, until it was as tall as a

Colorado mountain peak and she fell off, fell down into a hole of hunger and despair.

If it weren't for the fact that her best and only friend, Tamara Walkov, was nineteen pounds heavier than Dell, the despair would've been unendurable. While they nibbled snacks the Walkov cook pulled hot from the oven after school, Tamara never let Dell forget that there was at least one person in the world who thought Dell was perfect.

"What's the use?" Dell would whine. "I'll always be fat and ugly. Every month I buy a fashion magazine and cut out pictures of the skinny models and tape them to my mirror. I start a new diet every day. I've got Russell Mullins reciting fat rhymes in my ears and my mother wagging her finger in my face. But nothing helps. I'll never be thin. I'll always be ugly and live in an ugly house and have an ugly little life."

And Tamara would disagree.

"Dell, you're not ugly. Okay, you're a little overweight. But ugly? Oh, God, I'd give anything to have your features. You've got everything—hair, face, eyes, coloring, shape. You're so lucky. *I'm* ugly. *And* fat."

It was true. Her skin was the color of a summer tan gone sallow. Her dark brown eyes were so close together and her nose so bumpily sloped that her face looked like it belonged on a large, bearded man. She had no neck, no waist, and no ankles. Though her clothes were expensive and even elegant, they were always too tight and wrinkled. Even her mother urged her to get "recontoured" by a plastic surgeon. Certainly they could afford it; Tamara was the richest girl Dell had ever known, richer than all of her relatives combined. But Tamara refused. Until she was thin, she refused to improve her facial defects. Her defects were her punishment for being so fat. But as long as Dell remained fat, there was no reason to change. They kept each other company.

"You're so lucky. You've got *things*. New things," Dell told her.

"You're luckier," Tamara told Dell truthfully. "If I lost weight, I'd look *better*. But you! Already you're as tall as a model. Someday, you're going to be gorgeous, and I just hope you'll still like me then."

"How can you even think such a thing? You're my best

friend. I tell you everything,'' Dell protested, hoping that the force of her objection hid from Tamara the embarrassing truth. For if and when Dell ever emerged as gorgeous, she knew she probably wouldn't remain friends with Tamara. Tammy was too far from perfect.

But her house! Ah, Tamara's house was such a marvel of space and style that Dell was sure that if only she lived there, she'd be utterly transformed. If she had a room like Tammy's, so modern in brown and turquoise . . . if she owned merely the chocolate velvet bedspread or the turquoise formica desk that spanned one entire turquoise wall and had nothing on it but three miniature, narrow-necked vases . . . if she could have brushed her teeth each morning at her very own turquoise sink . . . if she could've patted her skin dry with just one of those thick, brown towels, then her beautiful surroundings, she was certain, would force her to become beautiful, too. Inside and out she would match her exquisite things; she would measure up. If only she possessed perfection—lived in it, sat on it, slept with it—she would *become* perfection. Surely her things would transform her. It dismayed her how Tammy could remain so ugly in a world of such beauty.

She came to Tammy's house every day and put off reciprocating until Tamara revolted.

"I'm really hurt, Dell. We always go to my house. Why don't we ever go to yours? Are you ashamed of me?"

Shame, Dell thought. *It surrounds me.*

Of course she was ashamed of Tammy. She despised her best friend's faults almost as much as her own. And she knew that the kids at school held the pair of them in contempt. But there were other, deeper shames Tammy knew nothing about and that Dell never had to reveal before.

Even as they approached Littleneck Street and turned left onto Neptune Walk, Dell couldn't lift her arm and point her finger toward the fence and the house beyond it. She couldn't tell Tammy, "Well, this is it!" because she couldn't speak at all. She led the way, looking straight ahead, as if her house was up ahead, across the bay, miles from there. Then, suddenly, she stopped.

"What're you stopping here for? I've always hated this

junkyard. It's so ugly. And it stinks. Can't you smell it? C'mon, let's get to your house.'' Tamara tried to pull Dell along, but Dell stood frozen to the spot.

Very quietly she said, ''This *is* my house.''

When Theo called that night, Dell had almost finished the whole box of gold-wrapped chocolates. Seeing Theo that afternoon, feeling his arms around her, enclosing her as if he meant never to let her go again made her feel as if she were suddenly wrapped in a luxurious cashmere blanket. She was blanketed in such thrilling softness she actually felt safe. *At last,* she thought at that moment, *I've finally, really arrived. I'm there! And I'm safe. I'm— yes!—I'm loved!* But then, just as suddenly, he released her and the blanket turned into a sheet of ice, numbing her.

''Don't let go!'' she wanted to tell him. ''Just hold me! Hold me!''

But of course, she didn't. At the instant of Danny's arrival, Theo backed off, and so did she. She gave up. She had to, of course, but the feeling of defeat, of giving up, stayed with her, coloring everything.

Defeat. By the time she turned seventeen, she thought she'd learned everything about turning defeat into victory. But tonight, looking back, all she could see was Theo's arms reaching out to her, enclosing her and then letting her go. Leaving her completely, utterly empty. She reached for another chocolate but the dark, silken sensation in her mouth was gone in an instant. Gone, just as Theo was gone, in an instant. And all that was left was the calories, the thousands of chocolate calories she'd just consumed.

On the tenth ring, she picked up the phone and quickly swallowed one last bite of chocolate.

''Hello?'' She heard only silence. ''Yes? Hello?''

''It's . . . me, Dell. Theo.''

''Theo.''

Her hands flew to her hair, her face. She wiped her mouth, smoothed down her blouse, as if he could see her through the phone.

''Did I catch you in the middle of dinner? You sound like you're eating.''

''Dinner?'' Dell almost laughed. Some dinner, she said

to herself bitterly. ''Well, sort of. Danny's not home and—''

''Oh, he's not?''

''No, and I'm just standing here in the kitchen and . . . stuffing my face.''

''I do that, too, whenever I'm home alone for dinner,'' he said, eager to draw her into conversation. ''Erica leaves a cold plate for me, but I like to stand up and grab.''

She could picture him standing at the open refrigerator, a miniscule wedge of brie in one hand, a Baccarat flute in the other. The pale gold wine the exact color of his hair. Pulling tidbits from the cold shelves.

''Not like this, Theo,'' she said, on the brink of telling him. But what would she tell him? That tonight she'd sunk back and become the old Dell, fat and hopeless? That tonight she'd given up, something she vowed she'd never do. That she'd already lost Danny and today she'd lost Theo for the last time, lost him though she'd never once really had him for her own.

She'd have to tell him how tonight she hadn't worn her new black velvet suit out to dinner; she hadn't gone out at all because, as usual, her husband had called to say he'd be late—very late.

Alone. She was utterly alone. But how could she tell him? And out of control. All her years of rigid discipline down the drain, for now that she'd finished the chocolates, why not have some ice cream, too? Why stop at all? Why bother anymore?

''What's the use?'' her mother would wonder, defeated, and reach for another doughnut. Now Dell asked the same question with the same sense of defeat.

''We're alike, exactly alike. Oh, Mommy, I am truly your daughter!

No, of course she couldn't tell him any of this. So she locked her anguish inside her and spoke to him with a smile in her voice, revising what she'd been about to say into something light and casual, something that hid her despair.

''I mean, not the way I look tonight. I'm a mess. You caught me just as I finished a drippy sandwich and was about to wash my hair. My hair is as greasy as my fingers.''

Theo sighed. "Dell, I saw you five or six hours ago, remember? Your hair looked fine. Fine? What am I saying? Your hair always looks . . . like your own private sun on the top of your head.

Oh, God, he's being so sweet, she thought, *so unbearably sweet.* But why? Why was he calling her?

She was staring at the mound of foil chocolate wrappers on the platinum counter, thinking of all those calories, all that sugar and fat she'd just consumed. Too late!

Knowing this only increased her sense of futility. She gripped the phone as if she were choking it, but when Theo spoke again, she heard his voice above the pounding of her heart.

"Dell? Do you remember what happened today at the Embassy?"

She remembered. How could she forget the way he held her, the way he pulled her to him? What had he been about to say to her there at the door to the Embassy? He had literally swept her off her feet and up into his arms. That was no polite kiss from a colleague. But what was it?

Everything. It was only everything.

And afterward, she could hardly look at him. Never again, she was sure, would he attempt to reach her, to touch her the way he had today, moments before Danny arrived and ended it before it'd ever begun. Never again. The certainty of it felt like utter defeat.

Even Danny had noticed.

"Lighten up!" he whispered, elbowing her as the three of them wandered the dusty, half-finished rooms.

"Stop moping!" he hissed at her as they pored over plans, inspected wood stains and faux finishes. "Look at our darling Embassy." He poked her. "Look at it and *kvell!*"

In even higher spirits than usual, he swept everyone up into his cheerful storm. Everyone, that is, but Dell. He applauded the contractor for doing the impossible— coming in ahead of schedule. He joked with all the workmen.

To Theo, with glances at Dell, he said. "I leave you two alone for five minutes, and look what happens. What's with you, Theo? You should be singing. You should be delirious. *I'm* delirious. Not just pleased. Delirious. Now how often do you hear that from a client?"

It worked. Theo had to laugh. Animated by Danny's enthusiasm, he took charge of the tour of the rooms and began explaining the chaos around them.

"Jimmy, here, is the best carpenter in the business, in my opinion. You've never worked with him? Look at this walnut wainscoting he's putting up. Superb, eh? This entire second floor is really one elegant salon, the library opening to the living room, then to the dining room, and so on."

Dell tagged along as if pulled on a leash. It was not that she was unwilling; it was just that she was lost in her own reverie. She kept thinking of the exuberant line of a song she vaguely remembered: "He kissed me!" Perhaps it was from a musical. She vaguely remembered having seen it on Broadway quite some time ago. *He kissed me.* And it was everything—*everything!*—and now she was afraid. What had happened, she wondered, to her nihilistic resolve, her *why not* attitude? Back at Willa's Way Studio she'd asked herself, *Why not?* And answered it with the question, *Indeed, why not?* Well, what happened to that casual indifference? Vanished. Dissolved in a vale of fears.

Now she and Theo stood in their separate, well-designed kitchens, chatting in the jargon of harried marrieds. They invoked the names of their spouses with pointed informality, as if the four of them were old college chums, when in fact they both knew Erica considered Dell a hated rival. Yet when he said, "Erica's seeing a Billy Wilder film tonight—*Sunset Boulevard,* I think," she nodded eagerly as if delighted to hear Erica was having a night out.

"Danny loves old Hollywood films," she said. "He's out right now meeting with our rug man. At least, I think that's where he is. He wants an enormous Oriental for the second-floor salon. Or maybe a Bessarabian. The Sidney Greenstreet look. Danny must be unrolling every rug in the place. He's hours late." The more she talked, the more absurd her words sounded to her. Theo. He was beginning to make her angry.

Why in hell had he called? To tell her about Erica's cold plates, her favorite film directors?

Sorry, Theo, no time to hear about your wife, she thought with impatience. *I've got a mess to clean up—*

me. I blew it tonight. And if I don't pull myself together,
if I don't get back in control right this minute, I might
never find my way back. So give my regards to your wifey
and please, leave me alone.

She said nothing more, and the silence between them
filled up with regret. She thought he might hang up, never
again to sweep her up in his arms, to kiss her as he had
today, doubtless, delirious, determined to have her. Yet
she did nothing to prevent it. She waited for the click
and the dial tone.

But suddenly, he spoke. "I—I wanted to tell you
something today that I—"

She waited, not really waiting, not expecting, prepared to say goodbye.

"Dell, I have to see you." He strained to push the
words out. "Alone. Do you understand? Would you go
with me somewhere? Alone? Tomorrow? Could you meet
me?"

Unconsciously, she reached for a paper towel and began wiping her face, then her hands, then the phone and
the counter. She smiled at her reflection in the back-
splash even though it was distorted.

"Yes," she whispered.

Her answer stopped him for a moment. The simplicity
of it! Sweet and unhesitant. He wanted to savor it, like a
taste on his tongue.

"Yes," she said again, afraid he might not have heard.
"Yes," she said even louder, surprising herself.

She heard him laugh with delight and relief and heard
herself laugh back.

"Did you really say yes?"

"I did, I did!" She was as surprised as he was.

He laughed uproariously, and she joined him and the
laughter washed away the distance and the fear.

Suddenly, she caught sight of the crumpled foil candy
wrappers, but their laughter gave her the strength to turn
her back on the counter, to ignore it for now, and to say
to him, "You're not sorry, are you? I mean, now that I
said yes."

"Sorry? Are you crazy?"

She heard him give the name of a restaurant at a hotel
on York Avenue. A very small, private hotel. He suggested they meet at noon.

"Is that a good time for you?"

"Yes. Noon." She was trembling. She slid to the floor, then immediately stood up. She didn't know where to put her body. She sank back down to her knees.

"Are you sure?"

"I think so," she managed, and stood up again.

He caught her hesitation. "Please don't change your mind," he whispered. "I've thought of you—I think of you—often, Dell. You can't imagine how often."

"I didn't know. I never imagined . . ."

"Every day, Dell. Every single day."

"I thought that only I . . . and that you'd lost interest."

He thought of her every day!

"I could never lose interest. But when I walked away from you that first day, and then you ran from my office, well, I thought you'd had enough of me."

"But it was I who called you to do the Embassy." She was fishing for more lovely words, knowing now that he would give them to her.

"Yes," he agreed, "but I wouldn't let myself believe it was anything more than professional interest."

"Then what changed you? Today, I mean."

He took a long time to answer, and when he did, his voice quavered.

"I saw you from the third-floor window in your red boots and you made me smile."

"Oh."

"No, you don't understand. You made me *smile*. Again. You always make me smile. You somehow pull out of me a sense of joy I never knew was there. Today, it came to me—you make me happy."

His words made her hunger for more. She thought she could have sat there on the kitchen floor and asked him questions and listened to him give her lovely answers all night long. But suddenly she heard a noise—was it a key in the lock? Danny?—and her heart began to pound in shame and guilt. She had to hide these wrappers, throw them out. She had to get off the phone! She couldn't be caught talking to Theo, not this way. But was that really Danny at the door? She listened. Silence. But the mood was broken.

"Dell?"

"I'm here," she said, but she wasn't. She stood up straight and her voice was formal. "But I just noticed the time."

"I understand," he said, and he did. He smiled and said, "you were about to wash your hair. So . . . until tomorrow?"

"Yes, tomorrow," she said, but she was no longer sure. Fear had returned again. And the old doubts.

"Tomorrow, Dell. I'll see you tomorrow."

"Good night, Theo."

"Good night."

15

"I am not homosexual," Danny claimed, staring at the ceiling. He said it as a statement of fact, without defensiveness. He said it with an indifference that often, although not always, is founded in supreme self-assurance.

But Edgar Garson, staring at Danny's slim, slick limbs stretched along the gray carpet, felt he knew this boy now. He *knew* him, the whole of him.

"You're lying to yourself. Your heart, your soul . . . and your cock are gay, boy. You're as queer as I am. Maybe queerer."

"Hornier," Danny disagreed.

"Queerer."

Danny sighed and stroked his bare, hairless chest. He closed his eyes. "I get it up for women. I get it up for men. I can get it up for an original Louis XV escritoire, and if I ever go back to Pompeii I know I will come all over the wall paintings in the House of the Vetti."

"Ah," Garson sighed, "a true patron of the arts. What makes Danny run? Beauty! Danny is a lover of beauty." Spent, so exhausted he couldn't seem to fully catch his breath, he nevertheless felt strangely unsated. Greedily, Edgar Garson reached for Danny's inner thigh and began stroking it again.

"Don't be sarcastic, Edgar. You know exactly what I mean because you happen to bow before the same gods I do."

Danny opened his eyes again but he didn't look at Edgar Garson as he spoke. He didn't even feel Garson's hands on him. He gazed out his office windows at the light show the city put on nightly, remembering that once, he and Dell had lain here like this, gazing at the night and the electrical wonderland that took the place of stars. And years before that, there had been another night spent lying on a carpet, a scratchy, homespun Haitian sisal, when he thought he'd found love, and didn't even glance out the window because the only thing he could see, wanted to see was Clive. *Clive.* But now it was ten-thirty, too late for those memories, and his client was asking him a question.

"What gods, pray, are those?"

Danny turned to Garson. "Edgar, you love beautiful things. So do I. Except that with me, beauty is a carnal turn-on. I automatically want to fuck anyone, or anything, that attracts me. So, I truly am a *lover* of beauty."

"And I suppose it was my magnificence," Garson said dryly, glancing down at his rotund belly, "that you found so irresistible tonight." Better to be a realist and say it now, Garson told himself, before this boy hurt him. These boys, even the sensitive ones, could be masters of cruelty.

"You have a certain beauty," Danny allowed.

"Do you mean my exquisite script, my stylish signature that now graces your contract?"

Ignoring the sarcasm, Danny continued with his point. "Christopher Beene did a showcase kitchen for United Marble and I swear, when I saw that room a few weeks ago, I wanted to fuck it. I wanted to fuck the floor, the arches, the dado—everything. Every edge curled and bowed and ended in classical volutes. It looked like Michelangelo himself did the carving. And I wanted to fuck it and fuck it. I stood there panting. They were doing an advertising shoot and the photographer thought I was having a heart attack."

At that Garson grabbed for his own heart. A pain seared down the left side from his jaw to his ribs. At the center of his chest it clustered into a massive boulder, crushing everything—breathing, thinking, talking. Nothing was functioning. Everything stopped. Only pain existed, freezing him. The world turned blue. In less than thirty seconds it was gone.

"Don't stop," said Danny. He was staring out at the night again, back in his own secret world, but when Garson abruptly pulled his hand away, Danny wanted it back.

Wearily, Garson reached for Danny's thigh and began massaging it again. For a week he'd been having attacks of what he was sure was bursitis in his left shoulder. And indigestion as well. An annoying heaviness after every meal, even breakfast. And shortness of breath. An old man's afflictions for which Garson felt only contempt. He ignored them all.

"Why don't you answer me, Daniel?"

This sarcasm was taking a supreme effort. Talking at all, when his breath was coming out in short wheezes, was an enormous strain. But despite this, Garson went on goading Danny. Goading him to say it. Forcing him to tell the poisonous truth now, before it could sting him later. Or perhaps, just to hear this dear boy deny it again. Deny the truth and reassure him with sweet lies. Garson no longer knew what he wanted.

"Speak to me, dear one, of me. Enough of kitchens and marble counters. Am I, for you, a David? A satyr, perhaps? Or, heaven forbid, a monstrous Gorgon? But, if so, how, dear lover of beauty, do you get it up? And why?"

Danny looked at Garson, but it was dark and he couldn't see the old man's pallor. And the shallow breathing sounded to Danny like lust. So he took Garson's head in his hands and placed it over his stiffly curved cock.

"I think this says it all, Edgar."

It didn't, but why did this scandalous boy who gave so little matter so much? What did he really expect this Danny Dannenberg to say? Words of love? Hah! Before him Garson's own naked body spread out like some kind of enormous root vegetable, gnarled and hairy. But he didn't have to look down at his own knobs and bulges to know it was not for beauty, and certainly not for love, that Danny was here with him tonight. Even when Garson had been young and rather attractive, it had rarely been for love. They were all searching for it, of course, this love, until they found another partner, and then they settled for something slightly less.

No, this boy was strictly business, Garson decided. A businessman. Not unlike Garson himself. A businessman who put his business before everything, *above* everything. Who gave gifts of gratitude for the big orders, the profitable contracts, the prestigious clients. Perks, gratuities, contributions, payoff. Danny was his very own gift of gratitude. His weighty cock, his accepting anus, his tireless, glorious mouth were all gifts of gratitude. Had Garson not signed the contract Danny so indelicately pressed on him before he'd finished his first glass of wine, there would've been no gift to slowly, deliciously, expectantly unwrap. Garson knew this, knew it and knew it.

And yet . . . there was a certain intensity, a vigor in the way Danny fucked that had surprised him. Surprised and shaken him. Just when Garson's body was beginning to fail him, his sense of power was being reawakened.

He loves it. This boy really loves it. With me!

Knowing this gave him strength, gave him breath. He pumped his head up and down, his nose snorting air in and out while he supported his weight on his aching left arm. He didn't bother to play with it with his tongue, to lick it and lap it. He took the tip of Danny's cock back, back to the wall of his throat and locked his lips tightly around the shaft. Then he rode Danny's cock with his mouth. Like a cowboy on a horse, he thought. Giddyap! He could feel Danny's hips lifting off the floor, lifting to meet him, but he would need a rest before he finished him.

"Oh, don't stop," Danny groaned. "Don't stop. Don't stop!"

It made Garson smile even as he rested his head on Danny's belly and panted for air.

"In a moment," Garson managed. He was amazed to see that he was entirely hard.

Danny noticed, too. "Want to have yours first?"

"Not at all," Garson insisted, shaking his head. "Not at all, actually."

The way Garson pronounced the word actually reminded Danny of Clive. Clive Sumners. Until tonight, no one else had ever pronounced it just like that, in four distinct British syllables. Tonight, everything seemed to remind him of Clive. Actually . . .

"Actually, I'm musing on the way that you come. The way that you come with me, for I can't believe you're like this with everyone," said Garson. He would need to rest a few minutes more. His heart was still beating wildly. Too wildly. "Like you're being electrocuted."

Danny smiled in the dark.

Garson let himself go. He dropped all sarcasm and

closed his eyes. "Electrocuted. And it is I who pulls the switch." The thought of it made him want to. He turned to face Danny. "Shall I?"

"Not yet," said Danny, and quickly turned Garson over. "I don't want to be selfish. First you." He unrolled a condom.

"Selfish?" Garson gasped as Danny entered him. "You don't understand—"

"Don't I?" By now, Danny was sure he understood every nuance of gratitude. Tonight, Garson had made him rich and now, Danny was making Garson happy. Doubly happy. That's how grateful Danny was feeling.

Weakly, Garson tried to protest. "I can't possibly . . . there's no strength . . . for another . . ."

"No?"

"Oh, God."

"Yes?"

"Yes, Yes! But oh . . . God . . . wait . . ."

"Wait? You don't want to wait. I know what you want. This is what you want. Isn't it? Isn't it?"

"Please—"

"Mmmm."

"Help. Oh, help."

"Here it is. Here's your help. Take it, baby. Just let it come."

"Something's terribly—"

"Stop thrashing, Edgar. Move with me."

"Unh."

"Just move with me. You're almost done."

"Having a—"

"I know."

"Having—"

"Yes."

"NNNNGGGHAAAAAAAH!"

"Oh, yes, Oh, yes."

Heart! Heart! It's over. Over! he thought he cried as the pain sliced his chest in half. *Tina,* he remembered.

Oh, please keep this from her. Don't hurt her again, he thought he said. But no sounds came out at all. Edgar Garson's last words were silence.

16

It was dark and silent. Too, too silent.

"Talk about electric orgasms. Edgar, you were mega-volted!"

Danny lay on his back, trying to joke, but the sound of his own solitary laugh echoed back to him as false and slightly hysterical. He closed his eyes but immediately opened them and found himself staring at the underside of his desk, the massive slab of rose and gray polished granite. The underside was unpolished; it looked, from his position on the floor three feet below, like the roof of a snug and sheltering cave. Almost habitable. Fleetingly, he wondered what it would be like to just crawl in and stay. Then he noticed the silence again. It enveloped the room as commandingly as loud noise. He had to rouse Garson.

"Edgar, we really mustn't fall asleep. Not here."

Silence, occupying every square inch of the dark, dark room, answered him over and over again, paralyzing him. Dully, he stared into the cavelike black void under his desk. After several minutes it looked more and more inviting. Protective. *I could crawl in there right now with just a futon,* he thought deliriously, *and in the morning Angie could leave a tray of croissants and coffee for me and hold all my calls.* His heart was racing wildly.

"Come on, Edgar. It's getting late. Time to go."

Edgar Garson gave no response. He lay on his side, facing away from Danny on the gray industrial carpet, and Danny had not yet looked at him. As long as Danny didn't look at him, he could tell himself that any moment now his client was going to stand up, get dressed and get *out* of here. He could even touch Garson; he just couldn't look at him.

To prove it, Danny stretched his leg straight out and

when his toes found Garson's bare buttocks, he tried to prod Garson awake.

"Please, Edgar. Please!"

The flesh was as yielding as a sponge, but unnaturally cool. At this hour the building's heat was turned down and the office was chilly, but Garson's flesh was as raw as a side of beef hanging in a butcher's refrigerator. Instinctively, Danny recoiled and pulled his foot away, but he refused to allow himself to feel fear. Fear was an admission that something was terribly wrong. And nothing was wrong, Danny told himself. Nothing. Except that Edgar the bitch was carrying things too far.

"Get up, get up, you goddamned queen!" he exploded, shouting at the ceiling, his arms folded tightly across his chest. "Enough! I'm waiting. Why don't you answer? Why don't you stop this . . . this . . . what is this, anyway? A game?"

He waited, but Garson didn't answer. Still, he waited, still unable to make himself look at Garson.

"Get up!" he shouted again, and then told himself, *Stop shouting or you'll scare him. You could make him worse, if he's not already . . .*

Shouting had never been Danny's weapon. He ruled, but never, he liked to think, through force. In fact, on those few occasions when he lost control and shouted at his staff and they cowered, he could hardly forgive himself. No ordinary despot, he much preferred to inspire in them reverence, a slavish devotion. Monarchs, he believed, so surpassed all others, shouting should have been unnecessary.

"Please, Edgar," he whispered this time, staring into the beckoning cave under his desk. Sitting up, coiled, chin on his knees, he rocked back and forth for ten minutes more. In front of him the mouth of the cave grew wider, as if trying to accommodate him. But of course, before he'd crawl in there, the place would have to be completely done. He'd do it, he thought, as an underground den of stone. Lots of fur rugs, hand-woven blankets, leather, heavy wood pieces. Rustic, unfussy. And such a relief after all the shirred, swagged, ruffled, ruched, ribboned, and tasseled treatments he'd been designing lately.

He was dreaming while he listened and waited, but

without much expectation. And then with none at all. It was time to act.

He crawled over to Garson, who still lay on his side, and pressed his hand to Garson's back. Garson fell over onto his stomach.

And Danny's own stomach plummeted like an elevator whose cables had snapped. For too many precious minutes now he'd been lying on his office floor—waiting, just waiting, he told himself—avoiding looking at Garson. Now he could avoid it no longer. Gently, he shook his client's shoulder.

"Edgar?"

When Garson remained still, Danny quickly turned him over onto his back and finally looked into the old man's face.

"Oh, God. Oh, God. Oh, God," he intoned. "God help me."

Garson's eyes were wide open but unseeing. His jaw hung slack and his white pompadour fell flat over his forehead like a waif's scraggly bangs. Danny didn't have to listen for Garson's heartbeat; he knew what he'd find. He had only to look at Garson's frozen face to know he was finished. And his neck. Oh God, his neck! Gone from flame to ash so soon.

Finished. He knew now that Garson was finished, yes, but he still couldn't, wouldn't accept it. He wasn't going to let Garson do this to him.

"No way, Edgar," he said out loud, shaking his head. No, he wasn't going to take this. He was going to awaken and revive Garson. Yes, yes, awaken him. He wasn't going to allow Garson to do this to him.

"Not to me, not to my carpet, not to my office, not to my future, not to my life," he declared, all in one breath. "You will not fuck me, Edgar, do you hear? Not now. Not when everything is so close to being perfect. No way. I won't let you. Edgar, listen to me. You're getting up!"

And so, though Edgar Garson had been dead for perhaps twenty minutes, it was only now that Danny could finally face him, that he was driven to try to save Edgar Garson's life.

Bending over the inert form, Danny pinched Garson's nose shut and blew air into his lifeless mouth. He counted to three, came up for air on the fourth count, and pressed his mouth back down over Garson's for a count of three again.

Breathe, you old queen.

Breathe, you son of a bitch, you daughter of a bitch. Breathe!

With every breath he pumped into Garson, Danny frantically willed him to breathe. Furiously. Violently. And when he didn't respond, Danny cursed him, as if Garson were pulling this stunt just to be contrary. The fury held off the tears.

There'll be no tears because he will *awaken,* Danny told himself. *He will. He must. And if he does wake up . . . no,* when *he does, dear God, I promise, I promise, I'll never . . .*

He climbed over Garson's inert torso, but tears were welling up in Danny's eyes no matter what he told himself. *What am I going to do?* he asked himself but there wasn't time for an answer because, he told himself, he had to save Garson.

Straddling Garson, Danny momentarily broke down, sobbing "Oh God! Oh God, help me!" But then he bent down and smothered Garson's gaping mouth with his own.

He could taste Garson's sour breath, feel Garson's cold, rubbery lips as he exhaled every atom of his breath down Garson's throat. Then, gasping, he sat up. It was then that he caught sight of his swelling penis pointing straight at Garson's neck. It made him want to scream or retch. He did both.

17

Grapefruit and homemade granola every morning and what had it done for him, Christopher Beene asked himself. At forty-nine, he should look better than this. Down in Washington, when he'd redone the president's residential quarters, he met white-haired senators who brushed their teeth in bourbon, drank it for breakfast, went to the office already drunk—and still looked younger than he did. Leaning stiffly into the bathroom mirror, he examined his sunken face and noted another odd brown spot on his nose, similar to several that had appeared on his legs some weeks before. Unmistakable signs, but no time tonight to soak them in a bath of self-pity. Danny needed him now and Christopher would find the strength to serve him. Somehow. At least he wasn't feverish. Usually, Christopher sunk to his lowest point around three in the afternoon. Danny's call, though it awakened him, caught Christopher Beene at his best time: midnight.

He knew he should hurry. Danny's emergency, now that he'd committed himself to it, required haste. Yet, unable to stop himself, he glanced once more in the mirror, propelled by a vanity so grossly inappropriate at a time like this that he wondered if his sarcoma had spread to his brain.

"Ludicrous!" he exploded at this reflection, and fled to his custom-fitted dressing room where he forced himself to put on unmatched, jarring pants and shirt as penance.

Danny's hysteria still rang in Christopher's ears.

"I need you. It's Danny. Christopher, help me! God knows why you've given so much to me. I have no right to ask for more. But there's no one else. I can't tell Dell. She, above all, can't be told. You're the only one I can turn to."

Danny certainly knew the way to his heart. Nevertheless, Christopher could hear in Danny's voice and manner something he'd never heard there before—raw terror—and it was alarming.

"What happened?" he asked quickly and heard Danny stifle a sob.

"I've got Edgar Garson here . . . and he's dead."

"Dead?"

"He—he died on me."

Dead! Damned right, you need me. Christopher's mind, along with the rest of him, was coming slowly awake. He reached for the hand-painted bedside lamp and turned it on. No one lay beside him; no one had for over three years. He was done with desire, but, by God, he could still be useful.

"When?"

"When? I don't know! I've been sitting here in my office—I'm under my desk, would you believe this?"

"Why are you under your desk?"

"Because I'm going out of my mind, that's why. I'm literally under my desk, shivering, and Edgar's on the floor, too—for I don't know how long—and I swear he's turning blue right before my eyes. I don't know what to do. Poor Edgar. I tried to save him. I really tried, but it was too late."

"Heart?"

"I think so. Christopher, we . . . were . . . you know . . . when it happened."

A sharp little bullet of jealousy shot through Christopher Beene's heart and exited, leaving an invisible wound. Even now, it still hurt to share Danny with anyone. When Danny accused him of being too possessive, Christopher argued, "I'm protective, not possessive," convincing no one and changing nothing.

But the truth was that he really did want to protect Danny. This was a love different from any he'd known. It was not Danny's body he wanted—indeed, for the last three years he had wanted no one. Once he knew he was lethal, it deadened all desire.

But even way before that, he'd faced the fact that he and Danny were never to be lovers. Employer, counselor, colleague, mentor, yes. He'd been all of these, and more, to Danny. But never his lover.

Perhaps, he reasoned, that worked out for the best. While lovers came and went, Danny remained permanently fixed in his life. Even after Danny's marriage to the tall redhead, Wednesday nights were still *their* nights, a custom begun almost immediately after Danny left his shop to join Leonard, Melton, Inc.

How worried he'd been then that he was losing Danny forever.

"I haven't taught you everything. There wasn't time. You'll need help," he warned. "Call me."

When Danny did, overwhelmed at the big, competitive company, Christopher insisted he come to dinner that night. They tackled Danny's first three design projects doing one a week. By the end of three weeks, the Wednesday-night custom was in place.

To be of use—perhaps that was all he'd wanted then. Or had he felt this dark devotion, this paternal pull, right from the start? From the minute he noticed the tall, skinny kid amble into his shop? Was it Danny's first words—"It's so beautiful in here. I wish I could stay forever"—that had instantly melted him? He could not remember. He only knew he had an end in mind now, filled with purpose. Before he went out of this life, he wanted Danny's future in place. Instead, it was in shambles.

"Have you told anyone?"

"No one. But I'm calling the police as soon as we hang up. I should've done it ages ago."

"The police will be called, of course," Christopher said slowly. A plan was forming, an end he could almost see. "But not yet."

"Not yet? I've waited too long already, haven't I?"

Christopher ignored him. "First, tell me something. Do you still have that hideous fiberglass cauldron, the mock terra cotta tub near your window, filled with those boring reeds?"

"Christopoher, why are you asking—"

"Remember I said it looked like a deep fryer for cannibals and you said it was a gourmet steamer for the upscale flesh-eater? You got it out of a window display and kept it, I was always convinced, just to irritate me."

"Of course I remember. It was the day you came to see my new offices downtown. So what?" Danny's exasperation spilled over. ''We're wasting time. I'm drowning here and I don't know what to do. I can't think straight—''

''I know,'' Christopher said, nodding into the phone. ''I know you can't,'' he added gently.

He was fully awake now; his brain was whizzing ahead, careening like a race car taking a sharp curve. It was a lovely curve, like a Greek volute that curled back in on itself, and he followed it to its end. Then he sighed, satisfied. *It would work.* He saw it all, the whole map and the route he would take to the end . . . and the purpose for living on a little while longer.

''Let me think for you, Danny.''

Christopher Beene drove to the entrance of Danny's building, just as he told Danny he would. Then he walked to the pay phone at the corner.

''I'm here,'' he said into the mouthpiece. ''I'm coming up.''

''No! No, don't!'' There was alarm in Danny's voice. ''I forgot about the nightman in the lobby. We can't risk him seeing you.''

''Damn!''

''Wait for me in your car. Once I'm outside the building—''

''I'll be ready. But can you manage everything up there all by yourself?''

Danny sighed. ''I'll manage.''

He was dressed now, and calmer. Not numb anymore. The numbness left him when he decided to call Christopher. His head was clear and he could think, but he could feel now, too, and what he felt was a sadness so wide and deep that already it was changing him, transforming him, and he knew he'd never be the same again.

''It's you,'' he said into the phone, his voice, his heart breaking simultaneously, ''who'll have to bear the major brunt. Are you still sure you really want to?''

''We've been over all this. I told you, I'm sure. Surer than I've ever been about anything. Now let's get off the phone and get on with it.''

Danny hung up and set to work. Grunting, he clasped Garson around the waist and lifted him onto the mouth of the fiberglass urn. For a split second they were face to face, Danny and the cloudy-eyed Garson. Then Garson's naked body arched backward and slid down, head first, into the huge bowl. But the feet didn't fit. They stuck straight out like thick stalks some florist had arranged in the fake earthenware vase, and Danny had to bend them and press down on the knees and ankles until they finally cleared the urn's lip.

The effort, and the horror, of lifting Garson, pushing and pressing his flesh, soaked Danny in sweat and made his shoulders curl in revulsion. But more than the effort, and the horror, was the sorrow. He was draped in a sorrow opaque as black crepe, and as lightweight. It didn't impede his movements, which were swift and crisp, but he worked in darkness, and the darkness was his own remorseful, mournful sorrow.

When he finished with Garson, he remembered his next task, and went directly to the large storage closet in the back office.

"You'll need something to cover the mouth," Christopher had warned him earlier.

"You mean Edgar's mouth?" Danny asked dully. It was midnight and Danny had been struggling to understand all the directions Christopher was hurling at him over the phone while, at the same time, struggling to prevent Christopher from making this enormous, beneficent sacrifice. But to prevent it, he'd have to refuse it . . . and he'd already reluctantly accepted. It was then that the sorrow had begun.

"Not Edgar's mouth. The urn, the urn!"

In the closet, on a shelf loaded with lamps, vases, accent pillows, platters, and a set of black satin bedsheets, Danny found what he was looking for—a Hopi blanket. He'd bought it for a client on a whim, a bad practice. Naturally, the client hated it. Clients, Danny knew only too well, insisted on the illusion that they were in charge, that only they decided what got purchased. Nevertheless, even now, Danny still loved to shop (no longer with Dell, of course; they were much too busy), and buy on impulse, neglecting to clear with his clients if he spied an item he knew was ideal for a certain room. Occasionally, a client would balk, and the item would wind up in his closet, adamantly refused, like this multicolored, expertly woven Hopi blanket.

He brought the blanket back to his private office and tucked it tightly into the urn's mouth. Then he stood up and looked around him. Edgar Garson's clothes lay strewn about the floor.

"Oh, my God!" he cried out with a sob. More than Garson himself, Garson's clothes—expensive, crumpled, and forgotten—summoned forth Danny's deepest pity. The forgotten clothes made him remember the man.

"Oh, Edgar," he whispered over the clothing on the floor. "You poor, ridiculous, old man. I'm so terribly sorry."

He could allow himself only a minute to mourn the last remains of Edgar Garson. Then he had to set to work again, but now with an added and troubling concern: What other blatant clues might he have overlooked?

On the floor beside the urn, he carefully spread out Garson's lavender cotton dress shirt, and in the center placed Garson's folded suit, his black and lavender socks, underwear, his purple satin tie, shoes, watch, appointment book, and billfold. Under a shirtsleeve he found Garson's keys, which must have fallen out of the pants, and he added them to the pile. Then he gathered up the shirt ends into a bundle, and stuffed it, holding the blanket aside, into the urn. When he had retucked the blanket, he looked around him once more.

He checked his granite desk and crawled underneath, where he'd hidden out for a time. He tidied the sofa pillows and carried the wineglasses and sandwich wrappings to the office kitchen. After the garbage was thrown away and the glasses were washed and dried, he washed and dried his own face, but immediately the sorrow engulfed him. He didn't know for whom he felt the saddest—Edgar Garson; Garson's wife; his own wife, Dell; Christopher Beene . . . or himself. He cried for everyone.

Standing in an unheated doorway, Christopher Beene shivered in the chill of the early March night. He knew he'd just checked his watch, but he couldn't help looking at it again. Five minutes had gone by since he'd last looked at it at one o'clock, and he tried to convince himself that in a short while they'd be finished with this business. Except, of course, that he knew he'd never be free of it now. Ruin awaited him, nothing else. Ruin for the remainder of his short life.

From the dark doorway, Christopher could see into the glass-walled lobby of Danny's building across the street. The nightman was plainly visible, sitting on a leather bench, reading a newspaper. If only he'd fall asleep or go make his rounds! But as long as Danny didn't let the nightman near the urn and rolled it out the front door himself (Thank God it wasn't real terra cotta or it'd weigh a ton!), Christopher surmised he'd be able to get the car door open and help Danny load without being seen.

Danny. Such flaming talent, such an unerring eye, such energy, Christopher mused, remembering the young Danny in those first weeks at his shop. And the questions he'd asked! Why, why, why!

"Why did you price this sofa lower than this bergère?"

"How do you decorate a room? What do you do first?"

"Why don't you advertise?"

Later, when he'd return from buying trips, he'd find that Danny had turned the entire shop around, moving furniture back upstairs, creating space for several coordinated homelike mini-settings.

"Now the customer can see how the pieces would look in a room, a room decorated by experts like us!"

Christopher had to laugh when he noticed that on a French writing desk Danny had placed a prop of a client's checkbook, with a check already made out to Christopher Beene Antiques & Design for the vast sum of five hundred thousand dollars.

"Ah, Danny!" Christopher groaned, remembering everything. He sent Danny to night school, he sent Danny to Haiti, he sent him on buying trips. He even dressed him, buying Danny a winter coat the first year, and entire outfits the second year. And why not? he asked himself. Danny was the hardest-working, most eager, talented, ebullient, enthusiastic young man ever to come into his life. Until now, Danny's very presence filled him with pride. He'd been so proud of Danny . . . until now.

Christopher looked across the street into the glass-walled lobby. He saw Danny rolling the urn out the door, and sighed bitterly.

My poor boy, he thought. *My poor, hungry, hungry boy.*

With the front seats rolled all the way forward, the back of the capacious Rolls snugly accommodated the upright urn. Of course, Christopher could see nothing in his rearview mirror, but he drove slowly uptown to his shop on Madison Avenue while Danny, scrunched up against the dashboard, drummed nervously on his folded knees.

As soon as they pulled into Christopher's custom-designed private garage and loading platform, Danny jumped out and wheeled a flatbed dolly over to the car. Together, the two men pushed and tugged, but the urn wouldn't budge. They switched places; Christopher pushed while Danny tugged from the open car door on the other side.

"Pull harder," Christopher commanded weakly, and leaned against the car for a rest.

Danny paused, too. "If it went in, it should come out, but it's not worth the effort. You go up and rest. I'm going to lift Edgar out down here." He spoke to Christopher over the roof of the car.

"I'll help you. I just need a minute."

"It's all right. I can do it. Go upstairs."

"You can't fit both Edgar and the urn on the dolly. I'll carry the urn. It's light."

The urn! If it weren't for Christopher, Danny would've left the empty urn in the car, another glaring clue. *What else have I forgotten,* he wondered wildly. *What else?*

When Edgar Garson had been rolled up inside the blanket and placed gently on the dolly, Danny was able to pull the urn easily from the car. He carried it over to Christopher's side and handed it to his exhausted friend.

"Don't forget Edgar's clothes," Christopher reminded him, pointing to the bundle Danny had forgotten. "What would you do without me?"

"Probably kill myself."

At that, Christopher laughed heartily. "Not you. True despair is something about which you know nothing."

Danny shook his head and said quietly, "I learned all about it tonight." Then he placed an arm around Christopher's bony shoulder. "Let's go up, my friend."

Edgar Garson lay peacefully where they'd laid him out on Christopher's silk voile-draped four-poster bed. Half of the urn burned acridly in the fireplace opposite, and half in the living-room fireplace. Garson's clothes were scattered randomly on Christopher's rare Savonnerie carpet and his pocket accessories now sat on a marble-topped French bedside table.

Christopher called directions to Danny from his daybed, conserving his strength for the final and loneliest siege that was yet to come.

"What did you drink? Chardonnay? All right, open a bottle of that French burgundy and pour some down the toilet."

Danny did as he was told.

"Wipe off your fingerprints and then hand the bottle to me."

Christopher grasped the bottle with two hands and placed it on the glass-topped column relic that served as a coffee table.

"Open the windows and throw some of those pine branches on the fires. And then put Edgar's fingers on a wine glass."

"I don't want to touch him again."

"Do it."

Tending the fire with his back to Christopher, Danny spoke with awe. "How can you think with such precision? I'm a walking zombie."

"We're almost finished."

"You still have that phone call to make."

"After you leave," Christopher told him, and searched the room for another task to assign Danny to keep him a little while longer.

"We have to get rid of the blanket."

"I'll dump it outside." Danny sighed. "Some lucky scavenger is in for the find of his life."

Then there was nothing else for Danny to do, no reason for him to stay any longer. It was important, in fact, that he leave so that Christopher could make his call. But he lingered, hoping Christopher would think of one more detail for him to attend to. But there was nothing else to be done.

The two men looked at each other, and slowly Christopher rose and held out his arms. They embraced tearfully, patting each other's back for comfort. When finally they pulled apart, Danny thought of one last thing he wanted to say.

"You are the father I always wanted."

"And you, Daniel Dannenberg," said Christopher, "have always been my son."

"Oh, God, how can I let you do this?"

"Haven't I always taken care of you? Let me, this one last time."

"But how can I ever—"

Christopher silenced him with his hand. "You're my darling boy, my Danny boy. You always have been. You always will be."

"Oh, Christopher. I love you!"

"Thank you. Thank you for letting me hear it. Thank you for being my darling boy."

And then, for Christopher—and for himself, too— Danny said it one last time. "I love you."

The phone call, made as soon as Danny left, wasn't as difficult as Christopher had anticipated. He'd rehearsed in his mind so many times what he would say to the police that he recited his announcement flawlessly.

Then there was nothing to do but sit back and await the police, the ambulance, the reporters and photographers . . . and the ruin.

He sunk deeper into the cushions and closed his eyes. Several of his most illustrious clients paraded by, and the grand homes he'd done for them, the rare pieces he'd sold to them. Inlaid bureaus and hand-painted screens floated by, and teardrop chandeliers that had once hung in Viennese palaces. The great antiques merchants of Europe, colleagues all, shook his hand, and the president of the United States gave him a bear hug.

"My name!" he cried out as they faded away. *My name*, he might have said again, but the doorbell rang and he could keep his eyes closed no longer.

18

Theo woke up, as usual, thinking of Dell. He had massive projects on his desk, work that could keep him busy round the clock for the next three years, but what he thought of before he even opened his eyes was Dell's ears. Pink ears. Delicate and translucent. And her belly, which he had never seen. Yet he saw it in his mind, her belly as some early temple, a flat, smooth plane punctuated by a deep, dark navel and a pelvic post on either side. But was the skin white and ornamented with a frieze of freckles like her face and arms, or pink and unmottled like her ears? Today, finally, he'd know. Today . . .

He looked down at his erection, and immediately it withered.

Don't! he told it, but it defied him once again.

You must be out of your mind, he told himself. *A few pathetic erections and you think you're ready.* What would he tell her, what would he do when he shrivelled up right before her? What would *she* do? Pity him, yes. Because she was kind. If she weren't kind, she'd look at him with disgust.

Unmindful of Erica lying beside him, he decided to phone Dell and call the whole thing off. He could say, "When I called you last night, I didn't know my clients were already on a plane to New York. Now it's too late to cancel today's meeting. I'm terribly sorry."

He could call her from any one of the other nine phones in the cliffside house overlooking the Hudson River; Erica, a heavy sleeper, would never know. With the covers thrown back, his head off the pillow, he was seconds from padding down to the first-floor phone in the kitchen when he reversed his thinking.

Sinking back, he asked himself, *What makes you think*

she'll let you take her to bed? Just because he'd booked a room in the hotel? She didn't know that. She expected lunch, nothing more. No, she expected more. She told him on the phone last night, she'd been waiting, too. For him.

And once she was in his arms, once he could touch her, taste her . . .

He ached with wanting to get his nose into the folds and pits of her, to become so familiar with her body's odors he'd be able to identify them with his eyes closed. His fingers twitched at the thought of touching the wiry hair of her pubis. Was her bush red? Gold? Black? He watched himself stiffening and thickening again at the thought of stroking her secret lips. Listening, he could almost hear the squishing sound they made. Then, then he'd be ready.

Grinning down at his brand new erection, he stroked it and said out loud, but very softly, "That's two, you big fucker. You're ready."

It was all he had to hinge his hope on. That, and the fact that only Dell could spark these feeble surges of life. It no longer mattered that he might expose his secret deadness to her, even though the fear of just that had haunted him for over two years. It no longer mattered because he no longer believed he would fail. Last night he had come in his own hands. This morning he awoke to an erection while thinking, dreaming of Dell. And now, another. Dell and his cock were already inextricably linked. All he had to do was think of her and his cock got hard. It had been that way ever since he met her, but lately, he often stayed hard. And last night, he came.

He was ready. He was almost sure of it. Today he would have her. Today he would know, once and for all. Was he a dead man, or could he be brought back to life?

Cara! Forgive me!

Morning, for Dell, came slowly, after an entirely sleepless night. The night was like a pie of fear; every couple of hours she polished off another portion of anxiety, then moved on to the next wedge, nibbling her way through the night.

An hour before dawn she was chewing on doubts about

her lingerie. It was brand new, but bought not for today—when would there've been time? Theo had phoned, after all, at nine o'clock last night. No, the lingerie was bought three weeks ago and still lay carefully folded between layers of its original tissue in her drawer. Never worn. Waiting in silky suspension, perhaps for just this rendezvous, to be christened. Or could she have meant it for Danny, to entice him on some rare night when he was home? Doubtful, she concluded. She had no effect on him anymore.

No, she bought the lingerie on impulse, in a sudden spasm of euphoria. She had a weakness for lingerie, for gowns of satin and tap pants lined in imported lace, for robes that belted silkily over the body and bras delicious as beribboned cupcakes. All this she saw displayed in the window of the tiny, lacey shop and couldn't resist going in. But by warning the saleswoman, "I'm really only looking," she hoped to prevent any more impulsive, lavish, out-of-control spending. And she already owned more nightgowns than she could wear in a month! But when her fingers touched the creaminess of the silk satin, they wouldn't let it go. She had to have it! It didn't matter that it wasn't on sale—its exorbitant price added to its allure. When she was a girl she slept in pajamas so worn they tore each time she put them on. Now she bought this satin lingerie because she could. Because it was extravagant and utterly impractical, she had no need of it.

Except of course, that now she did. The problem was that it was powder pink! Shouldn't she wear black? Or red? What did women wear to a rendezvous? She could call Jackie; she would know. But she didn't want to hear Jackie's suppressed glee. "Aha! An affair. So the perfect couple's having trouble after all."

Perhaps she should wear no undergarments at all. Nothing. Upon arrival, she could register and then go directly up to the room she'd secretly reserved at ten-fifteen last night, using her own credit card and her own name. Then, according to the plan in her head, she could phone down to Theo waiting for her in the hotel restaurant and ask him to come up. And flash her nakedness immediately.

No, she decided. Too brazen. Then she almost laughed

at herself. Too brazen? What do you call renting your own hotel room in your own name?

With dawn came the certainty that her eyes would be puffy as a frog's after her sleepless night. In the bathroom were gels and creams and herbal pads that promised instant repair, but would do no good, she knew. Once her eyelids puffed, they stayed swollen and red for the entire day and eye makeup only made the edematous condition worse. But she couldn't go without eye makeup. She'd sooner not go at all! Indispensable as her house keys, eye makeup unlocked the color, emphasized the catlike shape of her eyes, and darkened her lashes. Overall, it improved her face drastically, making her appear, she conceded, somewhat pretty. Without it, she felt dull and impossibly plain.

Lipstick, when she was a little girl, was the first and most coveted cosmetic in the feminine arsenal. In those early years, she loved blotting her lips on a tissue and leaving behind a perfect impression of her bright red, wide-open mouth. Now, she often went bare-lipped, but never, ever bare-eyed. She wore eye makeup everywhere, except to exercise class. But even then, her lashes were coated with mascara, for she rarely removed it. Only when her lashes were stubby and stiff as a toothbrush, and flecks threatened to fall in her eyes, did she cream it all off and begin again.

Cosmetics. She could stand for hours at those mirrored counters lined with jars and vials, sniffing, dabbing, daubing, inhaling the promise, believing the pledge rolled up inside every gold metal tube. She powdered herself with the dust of an old, familiar demand: *Improve! You can do better. Just try harder. And use our revolutionary formula to cover up your imperfections and become flawless instantly.* Eagerly, she obeyed, toting home hope in a new shade of hunter green, rubbing in camouflage from an enamel compact.

Jackie Knight, who made her living preaching sermons according to the beautician's gospel, was always at Dell to switch to sable-brown mascara, bronze blusher, blue mud facials. Dell did, but still, perfection eluded her.

"Don't you think my eyes stand out more with black mascara?"

"Black is too harsh for you. Stay with the brown."

"I like your new haircut. You look so great in short hair. I could never wear mine that short."

"But you could go shorter than you're wearing it."

"That's the problem. How much shorter?"

"One and a half inches. No more. No less."

Together, they examined each other minutely, and announced each improvement they noted, proof not only that they cared, but that they were approaching ever closer that flawless state just to the right of their reach.

Yet, for all her faith in face paint, in the gray light of dawn, Dell actually now considered going to Theo with a clean-scrubbed face. Bare even of mascara. Then she grimaced. It wasn't that the thought of baring her face to Theo was so unpleasant; she actually yearned to bare all of herself to him—all the fear, all the old shame. And yearned to believe that Theo just might be entranced enough to accept her, all of her. To accept her with such infinite grace that she wouldn't have to hide anymore. But the paradox was that to enchant him she'd need makeup, and plenty of it.

She looked at the silver framed clock on the pistachio-green skirted table: 7:01. Danny moaned in his sleep beside her. She'd heard him stumble in at four? Five? It didn't matter. Preferable, really. That way they didn't have to argue about it. Feigning sleep was easier. These days, more often than not, she slept through all her encounters with Danny. Or pretended to.

But she didn't want to think about Danny now. She didn't want to wonder where he'd been until four or five in the morning—and with whom. No explanation he offered had ever satisfied her, and no amount of anxiety or tears had ever abated his random nocturnal disappearances. Oriental rug merchant, indeed! They both knew his excuses were absurdly flimsy. It was insulting that he didn't even bother to lie effectively. Yet what right had she to demand the truth?

But thinking of Theo produced no sense of relief; in fact, it actually increased her anxiety. Marriage, she realized, even the most miserable marriage, was easier to endure than adultery. Somehow she'd survived three and a half years of marriage; she didn't think she could endure five more hours waiting for her affair with Theo to begin.

Noon, however, finally came to them both. Later, they would laugh, each accusing the other of being the most nervous. But the truth was that they both arrived five minutes early, each with identical anxiety and identical missions. And identical empty black nylon overnight bags.

He stepped up behind her at the hotel desk and heard her say, "I reserved a room. My name is Mrs. Dannenberg."

He stepped to the far end of the counter while she filled out the registration form. When the clerk finally looked at him, Theo bellowed, "And *I* reserved a room. My name is Glass."

She neither gasped nor turned to look at him, but he saw her drop her pen when she heard his voice. A slow blush crept up her neck to her cheeks, but she didn't falter when she asked the clerk, "Was that room 448?"

"Yes, Ma'am. Room 448. The number's right here, on your key. And yours, sir," the clerk said, moving down the counter to Theo, "is 442. If you wouldn't mind sharing a bellhop, I can send you both up right now."

Standing directly behind her in the elevator, Theo whispered, "I see you thought of everything. Well, which shall it be—your place or mine?"

"Yours," she whispered back. "I'm going to get a refund later."

Though all he could see was the back of her flaming neck, he knew she was smiling. But by the time she got to his room, she was tense again. She stood miserably in the middle of the room with her gloves and fur coat on, and didn't see how she'd ever have the nerve to take them off. That he too had reserved a room on his credit card, and therefore also had to use his real name, did little to ease her discomfort. Getting caught was the least of her fears at the moment. At the moment, taking her coat off was perhaps her greatest terror.

"I'm ordering lunch," Theo told her, reaching for the phone.

"Oh. I'm not awfully hungry."

Theo put the phone down.

"But a drink might be nice."

Theo picked up the phone again. "Champagne?"

Dell thought of the money they'd wasted on the extra

room. She knew she probably couldn't get a refund, but she said nothing about it. "Champagne would be lovely."

As Theo ordered, he motioned for her to take off her coat. She shook her head no. A look of surprise clouded his face.

"I'd like you to do it," she told him as soon as he hung up. It's what she'd planned to say but it sounded false, like the simulated seduction of a porno movie. Nevertheless, she felt she had no choice. She had to go through with it now, so she held her arms straight out like a scarecrow, but she couldn't look at him.

As Theo stepped toward her, he told himself to lock the door, but then remembered he'd have to unlock it again in a few minutes when the champagne arrived. He wondered if the room was too chilly, too light, too dark, too quiet, too musty, too obvious. He tried to calculate the square footage of the room, the height of the ceiling, the number of rooms in the hotel, the number of steps it would take to reach her, but he lost count of everything. He couldn't look at her either.

Then he was there, in front of her, and ever so carefully he undid the hooks of her silky pecan mink. Staring into the nut-colored fur, he had a sudden vision of *her* fur. He saw it. Pecan. This exact shade. He was sure of it. Grazing the fur with his fingers and wrists, he added to himself, *And this tactile.* If just touching her coat felt this good, touching *her* fur was going to be ecstasy.

Undone, the coat still hung closed over her body, even with her arms out like sticks. But she dropped her arms as soon as he gripped the lapels and lifted the coat up and back over her shoulders. It slid right to the floor.

Skin and pink satin. Bare arms and shoulders. He was staring at white breasts bursting out of pink satin. Then a bare midriff. Something hanging down from the bra. A forgotten sales ticket? Then pink satin again, tight over her waist and belly, loose and swingy at the top of her thighs. Lace.

He was standing so close to her he could hardly see her legs. Backing away, he took all of her in. When his eyes climbed back up to her face, he could see that her cheeks were flaming.

He flicked the hanging sales ticket. "New underwear?"

Twisting around, she saw what he was holding and tried to grab it, but he wouldn't let go.

"Oh, my!" he said in mock horror, flagrantly examining the price printed on the ticket. "You really spent all that for this tiny little thing?" He ran his finger along the flesh above the bra's lace. "And a little bare for a midday lunch date, don't you think?"

She broke away and collapsed, prone, on the bed, burying her face in the pillow. "I knew it. Oh, God, I'm so embarrassed. I knew I should've worn my little black dress. I've never done anything like this in my life. I know you're only teasing me, but you're right. How could I have been so . . . shameless!"

He wanted to smile at her discomfort and tell her how lucky she was. If by shameless she meant shame-free, then she was a truly rare spirit. He himself never felt free of shame. True, she had shocked him a tiny bit, but that was only because he was so afraid of himself, while she was so brave. He admired her bravery. He admired her buttocks. The sight of them, two balloons of pink satin, made him wince with desire. His fingers ached to get at her. *Slowly*, he reminded himself. Theo, don't blow this.

He joined her on the bed and stroked her back. "Are you really embarrassed?"

"Mm-hmm," she mumbled into the pillow.

"Well, as far as I'm concerned, you have my vote for best-dressed woman of the year."

She laughed and turned over and was about to try to choke him but the knock on the door stopped her. With no robe to cover her, she jumped from the bed and rushed to the bathroom in another fit of modesty.

Except that it wasn't the bathroom door she opened.

"I knew it the minute I heard the glasses tinkling on the tray, even before I saw his big, yellow eyes," she told Theo later, when the champagne was half finished and the pink satin had been flung across the room. "But by then it was too late."

"You still didn't have to let him in just because the door was half open," he teased. "You didn't have to stand there like a shameless hussy and say, 'Right this way.'"

"I was just trying to make the best of a difficult situation."

"Shameless hussy."

He had his mouth on her belly at last. Her belly was a field of freckles scattered like wildflowers over white skin. Sniffing, he could detect a faint, moist scent. Like morning. All the long mornings he'd spent wanting her.

They were naked on the bed, but still bantering. Suspended between awkwardness and passion, they joked their way through the chasm.

"Showing up in your underwear, parading in front of the bellhop. I never knew you were such a—"

She wouldn't let him finish. Her mouth was on his and her hands were in his armpits, pinching, tickling.

"Ow!" he cried out, aware of her thighs brushing against his erection. From the moment he unhooked the first clasp of her coat, he'd grown hard. Discovering her bare flesh in all that pink satin underneath shocked him into momentary softness again, even as he admired her audacity. But now, if anything, he was harder than ever. A selfish hunger made him want to ram it into her, just take her, just come, come for once, come for all those years without it. If he didn't take it now, he might lose it forever.

He pulled her on top of him, but when he saw her full breasts swinging above his face, he knew there was more of her he had to explore before he climbed inside her. Once he was in her, he'd come, and it would be over. He knew he'd explode the minute he penetrated her the first time. Already, he was bursting.

To Dell, his rapture was empowering. Even his nervousness at the beginning, when he could hardly look at her, was empowering. His fear gave her strength.

And then, when it seemed he couldn't stop looking at her, that gave her strength, too. But she held him off with games and jokes, which he played agreeably while aching for her. She knew that. He ached for her. And knowing it made her feel breathtakingly powerful. She could do nothing wrong; his desire for her was absolute.

Late that morning, it had come to her. After her sleepless night of self-doubt, it came to her, suddenly, that Theo wanted her as much as she wanted him. Knowing that, remembering it distinctly now from all the accumulated adoring and furtive glances he'd turned on her, all that he'd said and not said, she wondered how she could have tortured herself an entire night. The truth was, she now knew, she could come to him in smelly sweat-pants, with a face bare or painted like a clown's, and he'd still desire her.

Nevertheless, she took no chances. Knowing that he desired her, she dressed to entice him even more. Which was how she decided upon the bare lingerie.

Now, seeing him caressing her with his eyes as his hands caressed her body, she wanted more. More of him wanting her. She couldn't get enough of his wanting her.

Poised above him, she arched her back, which pressed her wiry mons veneris into his belly. When he groaned with pleasure, she slid down a little, until she was sitting directly above him, as he reached, stiffly and purple-veined, toward her.

In his hands, her breasts came alive, just as they had come alive, for a time, with Danny. Peeking out like the tiny tongues of two newborns, her nipples suddenly re-appeared after more than a year. In his hands, all of her had come alive, yet she wanted more of his hands, more. But she could feel him at the front door of her pelvis, pleading for entry.

"Please, oh, please, Dell." His hands were on her hips, urging her down into him.

She answered by lifting herself slightly higher off him.

"Oh God, please."

"Soon," she whispered, her eyes narrowing to slits.

There wasn't much will left in her to refuse. Holding herself above him so that only the crown of him touched her, her legs trembled with tension. Still, she resisted. His wanting her gave her the steel to resist.

She had never been wanted like this, not by anyone. He was almost mute with desire, waiting for her with excruciating, precarious patience. She moved slowly so as not to set him off, sinuously so as to arouse him even more.

"How soon?"

It didn't seem possible that his ardor could grow, yet she coaxed more heat from him, more. And exulted in his every shiver and sigh. To see him respond with such intensity inspired in her a kind of erotic creativity her body had never known.

"First tell me, is this what you want to do to me?"

Her tongue, red and erect, pushed out of her mouth thickly.

"Yes," he groaned. "Yes."

She found his mouth and forced her tongue in and out of it.

"This, too?"

Narrowed to a wet, tight chamber, his mouth received her like a woman, sucking her tongue into him, reluctant to let her pull out. He'd kissed off every trace of her pink lipstick and her skin looked raw, but he thought she'd never looked more beautiful. It was her eyes. Like the closed slats of a window blind, they let through one perfectly bright blue sliver of light. And of course, her magical tongue.

Abruptly, she sat all the way up. She towered above him, a priestess, a goddess, an ordinary woman who could make him laugh. She was master of his pleasure as well as her own.

"And this?" she asked, a finger buried inside her. Her imagination was an exact reflection of his desires.

He blinked in answer. For some time he hadn't been able to speak at all. Then, suddenly, neither could she.

When a tiny "Ooh! puffed from her lips, it wasn't so much a word as a sound. She made the sound again. And again, tormenting him into an unbearable frenzy. He had to have her. Now.

She felt him lifting her off him, turning her onto her back. No! she wanted to cry. There was more she wanted to summon from him, more her body needed to tell him. But as she felt him entering her, she heard herself cry out, "Yes. Oh, yes!"

She was high up, out on the ledge of a cliff. Without realizing it, she'd been climbing, climbing, until now she'd arrived. Momentarily, she was surprised to find herself there so soon. Then, nothing else mattered. She was there and she was about to fall off. She tried to tell him.

"I'm about to . . . ab . . . out—"

She wailed, dry-eyed, as she fell, wave after wave, into a steaming sea. From somewhere not far off she heard him following her, heard him sobbing, "Oh, Dell. Oh, God. Forgive me!"

And felt him, felt him inside her pulsing as he plunged

down into the same boiling deep. She clung to him, and he to her, as they dove, one after the other, like skinny-dippers in midair. Where they splashed down, rings of sensation radiated out in ever-widening bands. And that was where they lay, encoiled: in the center of that swirling eddy, even long after it had stilled and they were able to sleep, locked together, for a short while.

He awoke wanting to talk, to touch. His voice, like the tips of his fingers, whispered over her.

"I knew it would be like this with you. I knew it, and yet, I never expected this. Not this."

She thought of Danny, of awaking next to him, energetic and unreflective no matter how little sleep he'd had. Bounding out of bed, flicking on the lights, the news, the coffee, Danny carried her headlong into the glare of morning. With Theo, awaking was gradual, like dawn's imperceptible spread. She too had always known what it would be like, and she too was stunned that the reality could be so much larger than her fantasy. She was sure she could go on talking about it for hours.

"I know. Not like this," she agreed. "But say it again. Then tell me everything. Tell me . . . a secret."

He laughed out loud and hugged her tighter, but then grew serious.

"A secret?"

"Mmm."

"It's true I've wanted this . . . with you for a long time . . . but I really didn't know if I'd be able to . . . do it. To make love to you."

"Why not?"

He took a deep breath, yearning for a forbidden cigarette, and said, "I've been . . . impotent."

"You could have fooled me."

He smiled distractedly. "It was pretty real, for over three years."

"Three years," she repeated with hushed astonishment. "That's a very long time." Suddenly she remembered the uncommon sadness she saw in his brilliant blue eyes the first time she met him. That freezing day in February at the house in Southampton. She thought his tragedy had caused it. Perhaps his tragedy had caused this, too.

"You get used to it. Or you tell yourself you do."

"And your . . . wife?" As soon as she said it, she was sorry. Now Theo's wife was a presence, interrupting them again, entering the room. Even if Dell couldn't remember her name. "Was she . . . understanding?"

"I suppose so," Theo sighed. "In the beginning she hardly noticed. Neither did I, to tell you the truth. We were doing most of our mourning at night then, living our lives in the day. Maybe we still are."

"Mourning?" So the tragedy caused it.

He looked at her, hesitated, and looked away. "I thought you knew."

"I did, but . . . can you talk about it?"

He shrugged. "We had a daughter. Cara. She died."

She waited and after a while he continued, in a flat voice. "Two months. One night she just stopped breathing. It was a holiday weekend. Labor Day."

Labor Day! *Danny and I were getting married,* she realized.

"She was blue when Erica and I went to her. We had no idea. We stood by her cradle. We thought we were watching her sleep. It was all over before we had our coats on to race her to the hospital. Her death, like her life, was over in a flash." He snapped his fingers to illustrate what he meant, and remembered that all that long night and early morning at the hospital he kept snapping his fingers because the sound of that quick, dull thwick, more accurately than words, gave expression to death's incomprehensible swiftness.

It was then, he remembered, that Erica had made him promise he'd never leave her. Never.

He was lost in remembrance, and Dell held him carefully. That she lay no further burden upon him, she touched him with the delicacy of a fluttering eyelash. *I was marrying while his daughter was dying,* she thought. It was a weekend that changed them both forever. Now, he had lost his only child, and she was losing her husband.

Suddenly, she heard Theo laugh, but it was a laugh she'd never heard before, entirely devoid of mirth. He looked at her and said, "They call it 'crib death.' That's the nonmedical term. But you see, Cara slept in a cradle, so I kept arguing with the doctors, 'How can it be crib death if she slept in a cradle?' They said I was resisting accepting it. I still can't accept it, Dell. I don't know how.''

I have no right, he almost added.

Even now, he still had no right. It wasn't just his promise to Erica, the way she'd laid her life in his hands to become his responsibility. It was Cara. While she lay dead, what right had he to go on with his life, to search for happiness? None. Today, atonement had been suspended. *Cara, forgive me!* But he really couldn't permit this again . . . except that today was not yet over . . . and Dell was caressing him so gently and whispering into the down of his neck . . . and he felt her breath, like afternoon sun, warming his skin.

Her words were meant to console him, he knew, but he didn't want to be comforted. Today he'd come alive. He wanted it again. He wanted more of today, and more of her, and more of what he'd most forbidden in himself. *Just give me today.*

Dell looked at him in disbelief when he began to nuzzle her. ''Theo, are you sure?''

''It's up to him.'' He placed her hand where he wanted it. ''What does he say?''

''He says it's urgent.''

''It is urgent. There's so much lost time to make up for.''

''Not in one day.''

He wouldn't, he couldn't tell her this was all the time they had. He said, ''We could make a start.''

''Okay,'' she said, laughing. ''So, let's get the show on the road.''

He kissed her eager mouth and abruptly they ceased all talking for a while.

The room was dark when Theo reached for his watch on the night table. She watched him study the clock face.

It's over, she thought. Over so soon.

But he returned his watch to the table and turned to her. ''Let's order up some dinner. Unless . . . you have to get home?''

She shook her head.

''Good. Let's squeeze every last minute out of this day.''

It sounded to her as if this one day was all he expected, or wanted. Why else would he want to cram everything into it? But she didn't ask because she was afraid of the answer.

So, they ordered a tumbler of icy vodka, cold sandwiches of paper-thin roast beef on black bread with fat slices of onion and drippy tomatoes, grainy mustard and a sprinkling of capers, money-green and tart. They ordered asparagus thin as pencils and fried shoestring potatoes. And fresh figs and coffee and custard pastries. And snifters of cognac.

They ate in bed, feeding each other tastes from their identical plates, licking each other clean with their tongues. They finished everything. And only once did Dell pause to wonder, *Will I fit into my clothes tomorrow*?

But the cognac was sending warm, mellow messages to her brain. It was impossible to feel fearful when the cognac was crooning to her, "It's okay." Perhaps it wasn't the liqueur. Perhaps it was she—and she alone—who was telling herself, "It's okay. Everything's going to be all right." Reassuring herself, for the first time, that she needn't panic because she'd eaten heartily one night. "It's okay." And it was. She was not afraid. For the first time, she felt absolutely normal.

Tipsily she rose from the bed and stretched.

"Oh, God, Dell." Theo groaned, watching her. "You're utterly majestic. Yes, that's the word. Majestic."

Majestic! She drew herself up to her full, lofty height and vamped for him like a queen. "Her majesty requires a bath." It wasn't necessary to say more; she knew he'd follow her into the bathroom. And follow forever after, she prayed.

Giddily, they bathed in bubbled lavender water, locking knees, playing baby kissing games with their toes. They spent long, silent minutes simply staring, smiling, memorizing moles, colors, contours.

His voice, when he finally interrupted their silence, floated to her on a bath bubble, weightless and iridescent. "Tell me."

She didn't have to ask; she knew. And she wanted to tell him now. She wasn't afraid.

"Mine is a happy secret." She knew he was staring at her lips and she pursed them before continuing. "At least, it suddenly seems happy. And real. Until now, I hardly let myself think of it. But suddenly, I can actually see it. I had no idea of how much I've wanted it."

"Tell me," he said again, just as softly. "What is it you want?"

"My own design firm. To start my own business in my own space, with my own clients, my own ideas . . . and my own dreams."

"But why? I thought D & D was the hottest team in town. Why would you give that up?"

He didn't understand. She thought he'd get it instantly, but when he didn't, she felt herself begin to close up, constrict. Was she crazy? she wondered. Why did she tell him? It was wildly impulsive. She hadn't thought it through. So how could she explain it to him? She couldn't.

"Next time," she said, begging with her eyes. "Next time we're together, I'll tell you more." Then she tried to joke, "To be continued . . . next time."

But he seemed to wince whenever she said next time. And though he rose and lifted her with him and draped them both in a large bath towel and said, "I don't want this to end," he wouldn't—couldn't—look at her.

She wanted to say, "Then don't let it end," but she waited. She waited as they dressed and groomed and finally pulled on their coats. The pain, she noticed, had returned to his eyes. She waited as they said silent good-byes under the hotel canopy, blinking back paragraphs of unfinished thoughts.

They hailed separate taxis. Dell climbed in and looked at him one last time.

He touched her flaming hair through the open window.

"If only . . ." he began, and stopped himself. Then he sighed and said, "Dell, don't wait for me. I can't promise I'll ever be free. Don't . . . wait."

But she could not do otherwise. And although she cursed him, damned him in the backseat of the cab all the way home, she wept with emptiness, already missing him. She would not, however, give him up. Not now.

Not yet. Not so soon after finding him again. No, she would wait. And meanwhile, she would keep trying, just a little harder, a little longer, to be better, to be more perfect. That was where love was hiding.

19

Dell heard the sound of the television in the bedroom as soon as she entered the apartment, and her heart sank. Danny was home. Home watching television. How long, she wondered, had she been waiting for just this—to arrive home and find her husband curled up in domestic tranquility, waiting for her? Now, here he was at last . . . and she didn't want him here. She'd hoped to be alone to wail, to tear off her pink silk—

She remembered as soon as she pulled off her fur and hung it in the closet. There was no robe in the guest bathroom, no old shirt hanging in the coat closet. Nothing to cover her pink silk lingerie, her damning almost-nakedness. She had no choice, and perhaps that was best, she decided. Danny would look up from the bed and ask, "What's this?" and she'd have to tell him. *I will. I'll tell him. All of it. For once, the truth. And if he's repulsed by it, I've lost nothing, for he's no longer mine, anyway.* He was someone's beloved, for sure, but not Dell's. Nor was Theo. So she'd have no one and she'd be alone again, like always. But at least they'd be living honestly at last, and might even recover some shred of their self-respect. Yes, she'd tell him . . . everything.

But Danny had his finger to his lips to hush her as she entered the peach bedroom. Newspapers were spread across the peach quilt and the television volume was turned up high. She stood at the doorway and waited, but Danny never even noticed! He was listening to a report on the eleven o'clock news about someone who died at the apartment of—

". . . Christopher Beene, noted art historian, antiquarian, and design consultant who, three and one-half years ago, directed the interior renovation of the president and first lady's White house residential quarters.

"A private funeral service for Edgar Garson will be held tomorrow at an undisclosed chapel, according to a family spokesman."

Christopher Beene! Edgar Garson! Dell sat down on the edge of the bed.

"What happened?"

Danny flicked off the TV with his remote button and pulled the covers up under his chin. He hadn't yet looked at her, but even if he had, it wouldn't have mattered to Dell now, for in the wake of this terrible news she'd all but forgotten her own nakedness and the announcement she'd intended to make.

"Was that . . . your . . . Christopher Beene? And our Edgar Garson?" She glanced at the headlines on the bed. They informed her of the scandal in five or six words of screaming type, but still she asked again, "What happened?"

"Edgar Garson's dead, apparently of a heart attack. He was found in Christopher's bed," Danny said dully, staring at the blank television screen. "Poor Christopher. God help him."

"Poor Christopher!" Dell exploded. "That . . . pig! I thought he didn't take lovers anymore. How utterly irresponsible. He could've infected Edgar. I bet he never even told Edgar he was sick."

To Dell's utter amazement, Danny screamed on the top of his lungs, "Don't you dare! Don't you ever dare call Christopher irresponsible, do you hear me? Because you don't know, you just don't know what you're talking about! He's fabulously, outstandingly responsible, okay?" Then he began to sob. Dell patted his hand, wondering idly if he would have as many tears if he ever lost her. The thought made her begin to weep, too. Now Danny patted her hand, mistaking her tears as grief for Christopher Beene.

"Oh, it's so terribly unfair! You do see that now don't you, Dell, darling?" He reached over to the bedtable and pulled tissues for them both. "To drag poor Christopher's name through the mud like this when he didn't do *anything*. Just because his clients are celebrities and . . . and presidents! Edgar Garson died of a sudden heart attack last night. Christopher didn't infect him. Poor Edgar just . . . died, that's all. Isn't it terribly, horribly sad, Dell, darling? Isn't it?''

Yes, yes, she nodded, wanting to agree, wanting to cry for the sadness of it all, for Danny's loss, for poor Edgar's sudden death . . . and for Christopher Beene. But her mind kept going back to yesterday, to Wednesday night, to the strange event that ended with Edgar dead in Christopher's bed. Once Danny had told her Christopher hadn't taken a lover in years, and Dell not only respected that decision but also felt a great wave of tenderness and sympathy for Christopher. It was the first time she ever felt sympathy for Christopher, which was why she remembered it. So why did he take Edgar Garson into his bed last night? Why would he risk infecting Edgar now—for surely he didn't know Edgar would have a sudden heart attack? It didn't make any sense.

But Danny had called her darling. Twice. She couldn't remember the last time Danny had used the word. Or the last time he'd cried. Could it've been the night that now seemed so long ago, the night they first fell in love? Now, here were his tears again, and his dark, silky head in her lap. Like a darling, innocent boy he peeked up at her and asked, ''Still love me?''

''Do you still love *me?*'' she asked in tearful answer and, as always, waited breathless for his yes. Yes, and her life could begin again. Always, it had been this way. But what was she waiting for tonight? Another yes, yes, kiss, kiss? No, tonight she was waiting for the truth. The truth at last.

Their eyes locked, each waiting for the other to speak. Then, when they both might have spoken at once, the phone rang, leaving their identical questions, like premature twins, stillborn in the night.

It was Tina Garson.

''I know it's late . . . and that by now, you've heard.'' Her voice quavered as she struggled for control over her shame. ''I suppose the whole world's heard . . . by now.'' There was resignation in her voice now, too, but most of all, there was a certain dignity, and Dell had never admired Tina Garson more.

''I only just heard about . . . Edgar. I've been . . . away all day. Tina, I'm so terribly sorry.''

At the corners of her vision Dell could see Danny waving his hands, shaking his head no. For the time being, she ignored him.

"Yes, it's very sad, very painful," Tina agreed. "But I'm calling to ask a favor."

"Anything," Dell said earnestly, wishing she could reach through the phone and put her arms around Tina's narrow shoulders and comfort her. "Anything at all."

Danny was still shaking his head no, more vehemently now, and although she was beginning to get his meaning, she was also beginning to hate him.

"There'll be a small, private funeral tomorrow. Very small—I think you can understand why. But I'd appreciate you and Danny being there. It'd mean a lot to me—under the circumstances."

"Of course, Tina. What time is the funeral?" Dell asked gently, but at that, Danny turned almost purple, coughing and choking while telling her in sign language. "No! Tell her I can't go. Tell her I'm sick."

"Ten-thirty."

"Uh, of course I'll be there," Dell agreed, hesitating to glare at Danny. "But I'm afraid Danny's sick in bed with the flu. I doubt if he'll be able to make it."

Danny collapsed back on the pillows and sighed with relief. Dell turned her back to him.

"I understand," Tina said softly, but Dell didn't. And as soon as she said a sorrowful good-night to Tina, she turned on Danny, the tenderness and regret of a few moments ago gone now, all gone.

"I don't understand you. How can you be so callous? Edgar was your biggest client. You *must* pay your respects. You owe it to Tina. You must set an example for our staff. What will they think if you don't show up?"

He was lost. What could he tell her? He could never face Tina. Not now. Not ever again. And what if the casket were open? What if he were forced to see Garson's flesh one more time? Oh, he'd gag, he'd choke—he'd die! No, never again. His heart was breaking for all of them, but no! He wasn't going to the funeral.

"I can't. I can't possibly."

"But why?" she insisted.

"You don't understand because . . . you're so strong and brave. You've always been strong and brave, Dell, darling. I'm not. I can't bear these things."

Darling again. And he was calling her strong and brave. Suddenly, she noticed she was still in her pink lingerie, but she didn't care now. Did that make her brave? She had no idea.

"What . . . things?" she continued.

"All these tawdry, ugly things." He shuddered as he said it. "I can only exist in an environment of beauty." He touched her bare arm. "That's why I adore you. You're my jewel."

She shook her head no.

"Yes, it's true, it's true! I'm not like other people. I can't bear it. I can't!"

"So you want me—your jewel—to face the ugliness for you."

Sinking down into the pillows, he covered his eyes with his hands and groaned. "You know what? I think I *do* have the flu! My head is aching. My throat, too. Everything aches. Oh, Dell darling, be a nice nurse, my gem, and get me two aspirins, please. I'd be so grateful."

Dutifully, she marched to the bathroom. Disbelieving, she'd nevertheless nurse Danny anyway, for what else had they between them anymore except this pretense?

She examined her face in the bathroom mirror and noticed her swollen bottom lip. Theo! A sudden sexual flash of memory ignited her . . . and just as suddenly she extinguished it. *Put it away,* she chided herself. *Put him out of your mind. You can do it with chocolates; now do it with Theo. Place him up there on that same unreachable shelf. Do it now!*

With quick, ragged movements, she pulled herself free of the pink silk lingerie that would forever belong only to this day, only to him. Maybe she should send it to him, she thought with a bitter smile. Tell him: *This is yours now. I'll never wear it again. It was meant only for you . . .*

Wrapped in her peach robe, she brought Danny his aspirins.

"Ah," he sighed in gratitude. "And now, could I have just a teeny glass of orange juice, and maybe a cup of tea?"

You're strong, she told herself as she fixed Danny's tea in the kitchen. Strong and brave, isn't that what he said?

It was a new thought, but not unpleasant. So she'd do what had to be done. She'd go to the office early tomorrow morning. She'd take Angie with her to the funeral, and anyone else who wanted to go. Tomorrow night she'd pack. And Saturday morning she'd get on the plane with Danny for Milan. Surely, Danny wouldn't miss that. They deserved that award and D & D was going to get it, no matter what happened afterward.

"I want my own design firm," she'd told Theo. The thought made her tremble, but not so much with fear as with exhilaration. *My own space! But why stop there? Why not my own apartment, too? My own life? My own future!*

Oh, what was she saying, thinking? On Park Avenue, their unfinished Embassy was waiting for them. They were sinking hundreds of thousands of dollars in its renovation. In Milan, their award was waiting. And all over the city—indeed, all over the country—bare, sterile apartments and tired old houses were waiting just for them. They were partners, they were a team, and they were wanted. So what was she saying?

"Danny?" she called as she carefully carried his tray before her. "Your nurse is here with your tea!"

But Danny had fallen asleep, with the lights on and the newspapers still strewn over the bed. On his face was a look of such sweet innocence that Dell no longer saw the screaming headlines, no longer saw the lies.

"Still love me?" she whispered wistfully. "You never said."

"I'm going for *you*," Angie Romano told Dell in the taxi, "certainly not for Edgar Garson. He had a way of looking right through me as if I didn't exist. Never a smile, never a thank you. I'm not glad he's dead, but I can't say I'm sorry, either."

"I wasn't exactly crazy about him myself," Dell admitted, "but he was one of our top clients. It's Tina I feel most sorry for. When I spoke to her last night, she sounded so . . . alone. So in control, yet so bereft."

"I thought she loathed the guy." Away from the office, Angie could forget that Dell was her boss, and speak with her as a friend.

"She did—but she loved him, too. I didn't realize it

until last night. Her pride, you see, wouldn't let her show it.''

Angie fluffed her wavy, otter-brown hair and wondered, not for the first time, if she should quit her job. Of course she was underpaid and overqualified, but ambition had never driven her. And if she quit, she might miss the next chapter of the riveting Dannenberg saga. At D & D, she was immersed in a world infinitely more interesting than her own, a world of interior design—and interior designs. When Dell hired her, she was divorced, alone, far from her parents' home north of Rome—and she still was. But now it was Dell who could use a loyal ally—any minute the roof could fall in. For curiosity, for gratitude, and for Dell she would stay. And when the roof caved in, she'd be there, right behind Dell. And follow her anywhere for, in Angie, Dell had more than a friend. She had a disciple.

''Tina's a very proud woman,'' Dell was saying, drawing Angie back into the conversation.

''Well, I heard she wasn't too proud to work side by side with him in the business, despite his shenanigans.''

Angie's remark, however unintended, embarrassed Dell, reminding her that, unlike Tina, she'd let her marital problems interfere with her work. When the staff found her in her office this morning, there were cries of surprise. Lately she'd dreaded going to the office, because it was *his* office, not theirs. And perhaps that was why she felt compelled to defend Tina, even if it meant disagreeing with Angie, who idolized her. Suspecting a certain fragility behind Angie's heroine worship, Dell always tried to treat her gently. But it was Tina who she admired, for it was Tina who was, to Dell, the other side of herself.

''Garson Textiles is as much Tina's as Edgar's,'' she told Angie firmly. ''It was *her* money, I understand, that helped found the company. And through the years, she was instrumental in the company's growth. She was never Edgar's assistant, always his equal partner.''

''Then I wonder if she's going to honor our contracts, now that they've been signed.''

''The contracts with Edgar Garson were signed?''

Angie hesitated and pushed a loose lock of hair behind her ear. That Danny might not have told Dell that Edgar

Garson signed the contract—three contracts, actually—was a possibility too impossible to contemplate. Not when the signing took place the same night Edgar Garson died. And at the D & D offices. Not when they'd been reeling in this catch for so many weeks. She decided Dell simply must've forgotten.

"Yes, but you knew. You had to've known."

"Why is that?"

Angie didn't like the stricken look on Dell's face, but she had no choice. She continued, "Because the signing took place that night."

"What night?"

Why was she being so dense? Angie wondered. "Wednesday night. The same night that Garson was later found dead in Christopher Beene's bed. Edgar certainly was a busy little bee that night."

Dell's face seemed to relax slightly. "Oh, so you were there when he signed off?"

"No. Danny asked me to prepare the contracts, but I left work before he got back to the office and before Edgar arrived."

"So how do you know—"

"Dell, the signed contracts were on my desk Thursday—yesterday—morning when I came to work. I'm sorry. I was so sure Danny would've told you, it never occurred to me you didn't know. Even though you haven't been around the office that much lately, I knew how excited you were about this one. Everyone was. We all knew how big this is. Big money, big prestige, big publicity."

"It's not Danny's fault—he's been very upset, uh, in addition to coming down with this flu." How she hated lying for Danny! "Not only because of Garson's death, but the lurid way the press have treated the whole thing. Christopher Beene was like a—a father to Danny."

Yes, that's what he was—a father. A father, Dell suddenly realized. A parent, not a lover! Until now, she'd never been entirely sure. Oh, she'd wasted so much time worrying needlessly. It was all just as Danny had said it was. Hadn't Danny said Christopher was only a devoted friend? Yes, but then she remembered what he *hadn't* said. Why hadn't he told her he was with Garson at the office signing contracts the night Garson died? What was he hiding?

"I know," Angie agreed. "At first, I was surprised Danny wasn't more excited about the signed contracts yesterday. We all cheered him and applauded when he walked in yesterday morning, but it seemed to make him angry—and that's not like Danny. You know how he loves applause. But later, when I heard the news, I understood. And on top of everything, he was probably walking around with that virus all day."

"Danny was upset yesterday morning?"

"Mm-hmm," Angie murmured as the taxi stopped in front of the funeral chapel. "He was a wreck."

But the news didn't break until late afternoon. Yesterday morning she lay abed, angry with Danny again for coming home so late, anxious for her affair with Theo to begin. Theo! Yesterday felt like years ago. "Don't wait for me," he had said, as if that could obliterate everything, stop what had begun.

Her mind, as she climbed from the cab, went from Danny to Theo, from Theo back to Danny again. Images of yesterday morning kept flashing before her, alone and sleepless all night long in the big peach bed. Hearing Danny's key in the lock. Wondering if it was three? Four? More? Afraid to look at the clock. Afraid to know. Hearing him dress for work, neither of them speaking. Not a word.

Now she wondered, was he with Edgar signing contracts at three, four in the morning? Of course not. At that hour, Edgar Garson was in Christopher Beene's bed—dead. Then where was Danny? And why hadn't he told her he'd got Garson to sign? Why didn't he wake her up to tell her Garson was mad for her pagoda and her Oriental color scheme? Were they so far apart they no longer told each other even the good news?

In the beginning, there was only good news, or so it seemed. Every day another delight to celebrate. They knew how to enjoy the good times then. Now there was no news, it seemed, good or bad. If, however, Danny had awakened her and told her, would it have made a difference? Would it have made her hesitate one second in her rush to arrive five minutes early at the East Side hotel, to Theo? Could anything have stopped her? Even if she'd somehow known how it would end, that he'd rip her heart in half? She knew the answer but she told herself, not for the first time, to put it away. *It's over, you fool. Over. Everything.*

Angie paid for the cab, got a receipt, and hesitated. She didn't know whether to give it to Dell at a time like this. Not that she needed the money. Ever since her divorce, she received a generous stipend. But Dell was always telling her, "It's not the money. You're entitled to what's yours. Now you say it—'I'm entitled.'"

She handed the receipt to Dell. Dell stared at it.

"If you don't want to be bothered, I'll take the receipt back and put it in the petty cash file."

Dell didn't seem to hear her. She stared at the receipt for a long time and finally stuffed it into her pocketbook.

"Let's go in," she said, but she made no move and Angie, distraught, tried to take her arm. Gently holding her off, Dell insisted, "I'm all right," hoping to make it true by saying it. But she entered the chapel with a tight belt of dread cinching her middle, wondering if today was the day her life was about to end . . . or, finally, to begin.

Tina Garson stood starkly alone in the center of the hushed room. Angie entered first, dark and chic in a slim wool suit and a leather cape strikingly similar to Dell's. From Tina's puzzled expression it was clear she had no idea who Angie was. Only when Dell took Tina's hands in hers did her eyes become clear.

"Dell. Thank you. Thank you so much for coming."

Of the hundreds and hundreds of people Edgar Garson had known and done business with, few evidently were willing to come here today to mourn him. The room was almost empty.

Dell had to bend down to embrace Tina. "I'm so terribly sorry. Is there anything, anything at all—?"

"I'm all right," Tina insisted with the same stiff, held-in determination Dell herself had voiced to Angie earlier. Dell recognized the tone and almost smiled. *We're a pair, all right. A pair of bleeding survivors.*

"I'm all right because I have to be," Tina said, pulling away. "I have no choice, you see."

"You're very brave," Dell said, and meant it.

"Not really." Her voice was tight, controlled. "Edgar

left me with quite a mess. I've got to clean it up for the sake of our business. I mean, my business. I suppose I should start getting used to saying it.''

''Tina, I want you to know how sorry Danny is that he couldn't be here with you today. He's home with the flu and a high fever.''

Tina patted Dell's hand as if she was the one who needed consoling. ''Well, tell him I'm sorry. I wasn't very nice to him, I'm afraid. But now that I know I suspected—judged—him unfairly, tell him I found the signed contracts in Edgar's jacket and I'll honor Edgar's wishes and go ahead with the plans.'' For the first time, she seemed on the point of breaking. ''He always liked it when I let him have his way without an argument. God knows, that wasn't very often. This would've made Edgar very happy. It's my belated gift to him.''

''Don't be too hard on yourself,'' Dell said, giving Tina the kind of advice she herself usually found impossible to follow.

''Show me a woman who isn't too hard on herself, '' Tina said, almost smiling. ''Aren't you?''

Tina's eyes seemed to be boring into Dell's soul, exposing it. ''Yes,'' she confessed simply, to her own amazement.

''I thought so.''

Then a hot flush of embarrassment crept up her face as she remembered that yesterday, she certainly hadn't been hard on herself. Yesterday, her behavior was far, far from perfect. Oh, Theo!

Quickly, she changed the subject. ''Just remember, Tina, if you want to change your mind about the contracts, Danny and I will understand.'' She knew Danny would be furious with her, and perhaps that was why she said it. But she was glad she did. And she wasn't afraid.

Tina's eyes threatened to spill over with tears. ''You're really very sweet. I'll remember what you said, but I won't change my mind. However, I only want to work with you. Not Danny. Just you, Dell.''

Then Tina's attention turned to the next person in the small line behind Dell. But as she squeezed Tina's hand, Dell's glance traveled to the doorway and the anteroom beyond it. There she saw Theo and Erica Glass removing their coats. Stunned, she edged quickly to the back of the room. The world had suddenly shrunk.

"I can't stay," she whispered to Angie. "I've got to get back and . . . to see if Danny's all right. You stay. We should have someone here representing D & D. I'll speak to you later."

Before Angie could protest, she walked quickly across the back of the room, passing behind Theo and Erica, who were now on line, and made it out the door unnoticed. She hailed a cab in a voice that was a scream and told the driver, without thinking. "Take me home."

"Where's that?" he asked.

Home. She gave the driver the address of the Dannenberg apartment, but that wasn't what she meant. Home was somewhere else, back in Brooklyn. That was where her heart—and her pain—still dwelled.

Danny was dozing but his eyes opened when she entered the bedroom. Now that everyone believed he had the flu, he had no choice but to take the day off and behave like he was sick. He almost believed it himself. Exhausted, he could use the rest. And a little extra pampering from his magnificent nurse might make the day almost pleasant. That Dell had arrived home so early surprised him slightly, but he was pleased to have her company. He didn't want to be alone with his thoughts. Thank God for Dell. She'd make everything all right.

"So, did you see Tina?" he asked as he watched her slip out of her somber suit and change into a pair of olive silk slacks and a matching sweater. *Nice,* he thought, *but the tortoise jewelry is all wrong.* She should wear gold jewelry with the olive, gold at her ears and her throat. Oh, how he used to love to dress her! He'd pick out her outfits, down to the shoes and the tinted hose. Now he didn't dare make a suggestion, say a word. She wouldn't appreciate his offers of constructive criticism. Where once she would've followed his advice to the letter, followed him anywhere, now she insisted on taking her own path. Just to irk him, he was convinced. Why else wouldn't she want to be molded into perfection?

"Mm-hmm," she said, clipping on a pair of tortoise earrings.

"Well, what did she say?" Then he couldn't help himself. "Not the tortoise," he told her. "Gold. You must wear gold at your ears. And the bronze wedgies. Not those brown flats. And a gold-flecked lipstick—"

She whirled around and glared at him.

"Okay, okay," he relented, holding his hands in a gesture of giving up. "I was only trying to make you more—"

"Don't." She silenced him with a word. "Stop trying to make me into something I'm not. Just . . . stop it!"

He wanted to argue, *I don't want to change you; I just want to suggest a few improvements. How could that be bad?* But he didn't say it. He said, "Okay, what did Tina say?"

"She said to tell you she's going to do things the way Edgar would've wanted."

At the mention of Edgar's name, Danny looked away, but finally, he couldn't help asking, "And what is that?"

"She's going to honor the contracts. The *signed* contracts."

"Fabulous!" Danny sat up, slapped the mattress, slapped his thighs, slapped the mattress again. He didn't seem to catch her biting emphasis.

"But she's given the job to me. She wants me to head up the projects and says I'm the only one she wants to work with."

"Who cares about that? We're partners, aren't we?"

Are we? Dell wondered.

"That's so fabulous, I can't believe you didn't tell me first thing."

But Dell was ready. "And I can't believe you didn't tell me the contracts were signed."

"Didn't I?" He sank back down into the bed again.

"You know you didn't and I want to know why. Where were you Wednesday night?"

"How can you ask? After all that's just happened, how can you ask such a ridiculous thing?" His eyes were startled, hurt.

"When were they signed?"

"When? Who remembers? Who cares?"

"I care."

"Well, I care that Edgar's dead and Christopher's ruined!" His voice breaking, he said more gently, "I'm sorry I didn't tell you, but I had other things on my mind.

Now, will you shut the lights out and close the door? I'm going to have a nap.''

Chocolates. She yearned for the comfort of rich, silken chocolate, nut-studded with pecans. Or shopping. Shopping always lifted her up, sent her heart racing with elation. Like she felt at the end of an exercise workout. Filled with new determination and endless possibilities. It gave her a sudden admiration for herself, brief but thrilling. Where else could she find such comfort now, such self-assurance.

In Theo? But how long must she wait?

In Danny? How could she trust his "darlings," his "gems," anything at all when he wouldn't tell her about that night? About so many nights. She too had kept secrets from him, and a day of betrayal for which she'd always feel the sting of shame and guilt, though in truth he'd driven her to it. But Wednesday night was different—it was a matter of life and death. Where was Danny when Garson died? Only one thing was clear; Danny wasn't going to tell her. Not now; perhaps never.

Could she find comfort in work? Yes, but not yet. She couldn't bear going back to the office today now that she knew Edgar Garson had been there the night he died. With Danny.

But even before that, before she knew, she couldn't bear going to the office. To *his* office. They were *his* clients, *his* staff, *his* desks. Partners. Partners for life, he'd said. But she'd never been his partner; she'd only been his proof—his exquisite pearl of proof—that he was a man. Oh, D & D had been such a sham! Such a wonderful, brilliant, marketing concept that had nothing to do with Danny and Dell. Partners. Husband and wife. Why hadn't she seen it before?

Nervous, jittery, she was at loose ends. She could pack, she told herself. She did have a morning flight for Milan. And always before, she'd found a kind of comfort in packing. Fingering fabrics, folding clothes, coordinating outfits, fitting everything into neat plastic bags and miniature plastic travel bottles, and then crossing everything off on her list—all of it quietly satisfying, comforting. But not today. Today Danny was in the bedroom and she wanted to be in the same room with him about as much as she wanted to be locked in a room with a snake.

There was really only one place she wanted to be. Needed to be. It had been several months since she'd made the long trek back to Brooklyn, but she'd never really gone home. All her visits ended the same way, incomplete and frustrating. She never really felt she was home. Yet she yearned to return today, though she couldn't say why. For one brief moment at her wedding she thought she'd found what she was searching for, but the feeling vanished. She was still searching for it, but now she knew where to look.

"Mommy?" she said when she heard the voice of Gertrude Shay at the other end of the line. "I'm coming to see you. I'm coming home."

20

She was home. She was back once more in the old-fashioned kitchen with the enamel stove and linoleum floor of her childhood. The hand-painted Portuguese vase that had been her first decorating purchase sat in the center of the old formica table, where she too now sat opposite her mother. Ever since she'd left home for good, she'd brought back flowers for the vase. This time it was weeping hearts.

"You see?" she told her mother. "Each flower is like a miniature, melancholy heart."

"Such a sad flower," said Gertrude Shay with a penetrating look at her daughter. "I prefer the cheerful ones, don't you?"

Yes, she was home, but this wasn't how she'd imagined it. In the homecoming of her dreams, she saw herself embraced at the door by her mother's welcoming arms and comforting words assuring her everything was going to be all right. With her cheek pressed to her mother's pillowy chest, she'd listen to her mother croon a baby's lullabye and feel safe at last, safe!

But when Gertrude Shay came to the door, it was the bouquet of flowers she took into her arms, not Dell. The flowers between them, they pecked each other's cheeks, barely touching.

"What a surprise!" Gertrude exclaimed.

"But I always bring you flowers," Dell said, and then realized her mother meant her visit was a surprise. And it was, but Dell reddened and told her about the flowers instead.

Outside, a sudden rainstorm spanked the windows with wet slaps that echoed, for Dell, her mother's slap of disapproval.

"I think weeping hearts are pretty, but if you don't," she sulked, "I'll take them home with me."

Carefully, Gertrude told her daughter, "I didn't say they weren't pretty," and took the vase to the sink to fill it with water. "It's just that you seem so unhappy today, like those flowers."

"You noticed?"

Gertrude sighed heavily. "I'll make some coffee," she offered, secretly glad for the chance to stand at the stove and avoid her daughter's sullen accusations. *All I said was, Hello, what a surprise,* Gertrude thought, *and already she's angry. When it begins this badly, at least it ends soon. She'll stay,* Gertrude decided, *just long enough for the rain to stop.* She'd give Dell an hour. By then she'd thoroughly hate her mother again. So what was the use? Like so much in her life, Gertrude's daughter's visit had defeated her too.

Nevertheless, Gertrude poured the coffee and put out a plate of cookies and finally sat down opposite Dell.

"How's your tall, handsome husband, your Danny boy?" For her daughter, she tried to sound cheerful but Dell was sure the smile she flashed was really a grimace.

"What do you mean?" She was sure she'd heard a hint of sarcasm in her mother's voice, too, and felt her anger rise.

Gertrude sighed again. "I mean exactly what I said. How is he? You don't bring him here, so I was just wondering how he is."

This was why she'd come here, wasn't it? To talk about Danny. About the pain and confusion he was causing. Instead, she found herself defending him, protecting him from the same disapproval and disappointment her mother always had for her.

"I don't bring him here because you always look at him as if you suspect he's gay. You and Daddy always thought male decorators *had* to be gay. Well, he's not, even if you don't believe it."

It was true. Gertrude never could look at Danny without noticing certain peculiarly effeminate traits—one day it was his excessive, gushy speech patterns, another day it was his hip-thrust walk. Always, he kept her wondering, *Is he?* Dell didn't seem to notice what to Gertrude seemed glaringly obvious. Had love so blinded her that she expected everyone else to close their eyes, too? Indeed, Gertrude loved Danny, too. If Danny wasn't exactly ideal as a man, he was close to ideal as a son-in-law, turning many of her dreams for her daughter into reality. What Dell didn't realize was that Gertrude didn't dislike Danny—how could she when he seemed to so adore Dell? No, she just wanted an end to this uncomfortable pretense. She just wanted the truth.

Now Gertrude felt sulky. "Have it your way," she said, and reached for the cookies.

Dell watched as her mother methodically ate one cookie after another until the plate was empty of all but one. This Gertrude offered to Dell.

"One won't make you fat. Go on, have it."

"I can't," Dell insisted, barricading herself with her hands.

"You can't have even one? What kind of a diet are you on this time? You're thin enough, maybe even too thin. You look . . . gaunt. Are you starving yourself? It's dangerous, Dell. Being too thin is just as dangerous as being too fat. I've been reading about it."

"You're never satisfied. All my life you told me to lose weight. Now that I'm thin, you want me to eat."

"One little cookie is all."

"Ma, you don't understand. I can't have just one cookie because . . ."

She hesitated, the sentence hanging, unfinished, between them. The urge to flee, to just run out the door was so strong that she stood up, but then she surprised herself. She crossed over to the other side of the table and knelt down on the floor in front of her mother.

"I can't because I'm just like you. Once I start, I can't stop. The only difference is—I don't let myself start. The other night I ate up a whole box of expensive chocolates. I ate them one by one until they were all gone, just like you just ate those cookies. It was the first time in years that I completely lost control but it's what I most fear—losing control. Losing control of myself, my life, my husband, and ending up ugly with an ugly, hopeless life. And do you know what I thought to myself as I reached for another chocolate . . . and another . . . and another?"

Gertrude blinked but said nothing.

"I thought to myself that I'm just like you. Ma, we're the same!"

At last. Somehow she'd found the words that had eluded her all these years. She'd finally said it. Out loud. To her mother. And now that she'd said it, there was more, much more she wanted to say. But for this moment, it was enough. Enough to feel relief. And for her mother to at last know the secret that linked them. Yes, today she'd truly come home. She squeezed her mother's hands.

But Gertrude Shay pulled her hands away, appalled. The last thing she wanted was for Dell to inherit her misery. It was her mission to save Dell from her own fate. And hadn't she succeeded? Wasn't her daughter slim and beautiful, rich and successful, married to a dashing, brilliant man? A man diametrically opposite to Dell's father, Victor Shay. Just as Dell was Gertrude's opposite. They were nothing alike. Nothing. So why was Dell saying she was out of control, just like her? It wasn't true! She couldn't bear to listen to another word.

"You don't know how mistaken you are." Even to Gertrude, her voice sounded cold. But how else to create a distance? "You have none of my problems, thank the Lord."

"Oh, Ma," Dell pleaded, still on her knees. "Try to understand."

"I do understand. I understand this: You were always dreaming up palaces and decorating them for your dolls when you were a girl, and now you're going to live in one. A mansion! It's what I always wanted for you because I never had a real home, I never had anything. The day I married your father I knew the mistake I made but I didn't have the will to do anything about it. And unhappy though I was with him, I got used to him. Now that he's gone, I even miss him. I'm all alone. Maybe, if I had religion, but you know we were never a religious family. So, of course I'm depressed. But you! You have everything! My dear, you're nothing like me. If there's one thing I made sure of, it's that you wouldn't end up like me. And you didn't, thank the Lord!"

"But I did, Ma. I did!"

"How? By having a successful business? A handsome

husband who loves you? Beautiful furniture, elegant clothes, nice friends? How?''

''Inside, Ma. Inside.''

''Inside?''

''Forget appearances. Forget everything you see about me on the outside. I'm trying to tell you what I'm really like in here.'' She pointed to her heart. ''And in here.'' She pointed to her head. ''That's where we're the same.''

Gertrude Shay looked down at her daughter and stroked her glorious hair, smoothing it back so she could see Dell's face, see the good cheekbones and the freckles on her tight, white skin, see her strong mouth and her high, unlined brow . . . and see her eyes. Even Gertrude couldn't dismiss the anguish in Dell's wide, sage eyes. And fear that somehow she was to blame.

''You're . . . unhappy?''

''So horribly unhappy, Mommy.'' Tears welled up in her eyes and she buried her face in her mother's lap. Mommy. She never knew what to call her mother—Mom, Mommy, Ma. She assumed she always used them interchangeably but now, with her head in her mother's lap, she observed that she called her mother Mommy only when she felt close and safe. Which was why she used the term so rarely. And why she used it now.

''I didn't know. I had no idea. Tell me why. What's making you so unhappy?''

''Everything!'' Dell sobbed. ''My marriage is falling apart. Danny's . . . not the loving husband you think he is. Or the supportive, equitable business partner, either, for that matter. There's no Dell in D & D—it's all his. I want out but—Mommy, I'm so confused and so scared.''

Gertrude sighed but Dell said, ''There's more. There's another man. It's hopeless but I can't stop dreaming about him.''

Again, Gertrude sighed as Dell rushed on. ''And tomorrow, Danny and I fly to Milan and I haven't even packed yet. I dread sitting on a plane next to him for all those hours but I dread losing him, too. I live in dread and shame. I always have. Always.''

''Dread and shame?'' Gertrude repeated. ''You mean you ended up like me after all?''

''Isn't that what Daddy wanted—for me to be just like you?''

"He wanted the best for you. He loved you."

"No!" Dell shook her head violently. "He loved me when I was little . . . and fat. But he stopped loving me at seventeen, when I got thin and made up my mind to get out of Brooklyn, forever. Why? Why did he stop loving me?"

"He never stopped, but suddenly you seemed so grown up, so adult. With your own mind. So determined. The way you kept on that diet and saved your money and applied to colleges in the city. So determined, it was remarkable."

"But he didn't think it was remarkable. He seemed angry. Angry and disappointed. And I felt so terribly torn and guilty. And forever after that's the way it's been. I never knew what terrible thing I had done to make him stop loving me. I still don't, but I long for his forgiveness. And for yours."

"Why mine?"

"Because I didn't turn out the way either of you wanted."

"But you did!" Gertrude protested, baffled.

"No, Mommy. Not inside. In here there isn't a beautiful, successful woman—only a too-tall, too-fat, too . . ."

Gertrude Shay could feel her daughter's pain but it was all still terribly confusing. *She's exaggerating,* Gertrude told herself. Dell always was dramatic. What could she really know of shame? Didn't Gertrude make sure Dell would be different? Ever since she was a baby, she'd trained her to be independent, to rely on herself, and it had worked, hadn't it? Look at her. She came to her senses and transformed her life when she was seventeen, and she hadn't looked back since. Not even her father's sour puss could stop her. Oh, how he'd mope around and sulk and shake his fists when his baby flew the nest. "It's your fault," he'd say. "You're the one who gave her these ideas. You're the one who painted her lips and told her to fly away. It's your fault she doesn't listen to me. Now I can't even look at her. She's not my little girl anymore."

Maybe he couldn't stand that she was growing up, becoming a woman, but Gertrude was glad. Gertrude was glad to watch her take control of her life, make her own decisions. Become independent. Maybe too independent. She kept her life carefully guarded, but anyone could see it was a charmed life. So why this doom and gloom? And yet if Dell was exaggerating, why was the agony so real in her baby's eyes?

"You said you're filled with guilt and shame. Are you . . . ashamed of me?"

Slowly Dell stood up and held onto the back of her chair, choosing her words carefully to avoid offense yet not to avoid the truth.

"Maybe I was. I don't know. But I'm not now." She sat down and reached across the table and took her mother's hands in hers. "I know you wanted something better for me. But Mommy, you hated yourself so much that you wouldn't let me love you. I felt that you wanted me to hate you, too!"

Gertrude dropped her eyes. "And . . . do you?"

"I hated the way you lived your life. And that you were so depressed. I hated the way you and Daddy fought all the time and how you always gave in, gave up. You were so afraid I'd grow up and become like you that you made me afraid of it, too. But I didn't hate *you*. I wanted you to be proud of me. That's why I tried so hard to please you. I loved you. I always loved you. Always."

Now Gertrude, who hadn't cried in the five years since her husband's funeral, who thought she'd dried up and lost the ability to weep, just as her womb and her ovaries and her skin had dried up, felt tears pouring out of her eyes, a cleansing sea of tears.

"What have I done to you? I thought I was saving you, but look what I've done!"

"Don't, Mommy. Don't blame yourself. I just want you to understand me. I could never make Daddy understand. When I tried to make something of myself, he—he seemed to resent it. And then I'd feel so guilty. But I always loved him. And I always loved you."

"You know that I love you, too, don't you? Maybe I never told you often enough, but I do. With all my heart. Oh, my dear, dear Dell!" Gertrude sobbed. "It hurts me to see you so unhappy. Your father's gone now; he can never make it up to you. But what can I do? How can I help you, my darling?"

"Oh Mommy!" Dell cried, and collapsed into her mother's open arms. "You already have."

Gertrude shook her head no. "Not enough. Not yet. Oh, my poor girl. I've made so many terrible mistakes. So many. I was so blinded by my own bitterness, I couldn't see what I was doing to you. Can you ever forgive me?"

They stood now at arm's length, grasping each other's hands, gazing directly into each other's weeping eyes.

"If you'll forgive me."

"It wasn't your fault," insisted Gertrude with vehemence. "You were never to blame. Never! But I have so much to make up for. Will you let me try?"

Through her tears, Dell began to laugh. What a question! She'd only been waiting to hear it her whole life. To which there was only one answer. Yes! Yes, waiting on her lips, yes waiting on her tongue and in her heart. Yes, at last!

"You see?" Dell said, weeping and laughing at the same time. "You've made me happy already."

But Gertrude was not yet ready to laugh with Dell. She knew what still lay before them. "You have a lovely laugh. I love to hear it. But when you don't feel like laughing—and there'll be times in the days to come when you won't—I'll be here if you need me. You're not alone, and neither am I. We have each other." Now Gertrude smiled. "And I'm the luckiest mother in the whole world because I found my daughter again. Or was it you who found me?"

"Maybe we both did."

"Yes, you're right," Gertrude agreed. "We both did."

As the taxi emerged from the Battery Tunnel, all of lower Manhattan seemed to Dell to be shrouded in an indecisive mist, neither rainy nor dry, not unlike her own ambivalence. Was she ready to go home and see him— or not? she asked herself over and over, in time to the *whisk, whisk* of the window wipers as the cab crawled through the rush-hour traffic.

"Not!" she suddenly announced out loud.

"What was that?" asked the driver.

"Uh, *not* the address I gave you. I'd like to go to Sutton Place instead, please." She gave the driver Tina Garson's address and sat back, pleased with herself. Leaving her mother's house, she possessed such a fount of well-being, it didn't seem possible it would ever evaporate, least of all so soon. But the thought of going home to Danny had drained the pool of warm love in which she'd been floating, leaving behind a raw, dry bed of dread. Until she changed her mind.

This was the Garsons' old apartment, from which they planned to move when the new, nineteen-room penthouse with Dell's Chinoise scheme was completed. But to call it old was to call a Ming Dynasty vase old, or a Savonnerie carpet. Small, certainly, compared to their new apartment, it nevertheless occupied an entire floor of the building, with ten high-ceilinged rooms, many of them paneled in pecan and facing the East River. A maid in black uniform with white ruffles opened the door for her.

"Mrs. Garson is meeting with her lawyer in the library. Would you care to wait in the living room?" she said, leading the way through a gallery with small but important works of art, and into a room done in cream and white with all the color concentrated in the massive, explosive paintings on the walls. No one, however, was there—not in the living room, nor the dining room, nor the garden room, nor the breakfast room. Circling back to the living room, Dell remembered that at the funeral a small sign on a stand announced that Tina Garson would be holding a reception here at her apartment from one o'clock until nine. It was now five-thirty. Where was everyone?

When the maid brought her a cup of coffee, she asked to use the phone and was directed to a cream instrument beside a cream silk sofa plump with down. When she heard Jackie Knight's voice, she sat back and smiled.

"How would you like some company?" she asked.

Ignoring the question, Jackie had one of her own. "Where were you this morning? You've never missed an exercise class in your life."

"I know," she said with some regret. Regret for the missed class, but even more for her rigid adherence to these compulsions. In the past two days, however, a new desire had been quietly taking hold—a desire to let up on herself. So far, she hadn't fallen apart or run amok, as she'd always feared, but she was maintaining a close watch on herself nevetheless.

"Are you okay?"

"I'm . . ." Dell hesitated. "Jackie, can I come over, or are you still working?" Usually, on Fridays Jackie remained at home and typed up her interviews.

With a mysterious laugh, Jackie said, "You have no idea, do you?"

"No idea of what?"

"Of where I am. I'm in my new home. I'm at Dom's. I moved in last night."

"But I dialed your old—"

"I know. I had the number transferred. And now I'm in the kitchen trying to fix a pasta Genovese from a recipe Dom's mother gave me."

"You? Cooking?"

"Shut up."

Dell laughed. "Okay, but I can't believe it. And I can't believe you really moved in."

"I tried calling you all day yesterday to tell you. Where were you?"

Again, Dell hesitated. "I've got a lot to tell you."

"Mmmm!" Jackie made a sigh of approval, but whether it was for her pasta sauce or Dell's hint of juicy news, Dell couldn't say. "Come right over."

Just then, the door to the library opened and a man emerged, his back to Dell. He was as tall as Danny, but broader. Indeed, his shoulders seemed to span the entire width of the doorframe.

"Are you sure? I don't want to intrude. It's only your second night," she said softly into the phone, but her eyes were still on the man's broad back.

"Don't be silly. Dom loves company and he's eager to see you—to see Danny, too. So come right now and just step over the cartons and suitcases, okay?"

Hearing Dell's voice, the man, who was saying some last words to Tina, closed the door and turned. Then everything simply stopped and Dell stared at him, transfixed. Coffee cup suspended in her hand, halfway to her lips, she sat motionless as a mannequin, her eyes luminous as glass.

"So? Dell, are you coming?" Dell heard Jackie ask her, but while he stood directly in front of her, everything else ceased to exist. She could only continue to stare at him. Nothing else.

His face was strong, weathered, like fine leather. His hair was salt and pepper and slightly disheveled, as if he'd been out on the windy range herding cattle, on a horse. Even in a business suit he looked like a cowboy, a rancher. *It's the Western boots,* Dell decided, and looked up into his eyes. *Intelligent,* Dell thought. *A handsome face, rugged, but the eyes are intelligent. And kind, definitely kind.*

He too was staring.

Dell finally forced herself to drop her eyes and tell Jackie, "I'll be there in half an hour. And I'll be coming alone."

Her hand trembled slightly as she replaced the phone on its cradle and she couldn't make her eyes look anywhere but in her lap now. She prayed for him to say something, anything, and finally he did.

"Hello, I'm Rip Stone."

"Oh? I thought Tina was meeting with her lawyer."

A miniscule smile barely curled the corners of his mouth but his pale gray eyes squinted with amusement.

"Never heard of a lawyer with the name of Rip before? Well, that's okay. Lots of people say I don't exactly look like their idea of a lawyer, either." It was clear he meant that she was one of them. He seemed to know exactly what she was thinking. He was teasing her. But before she could deny it, he put her at her ease. "Tina will be out in a few minutes. We just had a few matters to go over."

Then, for the first time, he seemed to notice his surroundings. "This place really emptied out. It was packed an hour ago."

Dell stood and held out her hand. "I'm Dell Dannenberg."

He reached across the coffee table that separated them and found her hand. He didn't let it go. He didn't let go of her eyes, either. "Hello, Red," he finally said. "What took you so long?"

She was about to look at her watch. Then she realized what he meant. He didn't have to say, "I've been waiting for you to come into my life," or something equally trite. Just the question, quietly asked, "What took you so long?" She got it. And although she didn't know it, not yet, not with any certitude, it was how she felt, too.

He let the question remain unanswered and slowly strolled over to the alabaster banquet that served as a bar. For such a big man, he moved with surprising grace. There was a certain grace, too, in the way he spoke. An informal ease, a certain familiarity, yet without a trace of rudeness.

"Care for a drink, Red?"

Dell nodded yes. Red. Automatically, he'd nicknamed her Red. As if he'd known her for ages and was just waiting for her to get here. *What took you so long?*

"Say, 'I'd love a martini, Rip,' " he said.

Dell shrugged her shoulders. Okay, she'd play his game. "I'd just love a martini, Rip," she said, exaggerating the words.

Rip slapped his thigh. "What a coincidence! A martini happens to be the only drink I know how to make. Uh, vodka martini, right?" He nodded his head up and down to indicate that she should say yes, making her laugh.

"Definitely!" Though she rarely drank anything more than a glass of wine, this had been a long day and his vodka martini was sounding better and better.

"Now, Red, come on over here and watch this because this is my secret recipe. Been in the family for generations."

But when she joined him at the bar, he stopped what he was doing and just stared at her. She could feel herself beginning to blush, so she asked casually, "What's your secret?"

"Preparation. Careful preparation," he said, and went back to work, dipping the glasses into the ice bucket and packing the shaker with more ice. "I used to think only my work required careful preparation, but after some years of marriage, I find myself single again, making my own martinis, cooking my own dinner, and I've learned—" he paused to carefully measure the vodka and vermouth—"that chaos is simply the absence of preparation."

"On the other hand," Dell said, watching him ever so gently shake up the liquor and ice, then strain it into the cold glasses and top them with a thin twist of lime peel, "there's a danger in being too cautious and squelching all spontaneity."

He gave her a long, penetrating look and handed a

glass to her. ''That's true,'' he agreed softly. ''There is that danger as well.''

They clinked glasses and Dell took a sip. Then another. ''I speak from personal experience.'' She took a large gulp. It was the single most splendid martini she'd ever tasted, bitingly cold and dry, mellowed with the faint fragrance of lime. But it wasn't the liquor that gave her the courage to say, ''I've always been so afraid of losing control that I became overly cautious. But recently—very recently—I've been loosening up a little, taking some risks. It's scary . . . but . . . exhilarating.'' It was this bear of a man, this Rip Stone, who drew the words out of her.

He nodded as if he understood. Then he put his elbows on the bar, leaned close to her and said, ''Tell me more, Red. I want to know everything about you. Let's go out to dinner and you can start at the beginning and—''

She was laughing but already her hands were signaling him to stop and her head was shaking back and forth, no. Oh, he was a delightful man, this Rip Stone. He had such a delightful way of putting her at ease. Never had she felt more her self, her *best* self. Which, of course, was ironic, for she'd just told him of her worst self, the part she'd always kept hidden—and yet he'd asked her out to dinner! Yes, this was delightful, maybe even glorious. But it was utterly impossible. Already, her life was more complicated than she could bear.

''I would've loved it, but I'm afraid I can't,'' she said with genuine regret. ''I have an appointment and I really must go now.'' She rang for the maid, who brought her coat, and avoided his eyes.

But then he was beside her at the door.

''Please tell Mrs. Garson I'll call her,'' she told the maid, who nodded and left. Then Dell could avoid his eyes no longer.

''Good-bye, Rip.'' As soon as the words were out of her mouth, she regretted them. She saw the flash of disappointment in his eyes and held out her hand to him. ''I mean, good-night.''

He looked at her hand but this time he didn't take it and hold it. This time he didn't touch her. Or speak. He just stood there, staring and smiling at her. And it was only after several minutes had gone by that Dell realized she was doing the same thing. The realization embarrassed her. To mask it, she insisted she really had to go.

He nodded and held the door open for her. "We will meet again, Dell Dannenberg." He said it as a promise. "Soon."

She knew he was standing at the doorway, watching her as she waited for the elevator.

"Hey? Red?" he called just as the elevator door opened, making her look back at him one more time.

"Nothing," he said and waved her on. "I just like saying it. *Red.*"

She floated down to the street and dreamily made her way out into the night. Jackie's—or rather, Dom's—apartment was only six blocks away but when she arrived she had no memory of the walk. Her mind had been somewhere else.

It was Dom who greeted her at the door. "Come in, come in," he said, hugging her, pulling her, patting her as he led her into the living room. "Welcome to mia casa. You're a famous decorator. So what do you think?"

Everything was black, or bright pink. The wall-to-wall carpeting was black, the sofas, chairs, and lampshades were black. Even the bookcases were stained black, with brass trim. The toss pillows were bright pink satin.

"Don't answer that, Dell," Jackie said, entering with a platter of hors d'oeuvres. Then she smiled wickedly at Dom. "On second thought, tell him. Maybe he'll listen to you."

Dom was short and pudgy, not at all like the smooth, cold men Jackie had dated in years past. More like a lovable clown, and he seemed to relish the prospect of being teased by *two* women. With a wink he signaled Dell to go right ahead.

"Let's see," she ventured, dead-pan. "A Las Vegas brothel. No, a Reno divorce parlor. No, I've got it—this is a Florida funeral home!"

Dom burst into laughter and sat down beside her and hugged her again.

"I love her," he said to Jackie while kissing Dell on the cheek. "I'm crazy about her. And did you hear? She thinks I have great taste!"

Dell refused the glass of wine Jackie offered with, "I've had more than enough already, but thanks." Then she simply couldn't resist teasing Dom one more time. "Ah, Dom," she said drolly, "great taste doesn't describe it."

The apartment's decor was so appallingly hideous that Dell wouldn't have dared mock it in other circumstances. But Dom and Jackie seemed to have no illusions. Not only did they laugh at themselves, but they invited her to do the same. What remained incomprehensible was how Jackie, who put such a high premium on beauty, both personal and environmental, had wound up here with this man, and with no regrets and no shame. She thought of her own childhood and the house that had made her cringe for so many years. "Are you ashamed . . . of me?" her mother had asked. If only both she and her mother had possessed one ounce of Jackie and Dom's carefree insouciance, the heavy burden of shame they carried would've been lightened. But it wasn't too late, Dell thought with determination. It was really just the beginning . . . of everything.

"The truth is," Jackie said, turning serious, "Dom promised me I could redo the place . . . without interference."

Gesturing with his hands like a true Sicilian, Dom added, "Hey, I'm a businessman. I have a nose for business but I lack an eye for style, as you've noticed," he smiled, revealing a subtle depth of sophistication that belied his surroundings. "So, although I'm blind, I'm not stupid. I'm leaving the aesthetics to the experts." For emphasis, he patted Jackie's backside as she sat down on his lap.

"And that's where you come in," Jackie said, jumping up again to lead them to the table.

"Me?" At the sight of the huge bowl of pasta, verdant with fresh-chopped basil that Jackie brought from the kitchen, Dell allowed Dom to give her a small glass of wine after all. This was a celebration, she knew, and she wasn't going to miss it.

"We want you to do it."

Another client! Dell stood up. Oh, yes, this was going to be quite a celebration.

"I accept—that is, if you're willing to hire only one 'D.' "

Jackie and Dom looked at her, uncomprehending.

"I don't know when, and I don't know how, but I'm going out on my own. I'm starting my own design firm."

For a moment, Jackie stared at her, mouth gaping. Then Dom yelled "Bravissima!" and Jackie screamed "I don't believe it!" and clapped her hands enthusiastically. That her friend was eager to hear more was obvious, but Dell refused her gently, shaking her head.

"That's all I can say right now. Tomorrow I'm going to Milan. Perhaps there'll be more news when I return."

"In that case," said Dom, "sit down and let us send you off with this wonderful dinner my beautiful Jackie has prepared. It's a recipe from the north, but my mother always made it when I was a boy."

Dell remained standing and raised her glass. "I can't wait. But first I must toast the two of you. To you, Jackie, my dearest friend, and to you, Dom—may your happiness, which is so huge that it even makes this all-black room seem sunny, be everlasting."

There was much laughter and eating for the next hour, but finally, Jackie could contain herself no longer. "Dell, what's really going on with you? I swear, if you don't tell me, I'm going to burst."

At that, Dom excused himself. "You two have things to say to each other and I think we'd all be more comfortable if I went into the bedroom and watched the last half of a game I've been looking forward to all day. *Ciao,* Dell," he said, squeezing her shoulder, "and take all the time you need. Jackie and I have the rest of our lives."

"He's a gem," Dell said when Dom had closed the bedroom door.

"Can you believe it!" Jackie agreed. "This from a man who couldn't make any commitments a year ago!" But then she leaned forward on the uncleared table and said, "Okay, Dell, I'm listening."

"Oh, Jackie," Dell sighed, "I don't know where to begin. I feel so lost—and yet, I also feel so strangely light and free. I'm so desperately confused. Can you help me figure out what to do?"

"This is the first time you've ever asked for my help, but I never gave up on you. I always knew we'd become really great friends. And tonight we have."

"I love you, Jackie."

"Me, too," Jackie smiled and impatiently motioned

for Dell to continue. ''Now tell me everything. We may not solve your entire life tonight but at least we've found each other. And there's always tomorrow.''

We've found each other. That's what her mother had said. What a day! Suddenly, Dell smiled, too. Jackie was talking without her phony southern accent. She too was becoming her own real self, Dell thought. It was truly a new beginning for them both.

21

"Who's this?" Danny asked, immediately recognizing that the voice answering Christopher Beene's phone belonged to a stranger.

"Who's *this?*" the voice answered back.

The voice, the question, the attitude all conspired to push Danny into a full-blown, heart-racing, stomach-churning fit of anxiety. He was already on edge from a morning of last-minute packing and the mad dash to the airport with Dell maintaining a stony silence beside him. Now he was over the edge. Drenched in perspiration and dread, he thought, *Oh no, is he dead, too? Or even worse—God help me!—has he found someone else to adore?*

"I wish to speak to Christopher Beene," he said, drumming on the glass phone booth door in the airport terminal.

"Who shall I say is calling?"

"Just tell him Danny."

"I have a Daniel Dannenberg on my list. Would that be you?"

The drumming turned to pounding. "Yes!" he snarled, shocked that after all their precautions, Christopher would give his full name to a complete stranger.

"One moment please."

"Who *was* that?" Danny demanded as soon as Christopher came to the phone.

"Nurse Robert. A lovely boy."

Danny groaned inwardly. Was that remark of Christopher's a taunt? If so, then his worst nightmare was coming true. But he said *Nurse* Robert. What was going on?

"You gave him my name."

"Had to."

"Why? And when did you get a home nurse? Has something happened?"

"Just a little tired. I'm all right. And this new medicine I'm taking feels very promising. Nurse Robert takes good care of me. Won't let me talk to anyone not on the A-list."

"Yes, I know. But are you really all right?" What he really meant was, *Do you still love me? Can you ever forgive me? Am I still your darling boy, your one and only son?* And not being able to ask, he imagined the worst.

"Absolutely," Christopher said, but his voice was weak.

"I've felt. . . . terrible about not calling, but we did agree—"

"Yes, so we did. And right you were."

"But I just had to speak to you before I left. Did you forget I'm off to Milan this morning?"

"I didn't forget."

"Well, I just thought that now that the funeral is over with and the news had died down—"

"Oh, dear. Here's Nurse Robert with something ghastly for me to swallow again. I'll have to go now."

"All right, but please take care of yourself. Remember, in two months is D & D's opening at the Embassy. We've got two crews working overtime. You've got to be there, so you must use this time to get strong. I just wish I could visit—"

"I'll be there. I promise. Got to go now. Ta-ta."

It was inevitable. Dell realized it the instant she noticed them, and told herself that of course it was to be expected that they, too—they *two*—would be here this morning, taking the same plane to Milan. He, after all, would be receiving his own award, one of the most prestigious: Architect of the Year, International. So, of course.

But during all of Thursday together, she and Theo had never discussed it. So little, really, had been discussed. Now, waiting for Danny to get off the phone so they could board, she hid behind a column, thinking she'd spent more time hiding from Theo than being with him. When would she have had enough of this?

She was angry at herself. Yesterday had been a day of

miracles but today she was angry with everyone, most of all herself. She should've known, she told herself. She should've been prepared. But she wasn't. And therefore, seeing Theo and his small blonde wife striding toward the international departures gate made her heart break loose and plummet wildly down a straight shaft to her stomach. She ached at the sight of the two of them and backed further away until—

"Watch out!" someone called behind her. But it was too late. She backed into two suitcases parked beside their owner, who grabbed Dell as she began to fall. With one leg in the air, half-sitting on the suitcases, Dell came face to face with the stranger and almost flopped over again.

"Tamara!"

"Dell!"

The two women squealed and screamed as Dell struggled to her feet. Then they hugged and squealed like schoolgirls—which was exactly what they had been the last time they saw each other.

"You're—half your size. You look wonderful!" Dell lied.

"No, I don't. I'm still the same old fatty," Tamara Walkov said good-naturedly. "But you really do look wonderful, Dell. Never gained it back, I see."

"No," Dell shrugged, "but that's not important. It's just so great to see you again."

After high school, Tamara had gone off to the University of California while Dell had remained in the East, and the two quickly drifted apart. But though older, Tamara looked essentially the same. Still the same sallow complexion, the same close-set eyes, and almost the same expensive and wrinkled clothes.

It was Dell who had changed. It was she who'd stopped writing to Tamara, ashamed of her homely friend. She still couldn't help noticing Tamara's bulk, but now she didn't care.

"It sure was important then, wasn't it?" Contained in Tamara's question was a subtle accusation, which Dell acknowledged with great tenderness and some regret.

"Too important. It's now—what?—almost seventeen years? And I'm still struggling to put things in proper perspective. But I like to think I'm a little wiser than I was then . . . and not half as unkind.''

''You were never unkind,'' Tamara disagreed and gave Dell another hug. ''You were just very . . . young.''

There was so much to ask, so much to tell, but they each had planes to catch.

''Call me.''

''I will,'' Dell promised.

''I'm in the book. Still under Walkov. I kept my name when I married.''

So Tamara had married! Out of the corner of her eye, Dell could see Danny pacing the terminal, searching for her, but she couldn't pull herself away from the first true friend she'd ever had. Tammy. Once, she could tell her anything.

''My married name is Dannenberg. Unfortunately,'' she heard herself say, ''I changed it.''

''My husband's name is Berringer. Gillian Berringer.''

''Not . . . *the* Gillian Berringer? Berringer Vineyards?''

Tamara smiled. ''That's the one. We live in California but we maintain an apartment here, too. I'm vice-president. And what do you do now, Dell?''

''I'm an interior designer.'' She was about to add, ''With my husband,'' but she didn't.

''This is really amazing. I'm flying back to California to start interviewing designers. We're building a new chateau at our winery and we need a plan for the residential interiors. Oh, Dell, wouldn't it be thrilling if—''

''It's already thrilling just finding you again. I mean it. I'm overwhelmed.''

''I know. But just think . . . you could fly out, do our chateau, and we'd get to see each other every day.''

''I'm leaving for Milan in one minute. Let's talk about it in a few days when I get back.''

Once again, the two women hugged. ''Don't forget,'' said Tamara. ''Call me. My California number is on the message machine.''

''The minute I return.''

Tamara watched Dell go off. At the last minute, she suddenly called out, ''Dell!''

Dell turned.

"Just tell me. . . . what size are you now? A four?
Am I right?"

Dell shook her head but Tamara couldn't hear her answer. The last call for boarding Flight 803 for Milan
drowned out her words. A crowd of travelers rushed by
and all Tamara could see of Dell was her long, gloved
fingers raised high in a last wave of good-bye. Then she
was gone but this time, Tamara knew, only for a little
while.

They sat side by side on the spacious seat of first class
like two strangers faced in the same direction but traveling in different worlds. The continuous hum of the engines, the hours of enforced inactivity, and the exhausting
events of the last few days put them both in parallel states
of sedated reverie, separated by the distant and unique
melancholy they each were feeling.

All day yesterday, Danny had lain in bed, thinking.
Now he was doing it again—or rather, the thoughts were
doing it to him again. Ugly thoughts, horrible memories.
He kept feeling Garson's cool flesh on his fingertips. He
kept seeing Garson's white buttocks, and then his legs,
like stalks, sticking out of the urn. Remembering how he
had to push them, lean on them to stuff them inside. And
then poor Christopher taking over, thinking of everything, and calling him "my son."

How could he live with it? How could he go on? The
ugliness of it all!

If only he had Christopher to turn to. But Christopher
was avoiding him, that was obvious. The question was
why. Was he avoiding him in order to protect him . . .
or because Danny had so completely stripped him that
even the core of Christopher's devotion had been cut
away?

Even his darling Dell was avoiding him. All day yesterday he kept hoping she'd come home and crawl into
bed with him. Have a pretrip sendoff. He'd transport her
to the airport terminal. "It's completely empty and while
we wait for the plane, you sit in my lap on one of those
awful molded plastic seats. I hike up your skirt and spread
your panties to one side . . ."

But last night it was he who was sleeping when she

finally came home. Her packing awoke him. Where had she been all those hours?

"Where were *you* Wednesday night? Where were you all those hours when Edgar Garson was dying?" she countered, sending him back under the covers, back under a pastel rainbow where all the colors were soft in the caramel sunlight . . .

From Dell's seat, neither Theo nor Erica Glass were visible, but knowing they were somewhere on the plane preoccupied her with alternating wishes: to hide, to find them, to hide, to find them. For the first hour, she hid, her trench coat pulled up to her nose. Then she told herself this was ridiculous. Unbuckling her seatbelt, she craned her long neck to scan the row of unfamiliar heads, looking for two she recognized. She wanted to find them in order to avoid them. That way, perhaps the only time she'd have to encounter them would be at the awards ceremony and dinner tomorrow night. But unable to locate them, she sat back and turned to glance at Danny.

He still had the face of a boy and the silky hair she used to love running her fingers through, but she could see the first fine lines of age around his eyes and a slightly tired sag to his skin, and she inwardly rejoiced. Knowing the extent of his vanity, even these small imperfections were guaranteed to annoy, to grate. And that was what she wished on him—nothing big, nothing tragic—just an insignificant, incurable erosion of his monumental ego.

"Some hors de'oeuvres and champagne?" the flight attendant offered and to Dell's surprise, Danny, who lived on diet cola, emptied his glass in a minute and asked for another. And another. After the third glass, he turned to her.

"What're you wearing to the awards ceremony?"

"I bought a black velvet dinner suit. You haven't seen it," she couldn't help telling him. For too long he'd been her guru, her magician, her dresser. Automatically, she heard herself ask him, "But it's short. Do you think I should wear it?"

"I think you should wear something long and very bare, but on top. Your legs should be covered."

"Oh," she said, crestfallen. He could still get to her . . . but only if she let him.

"I'll take you shopping. On the Via Montenapoleone.

You can wear your suit tonight. Chris—I mean, someone told me about a wonderful restaurant with the best risotto in the city. And afterward, we'll go dancing at Cafe Milano. I hear it's so chic that all they serve is champagne and caviar. Oh, Dell darling, let's have a fabulous night— the way we did on our honeymoon, remember? Please say you want to. Say you're not mad at me anymore. Say you forgive me.''

She didn't say that she forgave him, but she did manage a smile. She would try, she decided, one last time. In Milan. She would try to make it right, to make it work. Tonight she'd be what he wanted—his gem, his brilliante. And then, perhaps Danny would once again be for her—what? Once, he had been everything. Surely, there was still some magic left. Or was that all it ever was—a stack of cards, a rabbit in a hat, an illusion?

"It's not your fault. It was never your fault," her mother had told her yesterday. Tonight, whatever happened, she would try to remember her mother's words . . . and believe them.

Their room, larger than the master bedroom in their apartment at home, was papered in a marvelous old Italian paisley, and one wall housed a floor-to-ceiling, paneled armoire for their hanging clothes. Shrouded now in twilight and mist, the terrace still offered a spectacular view of the best of Milan. But what Dell liked most of all, aside from the hand-embroidered and hand-laundered bed linens, was the enormous bathroom completely tiled in an unexpected brilliant blue, with matching bathtub. It was there that she now soaked dreamily until Danny came in to join her.

"What're you doing?" she almost shouted as he began slipping out of his clothes. She knew exactly what he was doing, but no! It was too soon! On Thursday she'd bathed with Theo, sucked on his toes, washed his back. On Wednesday night, Danny had done God knew what with Edgar Garson. No. She was willing to try again, but she wasn't yet ready to take him into her bath.

Naked, he knelt his lean body before her and reached for the perfumed soap in the shape of a seashell. She held his hand and shook her head no.

"I can't. Not now. I need . . . quiet. To be alone.''

He didn't believe her. He climbed into the bath but as he did, Dell jumped up and out, splashing the brilliant blue floor with water.

"I'm sorry, but I just can't right now."

"But I need you!" Danny insisted and held out his arms to her. "Come back, Dell, darling. I need you."

She wrapped her wet and glistening body in a towel and told him steadily, "I have needs, too. So many nights I wanted you, needed you . . . and you were never there. So many lonely nights, hungry nights. Nights I was worried sick about you. Where were you all those nights?"

"Nowhere. Just . . . out. Just nervous and needing to keep moving. You know all that."

"I don't know anything! I don't know you, Danny. And you don't know me."

He followed her into the bedroom and watched her dress. As she clasped her black lace bra, he clasped her breasts in his hands. "You know this." Squeezing them, he sent a sudden charge of electricity through her, but she resisted. "And you love it."

"I did . . . once." She shook him off and pulled on her black velvet beaded suit. "Now I don't know what I love . . . or who."

He didn't hear it. It was the closest to honesty she'd come with him, but he was staring at her, entranced.

"Divine, Dell, darling. Positively, absolutely divine!"

He loved the suit, just as she had known he would when she'd bought it. Because he loved her most in glamorous clothes, in glamorous settings, the eye-catching redhead attached to his arm.

And Theo? How did he love her most? Why, the same, of course, she admitted to herself with brutal honesty. Almost exactly the same. As the eye-catching redhead attached to Danny's arm. Attached, yes. Unavailable, unattainable. Was that why he didn't approve of her wish to go into business on her own? Why he could not understand her need to leave D & D?

Somewhere in this hotel, he too was dressing for dinner. They were bound, she knew, at some point to meet. She only hoped it wouldn't be before tomorrow night. Already, she'd seen him again. Just as she and Danny entered the hotel elevator, she glimpsed Theo and Erica arriving. At the sight of them, she almost laughed out loud as she thought of the irony of being in the same hotel again.

They entered the dark, sedate lobby walking oddly. Theo, she noticed, as the elevator door was closing, was bracing Erica, trying to hold her upright. Nevertheless, Erica stumbled. But the image became clear to Dell only after the elevator began its slow climb to the eighth floor—quite obviously, Erica was completely drunk.

All during dinner Danny's fingers kept creeping up Dell's skirt, electrifying her thighs, while he whispered words of need and desire in her ears. It was the old, flamboyant Danny, making a public spectacle of their sexuality, making her giggle with embarrassment and heat. With their creamy risotto, fragrant with porcini and cheese, they sipped a Tuscan Chianti and nibbled on wet lips and pink ears.

Try! she admonished herself. *Try, for if you make it right this time, you'll have it all. He says he needs you. Believe him. He says he wants you. Believe him. Be there for him just this one time more. Look how happy you make him. Believe that he'll make you happy, too. And keep you from being alone.*

"We aren't alone anymore. Now that we've found each other," her mother had said. And it was true . . . but maybe it wasn't enough. So she would try with Danny once more.

She went with him to Cafe Milano, though she was beginning to yawn and longed to collapse between those exquisite Italian sheets. And she nodded enthusiastically when Danny squeezed her arm.

"Isn't this place divine? Isn't it fabulous?"

Cafe Milano was made for Danny but she couldn't help feeling a slight sense of foreboding in the dark, elegant club crowded with beautiful, haughty men and women, all dressed entirely in black. At least her velvet suit had found its proper home, she mused as they were seated at one of the tiny round tables set on a tier around the dance floor. Every table had its own bottle of expensive champagne in a silver bucket. On the table next to Danny there were two, though the silver-haired gentleman was apparently alone.

"How odd," Dell said, observing the dancers. Five striking women, each in an expensive black lace or silk dress, all wearing extremely high black heels, danced by themselves in slow, undulating movements to an American rock song. The DJ, clearly visible at his electronic table, wearing makeup and black jet earrings, blew kisses to the women.

"Don't you think that's odd?" she said again, but Danny wasn't listening. He was leaning over, talking to the silver-haired man at the next table. She clearly heard him ask Danny, in a heavy accent, "Would you like to dance, you gorgeous Americano?"

And then she heard Danny laugh, laugh with delight, before he turned back to Dell to check her reaction.

"Let's leave," she said.

"Don't be ridiculous. This place is fabulous. We're not used to this level of sophistication, this freedom. You've got to lighten up to appreciate it."

"I've got to go home." She rose and grabbed her black satin purse. There hadn't been time to buy a beaded one. "Stay if you want. I'll catch a cab."

He let her go. She couldn't believe it, refused to believe it even as the doorman called a cab for her, even as she climbed in. She kept expecting to feel his hand on her shoulder, to hear him say, "Wait. I'm coming, too. Do you think I'd let you go alone when all that's important is that we be together—and stay together?" Even as she paid the driver with her crisp, new Italian lire and pushed through the hotel's glass revolving doors, she expected that somehow he'd be there. With all his needs, all his hunger. That he'd have run, flown all the way, to be with her.

Instead, there was Theo. Alone. At the concierge's desk, writing a note.

"Dell!" he turned and smiled, his eyes taking in all of her with unhidden longing. "I was just writing you and Danny a—"

She touched his mouth with her fingers to silence him. Then she took his hand and led him to the elevator.

"What're you—where're we—?" he laughed, but she was silent, so silent that he mutely let her lead him where she wished, and all he could hear was his own breathing, heavy with desire, and her own.

They were at each other as soon as the door was closed, pulling off their own clothes, pulling at each other's, pausing to hurtle their bodies into each other in a quick collision of flesh and sensation. Then more pulling and stripping until their clothes littered the carpet like rags. In one swipe, he ripped down the blankets, exposing the pure white sheets, and pulled her down beside him.

Then he had to ask, "Is Danny—?"

"Not for at least an hour." Then she had to ask, "But how did you know we were here?"

"I asked the concierge. I figured the Academy put up all the foreign recipients at the same hotel and—"

There was no need to go on. Enough explanations, enough talk. He covered her mouth with his, he found her tongue, her breasts, her pecan mound, and entered her.

This time he didn't wait, this time she didn't hold him off. This time there was no time. So this time he gathered her up and took her, took her right there on the pristine sheets of Danny's bed, took her without stopping, without talking, until it was over. And this time, he didn't ask himself once, *Can you do it? Should you?* This time, there hadn't been a doubt. Now he was completely sure of himself. He was a man again. A man!

It wasn't until several minutes later that he became aware that Dell was crying. He touched her cheek which, unlike his, retained none of the heat or their recent passion. "What is it?" he asked, and covered her.

"My marriage is over." Her voice was flat, dead.

He sat up and sighed. He could think of nothing to say and despite his wish to comfort her, he couldn't help glancing nervously at his watch, still on his wrist.

"Yes," she said coldly. "Go. Go! Run! Get out while you can!"

"Dell, please try to understand," he pleaded as he pulled on his clothes. "Danny's due back any time now. He's staying here, right? Then your marriage isn't over. I don't want to cause a final break. My own marriage is teetering. Erica needs me. She's . . . not well. I'm completely confused. Please, Dell." He touched her cool cheek again. "You're so beautiful. Tonight, in that black suit, you looked . . . like a goddess. I wanted to take you on my arm and show you off to all of Milan. Show them the goddess who brought me back to life! Please, Dell. I want you. I need you. Forgive me."

And then he was gone.

They all said they wanted her, needed her. They all begged

her for forgiveness. But they never asked, What do *you* want? What do *you* need? And they never stopped hurting her.

Oh, how she'd love . . . a martini now. Yes, a martini, bitingly cold and dry. In bare feet she made her way to the blue bathroom, picking up clothes as she went, thinking for the first time since she met him—was it really just last night?—of Rip. Rip Stone. His martini had numbed her, and that's what she needed now—to be numbed down to her breaking heart.

Yet to her surprise, the reflection of herself she caught in the mirror was smiling. Rip Stone had made her smile. *Red.* Even now, she could hear his deep, confident voice saying it, calling her *Red,* making her laugh out loud. Theo said she made him smile, Danny said she made him laugh, but it was Rip, Rip Stone, who'd made *her* happy with just one word. *Red.*

Thinking of him, she continued to grin into the mirror. The sheer size of him made her happy. At last! A man who weighed so much more than she did!

But it was more than that. She stepped out onto the terrace for a look at Milan's old clay roofs and modern towers and remembered the way he'd looked at her when she told him she'd always been afraid of losing control. As if he understood, or wanted to. "Tell me more," he'd said. Here was a man who wanted to know her, who wanted to understand. Here, then, was a new kind of man—a man who might truly be able to care about more than his own problems. But tonight it was too late and yet much too early to know. There was still tomorrow to get through.

Tomorrow! This she did know—she would not stay in this room with Danny another night. She phoned the desk and arranged to have Danny moved into another room tomorrow morning. Then she had them connect her with the airline and moved up her return flight. What she'd do when she arrived home she didn't know. There was so much she didn't yet know. But she wasn't falling apart, she wasn't out of control. In fact, she was still standing, head high and with the barest of smiles on her lips. Then, exhausted, she climbed into the rumpled bed. Tomorrow she had to be up early. Tomorrow she was going shopping.

22

It was not the same. All morning she'd wandered the Brera district, exploring the once-a-month outdoor antiques market with its endless tables and stalls filled with everything from old postcards to important sideboards, but it wasn't the same. Today, shopping didn't thrill her, didn't transport her, didn't seduce her into forgetting a thing. She carried all her burdens with her. It wasn't Milan, it wasn't this flea market, which in former times, with its sellers barking "Dica mei!" and its astounding bargains, would've seemed to Dell like heaven. No, it was shopping itself that could no longer provide the magic. The reality of her life was just too . . . real. She was done with escaping.

Quickly, she hailed a taxi for the short ride back to the old city, where the streets were cobblestoned and the shops sleek and grand. For though the thrill may have gone, she did have to shop for a gown for tonight. Danny was right again, as he usually was in matters of taste, as long as it didn't involve his own tasteless behavior.

"What happened to you?" he asked her in the morning with innocent eyes. "I thought you went to the ladies room. I waited and waited, but you never came back."

That was when she told him she wanted him to move into his own room.

"But why? All because I misunderstood?"

Had he "misunderstood" for over three hours, assuming she was in the ladies room all that time, until he finally dragged himself back to the hotel? She didn't bother to ask, not only because it was useless, but because she wasn't entirely blameless herself. It was he who'd driven her to it, driven her into that wild, passionate escapade with Theo last night just as surely as if he'd pushed her into Theo's arms. It was he who'd raised her hopes once more and aroused her dying passion. And it was he who'd dropped her the moment she vowed to be his, dropping her down a dark hole of need and loss. Still, it was she who took Theo to her bed, and for that she knew she must bear some of the blame.

In ancient buildings housing high-tech boutiques, arresting window displays beckoned for her attention. But the streets were empty and the shops were dark. It was Sunday, she remembered. Everything was closed! Still she wandered, gazing at the designer fashions on the superbly coiffed mannequins posed, one after the other, like frozen party girls in the endlessly unique window tableaus. Finally, she came to a shop whose windows were empty and whose lights were on. Two women in jeans, visible through the window, were struggling to fit on a mannequin a skin-tight gown of emerald and gold. As one zipped up the gown, the other woman, a cigarette dangling from her lips, draped an emerald chiffon scarf, shot with gold threads, around the mannequin's bare chest and throat.

"No! We're closed," they signaled in sign language when Dell tapped on the window. Suddenly, all her travail with Danny was forgotten, her desperate interlude with Theo gone from her mind. The only thing she knew was . . . she had to have that gown! It was perfect. It was sensational. And it was necessary. This was an emergency. Already, it was noon. The cocktail reception was being held at five sharp. She drummed on the window.

The woman with the cigarette came to the door. Opening it a crack, she tried to explain in Italian that the store was closed, that they were just working on a new window, that she should come back tomorrow.

"Domani, signora," she said. And then again, *"Domani."*

But Dell shook her head no and pressed her palms together as if in prayer.

Per favore," she pleaded in Italian. Then in English she said, "Please. I'm desperate. I must have that gown for this eve—"

"Ah. Inglese," the woman interrupted, pleased. "I am studying now the English lingua. Are you Americana?"

"*Si*. I mean, yes," Dell nodded eagerly, seeing her opening. "From Manhattan."

"Ah, Manhattan! I love Manhattan. We go to New York in . . ." she held up seven fingers.

Dell helped her. "Seven."

"Yes, in seven months. We open there our New York shop."

"How wonderful!" Dell said, genuinely delighted for her. Then she did what Danny would've done—she pulled out a business card.

The woman with the cigarette studied the card. Then she call out, "Flavia! Come!" To Dell she said, "My sister is also *designatrice*, but not—how do you say?—pro—?"

"Professional?"

"*Si.*"

The door opened wider and the women shook hands and introduced themselves.

"Then you may need help when you come to New York." Dell wrote her home number on the card.

"This is really great," said Flavia fluently. "Please, do come in. Let us see if we can help you now."

Dell sighed. It was almost a miracle. If the gown fit, it would be a definite miracle.

"Which one?" Flavia asked.

"*Questa qui,*" the first sister answered for Dell, and stubbed out her cigarette. "This one. Is beautiful, no?"

"Is beautiful, yes! May I try it?"

The two sisters peeled the dress off the mannequin and led Dell to a dressing room in the back, Flavia warning her the dress was so tight that she couldn't wear any undergarments with it. "Take everything off. *Tutto.*"

Elena zipped Dell up and now Flavia lit a cigarette. The two sisters took turns studying Dell and smoking. In Italian they argued over whether to take it in at the waist, let it out at the hips, whether the chiffon scarf should be draped over Dell's shoulders or wrapped at her neck, the ends falling down her bare back. Dell let them do with her what they wished while she gazed at herself in the three-way mirror, not quite believing what she saw. It wasn't that she couldn't believe she looked beautiful—it was that she *did* believe it! Staring back at her was not so much a reflection of loveliness—though, indeed, she was splendid. Instead, what she saw were two eyes green as the gown . . . and as sparkling. Sparkling with pride and confidence without a flicker of self-doubt.

"Bella, signora," said Elena, and Dell smiled and lowered her arms.

"Before I alter it," Flavia hesitated, "do you want to know the price in American dollars? I have here a calculator."

Dell shook her head no. "I must have this dress, whatever the cost. For tonight." She put her clothes back on and gave them the gown. "Can it be ready in two hours?"

"Si," said Elena. "My sister has *magico* fingers."

"But I have much hunger," Flavia said, pressing her hand to her stomach. "I must eat something first."

Quickly, Dell grabbed Elena's hand. "C'mon." Then to Flavia she said, "We'll go out and buy some lunch. We'll all have a picnic right here."

"A picnic?"

"Lunch al fresco," Dell explained. "Meanwhile, you start sewing!"

They found a market about to close for midday and quickly bought prosciutto and cheese and tomatoes and olives and fat, crusty bread. By the time they returned, Flavia was almost finished. "You only needed *un poco*— a little here in the hips."

The only dressy shoes Dell had brought with her were black. But this time she just shrugged to herself, *Oh, well, they'll have to do.* Rather than racing all over town to find a perfect pair of green heels, or gold, she sat talking and eating with her new friends. And as she kissed them good-bye, she thought of the other saleswoman in the Madison Avenue shop that she'd also kissed. In all her years of shopping, she'd never taken the time to know any of the staff. Now, in this past week, she'd kissed three of them good-bye. They all, in their way, had become new friends. Oh, what a week, indeed!

A towering centerpiece of brilliant spring flowers bedecked the round table reserved for Americans, blocking Dell's view as she and Danny were seated. That Theo and his dainty blonde wife were already sitting beyond the centerpiece at the other side of the table missed her notice; there was so much to look at. The guests, re-

splendent in satins and ruffles and dark, elegant tuxedos;
the flowers; and, most of all, the astounding frescoes
on the walls of the great architect Aldo Pigno's villa,
where the awards ceremony was being held. But when
she heard Danny say, "*Ciao*, Theo," and saw him kiss
Erica's hand, she wasn't surprised. All evening, she kept
seeing them out of the corner of her eye, and kept finding
a way to avoid them.

At the cocktail party, she did it mostly by mingling.
As soon as she saw Erica's backless pink gown partially
draped by Theo's protective arm, she found a group of
Italians or French to surround her. For quite some time
she found refuge in a corner with the world-renowned
Swedish furniture designer, Lars Josephson, who'd rev-
olutionized chair construction in the 1950s. But when she
saw that bright pink gown heading her way, she began
backing out into the garden.

"Where are you running?" Aldo Pigno protested,
having just joined Dell and the Swede. "Finally, I am
standing next to an American Venus and what does she
do?" he asked Lars Josephson.

"She vanishes," the chair designer answered on cue.
"Perhaps back to her island of Melos."

"*Si!* She vanishes. But not to Melos. This one is all-
American and quite a beauty, no?"

"Very much so," Lars Josephson agreed, watching
her float away in her green strapless gown, the chiffon
scarf trailing behind her.

"I must find her," the architect confided to the old
Swede.

"And what will you do when you find her, you with
your dear wife and she with her tall husband?"

"You saw the husband? Tall, eh?" Then he shrugged
helplessly. "What can I do? She has put me in her
trance."

"Aldo, she's neither a witch nor a goddess; she's
merely flesh and blood."

"Ah, but what flesh!"

Lars Josephson shook his gray head dismally. "What
you men do to these poor women! You make them into
dreams. You pursue them until they swoon. Then you
notice their pimples and stretch marks and you're disappointed."

"*Si, si,* I know all about it, Lars. The endless quest for unattainable perfection," Aldo interrupted impatiently. He'd heard it all before, he knew it by heart, but he refused to believe it. There! He caught sight of Dell's fiery hair piled atop her head that already was several inches above all the others, and he went helplessly in pursuit while Lars looked on askance.

But Dell was weaving a zigzag pattern through the crowd, stopping to chat with the American president of the Association of Interior Designers, then with a group of Milanese experimental artists—and then, eluding everyone, she escaped to the ladies room.

It was only later, when Dell and Danny were called to the stage to accept their award, that she exchanged her first real eye contact with Theo and his wife. Rising from her chair, so did everyone else at the table, and she was forced to accept not only the kisses and congratulations of her colleagues, but of Theo as well. He kissed her on both cheeks, European style, but she saw that he held tight to Erica's hand all the while.

Nevertheless, Erica lunged forward, as if to embrace Dell—or possibly to pummel her—and Dell, startled, took a step back. But she caught, in that instant before Erica fell, face down, a strong whiff of Erica's boozy breath and the lost, blank look in her eyes.

Somehow, she made it up to the stage and listened, beside Danny, as Aldo Pigno chronicled the short but remarkable rise of D & D, highlighting its successes with slides of the firm's famous interiors flashed on the white screen.

"It now gives me great pleasure," she heard Aldo announce, "to confer upon these two attractive Dannenbergs—partners, by the way, not only in their dynamic American firm, but in marriage as well—our award for distinguished and innovative design."

She heard the applause but she couldn't remember anything after that. Did Danny make a speech? Did she? Did they hold hands like the loving married couple they were introduced as? How did she get back to her table? And how did their award get into her hands? She didn't know.

All she knew was that Theo and Erica were gone when she returned, before Theo could run up on stage and accept his own award, which was to have been the high-light of the evening.

The ceremony ended inconclusively, with the disap-pearance of its star, Theodor Glass and his unfortunate wife, and a brief announcement that his silver plaque would be held for him. The evening, however, continued on jubilantly.

There was dancing until the wee hours and Dell was kept in constant motion by a string of partners who wouldn't allow her to sit down. This had never happened to her before. Tonight she was . . . popular. Popular! It's what they called it back when she was a schoolgirl, but she could only imagine its delicious delight then. Not until tonight had she ever really been given so much at-tention by so many. Groups of men surrounded her—handsome men, distinguished men, talented men—all wishing to dance with her, laugh with her, be with her.

From the sidelines, Danny watched his wife boogeying on the dance floor with a mixture of pride and regret. Mostly regret.

"It's late," he told her when he finally caught up with her. "Let's go."

"I'm staying until the last waltz. You go. Your room is ready."

"Dell, this is ridiculous."

"I know how you feel. I felt exactly the same last night," she said pointedly. "Good-bye, Danny."

"Good-bye? Don't you mean . . . good-night?"

"I'm going back to New York tomorrow morning. I changed my ticket."

"I'll change my ticket, too, and go back with you."

"Don't," Dell told him emphatically.

"But I don't want to stay here in Milan alone."

Dell patted his shoulder in mock sympathy. "Speaking as someone who's had a lot of experience in being left alone, I'd say you'll survive. Unfortunately." Then she turned on her heel and walked away.

Later, Aldo Pigno was only too happy to escort her back to her hotel. He'd finally found her on the dance floor the hour before and managed to dance with her three times, including the last waltz. Bold though he was in his advances, Dell found him adorable and utterly harm-less. Almost a head shorter than she, his bushy eyebrows kept brushing her bare chest, tickling her and making her laugh.

On the way home in his limousine, he held her hand and told her, "Tomorrow you come for lunch. I'll send the car. But have no fear—we won't be alone. I'll invite some guests. You can even meet my priest, if you like."

"What a tragedy! How I would've loved it—but I'm going home tomorrow morning."

Taken by surprise, he cried, "No, it's not possible. My Venus is vanishing again."

"Then you must come to America and find me again. And I'll have *you* to lunch and you can meet my husband's rabbi, if *you* like!"

At the hotel, the concierge handed her a sealed white envelope along with her keys, but she didn't open it until she was alone in her room, for she had a suspicion whom it was from.

When the green gown had been hung up in its garment bag, her luggage packed except for toiletries, she finally crawled into bed wearing an oversize T-shirt. Then she read:

> *Dell,*
> *Forgive me. For tonight, for yesterday. I think I love you.*
> *Erica needs help desperately. So do I. When I find it, when I find myself again, may I call you?*
> *Theo.*
> *P.S. You looked utterly . . . petite tonight.*

23

It was finished. Not just the Embassy, but everything. Finished, Danny thought, but as Dell told him two months ago in Milan, he'd survive. And D & D would survive with him despite Dell's departure. At first, when she told him she'd rented office space, he felt a moment of devastation, as crushing as when his father once said to him, "I want nothing more to do with you." His face grew hot and his eyes filled with tears. Dell's stony countenance and dry eyes only made him feel worse. Once, his tears would've moved her. Now it was she who was all business. But he wouldn't allow her to make this ugly. If the purpose of his life was to dwell in beauty—to breathe it, think it, create it—then he would become its living symbol. He would show her how very beautiful he could be!

"Not only do I understand your need to establish your own professional identity, but I respect it," he told her solemnly. "And I want to do everything I can to help you."

His only condition was that she tell no one about her new company until after tonight.

"Let the D & D Embassy opening go as planned or my clients will scatter to the four winds."

Though she took note that he called them "my clients," she agreed, but with a condition of her own.

"After the party, I'm on my own." Even she wasn't entirely sure what she meant. Though for two months now the marriage was effectively over, it hadn't been discussed. Nothing had, and this was their first real conversation in ages. But Danny, posing and preening like a gilded monk, didn't press her.

He didn't press her then, but now, as he wandered up

and down the three floors of his mansion, he couldn't deny the sound of finality in the overwhelming silence.

Silence. After months and months of hammering, of drills buzzing, old windowpanes smashing to the ground, the constant screech of saws, the slaps of paintbrushes . . . silence.

Gone, too, was the dust. Months and months of dust—plaster dust, walnut dust, and ordinary New York soot. And garbage. Bin upon bin of refuse—old, broken tiles, sinks, mirrors, plaster board, one section of the third-floor ceiling, a defunct refrigerator, empty paint cans, crates and cartons—costing two thousand just to cart away.

Finished, all finished. The walls had new wiring, the ceilings new recessed spots. The first floor, D & D's new home, was almost unrecognizable. Six high-tech work stations, each equipped with state of-the-art design computers as well as ordinary drawing tables and custom samples files and shelving, formed a circle around a central, carpeted core, a Theodor Glass hallmark design.

Occupying the former dining room, the new conference room featured a tinted glass table two inches thick. Its four antique bases rested upon a sixteen- by twenty-five-foot Bessarabian rug with hand-woven oversize roses on a black ground. At nine the florist would arrive to fill the house with flowers for the opening party tonight, but now, at only seven in the morning, the table was lined with a collection of empty vases.

On the second floor the renovated kitchen gleamed with sunlight that streamed through the glass-roofed conservatory, past its French doors, and onto the white-glazed tiles. Malachite bullnose counters echoed the green of the plants in the conservatory and French copper pots gave a burnished glow to the room.

Only yesterday had the green-dyed leather, custom Chesterfield sofas finally arrived and been arranged in the living room, forming a *U* around the outrageously expensive shagreen coffee table.

Three bedrooms and baths on the third floor looked out over the glass roof of the conservatory and a small garden beyond.

Danny checked to see that there were soaps and guest towels laid out in the bathrooms, ashtrays discreetly placed on side tables. He stared at the custom-upholstered master bed with its tufted and rolled headboard, upholstered bun feet, and its five inches of extra padding . . . and winced. Neither Dell nor he had spent even one night in the bed together, though they'd moved into the house more than a week before. Ever since Danny returned from Milan, Dell refused to sleep in the same room with him, much less the same bed.

And after that, though Dell continued to speak to him, it was with the chilly formality of a complete stranger.

"We have a lot to do in the next two months," she told him one morning. "If it's agreeable to you, I'll organize our move from the apartment to the Embassy, and you can direct the plans for the opening. I won't be in the office today and I won't be home for dinner."

Now it was he who never knew where she'd been, or with whom. Of course, it wasn't the same thing as when he kept late hours and refused to give her explanations. If he kept part of his life secret from her, it was only to protect her. How could she, he asked himself indignantly, with her weak ego, her endless need for approval and love, ever understand his complicated life, his burning ambition and passions? To keep her from devastating feelings of rejection, he of course kept things from her. He did it only for her! He loved her that much. But what did he get for all this care and devotion? This ridiculous game of tit-for-tat. In dismay, he wondered when she would come to her senses.

Meanwhile, their lives had completely reversed. Now Dell met with *her* clients, closing her office doors behind them and not even bothering to introduce him. Now that she'd announced she'd taken new office space, he supposed they should divvy up the client list, but something held him back from offering.

Why offer, he reasoned, when she would never get the nerve to really leave. *Leave all this?* he asked himself, incredulous, as he weaved his way in and out of the six work stations of D & D's new headquarters. *And take half my treasure with her? Never!*

Like Christopher Beene before him, Danny had come to think of his A-list clients as his treasures, too. How he'd wooed them, flattered them, cajoled them, seduced them until finally, they were his! Yes, Christopher had recommended him most highly, but still he had to convince them, win them, take them over. He had done it. He alone. Now they were his. If she wanted to walk out, fine. She could leave . . . but with not one of his treasures. And that included the bitch, Tina Garson.

"Well, that's it. You're in business," said Rip Stone, taking the gold pen from Dell's hand. "Three signed copies for you, three for me, a set of corporate minutes, and—presto! 'House of Dell Shay' is born."

Dell tried to smile but she was too drained. "This was bigger for me than I realized," she admitted, and slumped down into the upholstered English chair, a rather fine though faded reproduction, opposite Rip Stone's English kneehole desk. When she'd phoned him exactly two weeks after she returned from Milan, two weeks after first meeting him at Tina's apartment, she told him her call was strictly professional.

"I need a lawyer and I have . . . personal reasons for not using my husband's attorney."

"I see," was all he said in his deep, rich drawl.

"Would you be willing to set up a new corporation for me?" she continued. "I'm going to call it 'House of Dell Shay.' "

"I can take care of that for you, yes."

He hadn't called her "Red," and although, by her formal tone she knew she was erecting a wall between them, she nevertheless was disappointed. Until she became aware that he wasn't going to say it, she hadn't realized that she wanted to hear it again. To hear him say *Red.* But she fought the feelings.

Just as she fought the electricity between them on the phone. It was as if the line carried not only their sound waves, but their heartbeats as well. Convinced, however, that the last thing she needed was another man in her life—even one who could, with one word, make her happy—she was determined to discourage any hint of romance. So far, she'd succeeded. In their two meetings at his office, the only subject other than her new business that they had discussed was his business.

Rapping his knuckles on his cluttered desk, he said, "As you can see, we're bursting at the seams here. My practice has been growing like crazy, knock wood, but I can't find anything anymore. My secretary says I should buy more file cabinets. But maybe a more ambitious solution is needed.'' Then he paused before asking her, ''What do you think?''

Looking around her at the handsome but worn pieces and the inadequate storage files, the personal memorabilia like the Western saddle and the ornamental pair of spurs, she knew exactly what she would do—design an efficient office plan and throw out whatever couldn't be recovered or refinished. And although the saddle seemed to be of particularly fine leather, it too would have to go. But she hesitated telling him.

Go slow with this one, she warned herself. With Tina Garson, Jackie and Dom, and as of yesterday, Tamara, she had enough clients to keep her head above water. *Be sure before you take this one on . . . this time, be absolutely sure.*

So she simply said, ''Maybe you need larger office space,'' and he agreed, backing off. But now, today, with their immediate business completed, he approached her again, from a different angle.

''It's too late for breakfast, too early for lunch, so what should we do?''

Exhausted, her mind worked sluggishly to comprehend. ''Do?''

''To celebrate.''

He was right, of course. She didn't exactly start her own business every day of the week. This was the biggest event of her life, and it deserved acknowledgment. It deserved . . . a toast!

''Martinis,'' she said sheepishly.

''Martinis?'' he repeated in disbelief. He looked at his watch. She didn't have to; she knew it was only eleven-thirty in the morning. But then he smiled at her. A dazzling, warm, heart-stopping smile. ''Ah, Red, I knew it the minute I saw you.''

''Knew what?'' she asked, but she was smiling, too.

''I knew your problem was that you'd never met a man you could trust enough to ever let down your guard. You're plenty spontaneous. No one's ever taken the trouble to really know you, that's all.''

He could see that her face was flaming and that she was close to tears, so he handed the ladies' room key to her without a word, and while she was gone, he made martinis for them both.

When she returned, her cheeks were still pink but she was still smiling. He had made her happy with a word.

"To the House of Dell Shay," he said, clinking her glass with his. "And to you, Red. Congratulations."

The martini went directly to her head, freeing her to say what was in her heart. "Thank you Rip. For being more than my lawyer. For being my friend." She leaned toward him to kiss him on the cheek, but he pulled her closer until she was crushed in his embrace. For once she didn't fight her feelings for him. She allowed her body to melt into his and wrapped her arms around his neck. Then his lips were on her ear and he was beginning to whisper something that she passionately wanted to hear. Except that . . . the phone was ringing!

"Damn!" he exclaimed, and he let her go. He picked the phone up and barked into it, "I told you to hold my calls." Then he paused, listening, and nodded. "I see," he said, and sighed. "All right, I'll be with him in five minutes."

Turning back to Dell, he said to her gruffly, "I'm sorry, but I've got a court appearance on Monday and a desperate client waiting to see me. How 'bout letting me make it up to you by taking you out to dinner tonight?"

"I can't," she said, hesitating before telling him the rest. "Tonight, D & D is having its own celebration for its new offices. It's an open-house party at the Embassy." Then she hesitated again. Until now she hadn't wanted to mix her old life with her new one, but already the lines had blurred. New friends, new clients would be at the party—so why not Rip Stone? Besides, now that he'd filed her Certificate of Incorporation with the Secretary of State of New York, the need for secrecy was over. Danny was just being slightly paranoid. News of the split-up of D & D would cause barely a ripple, she predicted. And the faithful and adoring—his clients—would only cling closer to him as a result. So while she'd honor her promise to Danny tonight, she would no longer hide.

But what about her feelings for Rip? Should she hide them? What were her feelings, anyway? He had said she was "plenty spontaneous," but she just hadn't met a man she could trust. Perhaps tonight was the time to find out.

"I'd really love you to be there," she said shakily, but his eyes steadied her, and she even managed to jokingly trap him with, "And you can't plead it's the last minute because you already told me you're free tonight."

He accepted the invitation with a small bow and walked her to the door. Then he suddenly grasped her shoulders and pulled her to him again. He didn't kiss her, he just gazed at her. "Red, oh, Red!" was all he said, but it was more thrilling than the dizzying rhapsody she'd known in those first heady days with Danny . . . or with Theo. Thrilling, yet somehow calming. Calmly, she walked out of his office and into the sunlight. Magically, her exhaustion lifted. She felt strong and free. She felt she could walk miles. She could walk all the way to Second Avenue and Eighty-ninth Street, to her new office, to the House of Dell Shay.

Angie Romano looked up from a temporary desk made of a plank and two sawhorses and smiled when Dell entered.

Dell smiled, too, but she scolded. "What're you doing here? It's bad enough you come here after work at night—and now you're giving up your weekends, too. What am I going to do with you?"

Angie ignored her. "Guess what?"

Dell scanned the large loftlike space, from its white-painted pressed-tin ceiling to its bleached-oak floor, but the room looked just as it did yesterday. Bare.

"I give up," she said, not noticing the rectangular box amid all the paper coffee cups on the plank.

"I picked up your stationery on the way over. It was ready."

"Ooh, let me see!" Dell opened the box and lifted a letter-size sheet from the pile. For three weeks after she placed the order with the printer, she kept calling up and changing the design of the letterhead. She made it larger, smaller, bolder, and finally starker. But now she wasn't sure she'd made the right decision. All the letters were in lower case, very small, very discreet—but was it right? Was it perfect? A perfect reflection of her and her new firm? All her old doubts had returned. Now that she'd designed her own logo, it was time to tackle the biggest project—designing her office. But how could she when she still wasn't sure if she liked the logo?

"Don't you like it?" Angie asked.

"I don't know."

"Well, *I* do. I think it's modern and elegant. It's—*you,* Dell! And I can't wait to type my first letter on it on Monday."

"Monday! But you haven't even given Danny notice yet."

"Yes, I did. Last week, as soon as you asked me to work for you."

"Oh," said Dell flatly. "He didn't tell me."

He didn't tell her, Dell realized, because he didn't believe it would happen. He was waiting for her to come back to her senses, to come back to D & D. To come back to him. Instead, she didn't know how she'd endure even another night living in the Embassy. Living with him. For two months she'd put off thinking about her marriage while she concentrated on forming the House of Dell Shay. And for some reason, she'd put off the design of her new office. The two were somehow linked, but she wasn't sure why.

"Can you stand working in all this—emptiness?" she asked Angie, reminding herself that with Angie now on the payroll, too, she'd have to start earning money fast. Thank God for Tina Garson. She was coming in with a check on Monday.

Then she realized what she'd just said to herself—thank God for Tina Garson. Not thank God for Danny. Yes, she was truly on her own!

Thank God, she said again to herself, for all the lovely women in my life. Thank God for dear, sweet Angie, here. And for Jackie. And Tina. And Tamara Walkov.

And thank God for you, Mom, she said under her breath. *Most of all, for you.*

"Monday, we're going to get you a typewriter, and next month, a computer. But no more work for today. I'm going home to have a nap before the party. And when I wake up, I'm going to do my mother's hair. She's coming early so I can dress her. And then we're going to sit down like two ladies and have a martini. Someone I know taught me how to make them. Now let's both get out of here!''

The red in Gertrude Shay's hair had faded and there wasn't time for a color rinse, so Dell twisted her mother's limp strands into a French knot and stood back to survey her handiwork. Already her mother's face had been transformed with powder and blush and jade-green shadow and pale coral lipstick. Now all she needed was a pair of earrings to emphasize her new, sophisticated hairdo. Dell clipped pearl teardrops to her ears and pronounced her mother "a knockout."

Gertrude's laughter traveled out the open windows and into the balmy spring evening. Perhaps all the way to Danny's room, Dell thought sadly. Between their separate bedrooms, their own separate worlds, the huge master with its unoccupied custom bed reposed in darkness and silence like a sealed tomb, shrine to their lost love.

"Do you know what today is?" Gertrude asked her daughter as she reclined on the down-filled English chaise and watched Dell dress. "You don't, do you?" she said again for emphasis and sipped her martini in the long-stemmed glass.

"Of course, I do. It's May seventh. It's—oh my!" Dell gasped. "My birthday."

And not one card, she thought miserably. *Everyone's forgotten—including me.* However, she had only herself to blame for, unlike Jackie, who began reminding everybody two months in advance, Dell always insisted birthdays were for the very young and the very old. Mature adults shouldn't make birthdays obligatory.

"I don't need a cake and balloons. And I don't believe people should feel obligated to buy me useless presents. A thoughtful card will do—if my loved ones happen to remember," she'd repeated so often that now, it seemed, her words had been taken literally. No one happened to remember . . . and she was disappointed.

She undid her ivory silk dressing gown and pulled on sheer, green-tinted pantyhose. Then she stood naked before the tall Federal pier glass and her mother sighed.

"My beautiful baby. You have the body of a teenager. You know, I never knew what it was like to have a young, firm body. I didn't want anyone to see my big old cow's breasts and my flabby thighs—not the doctor, not your father, not even you. But seeing you now, I can almost imagine what it might've been like. It's your birthday, but it's you who's given me the better present—you. Anyway, happy birthday, my dear.'' She held out two small packages as Dell pulled on the strapless green gown that had been such a triumph in Milan. ''But don't open them now. Wait till later. Let me zip you up and then we can show you off to your handsome husband.''

Danny. What did her mother know, suspect? Certainly, their separate bedrooms were a sign that something was wrong, but this wasn't the time for tearful confessions. She placed her mother's presents on the antique lowboy and slid into the one new purchase she'd made—green ribbon high-heeled sandals banded in gold. Then she took her mother's arm and carefully made her way down the original ornate staircase in her new and terribly uncomfortable shoes. Danny was waiting for them at the bottom, beaming with pride.

''My bride,'' he cooed and tried to take Dell in his arms but Gertrude saw how her daughter grew rigid at his touch. Danny, however, was unfazed.

''Gertrude, you look gorgeous!''

Once again, his excessiveness had the opposite effect that he'd intended, and Gertrude, too, shrugged him off, embarrassed. It was baffling. He was being his most charming. If he did say so himself, he was, well, superb. But even a great actor can't perform in a vacuum. He had, however, one last stratagem which he'd meant to save for later, but it wouldn't hurt for Gertrude to witness this. Maybe she'd even give Dell a nudge and then he'd finally get his due from the two of them—applause.

Taking a small box from his coat pocket, he held it out to Dell, but spoke only to Gertrude.

''I absolutely worship you daughter. She is a rare, rare gem whose brilliance, I always recognized, needed a proper setting. Which is why I've given her this.'' He held out his arms to encompass the mansion.

''I thought,'' said Gertrude Shay with cool precision, ''that this house was earned by both of you, a gift to each other.''

Unruffled, Danny said smoothly, ''That's true. From

the day we took our vows, Dell has been my partner . . .''
Then he turned to Dell.

". . . and always will be.'' He clasped the box into
her hand. "Happy birthday, Dell, darling.''

"I think I've seen that dress before, which is a good
thing because I didn't get to see enough of it last time,''
someone was murmuring into the back of her neck. She
knew that seductive, familiar voice—even her spine tin-
gled in recognition. Theo! She turned to face him.

"Hello, Dell.''

He was dressed all in black, which made his blond hair
appear even lighter and his perfectly square, perfectly
white teeth gleam almost too brightly. He had shaved off
his moustache.

"I almost didn't recognize you without your—'' she
gestured toward his upper lip. During these last two
months she'd let Danny deal with completing and fur-
nishing the Embassy. Until the day she moved in, she'd
hardly gone near the place. This was the first time, then,
that she'd looked into Theo's lapis-blue eyes since Milan.
If she let them, those eyes could probably still make her
heart stand still and her skin blush a hot pink. But she
had no intention of allowing those eyes to get anywhere
near her heart. She looked past him to the crush of people near the door.

"When did you arrive? I didn't see you come in.''

"How could you've? There must be close to a hundred
and fifty people here already.''

Surrounded on all sides, Dell could only smile and
shrug. Almost all of the faces were familiar to her, and
it was impossible to stand there for more than five
seconds without being kissed or embraced by some
colleague, client, supplier, artisan, contractor, or manufacturer she'd known or worked with before.

Theo was urgently trying to tell her something, but she
was being hugged by Angie Romano and Jackie and
Dom, who'd all arrived at the same moment. Angie
wouldn't let go of her hands and stared at her with wide-
eyed idolatry.

"That's the single most beautiful dress I've ever seen.
Where did you get it?''

The question directed everyone's attention to the gown,

one long, breathlessly tight lick of lollipop green that pushed Dell's bosom up—and almost out of—two strapless sweetheart cups. Draped over one shoulder was the gold-shot chiffon scarf and around her neck she wore an antique emerald and gold choker. Jackie fingered it admiringly.

"This looks real. Is it?"

Nodding, Dell almost had to shout, "It's a present from Danny—but I'm not keeping it."

She hadn't wanted to accept it, despite its beauty. But Danny insisted she wear it tonight.

"For me. For D & D. For all that this night means."

Even her mother exhorted her to keep it. "Such a beautiful piece. Look how it goes with your dress." Then, in a whisper, "Can't you see how hard he's trying?"

"Yes, I see." But her mother didn't know that it was too late. She thought there was still hope, still time; perhaps, until this moment, Dell did, too. That it was too late—years too late—was a realization that had only just penetrated her mind. Until now, it hid in her heart. Now she knew with certainty, with finality, but she would need a little time before she could speak of it. The necklace, however, would have to go.

"I'll wear it tonight—but only tonight. After that, it's yours. And what's mine," she added somewhat cryptically while her mother looked on helplessly, "I'll claim at the proper time."

So now you know, her mind kept repeating as she floated through the crowd, seemingly serene. *Too late. Too late. Too late.*

Leroy Delray, the perfume manufacturer whose New York headquarters D & D had done two years before, grabbed Dell's arm and led her to the French coffee table in front of the green leather Chesterfields.

"I want this. I need this. What is this?"

"It's sharkskin."

"Sharkskin. I love it. I want one."

"In the 1920s they called it shagreen. It's very rare."

"All the more reason to have one."

Dell nodded. She understood. Wasn't this exactly what the renovation and redecoration of the Embassy was supposed to do—make everyone drool? Make them think

Danny and Dell now had it all, had perfection? Make
them think D & D could create an ideal heaven for them
where they too could live in expensive bliss? Wasn't this
what she'd always wanted since she was a girl—to create
ideal rooms and fill them with perfectly beautiful things
and make people happy? Yes, but something was wrong
with the question. And the solution, as ever, eluded her.

She drifted up the stairs to the third floor, where Theo
and Danny were giving a group of journalists a tour of
the house. First Danny motioned to her, then Theo. Each
had something urgent he wanted to tell her, wanted from
her, but they didn't know what she now knew—it was too
late, much too late.

On the second floor she found Jackie and Dom talking
to her mother. Gertrude Shay clung to her daughter's
hand.

"I'm worried about you."

"So am I," said Jackie. "Why aren't you keeping that
incredible necklace? This really worries me."

But Dom made her laugh. "I'm worried, too. I'm worried I'm gonna be standing here when you fall out of that
dress and then you'll be too embarrassed to look me in
the eye again and you won't make our apartment as pretty
as yours—and then Jackie'll be mad at me!"

Everyone was eating and drinking, and though she herself had no appetite, Dell made her way to the kitchen to
check on the food. It took more than half an hour to get
there. By the time she did, she had lipstick kisses all over
her face and a blister on both feet. Above the heads of
everyone she thought for a moment she recognized a
shock of salt and pepper hair and the shoulders of a bear,
but she lost sight of him and collapsed on a chair at the
huge malachite country table.

"Can I get you something to drink? Eat, Mrs. Dannenberg?" waiters asked her as they scurried around her,
carrying out platters of hors d'oeuvres. She just shook
her head no.

A chef was refilling a bowl with fresh crab salad, pulling the delicate white meat right from the chilled claws
and into the mixture. He stopped to drain a huge sieve
of sweet potato chips deep-frying on the stove. As soon
as he dropped them into two lined baskets, a waiter
placed them on trays beside dips of garlicky mashed egg-

plant and extra-hot and thick chili and carried them out. The kitchen was busy but well organized. She wasn't needed. Slipping off her shoes, she wandered out to the glass conservatory where a brand-new jungle of gigantic palms and tropical flowering plants looked like they'd been growing there for years. It was mostly dark, with just a few well-placed uplights illuminating the flowers. She was thinking, *This is the best room in the—*

When she thought she heard someone sobbing. She moved closer to the sound, and then saw him. It was Danny. Half-hidden behind several palms, Christopher Beene sat slumped in a wheelchair and Danny's head was in his lap. The cries that came from him, hoarse and pitiful, were like those of an animal whose foreleg had just been chopped off. Afraid that the kitchen staff might hear, Dell checked that the door was closed. She herself was about to leave when she heard Danny speak, his voice breaking again and again.

"If I knew—if I believed that this was the price I'd have to pay for you saving me, I never—ever—would've agreed to let you put Garson in your bed. I would've kept him where he belonged—where he died—in my office. And I'd have taken my lumps. Because they never could've hurt as much as this!"

"Oh, Danny, Danny," she heard Christopher groan. "You know I love you. You know you're all I love, all I have. What more do you want of me?"

"And—I—love you."

Again, Christopher groaned mournfully. "I know. And I'm here. Didn't I keep my promise? I'm here."

"But you'll really never come again?" He was sobbing again, rattling the palms. "You mean it—that we'll never—see—each other again?"

"You have a lovely home and a . . . lovely wife. I saw her before and she really is quite . . . spectacular. Enjoy your life. This is what we did it for, didn't we? All this. I can only taint it. Everyone shuns me now. So let it go, Danny. Let *me* go."

"I can't. I won't. I'd rather give all of this up."

Christopher's laughter filled the room.

"All right then," Danny pressed on. "I'll give up Dell. That's what you've always wanted, isn't it? I'll give her up."

Dell stepped forward. "That won't be necessary. *I'm* leaving you!" Then she gave the two startled men her biggest, brightest grin and about-faced, leaving them to stare at her bare, straight back as it vanished from their view.

The grin, of course, faded as soon as she made her way out of the kitchen and into the crowd. It wasn't replaced by tears—she felt no need to cry. She felt simply empty. Nothing at all was left.

In her bedroom she found the peace and quiet she craved. Her mother's two presents were still where she'd left them and now she unwrapped them, the larger one first. It was an enlarged and framed photograph of Dell, six years old, sitting on her mother's lap. The note said, "You are not alone. You'll always be welcome on this old lap of mine."

The second gift was a surprise, a ring of rare beauty that Dell had never seen before, though her mother wrote, "It was my mother's—the only thing she left to me. And now it's the only thing of value I have to give to you."

Things of value, Dell mused to herself, and worthless things. Who could say except oneself? Unclasping the antique necklace Danny bought for her, she laid it in its rectangular box like a body being put to rest. Then she slid her mother's gold ring onto her finger. She knew she'd never take it off as long as she lived. Her mother was wrong, of course; she'd given Dell numerous things of value, priceless—

"So this is where you've been hiding!"

Abruptly, her peace was shattered. She turned to see who'd found her out, and smiled.

He smiled, too, and his handsome, rugged face reddened slightly. "Everyone's looking for you. It seems there's a big birthday cake but no birthday girl to blow out the candles. You didn't tell me it was your birthday. No fair," Rip Stone scolded her, but he was still smiling.

"I didn't want a big fuss."

"Well, there's going to be a big fuss if you don't blow out those candles. Shall we go now, Red?" He held out his arm.

Red. He was wearing those cowboy boots again. Downstairs, Danny was waiting. And Theo. No, she didn't want to go down there just yet. She wanted to stay right here and ask Rip something. "Tell me about those boots."

Looking down at his feet, he gave a mock shrug. "Way'll, this ol' boy is from Texas, y'hear?" he said, laying on the accent extra thick. When she laughed, he continued in his normal speech. "And back home, everybody wears these here boots. And Stetson hats. I gave up my Stetson in law school, but I couldn't give up my boots."

"Why not?"

He'd been slouching against the door, but now he stood up straight and looked at her as if she were mad. "Give up mah boots? Why, it'd be like you giving up your beautiful red hair. They're a part of me."

She nodded. She understood, and now it was time to go, but still she lingered. His words ". . . your beautiful red hair" echoed in her ears. They were sweet words, delicious, making her want more of them.

"Do you have anything else to tell the birthday girl?" she teased as she circled in front of him, but he refused to look at her.

"My grandmother once told me that a woman's beauty should be judged first thing in the morning, just as she awakens. It is only then that her true face is revealed."

"Oh," she said, deflated. When would they ever share a morning like that together? Never?

Suddenly, she felt his warm hand on her cheek. He was looking at her, right into her. "What is it? What's making you so unhappy?"

"Is it that obvious?"

"To me, yes."

Giving up the bright pretense, Dell slumped on the edge of the bed, her head in her hands. "My marriage is finished as of tonight. But it was over way before this. Years, in fact."

"Yes, I thought so," Rip conceded and sat down beside her on the bed.

He'd guessed the truth and she was relieved. Now she didn't have to hide any of it—not from Rip. "Tonight, I'm leaving this house and I'm never coming back."

"Where will you stay?"

Dell shrugged. "A hotel. Or with friends. Just until I can find my own place, my own life." Suddenly filled with nervous energy, she jumped up and began throwing clothes into a soft leather bag. With symbolic finality, she meticulously zipped it closed.

"Would you like me to carry that for you?"

"No, I'd very much like to do it all myself," she said, breathing deeply with emotion.

"Yes, I thought so," Rip said for the second time.

"You understand completely, don't you?"

"Yes, I think I do. I've been there myself."

"Yet there's nothing . . . you want to tell me . . . about what I should do and how I should do it?"

"My grandmother once told me that if it's not broken, don't fix it."

"I like your grandmother."

"You're going to be fine, Dell."

"I wish I felt as sure as you are." What she really wished was that she could just collapse in his powerful arms and let him take charge, take care of her, do it all for her. But even if he'd agree, deep down she knew it'd never work. Because it was she—and she alone—who had to take these first difficult steps. If ever she was to become truly independent and free, no one else could do it for her—not even Rip Stone.

She knew all this, and yet how she wished she could at least keep him beside her. Already, she missed him. This was a necessary but solitary journey on which she was about to embark, and she knew neither how long it'd take nor where it'd end. She didn't know if he'd still be waiting, or even if she'd want him to wait. She only knew it was time to begin and that already she missed him, missed him woefully.

Hoisting her bag with one hand, she held out the other to Rip.

"I wish—" she began, stopped herself, then started again, this time with determination. "I'm going down now to blow out my candles and make my wish properly. This one's too important not to play by the rules. Then I'm going to collect my mother and her things and treat her to a night in a hotel. After that, I just don't know."

Comprehending her meaning, he couldn't mask his disappointment. Nevertheless, he took her proffered hand and squeezed it tightly before he let her go to make her own way, as she wished.

"Thank you, Rip, for coming tonight. And for being here for me. Oh, I'm so sorry it's ending like this—before it ever really began—but I hope you understand," she exclaimed and passed in front of him and out the bedroom doorway.

"It hasn't ended. It has only just begun."

She turned back to face him and dropped the bag. "How can you be so sure? At this moment, nothing is clear to me. I don't want to hurt your feelings, but I—I just can't make any promises."

"I can."

"No, don't. No promises."

But he didn't listen to her. And she couldn't help admiring him for it.

"Look, Dell, maybe it isn't the best timing. Maybe I did meet you at just about the most unsettled moment of your life. But there will come a time when the pain will lift and the mist will clear. And I can promise you this— I'll be there, waiting. I ask nothing of you but that you understand that I'm going to wait, for as long as it takes."

Once, Theo had told her, *Don't wait for me, Dell. Don't wait.* Now she wanted to say these same words to Rip. But when she looked at him, he was holding his finger to his lips to silence her and in his eyes she recognized a determination equal to her own. He would not be easy to dissuade. Then, as if to prove it, he strode swiftly past her and escaped down the staircase, leaving her with his promise. A promise, she knew, that he'd never forget . . . and that, despite herself, neither would she.

Now she was truly on her own. With her hands trembling only slightly, she carefully lifted the skirt of her green gown in one hand, grasped her overnight bag with the other, and made her way down to the large group of well-wishers.

Danny was waiting at the foot of the stairs, waiting to play his role once again and escort her into the room. Perhaps no greater actor ever existed, she observed coolly. Even now, after all that'd just happened, he could perform his role of devoted husband with seamless artistry. But he did hesitate when he noticed her bag.

"So now I know the truth. All of it, at last," she told him with quiet finality.

Gesturing to the bag, he said, "That's why I didn't tell you. I was sure you'd overreact and do something like this if you knew."

Dell shook her head. "No, you're wrong. If you'd come to me, told me, I might've stayed—for you. Instead, I had to hear you promise Christopher Beene to give me up, to offer me as a donation, like I was some unimportant piece of furniture in an estate sale. But of all the unforgivable things you've done, that wasn't even the worst. The worst is that you dare to stand here now, ready to play my leading man!"

"Dell, not now. They're waiting—"

"Stand aside! This is *my* show, and you, my darling Danny, have been written out. So stand aside. I'm about to make my entrance—alone!"

24

End-of-summer light baked the exposed side of Danny's cheek awakening him on a goosedown pillow wet with perspiration, despite the chill of the air conditioning. Last night he'd forgotten to unhook the tiebacks over the master bedroom's polished linen Roman shades. And no wonder, he smiled to himself, squinting at his jockey shorts soaking up a puddle of spilled red wine on the uncarpeted walnut parquet margin of the floor. But those damned perforated linen shades were a disaster. That they were originally Dell's idea took some of the sting from a design failure he could ill afford to make, since it was his own money he was playing with here. Dell had had the ridiculous impulse to redo the bedroom of their last apartment shortly before they were to move to the Embassy. Of course, he nixed the plan, but he stole her idea for the shades, forgetting that his bedroom faced east.

Dell. He really should call her. It was their first ex-anniversary, Labor Day weekend. Or fax her. "Hi Ex! Happy Ex! Ex-love, Danny." She'd probably be in the office to receive it, slaving away even on a holiday weekend. Through the grapevine, he heard she'd spent this year and a half working like a demon. House of Dell Shay was being talked up in the trade. *The New York Times Magazine* featured one of her projects, a California winery, in a two-page spread. How was she getting the clients? In a gesture of generosity, he agreed to let her take Tina Garson with her after all, but none of his other A-list clients. So how was House of Dell Shay getting so hot so fast?

It was not yet, of course, a rival to D & D. An established firm now, with vast projects and healthy profits, Dell's defection caused barely a ripple, to his immense relief. But what he did best, what made him a master, was client wooing. Dell, insufferably honest, had none of his flair. So how had she done it?

He'd seen it with his own eyes only this past June, but he still didn't really believe it. It was at the New York Designers' Show House opening, a glittering black-tie affair. For several years running D & D had been the featured design firm, and as such was assigned the largest room to redecorate, while the younger designers had to be content with a small guest room or study. Though it always wound up costing Danny a bundle, even with loans and outright gifts of fabrics and furnishings, the publicity made it all worth it. This year, however, with the divorce and running D & D without Dell and all the new business flowing into D & D's Embassy offices, he declined to do a Show House room—but of course he was invited to the opening anyway.

It was on the tour of the rooms that he saw it—Dell's fantasy child's bathroom and all the commotion it stirred in the usually sedate crowd. Everyone was pressing and peering into the bathroom doorway, sighing and laughing and "oohing" with dreamy adulation.

"She's a genius. And look at her. She's gorgeous, too," the woman in front of him gushed.

"Where?" her companion in a sleek Galanos gown asked.

"She's standing at the far end, by the window."

"I can't see anything but a sea of heads in front of me."

"Well, just look at what she did with the tub. Look at the miniature hot-air balloon floating above it with all those pastel ribbon streamers. Charming, isn't it?"

"Ooh, I see her! My God, she's fabulous!"

"Here, let's take her card from the soap dish. Such a clever detail."

"Let's see, House of Dell Shay. I know that name. Wasn't she connected with another firm?"

"D & D," Danny muttered behind them. "D & D."

Turning to him, the woman in the Galanos nodded. "Yes, something like that. Not that it matters. Dell Shay. That's all I need to know." Then she tucked the card into her silk evening bag.

Yes, Danny had seen it with his own eyes. For a year he'd heard rumors that Dell was creating a sensation and tonight he'd seen it. But he didn't see her. He left her to the throngs still waiting to meet her and returned to his own realm, his Embassy, where he was still preeminent.

Here, in his magnificent mansion, Dell's success barely intruded. If indeed it was success at all. He still didn't believe it. One of these days, he'd have to find out for sure. Take Dell to lunch and find out the real story. Maybe even dazzle her again over a plate of lettuce leaves. Spark some of the old adulation in her eyes instead of this—this indifference! This insufferable independence! This immunity to his charm. Yes, he'd have to take Dell to lunch.

But not today, he thought lazily, yawning and awakening his companion in the huge, upholstered bed. For a short time after Dell left and Christopher Beene died, he tasted true loneliness and ugly despair. Oh, it was horrid! Such a painful time. But he wasn't meant to live in a gray, colorless world. An artist required stimulation. He was an artist, a master. To create beauty, he simply had to receive beauty.

He stroked the mound the young man's rump made under the Egyptian cotton sheet. *Let it go better,* he prayed, *this time.* Last night he had had too much wine. It had been a lovely night, a delicious night—except for the end. There had been no end, no release. He couldn't climax. It was the wine, he was sure of it. Just like the other times.

So stop the drinking, he chided himself. But without the wine, he knew he'd be even more tense and frustrated. Even now, sweat poured out of him, and not all of it was due to the sunlight. A teeny-weeny glass of Côtes du Rhône would take the edge off. Just a sip, and then he'd do the draperies over the damned shades.

Leaving the bed, he found a second bottle and poured himself a glass.

"Come back to bed," the young man whined adorably. "It's so big and I'm so lonely."

"In a minute," said Danny, emptying the glass. Then he poured a teeny-weeny bit more. After some minutes, he forgot about the shades altogether.

At dawn, the wide, white endless Fire Island beach was deserted and silent, except for the crash of the waves and the rush of the surf pulling back out to sea. To Dell, it was the best time to enjoy the beach, but none of her houseguests was willing to be awakened in the dark just to see what she meant about watching the sun rise over the water.

"Tell us about it at breakfast," they said last night at dinner under the stars on the vastly enlarged cedar deck.

"Here," said Jackie, passing Dell her camera. "Take pictures."

"Right. Take pictures," Dom agreed. "Just don't wake us." He patted Jackie's belly. "Baby Dominick here needs his sleep."

"Dominique!" Jackie insisted, poking her husband with her elbow.

"I pass, too," Tamara Walkov Berringer said, and her husband Gillian seconded her vote.

Even Gertrude Shay said, "Dell, dear, you won't mind if I don't join you, will you?"

Dell just shook her head, depleted by the flood of demurrals.

But now, sitting on the beach, coffee cup planted beside her in the sand, it was just as well, it seemed to her, that she'd been given this time to be alone and reflect. The serenity of this setting, however, did nothing to soothe her inner turmoil. If anything, she felt more agitated.

It was Rip, of course. Rip Stone. She told herself to think of something else, to think of the remarkable year and a half she'd had, all the hard work and how it was beginning to pay off. But it was no use, and finally she surrendered and allowed Rip Stone to possess her mind completely.

Arriving late on the last ferry, after they'd all had dinner, he was strangely quiet when she came to the dock to meet him.

It had been an impulsive call, a last-minute invitation she'd made to him, and he was clearly astonished. He was her business lawyer, so of course there'd been contact over the past year and a half—but exclusively by phone or mail. Amazingly, they hadn't set eyes on each other since the Embassy party.

Then, suddenly, there he was in a khaki safari jacket and his cowboy boots, the hard lines of his face still made stunningly attractive by the warmth and kindness in his eyes. But he didn't gather her up in his arms, he didn't enclose her in those shoulders the size of a bear. ''Hi,'' was all he said. ''Hi,'' was all she said back. Then she dumped his bag onto the red wagon she'd brought to the dock and they set out on the dark, quiet trek over the rickety boardwalks to her house on the beach. But she was disappointed.

What did you expect? she asked herself, pulling the wagon behind her, glad to have something to do beside walk in awkward silence. On an island without cars, wagons had become the new beasts of burden.

You call him up out of the blue at the last minute . . . yet he accepts your invitation. Then he races to catch the last ferry . . . and arrives slightly subdued. So he doesn't throw his arms around you. So he doesn't repeat the promise he made to you more than a year ago. Maybe he's waiting to see how you feel. Or maybe . . . he forgot.

Near the house the overhanging beach rose and poison ivy narrowed the path. Neither the moon nor the brightly lit house could be seen where the boardwalk ended and the private path turned to sand, and they walked on in complete darkness. Then, by accident, his shoulder brushed hers.

''Sorry,'' he murmured, but she wasn't. The contact felt to her like an electric volt, shocking her system awake. It was the undeniable proof of attraction. It was why, she now knew, that she'd invited him. She had been powerfully, intensely attracted to Rip the day she met him at Tina Garson's a year and half ago . . . and now she knew she still was.

The feeling only intensified at the crowded house.

''You missed a great meal, Rip,'' Dom told him after the introductions were made.

''Dell made barbecued chicken, barbecued ribs, barbecued everything,'' Dell's mother boasted. ''Do you like barbecue?''

''Mrs. Shay, I was born in Texas, home of barbecue. Down home I'm known as the barbecue king.'' He picked up a leftover chicken leg cooling on the counter and bit into it. ''Yes, ma'am, your daughter must have a little Texas blood in her. This is the real thing!''

Gertrude Shay beamed and Dell blushed and everyone else laughed.

Then they teased him about the sleeping accommodations. "Since you're the last to arrive, you get the last bed in the house. Actually, not _in_ the house. On the screened front porch. Hope you're not afraid of wild animals."

"Or worse. Early risers, for instance. Dell is queen of the dawn," Jackie warned him. "Tell her not to slam the screen door when she goes off to see the sunrise tomorrow."

At last he had looked at her for one long, quiet minute, turning her cheeks the color of fire. "Queen of the dawn, is she? Well, we'll have to see about that."

But he didn't stir when she passed him on the way out to the beach this morning, not even when the screen door squeaked.

And that's what had thrown her into this turmoil. For the hundredth time since Rip had arrived, she was disappointed. Oh, why had she invited him? Perhaps, she mused, making herself smile, it was only to please her mother.

"I like that lawyer of yours," Gertrude Shay had whispered when they climbed into the twin beds in the room they were sharing for the weekend.

"He's not mine."

"Isn't he your lawyer?"

"Well, yes," Dell conceded.

"That's all I meant," her mother said innocently, but as she turned out the light, Dell saw that her mother had a knowing smile on her face.

Soon now, she'd have to get back to the house and begin preparations for breakfast.

"Breakfast is a help-yourself affair around here," she had announced last night before everyone went off to bed. Still, there were the cereals and bowls to lay out, the baskets to fill with muffins and rolls. And of course the indispensable coffee to brew.

Coffee made her think of cappuccino and cappuccino made her think of Angie's housewarming present—the gigantic expresso machine that she'd taken with her when her divorce became final in July. Now it sat in her new kitchen, unused. She just didn't have the time to prepare cappuccino in the morning anymore.

For a year and a half all she'd done was work, work work. This weekend was the first time off she'd taken. Not that she was complaining, however. She'd loved every minute of it and was just as thrilled as her clients when an interior was completed successfully. Thrilled, yes, but no longer obsessive. Something profound had altered her perspective and she saw it most clearly in the way she now approached her work.

Gone now was the driving self-doubt that made her question, "Is it perfect, really perfect? Will they hate it? Can't I do better?" Now, she knew. Immediately, instinctively she knew. When an interior was done right— balanced in scale and proportions, respectful of its architectural or spatial surroundings, appealing visually and texturally, skillful and efficient in its solutions of storage and space problems—she knew. And could say, "Yes, this is a success." But not perfect. Never perfect. It was this that she'd finally learned.

Even a house filled with priceless antiques, custom draperies and details, museum-quality art and rugs, crafted finishing, and a state-of-the-art kitchen is still essentially empty. Empty! Cluttered with things, it still has no heart, no love . . . until the people who live there give it its humanity.

It was this slow realization that freed her in her work. Her personal life was another matter, however.

Jackie was at her all the time. "You've got to get out, date. You're becoming a drudge."

Even Angie Romano, whose idea of paradise was working beside Dell every day at the House of Dell Shay, couldn't resist offering advice, too. "Now that you got me to enroll in my night classes at the Design Academy, I realize how limited my life was before. I've made a whole new circle of friends at the school. Maybe you should follow your own example and get out more yourself."

But for the first time in her life, Dell had more friends than she could handle. She had old friends and new friends, like the Milanese sisters who'd opened a boutique in New York, and the marvelous woman on Madison Avenue whose clothes she bought exclusively now—when she had the time. There had even been a few dates with men, though they found her somewhat distant and wary of serious involvements. Eventually, they stopped calling.

"You're gun-shy," Tamara told her.

And perhaps she was. After her affair with Theo fizzled out and after the painful dissolution of her marriage to Danny, she was afraid to take the risk again. Yet she'd invited Rip Stone here this weekend. Last night, on the path of sand when his shoulder brushed hers, she realized she'd invited him because she was ready. Ready to take a risk, perhaps even to fall in love.

But was he even interested? He was here, yes, but where was his heart? She wasn't sure.

And then, suddenly, at that exact moment of worry and doubt, he was there. Appearing silently, the sand muffling his footsteps, he towered over her, blocking out the sun so that she didn't have to shade her eyes to see him. How did he know? Had he somehow sensed she was thinking of him? It was as if a breeze or a seagull had carried her thoughts back over the sand, over the high dunes and onto the porch, awakening him and making him run down to the beach to answer her. Yes, it was as if they had some sort of secret telepathic wavelength. One minute she was thinking of him—and the next, she was looking right at him.

"I see I'm too late," he said dropping down beside her.

Thinking he meant he was too late to see the sunrise, she shrugged. "That's okay, there'll be another tomorrow morning."

His eyes were still slightly creased from sleep and she could see that he hadn't taken the time to shave. When he stretched out his legs beside hers, she noticed how masculine they looked in contrast to hers, which were so much whiter and slimmer. And, of course, freckled. There was power even in his thighs. He was staring at her.

"How long have you been up?"

"A half hour," she estimated.

"Then perhaps I'm not too late after all. A half hour is still in the ballpark."

"For what?"

"To see your real face. Remember what my grandmother said?"

"Ah, yes!" Dell said. She remembered every word . . . and now, it seemed, so did he! But the way he was scrutinizing her face made her uneasy, so she bantered, "Well, this is my real face. Even your grandmother would agree. No makeup. I haven't even washed it yet. So, counselor, what's the verdict? Am I—?"

He didn't let her finish. In that instant between the beginning and unfinished ending to her question, she saw what he was about to do, saw his face coming toward her, saw his lips searching for hers, saw it all. Then he kissed her and she saw nothing more. Only felt his kiss. Nothing else existed. Sight and sound faded. Time stopped. And remembrance. And the sun was eclipsed and the sea was stilled.

He kissed her with such force, such intensity that she fell backward on the sand, and he with her.

He wouldn't let her go.

His mouth devoured hers, reaching into her, drawing her out, hardly letting her breathe. He kissed her as if he'd been waiting for this his entire life. *What took you so long?* He kissed her endlessly.

They lay in the sand, their bodies curled into each other, pressing closer, closer. There was no sun to burn them, there was no time to rush them. There was no sand grinding into Dell's hair and her back and the folds of her pink velour bathing suit. There was nothing but this endless kiss.

He might never have let her go but an early riser and his dog passed them, and the dog stopped to lick them, to give them his kiss, and their laughter temporarily broke the spell.

Half-carrying her back to the house, he said as he nuzzled her ear. "You passed my grandmother's test, by the way."

"Yes, I got that impression." But to herself she said, *Thank God for his grandmother.*

Later, in the packed and noisy house, they could find no corner of privacy and had to be content with hidden touches, quick caresses, a glance or two of infinite longing, fooling no one.

As Dell loaded the dishwasher with the last of the

breakfast dishes, he came up behind her and might have pulled her tantalizing pink suit off her if Jackie hadn't walked in on them, carrying some forgotten coffee cups.

"Listen, you two. We're taking the early ferry home. Tomorrow's a work day again. But you two stay. We'll see your mother home."

Tamara poked her head in the doorway and seconded the motion. "I'm going up to pack our few things now."

Dell loved them all but she was in no way sorry to see them go. With Rip's hands all over her, and her lips all over him, she never could have served the large late lunch she'd planned for them, anyway. She could hardly keep Rip off her long enough to say good-bye.

"Why don't we stay until tomorrow? Take the day off?" he suggested as they stood on the dock, waving to the departing ferry. "I know you can't. I can't, either. But I will . . . if you will." He held her loosely around the waist, but his hand kept slipping to her rump.

Dell tried to think it through rationally. "Certainly, the Labor Day traffic will be unbearable."

"Insufferable. We really should avoid the traffic," he agreed, leading her off the dock, dragging her red wagon behind him.

"And unless we stay, all that food I didn't serve will go to waste."

He nodded agreeably. "It will rot and decay, bringing vermin and lice."

Laughing now, with his arm tightly around her, she added, "And I really don't have to be in the office tomorrow. I was going to shop for a crib for Jackie and have two lampshades made up for a client—but that can wait."

"Lampshades wait extremely well. They're famous for it."

He walked her quickly over the low boardwalk, past the bushes of bayberry and beach rose and fiery red poison ivy, up the sandy walk to the house. Wordlessly she let him lead her inside, to one bedroom after another, searching for one that wasn't stripped bare. But the only bed that still retained its blanket and linens was his, on the porch.

"Oh, we can't! Someone might see," she protested when she saw where he was leading her.

He silenced her with a kiss. "Trust me." Then he hung the blanket as a baffle over the screen, leaving them just the top sheet. Certainly, it was warm enough . . . and in moments it would become warmer still.

But first he led her to the enclosed outdoor shower on the back deck. Then, as the cool water sprayed over them, he slowly peeled off her pink velour suit. There was no roof to the enclosure, and streaks of sunlight glinted on her cheeks, her shoulders and the pink, protruding tips of her erect nipples. Every part of her that the sun touched, he kissed. And then the parts where the sun couldn't reach.

He shampooed her glorious hair and soaped up her freckled body and then stood back to watch as the bubbles washed away, leaving the silky nymph of his dreams.

"Now you," she said and got on her knees to pull his black bathing suit off. But when she saw that part of him aiming straight at her, as erect and insistent as her own bare nipples, she decided to remain there on her knees . . . for some time.

"Dell, I love you," he groaned. "I think I've always loved you. Always. It just took you a while to reach me."

What took you so long?

She could not remember how they got to the bed on the porch, whether he carried her or they ran naked and laughing. All she could remember was what it was like once they were there, lying beside each other, tasting, probing, melting, combusting into liquid fire.

He was the lover of her dreams, as imaginative as Danny, as suppliant as Theo, but more. And it had nothing to do with his size, although later—much, much later—she would joke, "Now I know what they mean when they say everything's bigger in Texas."

No, it was something more, something that both Danny and Theo lacked, and only Rip possessed. Completeness. Rip was to Dell the only complete man she'd ever known. He was sure of himself in a way that could never be confused with arrogance or bravado. And he had an integrity so pure and true that he inspired in her not only complete trust but also the highest sort of admiration. He was a man, as a politician might say, of character.

Which was what made him such a divine lover. This was a man who did not need Dell to enlarge his mascu-

linity or massage his ego. This was a man who liked who
he was and knew what he wanted. And he wanted Dell.
She knew that now. She was sure of it . . . and sure of
him.

So when he said, "I want to watch you as I touch you.
I want to learn every secret corner that gives you pleasure," happily she let him watch, let him learn. But for
her, she now knew all she needed to know. She was at
last content.

25

"All I'm asking at this point is that you give me the nod to continue."

It was Wednesday morning and Dell, suntanned after the long Labor Day beach weekend and sleek in a silk suit, scanned the faces of the group of politicians, housing agency and finance administrators that she'd finally assembled after months of deliberate networking and shameless pleading. That no one was yawning or daydreaming—indeed that every last one of them seemed rapt—encouraged her to continue.

"A nod is all I need—nothing formal, nothing signed into law—for the idea to proceed. Because that's all it is at this stage—an idea, a beautiful idea to bring beautiful housing to the poorest of this beautiful city. And it won't cost you a dime!"

They wanted her to elaborate on this as they flicked through her proposal, which each of them had before them.

"I mean to accomplish this extraordinary venture entirely through the donated design and building resources of this city, and by the hands-on labor of the homeless themselves. Tremendous excitement has already been generated over this past year. More still needs to be done, but I need to know you're with me so far. So, ladies and gentlemen, do I have your go-ahead?"

Then Dell sat back and waited. She'd spoken nonstop for twenty minutes, carefully laying out her plan step by step, from the "name" architects and designers who'd form a pro-bono team, to the industry volunteers who'd train and supervise the future tenants. Contained in the proposal were copies of the letters she and Angie had written, and the promises of help they'd received. Looking back, she remembered a time when she never thought she'd be able to head this project herself. A man was needed, a famous man. Theo. But that was before she'd begun to believe in herself, before she'd begun to make her own dreams real.

Now, as one head after another nodded up and down, the serious, even stern, faces breaking into smiles, Dell repeated again what she'd told herself so many times since the night she walked out of the Embassy on her own: *It was all worth it!*

The House of Dell Shay was in a brownstone on a side street, west of Second Avenue. Her apartment was only three blocks north, but Dell headed straight for the office after her meeting. The office was where she lived—she used the apartment merely to sleep and change her clothes. It was a large, bright space, but unlike the office, which she'd finally finished decorating, the apartment remained essentially empty. For a short while, faced with designing an office–showroom all her own, she suffered the same paralysis Danny had experienced when D & D was born. Like Danny, she too got over it, and did it all on her own.

But the apartment remained empty not out of paralysis but indifference. So little time did she actually spend there that she thought of the flat as somehow temporary, impermanent as a motel where she happened to be spending her nights right now. She had a vague sense of waiting for something to happen—a move, a change— that kept her dangling. Meanwhile, she made House of Dell Shay her home, and that was where she put her energy.

She heard the phone ringing and Angie's silken voice answering it as she opened the door and entered the Pompeian red reception area. Two tall Tibetan painted wood figures stood as sentinels beside the japanned desk, and behind it, phone to her ear, Angie was motioning with her head toward the Italian gilt chair in the corner. There Theo sat, his eyes as deep a blue and sad as ever. A magazine, unread, fell off his lap as he stood to greet her.

''I know I don't have an appointment. On an impulse, I decided to drop by and see for myself what all the fuss was about. Very impressive,'' he said, gesturing stiffly.

"If I remember correctly," she couldn't help saying, "you weren't exactly impressed with the idea of my going out on my own at the time."

"No," he admitted, dropping his eyes. "But if it's any consolation, I can see I was quite wrong. Is it too late for an apology?"

"Of course not," she quickly consoled him. "Apology accepted." But in the dead quiet of her heart where bare truth dwelt, she could hear the certainty of her feelings echoing loudly. It was indeed too late. Far too late for Theo and Dell. And now, seeing him again, all she felt was the relief of a final resolution. It was over.

"How are you? Are you free to let me take you to lunch?" He was pursuing her as if he didn't see the truth in her eyes. And perhaps he didn't.

But Dell glanced at Angie and asked for her phone messages, not answering him directly. There was no one on the pink slips to whom an immediate return call was necessary, but Dell managed to roll her eyes and sigh as if each one was not only an emergency but a disaster.

"Oh, dear! The Lavins don't like the color of their bedroom walls?" Angie, just catching on, managed a nod, and Dell said, "I'd better get over there right away . . . And Tamara called from California?" She was with Tamara only two days ago on Fire Island. Probably she was calling to thank Dell for the weekend visit. But Dell, all business, said, "I'll call her before I leave for the Lavins."

She looked up at Theo and shrugged. "I'm sorry, but it looks like I've got a full agenda." She walked him to the door. "Let's do it another time, okay?"

He took her hand. Now he knew what was happening, but she was letting him down so lightly, he could hardly feel the pain.

"Be well, Dell."

"You, too. It was grand to see you again. I mean that. Grand." Then she kissed him on the cheek. Good-bye.

And it *was* grand to see him again. Grand to say good-bye. Grand to be alive. But there really was one phone call she had to make, only one person she wished to speak to right now. And for this one, she closed her private-office door.

As soon as she heard his voice, she smiled.

"How'd it go?"

"They gave me their nod of approval, just what I wanted," she reported, her voice filled with joyful triumph.

"Hey, that's great! I'm happy for you. I'm so proud of you." Then, after a pause, he added, "Don't you think this calls for a celebration?"

"Hmm, perhaps. What do you have in mind?"

"A repeat of last night might be nice."

She played innocent. "You mean, taking the ferry back to the mainland and then driving home?"

"I mean after that."

"Oh, you mean ordering up Chinese food and eating it in bed?"

"Yeah, a repeat of that . . . and everything after."

"Same egg rolls . . . and everything?"

"Same . . . everything. You take care of the menu and I'll take care of the . . . uh, entertainment."

"That sounds fair."

"One more little thing," he added.

"Yes?"

"Your bed's too short for me. Last night my feet hung over the edge."

"I'll take care of that immediately."

And she would. Only five days—and only five nights—but already there wasn't anything she wouldn't do for him. Anything to make him as happy and alive as he made her. A new bed. Yes! Now she could begin. Now she could begin to furnish her house, to make it a home. It was a project, she estimated, that might take years—preferably a lifetime. For this time she'd do it right. This time she'd fill her house not with perfection . . . but with love.